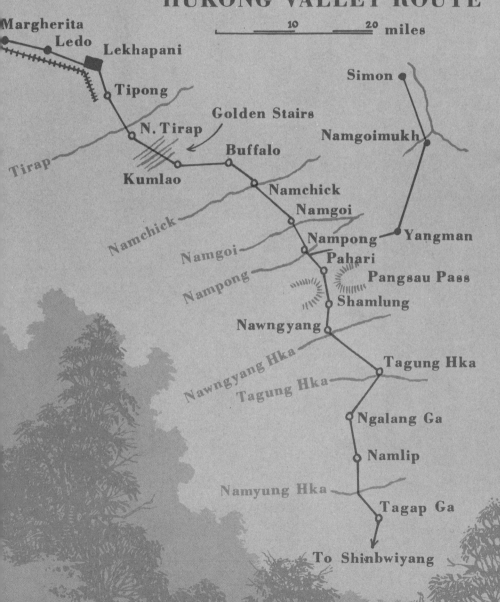

SKETCH MAP OF HUKONG VALLEY ROUTE

10   20 miles

Margherita
Ledo
Lekhapani
Simon
Tipong
Golden Stairs
N. Tirap
Namgoimukh
Buffalo
Tirap
Kumlao
Namchick
Namgoi
Namchick
Nampong
Yangman
Namgoi
Pahari
Nampong
Pangsau Pass
Shamlung
Nawngyang
Tagung Hka
Nawngyang Hka
Tagung Hka
Ngalang Ga
Namlip
Namyung Hka
Tagap Ga
To Shinbwiyang

Hampshire

the golden stairs

Cecilie Leslie

One of the consequences of the Japanese invasion of Burma was the tragic 500-mile march of thousands of Anglo-Burmese refugees through the jungles in the monsoon rains. Their goal: Kumlao, a clay mountain with 1,000 steps (the deadly golden stairs) cut into its steep side and leading to India and safety. Few survived the ordeal.

For many, the base of the mountain was the end of hope, a graveyard that claimed the lives of thousands of exhausted, diseased and despairing men, women, and children. Here, Monica Wadley's diary was found, an extraordinary document, the lonely outpourings of a desperate woman who schemed for love and marriage, and lost; who sought revenge, and found it. And lost again.

(continued on back flap)

THE GOLDEN STAIRS

CECILIE LESLIE

1968

DOUBLEDAY & COMPANY, INC.

GARDEN CITY, NEW YORK

ALL OF THE CHARACTERS IN THIS BOOK
ARE FICTITIOUS, AND ANY RESEMBLANCE
TO ACTUAL PERSONS, LIVING OR DEAD,
IS PURELY COINCIDENTAL.

AUTHOR'S NOTE

THE GOLDEN STAIRS, for my son, John Murray Leslie Hartley, is a work of fiction based on an historic situation, the fall of Burma from the first Japanese air-raid on Rangoon, December 1941, to the Hukong Valley Exodus from April to July 1942.

THE HUKONG VALLEY EXODUS, "that dreadful march which surpasses in horror anything of the kind in recorded history" (Compton Mackenzie's description of it in the official record, *Eastern Epic*), took place in a wilderness of malarious, forest-covered mountains intersected by seven mountain torrents in an area of North Burma that was, at the time, virtually unexplored and unmapped. About 40,000 men, women and children, Europeans, Indians, Anglo-Indians, Anglo-Burmese and Chinese attempted to reach India through the Hukong. About half died there. Among the survivors were many of my friends. My thanks are due to those who lent me diaries, letters, sketches, photographs relating to their experiences. In particular, I am indebted to MAJOR ALASDAIR RAMSAY TAINSH, who for four months worked up and down the Hukong rescuing people; ERIC BEADON, former Superintendent of Police, Magwe; and to MAJOR L. A. SUMMERSELL, Seaforth Highlanders, Commando Section of the Bush Warfare School.

Stream Mill
Chiddingly (Lewes)
Sussex, England

PRELUDE

July 1942.

In the Naga Long House of Kumlao, "Dukaba Major" worked methodically down the sleeping-platform, slipping his hand under each head, the most common hiding-place, feeling in pockets, probing among the bamboo leaves of bedding. Sometimes he found what he wanted, a clue to identity, in a message pinned to a shirt or a scrap of paper held in the tightly closed fist of the dead person.

He was a big young man, probably not yet thirty, but despite the impression of heftiness, seemed wasted, his bush shirt and shorts hanging limply against a bony body and looking many sizes too large for him. A square, handsome face, fair moustache, intelligent eyes of light, vivid blue, and an air of aloofness which some people, his C.O., for instance, described as truculent, "that truculent, insubordinate Waight," . . . this was the man refugees and Nagas of the Hukong called "Dukaba Major."

"Dukaba" in the Naga language means "Superior" or "Great Chief," and Hamish Waight may have been given this title because he first entered the Hukong at the head of a column, or because he was found to be "great" in another sense. As for "Major," the rank seemed proper judging by the crown on his shoulder tabs. However, judging by the rest of him he was not the type of major usually met with in the British Army. He could not remember when or where he had discarded his officer's cap.

In its place he wore an Abor hat, a cane-bowler with a brim. From his right shoulder hung a red Shan bag bulging with papers, disinfectants and bandages, from his left a water bottle whose webbing strap crossed over a cartridge-belt. From the rope round his waist dangled the revolver holster of a .45 Colt, a leather-sheathed kukri dagger, and a storm-lantern. He carried a long staff, wore hockey-boots by Bata, khaki puttees round his long, thin legs and a double band of red rattan cane below the left knee. Eastern Command could not have explained the significance of this red cane but any Naga or refugee could have done so: the red garter told them he was a Road Commander of the Hukong Valley who had crossed the Pangsau Pass.

Hamish Waight had trouble unknotting the bundle found beside an Indian clerk of about fifty. He carried it to the front of the hut, where he opened it and read the letter signed by Chandra Sunil Datta. The clerk stated he had been carrying the records of twelve companions who had died on the trek between Ngalang and Kumlao, about seventy miles. Datta had promised to carry these records to Calcutta so that the dependants of his friends would receive pensions. Fearing he was about to die himself, he had written the letter begging Dukaba Major to deliver the parcel to the Refugee Centre in Margherita. The letter ended, "My own records of service, pension schemes and provident fund herewith for benefit of dear wife, 6a Chowringhee Lane, Calcutta. Thanking you, Yours faithfully, Chandra Sunil Datta."

It was typical of many scores of messages already in the red Shan bag. Hamish attached his own scrap of paper to the bundle giving place—Kumlao, date—July 18, 1942, and approximate time of death, which he calculated by glancing at flies, flies' eggs and depredations of hatched larvae.

The clerk was the last one on the bamboo sleeping-platform, the chung, but there were still one or two below and the foolish Englishman, Robinson, under the entrance-platform. As he opened the clerk's bundle Hamish had caught a glimpse of Robinson lying with the basket under him, his face turned up so that water dripping through slats poured over his cheeks. Inside the hut there was a woman he recognized, Alice Something, who had kept a knitting shop in Maymyo. Her friends too had entrusted her with valuables, rings, bracelets, watches, gold crucifixes and gold chains. Alice had docketed each article, tying on scraps of labels with different-coloured wools.

When he had finished Hamish looked carefully into the corners. One never knew—the next one might be Jemma. It was always in the corners under chungs that women dumped children before abandoning them. It was under a chung in Tagap he had found the small Punjabi girl. The mother had wrapped her in a roll of canvas. Why? Usually they intended the children to be found and succoured by someone else, someone who might still have a little food or strength to carry a child. Hamish had toasted the little Punjabi over his campfire, turning her like a chicken on a spit before she had regained consciousness. He hadn't lost one child. It was the only boast he ever made. Of all the kids he'd collected up and down the track, he hadn't lost one. Sometimes he returned to camp with two perched on his shoulders, three hanging on to his staff and another couple clutching the tail of his bush shirt. The last two rescued, the night before, were English children. His orderly, Dil Tharpa, had reported seeing them peering out of a leaf shelter. The letter the mother had written was in the Shan bag.

"To whom it may concern: Mrs Harris, about to die, would be much obliged if her two daughters are given something to eat, not having eaten for six days. If they can be taken to relatives in Darjeeling, India, Mrs Harris would be much obliged. With kind regards and thanks, Sybil Harris."

He had at first assumed Mrs Harris, like others, had abandoned her children because she could no longer help them, but he had been wrong. The woman lay dead not far off in the undergrowth, where she had crept to spare her children the sight of watching her die.

Hamish climbed down the ladder to the midden under the Naga hut. Robinson could not have been dead for long because the Kumlao pigs had not yet found him. Hamish rolled him over to get at the straps of the big conical coolie basket. When he had first come across him sweating up the Ngalang climb he had asked, "What have you got in that? Whatever it is, chuck it out." Later he had found Robinson lying exhausted on the side of the road and had cut him a staff. "Get rid of that basket, or it'll kill you."

Hamish was certain the basket contained food or money. If it was food he proposed to strap it to his own back. A waterproof sheet had been sewn to the cane work, and it took time to remove it. When it was off, Hamish found the basket crammed with files—cardboard files threaded with tape-holding correspondence and papers of Rangoon Corporation. Robinson had carried them over three hundred miles and had died within a few miles of the Golden Stairs.

Hamish crossed the meadow of close greensward on which Kumlao, a typical Naga village on stilts, had been built. It wasn't a bad place, and of all the tribal villages, Naga, Kachin, Pinar had suffered least from refugee traffic, refugee looting and refugee dead. This was because it was on the summit of Kumlao, the starting place of the Golden Stairs and journey's end. Once a refugee realized he was within a few miles of the Golden Stairs, his courage returned and even the most demoralized no longer loitered. On a fine day, Kumlao, 2000 feet up, provided those who still had a stomach for mountain scenes with panoramas of Prussian-blue peaks, some to the north, touched with snow.

It was clearing, the grass straightening up, and the saturated earth had started its strange singing.

Now for the most depressing job of all, rooting in huts for those too ill to move, deciding who was worth carrying down the hill, and who was too far gone and must be left to die.

As Hamish crossed the refugee trail he took a crack at an old woman clanking along like a dustcart. She had a mania for collecting old tin cans. "Do you want another beating, mother? I beat you at Namlip and Shamlung, yet here you are again loaded like a dhobi's donkey. How are you going to get down the Golden Stairs like that?" She giggled and dropped her bundles. The moment his back was turned she'd pick them up again.

Yet he need not trouble about her. After three trips into the Hukong he had discovered the surprising fact that the toughest people were not the youngest. The kinds of refugees least likely to succumb were the old and mad, cripples, pregnant women and little children. On his first trip Hamish had marched the full extent, one hundred miles, of this dreadful Hukong, had crossed the seven Rivers of Death, climbed and glissaded over the clay slides of Kumlao, Nanki and Tagap and discovered the most cheerful and fittest refugee was a cripple who had slung himself along on wooden blocks strapped to his hands. As for the children, what their starved, shrivelled, scabrous bodies had endured was past belief. But then, Hamish wanted to believe the children in the Hukong were under some special kind of surveillance. His guilt over Jemma haunted him. It was responsible for driving him into the Hukong soon after he himself had walked safely out of Burma in early May.

Hamish paused at a hut where five people sat bunched under a soiled dhoti. He whipped off the cloth with his staff. Father, mother and three children sat with heads tucked between knees. "Dukaba Major Sahib, don't hit us! We can go no further. We are waiting to die."

"Get up!"

Whacks, prods, abuse, a couple of biscuits each from his pocket, and Hamish had set the demoralized family back on the path.

At the back of this hut Hamish turned out the pockets of a Mussulman wearing the high-necked blue-serge coat of an Indian servant. He glanced at three much folded and refolded testimonials from Memsahibs in Rangoon recommending the cooking—and character—of Mohammed Khan. Hamish scrutinized the shrivelled grey skin, hollow cheeks, and lips drawn back over the gums. There was something familiar about the features—could it be Mohammed Khan, Hugh Chapman's cook? It meant a great deal to Hamish Waight; for if Mohammed Khan had reached Kumlao, other members of Hugh Chapman's party may also have done so, and passed on down the Golden Stairs . . . Jemma, Mibs, Ken and that loathsome Wadley woman.

Hamish ran his hands over Mohammed Khan's clothing, found

nothing, but in the small of his back his fingers closed over a lump held in place by the string of the dead man's trouser cord. It was a packet wrapped in a leaf, a blue notebook. Hamish turned it over. "Letts' Diary and Account Book 1942."

Inside, in small handwriting, "This diary belongs to—

> *Monica Joan Wadley,*
> *7, Elsham Road,*
> *London W.14.*
> *Kensington 8007.*

In the event of accident please notify:

> *Mrs Arkwright,*
> *Helping Hand Agency,*
> *Brompton Lane,*
> *South Kensington (Kensington 1001.)"*

Hamish flipped through entries, reading some of them. The last one was written in early July, about a fortnight ago, and on the Ngalang Ridge. Hamish read and reread its final words: "Mibs—Jemma—Ken."

He put the diary down but for some time sat staring ahead of him.

Hamish did not look back as he walked into the forest at the far end of Kumlao meadow and started down the Golden Stairs. How he hated them. It was because of them that rations had not reached the forward camps and because of them that the gamest of the refugees, those who had endured the horrors of the Namyang crossing, the Nanki descent, the climb of the Pangsau, failed to reach safety.

The Golden Stairs were a series of steps, about a thousand, cut into the steep side of Kumlao, a mountain of clay. Though stakes had been driven in and bamboo poles laid across to secure each step, no drainage channels had been cut on the inner side. While the weather held, the steps proved helpful to refugee traffic. With the first monsoon downpour, however, the clay started to liquefy, and to move in slow-flowing ooze over the steps. The feet of elephants, mules, cattle and thousands of refugees did the rest. Clay was churned into the consistency of porridge and held between the stakes and poles of each step so that each one turned into a quagmire and death trap for any human being or animal who might fall into it. In some the yellow ooze lay six feet deep.

Refugees balanced themselves along the edge of the stairs, clinging to overhanging branches to keep themselves from slipping into the pits. If anyone fell in, he died there, and the forest walling in this cascade of clay prevented the disposal of corpses and carcasses.

By July, when Hamish was starting down the Golden Stairs, it was impossible to avoid stepping on human remains. Yet from this grisly place one could hear the hoot of a mine locomotive somewhere in the valley. The Golden Stairs were only a few miles from civilization.

He was halted by the sight of a soldier, a corporal of the Clerical Corps, who had fallen into a pit no more than three feet deep. He had been dead for at least three days and no one had bothered to remove the postcard hanging round his neck. On it he had printed his name—Cherry—rank, regiment and the address of his wife, who was evidently living in Simla.

Simla! Hamish removed the postcard, pushed it into his Shan bag and went down the steps. Simla, Army Headquarters! The place where preparations were going on for the next campaign before this one had been cleared up.

Head down, absorbed by his hatred of Simla and its officials, Hamish heard a cry and looked up. Two children hung like bats from a tree. Slimy clay slithered down their bodies and dripped off their feet. An old woman sat on the bank nearby with a third child across her knee. This one was vomiting clay.

"I'll take her."

Hamish pressed his water-bottle to her lips. "Don't drink, swill it round your mouth and spit."

Her body felt as light as an insect's. He cleaned out her nose and ears and, as he dabbed at her eyes, noticed her lashes were gummed together with slime.

"Jemma? Don't you know me?"

She regarded him with vacant eyes. Ken and Mibs, still dripping mud from the tree, stared at him in the same silent, apa-
thetic way. Only the old woman cried, "Waight, Sahib! S.P.
[Superintendent of Police] Sahib! Aye! Aye!"

"Didn't you know I'd been looking for you? For weeks—months!
Now I've found you, you'll be okay. I've got a bungalow ready
for you in Margherita. Baths, clean sheets and lovely, lovely
chow—you'll soon be okay."

He was talking for the sake of talking because he was shocked
by their appearance.

They were covered in sores, many infected and suppurating.
These were Naga sores which would take months to heal. Ken
had blue rings under his eyes, and his hair was as long as the
girls'. Shreds of a shirt and shorts lay plastered against his skin.
Hamish couldn't make out what Mibs was wearing, a material
that gleamed strangely white where it was not smeared with
mud. Parachute cloth! Jemma's dress was made from a sack, with
holes cut for head and arms. None of the children had shoes
or appeared to possess anything else whatever. Hamish wondered what they had used for covering at night on the freezing
summit of the Pangsau.

"Haven't much to say for yourselves, have you? Doesn't matter. Let's go. Mibs and Ken, walk behind me and hang on to the
rope round my waist. Fatima, hang on my stick. And you, Jemma,
I think I'd better carry you." He whisked her up on his shoulders.
"Hold my head, not my neck, or you'll throttle me."

He tried to sound cheerful, but remembering what he had
read in Miss Wadley's diary, he was filled with sadness. Where
was Hugh? What had happened to the sweeper, Nidhi Singh,
and where were the two Indian youths, Hanif and Ja-Bo, sons
of the two servants? He wanted to ask questions, but the strange
muteness of the children kept him silent.

Hamish was not surprised to spot among the refugees clustering at the foot of the Stairs a few of the original group of
Kaikun refugees. There was no sign of Hugh Chapman, but

the sweeper Nidhi Singh was there with his son Ja-Bo and the other youth, Hanif, son of the dead cook. They were squatting together, passing round a crude waterpipe made from a coconut shell. Fatima hobbled ahead towards them. Hanif, who was her grandson, saw her, but did not bother to get up, nor did Nidhi Singh rise to greet Ken, who had also limped forward. Then an odd incident occurred. Ken, the gentle boy, snatched the pipe from the sweeper's hand and shouted at him,

"Now you shan't beat us anymore, Shaitan. Waight Sahib's here and he will beat you."

Ken kicked the sweeper in the face. The big black-skinned Dom let fall the pipe, gave a shout and clouted the boy, grabbing his foot so that Ken fell on his back with a thud. Almost simultaneously Nidhi Singh caught sight of Hamish. He gawked, and rose awkwardly.

"Sahib!" A humble salaam, an indecisive offer to help lift Jemma from Hamish's shoulders.

So the sweeper had been beating the children! Did that account—partly—for their cowed manner? Though Hamish held the man's eyes in a hard angry stare, he made no comment. After three trips into the Hukong, Hamish had no sentimental illusions about refugees nor romantic notions about methods of rescue. He himself had been beating people up and down the Hukong: in times of crisis it was the quickest way of forcing obedience and it was the only way of rallying the demoralized.

There was still a mile or so of black stinking swampland to struggle through before reaching North Tirap, an outpost of civilization. Here in a small fort manned by the Assam Rifles, refugees in urgent need of attention could be treated in the barracks which had been converted into a hospital.

"You three—report to the Army Sahib. I'm not putting you on a charge, though you may deserve it. I want that boy's boil lanced." And—he wanted to be rid of them. In fact, Hamish was itching to lance Ja-Bo's boil himself. Last week, at Shamlung camp, with a razor blade he had opened up a similar knob on the head of a Chinese colonel—one of Stilwell's. He had extracted 350 half-inch maggots of four different species. It was one of scores of minor emergency operations Hamish had performed with the razor blade and common sense, and without any medical qualification whatever.

The road improved as it descended into the Tipang Valley. Round a corner they came upon the first wayside stall with Tipang women traders selling "Zu," Naga rice beer. Round the next corner they saw a bungalow, a white man's bungalow with a verandah netted against mosquitoes, servants in white uniform, a gardener watering a bed of cannas.

"The mine manager's bungalow. Now it's only ten minutes to the railway station."

While the voices of other refugees rose in excited chatter, exclamations, laughter, the brooding, silent indifference of the children did not lift. At the railhead Hamish helped his small party into one of the rail cars, placing the children so that they sat with their backs to the familiar hateful jungle and looking out over tea gardens, a tea-garden factory, a small bazaar with stalls selling pots and pans, cloth, umbrellas, spices and canned foods.

"Happy?" Hamish gazed into Jemma's eyes. There were white flecks in the corners—a sign of vitamin deficiency—but he imagined he detected a little more animation. Hamish persisted, "Don't you and Mibs fight anymore?"

Ken answered for her. "You don't understand, sir."

"I do. I know all about it." He put his hand on Jemma's shoulder, and then on Mibs. "Don't worry. It'll be all right."

"Will it?" Ken was sitting in a characteristic attitude, hands pressed between his knees. "Will it really, sir, you see, we . . ."

"I know. I don't want to hear about it and I don't want you to talk about it—to me or anyone."

"Yes, sir."

From the other side of Ken, Mibs's voice came softly, "But I'm glad, I don't care—I'm glad."

The rail car took them to Lekhapani, where they climbed into a train.

"Last time I was in a train was with Dad," Ken said.

The journey from Lekhapani through Ledo to Margherita was a matter of a few miles. The Jemma, Mibs and Ken Hamish had known in Kaikun would have been climbing over the seats, hanging out of the window, jigging about with curiosity, exclaiming at the tea gardens and asking questions. But these children behaved like old people, gazing with incurious eyes over the scenery. On Margherita railway station there were a number of officials, refugee administrators, reception-camp officers and volunteer women helpers from different organizations. There were also reporters and photographers from vernacular newspapers and English papers printed in Calcutta.

"They don't want to be photographed," Hamish said roughly.

"Are you the famous Major?"

"Come along, kids." He tried to push past the pressmen, but when one of them pointed a camera at them he said, "We're not in the least interesting, you know—but I'll tell you who are, on condition you leave us alone." Cameras were lowered. "See those Rip Van Winkles getting out of the train?" Hamish pointed to three Englishmen with long hair, long beards and long nails, but who nevertheless retained a dignified bearing, as well as servants and coolies laden with baggages. "I last saw them in April, in a courtroom in Katha hearing appeals. They had no idea the Japs were forty miles away. I had to tell them to scram. They are High Court judges from Rangoon."

Having diverted the pressmen, Hamish warded off solicitous officials, each anxious to give him a lift to the Golf Club. It was in the Golf Club, now the Evacuee Reception Centre, that the derelicts of the Hukong were divided and subdivided, and sent to different camps appropriate to their social and racial classification.

"No, I don't want a lift. Yes, the boy is Anglo-Burmese but he's not going to the Anglo-Burmese or the Anglo-Indian camp. He's coming with me, and so are the girls; yes, they're English. The old woman? She's Indian—a Muslim, but she's coming with me too. Against regulations? Too bad. She's still coming with me."

"Very well, Major!"

Dictating to half-dead refugees was one matter, but attempting to enforce the simplest regulation where the Major was concerned was another matter.

If the official was a white man he frowned but did not argue. If it was a white woman she looked affronted and, once the Major's back was turned, gave vent to her feelings. He had a nerve, really! He wore that ridiculous cane-bowler to make fun of them. As for the red-cane garters, that was to show *he'd* been over the Pangsau and *you* hadn't! You weren't responsible for the Hukong disaster. You were doing what you could, working twelve hours a day for the past three and a half months, sorting out these wretched, boring, whining refugees. What did he want? Did he want everyone to go to North Tirap where the corpses started, or up the Golden Stairs to show what heroes they were! Doubtless, they said, Major Waight considered himself a hero. Was he? They decided he was not, that his C.O. was justified in threatening him with a court-martial. After all, Major Waight, like everyone else, had a job to do in Margherita. There was a war on. The Army needed every man, all the transport, all the railway wagons, and all the food too. If hundreds of refugees were stupid enough to ignore Army orders and go trekking into the Hukong at the worst time, well, it was their lookout! It really wasn't Major Waight's place to look at you as he did and to make you feel—well, the way he made you feel.

As Hamish, Fatima and the children passed through Margherita, very few people, in fact, turned round for a second look at them. Walking skeletons in rags and smeared with clay were a common sight, arousing neither surprise nor compassion.

Hamish was therefore surprised when an Englishman rushed out of a house to greet him. It was Risley Hill, once Deputy Commissioner of Homalin, now a liaison officer with the Army.

"Hamish! It's good to see you. Are these the kids you've been hoping to find?"

Hamish nodded, smiling.

"I'm glad. Marvellous. But, you know the C.O.'s after your blood. There's a rumour of arrest."

"He wouldn't dare," Hamish said.

"No, I don't think he would. But don't go in again, that's all."

"I won't, not for a bit. Got to look after this lot, but once I've settled them . . ."

Risley Hill stared at the dirty children. "By the way—are their names Mibs, Jemma, Ken?"

"How did you know?"

Risley Hill continued to smile but his eyes were grave. "Did they start from Kaikun with a woman called Wadley?"

"I believe so." Hamish's manner became guarded.

"Did you know her?"

"Naturally, I knew her. I was S.P. Kaikun, how could I help but know her?"

"What was she like?"

Hamish did not answer straightaway. He lifted Jemma off his shoulders, then told Mibs and Ken to move on a little and wait for him. None of the children moved. Hamish let them be.

"Not a bad sort. But the kind who brings trouble on herself."

Risley turned with an overfriendly smile towards the children. "Now I'd like to ask you young people . . ."

"No you don't!" Hamish said. "They've had enough. I'll tell you anything you want to know."

"Did they get on with her?"

"The boy was devoted."

"*Was* he? Hum. Surprising." He moved away, beckoning Hamish after him. "They're wanted there . . ." He pointed to the bungalow from which he had appeared. Nearly all the Margherita houses were built on stilts. The lower area, between the wooden piers, was usually left open and used for storage, for cattle or as a garage. In this house the lower area had been enclosed by matting walls.

"It's a special court," Risley Hill went on. "Just been set up to deal with Hukong cases."

Hamish walked to the bungalow and stood looking into a room filled with people, mostly Indians. A crude dais with a table, the customary jug of water, pen tray, papers and an Englishman, whom he recognized as the Political Officer of Margherita, presiding: benches arranged on either side and some for the public near the door—a primitive courtroom. He said, incredulously,

"Are they really trying Hukong refugees?"

A look of vexation passed over Risley Hill's face—the same kind of look social workers directed at Hamish.

"Of course they're trying the blighters! What do you expect? You know what's been going on—robbery, looting, women abandoning children and—murder!"

Hamish glared at him. "Good God! Haven't you any idea what's going on in the Hukong?"

Risley Hill sighed. "I don't propose to start an argument. All I came to tell you is there's been a signal from North Tirap. An Indian, a sweeper, has made a very serious allegation against these children."

"Yes?"

"Murder."

"On what evidence?"

"Did you come across a Muslim cook—a Mohammed Khan?"

"Yes. He was dead. I recognized him. He was Chapman's cook in Kaikun."

"Did you search him?"

"He had some Memsahib's chits in his pocket."

"Anything else?"

"Such as?"

Risley Hill's eyes were boring into Hamish. "I gather there was a blue notebook, a diary belonging to this Miss Wadley. The sweeper says he found it and gave it to the cook."

"What do you want it for?"

"For the case."

"To furnish evidence against these children?" Hamish made no effort to conceal his contempt.

"If you found it, you're bound to turn it in."

"If I did find it, I would not. Get that straight. I went to the Hukong to help, not to judge. It's not the kind of place anyone can sit in judgment on anyone else."

THE GOLDEN STAIRS

1

Why did no one run for cover? Where were the air-raid wardens? And the shelters? Perhaps in Rangoon sirens were not used as warnings for raids.

Miss Monica Wadley was standing on No. 1 Platform of Rangoon Station, and the date was December 23, 1941. Tom McNeil, Ken's father, was there. With him was his friend, the big fair untidy man, Hamish Waight, also from Kaikun. These two young Englishmen were supervising the loading of her cabin-trunk and Ken's cases into the Kaikun compartment of the mail train.

Should she say, "That's an air-raid warning. We must take cover"? If she made a remark like that in South Kensington, people would have thought her daft, but then in South Kensington everyone would have taken cover by now. Why didn't they here? When the siren went, one or two heads turned, but there was no movement out of the station, and no one, Miss Wadley noticed, looked at the sky. Didn't they realize there was enough glass in the roof to kill scores of them? Hundreds were waiting for trains—cooking, sleeping, gossiping in family groups along the platforms, the greatest press standing round the third-class coffee stall. On the tracks, in full view of the public two men were relieving themselves, oblivious to trains, planes, bombs.

The siren's wail aggravated Miss Wadley's headache. She was

not the kind of person to take refuge in aches and pains when circumstances gained the upper hand, but this lack of organization was unnerving. It struck her as peculiar that Mr McNeil and Mr Waight, both officers of the Burma Government, should stand by the carriage smoking and chatting, ignoring the possibility that a bomb could hurtle through the station roof sending showers of murderous splinters upon them.

She went up to them.

"I'm worried about Ken."

It was the friend, not Ken's father, who said, "He'll be perfectly all right with Dil Tharpa."

"I expect he will, Mr Waight." Miss Wadley paused for a moment because she did not want to appear as if trying to snub him. But this was, after all, the father's business. She looked across Mr Waight at Tom McNeil. "This is a bit awkward for me. I'm still held responsible for Ken, as I've undertaken to deliver him to his parents—plural—and that includes your wife, as well. My responsibility only ends at your home in Kaikun, so you see . . ."

Tom smiled. "And I've upset things by meeting the boat."

"I'm glad you did. It's been a tremendous help. I'm also grateful for the lift in Mr Waight's car, and I'm sure the gentleman will look after Ken . . ."

Hamish Waight interrupted. "Dil Tharpa's my police orderly. He's the salt of the earth, one of nature's gentlemen."

Miss Wadley realized she had said something stupid, but was it necessary to call attention to it so pointedly?

"What I mean is, if there's an air-raid, Ken should be in the care of the person responsible for him."

"It's not an air-raid," Mr Waight said. This big fair man, with handsome features and strong physique, had a way of bringing attention back to himself. He seemed to assume authority and to dominate even when matters had nothing to do with him.

"Isn't it? It sounds like one to me. Surely that's an air-raid siren?" Miss Wadley failed to keep a certain aggravation out of her tone.

Tom answered, "Someone's pulled the wrong switch, Miss Wadley. You'll get used to this kind of thing out here."

"It could be a Civil Defence exercise." Hamish added, "If you like, I'll check with the Station-Master."

As he sauntered off, Tom said, "Some sort of Civil Defence was started here in October. Some V.I.P. came out from London to organize it. But this is nothing to worry about. Hamish and I were both around the Secretariat yesterday and both had a word with the Military Secretary. We would have heard if anything was blowing up."

"I hope you're right. But it doesn't alter my position."

"Nothing's going to happen. And if it did, my wife and I . . ."

"Yes, but there are my London employers, Mr McNeil. There's the Agency. They'd still hold me responsible. I should never have let him go off like that." She assumed the blame because she could not very well say, "You should not have let him go off like that." It was Mr McNeil who had given in to Ken's demand to get out of the car to do some Christmas shopping. Miss Wadley went on, "It was only a dodge, you know. I've got to know your son quite well after a nine-week voyage." She said this without rancour, and spoke with a softness in her voice that made Tom glance at her. "He tried it on me at every port—Capetown, Madras, Bombay, Calcutta. But he only got away with it the first time. After that I said, 'If you want to buy Christmas presents, young man, you can buy them with me. I won't interfere, provided you don't overspend.' That's what I should have said to him just now."

On the drive from the docks to the Station, Ken had suddenly announced, "I haven't bought a present for Ahme. Please, please, Dad, can I go into Orr's and get her a tortoiseshell comb?" Ahme was the Burmese word for "mother." Mr Waight, who was driving, stopped the car, and Mr McNeil calmly handed the boy a stack of notes—a hundred rupees at least. Having gained one concession, Ken had proceeded to wheedle others from his father, as Miss Wadley knew he would. He wanted to buy presents for—and there followed a list of people in Kaikun. Mr McNeil had handed over more money. Miss Wadley had tried to put a stop to the expedition by asking, "What about our train?"

Mr Waight had officiously taken upon himself to answer, "Plenty of time. Doesn't go till midday. Dil Tharpa's got a watch. He can go with him and see he gets back in plenty of time."

And so Ken had vanished into the jeweller's shop and they had driven on to the Station, parked in the yard, made their way to No. 1 Platform—and the air-raid siren had sounded.

Mr Waight appeared from the Station-Master's office.

"He doesn't know, but I'm beginning to think it could be."

"Why?"

He grinned at Tom. "Because it's just the sort of thing that would happen in Burma."

Tom shrugged. "The Japs are too busy in Malaya to bother about us."

What *was* happening in Malaya? Miss Wadley wished she knew. "Where can one buy a copy of *The Times*?" she asked.

"You can't—they're snapped up the moment they arrive. In any case, it wouldn't tell you much," Hamish said. What an extraordinary statement! Of course *The Times* would know! Tom McNeil said, "What Hamish means is, if there was a copy it would be dated October, probably shipped out on the *Circassia*, so it wouldn't help much."

Miss Wadley and Ken had sailed on the *Circassia* from Liverpool in October. Since then America had entered the war and Japan had joined the Axis partners. Miss Wadley had first heard of the debacle of Pearl Harbour over the ship's loudspeaker, and not until the *Circassia* called in at Capetown had she read about these events in a newspaper. When they called in at Colombo she had read of the sinking of the great British battleships the *Repulse* and the *Prince of Wales* in the Indian Ocean. When the *Circassia* tied up alongside Rangoon wharves early that morning, newspapers had been brought on board and she read of the Japanese invasion of Burma. If *The Times* confirmed all these unbelievable events, she would be forced to believe them, pull herself together and rid herself of this terrifying feeling of being without direction.

"Hey, you—is this a pukka raid?"

A slender youth in the uniform of a Boy Scout was passing down the platform. Round his sleeve he wore a blue band with the initials "C.D."

"Yes, sir. Sixteen anna raid, sir."

"What does that mean?"

"It means yes—according to him."

Miss Wadley asked the youth, "Where are the nearest shelters?"

"In the football ground, madam." He turned to Mr Waight. "Many planes is coming. Please, sir, help me to persuade these foolish ones to go to football ground."

"You'd better get hold of the Station-Master. Tell him to use the loudspeaker and order everyone off the platforms." Hamish added casually to Miss Wadley, "What about some coffee?"

"Coffee! We're going to be bombed! And Ken's missing!"

"Even if we were, we've loads of time. I'm thirsty. Coming, Tom?"

Mr Waight started towards a sign: "FIRST CLASS REFRESHMENT ROOM AND REST ROOMS." Tom McNeil hesitated. Miss Wadley asked, "How long between the warning and the planes?"

"No idea. An hour at least. The signal would have to come right up from Tennasserim, and Tennasserim is hundreds of miles south, where the tip of Burma dangles into . . ."

"I know," Miss Wadley snapped. Did he think she wouldn't know?

"It would come up by telegraph, and sending telegrams in Burma isn't speedy, particularly if it's a Burmese plane-spotter and the telegraphist is an Indian, as he usually is."

Hamish returned from the refreshment room. "I've ordered beer for you, coffee for Miss Wadley. Come along." They followed him out of the glare of sunlight into the Victorian atmosphere of the station restaurant.

For a moment it seemed to Miss Wadley she was back in London of prewar days escorting a schoolgirl or a schoolboy from one London station to the other. Mahogany furniture, gleaming glass-fronted cupboards, white tablecloths, polished cutlery surrounded them as they shared a meal accompanied by the muted thunder of expresses outside, couplings clanging as carriages were shunted up and down platforms and, now and again, the piercing noise of a locomotive's whistle.

The familiarity of the room soothed Miss Wadley. She would have liked to stay there. Its darkness and peace rested her eyes and nerves after the bewildering impact of Rangoon. But the moment she started to feel herself again, she straightened up, downed the scalding coffee and looked at her watch. Tom saw her do so. "I told Miss Wadley, even if the worst happens, we've an hour's warning." Hamish, equally unconcerned, added, "Depends if they climb or fall out of their trees, or if they decide they won't leave their trees. Out here, Miss Wadley, our plane-spotters sit in trees."

"Some of ours do too."

"Quite, but I'm sure you don't have the problems with plane-spotters we do. The latest one is that villagers are making some watchers lives so profitable they're deciding to become professional tree-men. In the East, Miss Wadley, anyone who acts in an eccentric way is not locked up, but considered holy and worshipped. We've just heard of villagers in a Tennasserim village who've mistaken our plane-spotters for holy hermits. They've been bringing them offerings of rice, fruit, flowers, and goodness knows what. The spotters are getting so spoiled, one of them has decided to take it up professionally."

Miss Wadley smiled politely. Totally untrue, she decided, and stood up. "I really must go back to where we left Ken." She waited, standing, while the men hurriedly finished their beer and paid the bill. She marched out of the restaurant ahead of them and then, to their surprise, did not wait to be shown the way but proceeded straight for the foot-bridge. The refreshment room was on the north side of the dozen or so railway tracks from where the foot-bridge connected with a main thorough-fare.

"We don't want to go that way or we'll land in Montgomery Street," Hamish said. "If you want to get to my car it's the other way, by the Kandaw Gate."

"You don't know Ken. He'll scoot off if he sees the car. The
only way to nab him is on foot."

Hamish looked irritated, glanced enquiringly at Tom, who
shrugged, as much as to say, let her do as she wants. But perhaps
because he was touched by her concern for his son, he tried to
be pleasant to her. "You call him Ken?"

"Don't *you?* I thought that's what everyone called him."

"Sometimes we call him by his Burmese name, 'Kyi Mint.'"

"When I went to Downderry, Mr Formby-Smith called him
'Ken.'"

"It doesn't bother me. On the whole I like 'Ken.' I expect
'Kyi Mint' was too much for an English prep school."

High buildings engulfed them in Montgomery Street, where
the temperature must have been ten degrees higher than in
the refreshment room. The impact of the street's chaotic traffic,
where handcarts, bullock carts, pedicabs, buses, cars and hundreds of barefoot pedestrians seemed locked in an inextricable
tangle, was almost too much for Miss Wadley. It was her first
experience of a bustling Eastern city street and filled her with a
sudden sense of fear.

"I'd like to go straight to the place where Ken left us. There
were some gardens on the left."

"Fytche Gardens? Then we should have done as I wanted—
gone by car. All we're doing now is to fight our way back towards
the station-yard."

"I'm sorry, Mr Waight. Can't we get a taxi?"

"Don't see one. We'll have to walk."

"What about a pedicab?"

"Wouldn't be seen dead in one."

Hamish Waight's abruptness increased Miss Wadley's feelings
of distress caused by noise, glare, stench, and agitation over Ken.
Her day had started at 4 A.M. when Ken, hanging upside down
from the upper bunk, had awakened her by his antics to watch
Diamond Point through the porthole.

If Miss Wadley's awakening was disturbed, she was disturbed
for the day. She liked routine. If she had been asked to say what
she most disliked in life, she would have answered the past six

hours on the *Circassia* when the delightful routine of life on board had become bedlam. Ken's dog, Butch, had been allowed up from the galley, and the boy and dog had gone mad, racing from one side of the deck to the other. When people were bothered with last-minute worries, they had got in everyone's way. From a thoughtful, pleasant boy, Ken had turned into a hateful one. Miss Wadley's three library books had disappeared from the cabin—thrown overboard, she suspected, by Ken. She had been forced to pack and repack the suitcases. No one had told her the breakfast sittings had been altered. Miss Wadley had arrived in the saloon to find breakfast had been served and cleared. As no more food was to be served before disembarkation, she had faced the day without the comfort of coffee and corn flakes.

"I don't mind how we get there, provided we do get there. Quickly."

Her tone of voice made Tom glance at her, and seeing the look in her eyes, he put his arm through hers. "I'll have to help you get through this, so hang on. Hamish, go ahead—act as a snow-plough."

It was Miss Wadley's first experience of fighting her way through a congested pavement in an Asian city. It gave her the same feeling of giddiness as watching superimposed scenes in a film. Not only vision but all her senses seemed to be exposed to simultaneous assault. Bicycle bells, temple bells, sizzling shriek of electric currents along overhead wires of passing trams, yap-yap of a street trader and the clanging from the side alleys where workers in different materials, brass, tin, iron, hammered away. The smells astounded her. The East, she knew, was supposed to be smelly, but she had no idea that the smells would rise like pillars in front of one, through which one had to pass with breath held in and handkerchief held to one's mouth. Rancid oil, bad fish and a peculiar tang, not altogether unpleasant, predominated Montgomery Street. She caught a whiff of peculiar pungency from a lane where an umbrella-maker was applying varnish to oiled brown parasols. The stench of bad fish, Tom told her, came from a street brazier where something was being fried. "Great delicacy—fried prawn paste." He laughed at her expression. She saw then his eyes were pale blue. Ken's eyes were black, so the boy must take after his mother.

"I'm quite tough normally," she told Tom McNeil, "but unless we soon get out of this I'm afraid I'll pass out." She felt him grip her arm. "No you won't."

"One incendiary would send the whole thing up." She looked up at a building covered in bamboo scaffolding, awnings of rushes and rickety timber balconies.

"Cheer up. Nearly there. You'll get used to it. Don't judge Burma by Rangoon. It's Indian." She did not understand what he meant until later. At the time she could only think the city was the most astonishing hotch-potch of East and West. On hoardings she read: "Moslem Children! Come Here for Circumcision." "Try Sri Churamani's Cure for Leprosy." "Are You Impotent? Cure Guaranteed or Money Back." The shafts of a handcart struck her, and she stumbled over something lying on the pavement. It was a moment or so before she made out a human being: quite old and a cripple whose stunted torso was no larger than a child's. He had been placed on a small wooden platform, his legs and arms arranged like the tentacles of an octopus round his begging bowl.

"Bhuk sé murtha!"

"What is he saying?"

"That he's dying of hunger. He isn't. Don't worry."

But she stopped, fumbled in her bag and threw him some money. "Bhuk sé murtha!" It was the first time she heard this cry which was to haunt her life in Burma.

They had been walking parallel to the railway lines, but where Montgomery Street crossed the wider thoroughfare of Sule Pagoda Road, Hamish led them to the left. "I'm taking Miss Wadley to the bridge for the view."

"Couldn't we leave it till later? At the moment all I want is . . ."

"I know. But this is also a good vantage point from which to spot Ken." Mr Waight was used to having his way, one could sense that. He led them where he wished, to the bridge over the railway-cutting. This was the place to see Rangoon, Hamish said, pointing to a gilded shaft which soared into the blue, its many-sided column catching the sun's rays. Miss Wadley had already passed this, the Sule Pagoda, on the drive to the station, and had been told it was a tenth of the size of the Shwe Dagon, the pride of Rangoon, which she had watched for more than an hour coming up the river that morning.

"Thank you for letting me see the view, Mr Waight. It's very nice. Now I want to go there." She pointed to the small park to the west of the pagoda.

"If Ken's anywhere he's down there." Mr Waight pointed to the shops, "or Burra Bazaar."

"I'm quite sure he'll be in those gardens. You see, people who've been in the blitz get conditioned. When the siren went just now, it was all I could do to stop myself running for cover. When Ken heard the siren he will have run for the slit trenches in those gardens."

"Slit trenches in Fytche Gardens! Are you sure!"

"I'm sure."

"Good Lord! I never saw any."

They were about to cross from the north side of Sule Pagoda Road to the pavement bordering the City Hall when they noticed people running out of banks, insurance offices and other buildings. Many stood on the steps of the City Hall shading their eyes with their hands. All stared at the sky.

High up in the milky morning blue, fifty or sixty silver specks were to be seen flying in formation. Miss Wadley started to run, Tom too, overtaking her, both hustling those who had halted on the pavement.

"Get inside! Take cover!" Miss Wadley called out.

Heads turned in surprise. What was the matter with this Englishwoman? Why was she running? Why didn't she stop to enjoy the spectacle in the sky?

"Get inside," Hamish shouted authoritatively at people thronging the steps. "That was an air-raid warning—and those are Jap planes." No one paid attention to this warning.

They ran until they reached the pagoda, then crossed the

street to the coco-palms and cloisters surrounding it. Hamish shouted in Burmese to the pongyis who were standing in the open, shaved heads tilted back as they craned at the sky, but they too ignored him. When they had again crossed the street on the far side and reached Fytche Gardens, Hamish was stopped by another Indian youth wearing the armband of the Civil Defence Service.

"Are you police officer, sar?"

"I'm a Superintendent of Police—but not of Rangoon."

"Sar, I am Air Raid Warden and these mens are laughing at me, not entering trench. Kindly enforce rules, Superintendent, sar."

He pointed to a group of richly dressed Burmese, whose clothes Miss Wadley saw were differently cut and of different colours to those of the Indians who had thronged Montgomery Street. The men wore pink turbans, tussore coats and long skirts or longyis. The women looked crisp in long-sleeved white blouses and pretty, colourful silk skirts. They were chirruping together, marvelling at the specks in the sky as if it were an air-display staged for the inhabitants of Rangoon. Like the Buddhist monks, these people ignored Hamish's warning.

A sound like thunder came rolling over the city.

"That's from the Botataung area."

"No, from Syriam. They're bombing the refineries."

"Where's Ken? Help me find Ken. He's not here. He should be here! Worrying about refineries and other people! It's Ken who matters." Miss Wadley stood at some distance from Hamish and Tom, looking down at two lines of slit trenches which were empty. Her voice was high and she made no more effort to control her anxiety over the boy, or her exasperation with the two Englishmen. Tom ran at once to her. "I'll take the trenches over there—you look in those." But she was now so distraught, she could only stand still and shout, "Ken! Ken! Ken!"

"That won't help, Miss Wadley. Please go and look."

But Tom was wrong. A school cap and grey flannel suit appeared over the lip of trenches partially obscured by shrubbery.

"Waddy! Here I am!" Ken raced towards her, threw his arms

round her, and for a moment the boy and the woman clung to one another. It was Ken who first broke away, grabbing Miss Wadley's hand. "Hurry! I can't leave Butch. She's mad scared. She's trembling. I always have to sit on her head in a raid." As he tugged at her he caught sight of his father and halted, looking stunned. "Crumbs, sir, I forgot about you. Sorry, sir. Please come too."

Dil Tharpa had also climbed out of the trench and stood to attention until they had all jumped in, then leaped in himself.

"What's that booming noise, Dil Tharpa?"

"Twelve o'clock gun, sir," the orderly said.

But it couldn't be. Hamish checked with his wrist-watch, and so did Tom. It was ten-forty. Again there was a muffled roar, and in the silence that followed an English voice said, "Look, darling, R.A.F. planes. Your Uncle Bob's in the R.A.F., and so is . . ."

An Englishwoman and her daughter, with an Indian Ayah, were strolling through the garden and, like everyone else that morning in Rangoon, gazing upwards.

"Those aren't R.A.F. planes but Japanese. Jump in here, quickly as you can."

Miss Wadley had recovered her composure now that Ken was with her and she could protect him. The boy was lying crouched over his dog's back, his hands pinioning her forepaws. Miss Wadley had rolled a handkerchief and placed it between his teeth and was shielding the back of his neck and head with her handbag. The Englishwoman peered down at them, but drew back. "I couldn't possibly. Dog's dirt, human dirt—it's filthy."

Miss Wadley stood up extending her hand towards the Englishwoman's small daughter. "Do you want her killed?" She pulled them both in, and Tom persuaded the Ayah to follow them. This one slit trench in which people were taking shelter was now causing as much interest as the "air-display." People ran across the gardens to goggle at them. Hamish tried to make a pretty Burmese girl take shelter by grabbing her hand. She let out a scream. "I will not there, mister. Detach me, please.

You are insane. Why you pull me?" Her voice rose, and a number of Burmese students ran to her help.

A line of foreshortened faces, eyes peering over the bumps of their chins, appeared over the trench. Staring up at them, Miss Wadley was struck by the background, the shining spire and belled cap of the Sule Pagoda rising out of coco fronds. Some of the students started to nudge each other. "It is impolite to watch. They are in trench to defecate."

Their laughter was followed by silence. A weird silence. Though the traffic was still moving round Fytche Gardens, it made no noise; though people were talking, no sound seemed to issue from their lips. It was uncanny. "It was a loud silence, Ahme," Ken said later, trying to pin it down. "You could hear it. You could hear no one talking. It frightened me. I shut my eyes and put my head against Waddy and held on to Butch. Butch was shivering; she had her nose in the back of my knee. All the time the silence went full-blast shrieking at us."

"It couldn't have shrieked, chaw lay. If you heard a shriek, it must have been the bombs," his mother replied.

Ken was emphatic. There was no whistling noise, no rumble and crump as there were during raids in England. Earlier, he admitted, there had been the sound of thunder, the kind of sound that came over the Kaikun hills before the monsoon. When the silence started, the only thing he was sure of was the jet of dust full of black objects. It swirled over the trench and palm trees, and some of it fell over the Burmese girl.

"She was quite dead," Ken told his mother. "When it was over we got out and I saw her. She was my first dead person. I saw my first Jap plane and my first dead person the same day."

2

As a boy, Tom McNeil lived in Scotland but went to school in England, in Sussex. His mother put him into the Royal Scot at Edinburgh for King's Cross Station in London. When he arrived, she told him, he was to get out of the coach and stand still on the platform holding up a card with the initials "H H" on a scarlet ground. On the back of the card was the address and telephone number of The Helping Hand agency. He felt an ass carrying out these instructions, more so when he was spotted from the other end of the platform by the Helping Hand, usually a tall, beaming middle-aged woman, holding a similar card, who bore down on him shouting, "Hello! Hello! Helping Hand—that's me!" The woman—not always the same one—took him in a taxi across London to Victoria Station, the station for the south, where she gave him lunch in the Grosvenor Hotel and then placed him in the school coach for Bexhill. One of them always pressed into his hand a bar of chocolate, which he suspected she bought out of her own money.

When the blitz increased in ferocity and the British Government sponsored schemes for the mass evacuation of school children from big cities, Tom and Hla Gale were faced with the question as to whether or not their son should be sent back to Burma. At a distance of six thousand miles it wasn't easy to know the wisest course to take. The headmaster had written to say that if things got worse the school would move to Dorset.

How much worse? What about rations? And Kyi Mint himself: was he frightened? Fit? And so on. Hla Gale was against approaching relatives for advice, so Tom, recalling these enterprising women, wrote to them. He had forgotten their address, but the agency was unique, and, sure enough, The Helping Hand, South Kensington, London, eventually found them. Indeed, where else but South Kensington would well-educated gentlewomen of independent means band together to solve other people's problems at a moment's notice and for a very modest fee?

Mrs Arkwright, the agency's principal, did not glance twice at the letter's Burma stamp. The mail that morning brought letters stamped in Egypt, Togoland, Canada and from five different provinces in India. Neither did the problem of a forest officer and his Burmese wife arouse particular interest. It didn't matter what sort of people, nor what kind of scrapes they got themselves into, provided the solution lay the right side of the law, The Helping Hand was prepared to take charge.

The difficulty facing Mrs Arkwright, however, was shortage of Hands. Ten staff Hands were out of town, escorting children, elderly folk, and two pedigree Angus bulls, valued £15,000 each, to Canada, India, the Lake District and (the bulls) Perth in Western Australia. Everyone, in fact, was booked, with the exception of Miss Wadley, and so, alas, Miss Wadley it would have to be . . . and that meant persuasion, tact, and wasting time, which Mrs Arkwright could not afford.

In the band of efficient amateurs Miss Wadley was the only one with a degree—not a good one, and not at Oxford or Cambridge, but a university degree all the same, in history. She had also had long experience in a firm of aircraft engineers.

A great pity she was not a staff Hand. Mrs Arkwright had at first thought, and had actually suggested it at their initial interview. Miss Wadley had, however, declined. She was really taking a rest cure, she said, recovering from, well, from a private crisis but needed something to do to break the monotony. She was unused to leisure, Miss Wadley said; she got depressed with nothing to do. "My work has been my life. Too much so, I'm afraid—that's half the trouble. That's why my leaving Burnett's knocked me sideways. I hear you have a variety of jobs, and that's just what I want for the moment—diversity to take my mind off myself. Of course, if you don't want me in a temporary capacity . . ."

Mrs Arkwright had been quick to assure Miss Wadley she had no intention of turning down someone of her qualifications; for as long as it suited her she was a welcome addition to their number as an Outside Helping Hand.

But sitting at her desk in the clean but dingy office off Brompton Road, Mrs Arkwright wondered if Miss Wadley had proved worth the trouble she caused. There were so many kinds of jobs she refused to do. Would this be another one? She recalled now indications of Miss Wadley's eccentricity at their meeting, which should have put her on her guard.

After University there had been a course at a Teachers' Training College, where Miss Wadley had gained a teaching diploma. "I did one year as History Mistress in a Worcestershire school but—never again!"

At the time Mrs Arkwright had smiled; now it made her frown. Why get a teaching diploma if you don't like teaching? If, the McNeil letter stated, The Helping Hand agency decided it was best for their son to return to Burma, the escort chosen to bring him home should be someone who would be willing to remain in Burma for at least four months—to help the boy catch up with the schooling he had missed.

Would Miss Wadley consent to teach him? Tiresome, prickly, unreliable Miss Wadley! Perhaps that wasn't quite fair. Tiresome, prickly, perhaps, but the Miss Wadley file demonstrated a fairly stable character with plenty of grit and no false pride. She had been with Burnett's twelve years, joining it at the age of twenty-three as one of the typists of the firm's typing pool. It had taken her only a year to rise through the three grades: Junior Personal Assistant, Senior Personal Assistant to the grade of an Executive Officer, that is Secretary. Within two years she had been, as she said, "annexed by the President. I was Sir Guy's Secretary for eight years, and when he became Chairman he made me his Personal Private Secretary, on a salary of two thousand a year." That struck Mrs Arkwright as a very good salary indeed. Miss Wadley had remained with the Chairman until he retired . . . no, that was not how Miss Wadley put it. "Six months after the Chairman's wife died I left." At the time Mrs Arkwright had been on the point of asking, "why?" What had the Chairman's wife to do with her? Had there been a strong attachment between the two women? If so, why leave six months *after* she died? Mrs Arkwright, however, had asked no questions because Miss Wadley had left the table, walking to the window where she had stood with her back to the room as if overcome by emotion.

During the year Miss Wadley had worked for them, Mrs Arkwright learned only a little more about her private life. Her parents, both dead, had left her comfortably off with a house in Elsham Road which she had turned into flats, occupying the top floor herself. Only once did she refer to her former employer, and then her voice sounded spiteful. "I heard today from the Chairman—that's Sir Guy Burnett, my old boss, you know. He's in Bermuda. Retired there with his wife and the son. How long have I been here? Twelve months, isn't it? Then, that's about the time he's been in Bermuda. The first letter I had, after three months, the bliss was wearing off. Now he says it's hell, deathly dull; he doesn't know what to do with himself. The son couldn't stand it—I knew he wouldn't—and has run away to America. Joined up."

The son . . . but "his wife." It sounded as if the boy was of a former marriage and the wife of a current, and therefore second, marriage. Well, so what of it? It wasn't of much interest to Mrs Arkwright, who wasn't a gossip. All the same, had it been anyone else but Miss Wadley, she might have asked a few questions. But with Miss Wadley one's attitude was always different, restrained, a little on edge. Mrs Arkwright wondered why. The look in her eye? The set of her mouth? Why did Miss Wadley give one the impression of being uncordial, resentful? As if, Mrs Arkwright thought, one had done something—goodness knows what—and she owed one a grudge.

When Miss Wadley arrived, Mrs Arkwright said, "Even if there were other Hands free, and there are not, I'd still appeal to you. This isn't the kind of problem anyone can solve."

"I really don't see why not."

"It requires a special kind of disinterestedness. For instance, I wouldn't be any good—I couldn't be objective in this kind of case. I'd be reminded of my own Simon, when he was small and went to prep school—far too early in my view. He was only seven . . ."

"This one's thirteen."

"I know. Seven—thirteen—don't think it makes much difference. They do suffer so. I've been haunted ever since. Just as the train pulled out I saw his face, so white, pressed against the window. He didn't cry but he looked awful—stunned—as if he had suddenly realized what was happening—that I was abandoning him."

"But you weren't. Good Lord, you were only sending him to school."

"It must have seemed like abandonment to him."

"Don't believe it. Boys are tougher than you think."

"It broke my heart."

"Maybe. But not his."

"I'm not so sure."

What did this hard little spinster know about children—or a mother's love? Mrs Arkwright was annoyed by Miss Wadley's rejoinders. To prevent herself retorting with similar rancour, she lit a cigarette and passed the McNeil letter over to Miss Wadley.

"The proposition of going to Burma, staying for four months, perhaps for the duration, is attractive, isn't it? No more air-raids, plenty of sunshine, and all the fun of a trip to the gorgeous East!"

"I wouldn't exchange the whole gorgeous East for one meadowful of buttercups. I love England," Miss Wadley said.

"So do I, but I must say I wouldn't mind a holiday from rationing, clothing coupons and Heinkels."

"Funnily enough, this past year has been a very happy one for me."

"I'm glad."

"I was so wrapped up in Burnett's, I neglected my own life.

The Chairman's problems all became my problems. I couldn't sleep for worrying over new projects, faults in designs, slumps in sales. I realize now that was a foolish way to behave. Since I left I've discovered people exist. There was just one person, the Chairman. There wasn't time for anyone else. He was such an overpowering personality—and so demanding. I didn't realize how lonely I'd allowed myself to become. Worked all day, went home whacked, fit only for bed and sleep. Now suddenly I've got time to discover how nice everyone is where I live in Elsham Road. Round the corner in Russell Street there are shops, and I've discovered the baker and the chemist knew my parents very well, and liked them. Some of their affection for them is rubbing off on me. If I forget my ration book they let me have whatever I want. And then—there's my flat. After living virtually for twelve years in an office and using my flat to clean my teeth in, it's funny finding how comforting your own rooms can be. Some of the shopkeepers come into tea with me. Once I used to dream about a beautiful house in Regents Park, a millionaire husband and entertaining in a big way, but that's all nonsense. Schoolgirl nonsense. I'm happy for the first time in my life."

Mrs Arkwright listened in some bewilderment. Far from outgrowing "schoolgirl nonsense," it struck her that a schoolgirl was exactly what Miss Wadley continued to be.

"From that letter, wouldn't you say the McNeils sounded a pleasant couple? Couldn't you be happy with them?"

"Hmm . . . Burmese wife. Suppose so. She'd speak English?"

"Certainly. I think she is the one who wrote the letter."

"She probably did. There are two signatures—'Thomas Mc-Neil' and 'Hla Gale'—and the letter's in the Hla Gale writing. But doesn't it strike you these two are at loggerheads? One wants the boy home, the other wants him to carry on at school?"

Mrs Arkwright gave her a quick look. Miss Wadley didn't miss much: that was the impression the letter had given her.

"And the query about homesickness. Bit late isn't it? He's been there a year. What's the point of raising it at this stage? He'd be over it . . ."

"Is any child ever over homesickness?" Mrs Arkwright asked.

Miss Wadley shrugged. "Don't they put it on for the parents' benefit?"

"Oh no!"

"Or to get their own way? A bit of misery is good for a child. Part of growing up. A child is toughened by suffering like everyone else."

Mrs Arkwright removed her glasses and polished them. There were facets of Miss Wadley's character she did not like to see, and would never understand. She said gently,

"But you like children."

Another shrug. "Some. On the whole, no, I don't like kids round me. So, I avoid them. If I do happen to get among them, I find myself getting rattled, tensing up. Can't describe it, really. As if all the chatter and uncoordinated movement took me apart too, disrupted me. You don't understand, do you? I can see by your face I've shocked you. But I've made no secret of it from the start, have I? I've always told you frankly, no jobs with children or animals for me."

"That settles it, then." Mrs Arkwright placed the McNeil letter in a file.

Suddenly Miss Wadley laughed. "Sorry! Haven't you realized— my bark's worse than my bite?"

Was it?

"And if you're pushed, I'll take this on. Don't want to, but I said I'd help you out, and I will. I'll take the train to Eastbourne this morning."

"You mean that? Well, thank you." She had nearly said, "Monica." Mrs Arkwright called all her other Hands by their Christian names.

"Thank you, Miss Wadley. Just one more point. If you decide the boy would be better off in Burma . . ."

". . . if. But I doubt it."

"I'd just like to know if you'll take on the other part—staying on to coach him?"

"You just don't know anything about me, do you, Mrs Arkwright? I gave my word. I wouldn't go back on it. What I like or don't like is nothing to do with it. Once I give my word—well,

I stick to it. In any case, the question may not arise. I'm not the one to go soft over schoolboys. They're heartless little brutes, you know. Discipline, air-raids, do 'em a world of good. I'm sure the McNeils' boy's best bet is to stay at school and get on with it."

3

Two snapshots of Ken McNeil had arrived in the letter from Burma. "Can't think why," Mrs Arkwright said, and there seemed to be no reason for them since the usual difficulty of identification did not apply to a boy who would be met in school.

After looking at them Miss Wadley came to her own conclusions. Parents, she had noticed, usually sent pictures of an offspring in "typical boy" activity, in the sea, up a tree, indicating thereby how they saw him and wished others to see him too. The odd photographs sent by the Burmese mother likewise seemed to hint how she too would like others to regard her son. One snapshot showed the boy leading a procession down a sunny country road. He was seated on a small caparisoned country-bred pony and was wearing an embroidered coat with some kind of fancy-dress crown on his head. On either side of him men carried long-handled ceremonial umbrellas and were followed by a group of barefoot boy musicians. The boys looked very young, with fringes and shiny topknots, and were probably his friends. They had halted to be photographed, drumsticks and cymbals raised. On the back of this snapshot the mother had written "Kyi Minh, age 12, setting off to religious Shinbyu ceremony (something like Christian Confirmation)." The other one was of her son standing alone dressed in robes similar to those of a Buddhist priest except that the exposed right shoulder was covered. He was holding a large black pot, as big as a bucket and shaped like a witch's cauldron. The crown was gone, so was all his hair. His shaved scalp accentuated comically prominent ears, giving him the look of a gnome. On the back of this picture were the words, "Kyi Minh, ko-yin (novice) in Deer Hill Monastery about to set out on morning round." In neither picture was the boy smiling, but the impression nevertheless was of a merry, chubby boy who had been told to look solemn and who, once the picture was taken, would break into laughter. This boy, as opposed to the one Miss Wadley had watched walking down the staircase, was handsome, with softly moulded cheeks and chin, lips that curved up at the corners, and a long, strong neck.

The only reasons the mother had picked out these particular pictures, Miss Wadley decided, was to emphasize that though her son was in a prep school in Eastbourne, he was still her son, a Burmese and a Buddhist.

"Ready, Ken?"

He had appeared in the hall and they walked together to the front door.

"By the way, is it 'Ken' or 'Kyi Minh'?"

He gave her a brief glance before lowering his eyes. In at the stomach, shoulders hunched, his eyes blank, there was little likeness between him and the boy in the snapshots.

"They call me 'Ken' here." It was surprising to hear him speak English without any accent, or rather with no accent other than that of a boy of the English upper classes, who widen certain vowels, and drawl their words.

"Would you like me to call you 'Ken'?"

"If you like." He sounded indifferent.

As they were about to get into the taxi she asked, "Where would you like to go?"

"I don't mind."

"Where do other boys go?"

"Home."

Miss Wadley told the taxi driver to take them to a restaurant or café on the sea front.

Ken sat down beside her, leaving a space between them, his school muffler tangled up with the straps of his gas mask. He did not look out of the window but stared at the floor of the cab.

Downderry School stood in the lea of Lullington Downs, below Windover Hill, in a lane signposted "No Through Road." Beech hangers and gorse thickets dappled tawny slopes surrounding the school on three sides. Approaching the old manor house down the "no through road," parents with a less practical eye than Miss Wadley's were impressed by a beautiful setting, solid-looking masonry and, above all, the tranquillity that broods over the rippling contours of all downland. One glance was enough for Miss Wadley to mark Downderry's disadvantage—not enough sunshine. It wasn't much after three, but the laurels and rhodo-dendron thickets bordering the drive were already soaking up darkness. Once out on the main Polegate-Eastbourne Road, how-ever, a ray of sunlight momentarily entered the cab; as soon as the road started to descend into the Old Town the atmosphere became moist. Soon the cab was crawling through a sea mist, and there was nothing to be seen but a few yards of pavement with sandbags heaped against walls.

"I was looking forward to catching a glimpse of the sea."

The taxi-driver told Miss Wadley, "At least there won't be any air-raids in this."

"Has it been bad here?"

"We've had our share, miss."

Suddenly Ken said, "I like air-raids. We go down to the cel-lars and drink cocoa and have sing-songs."

"Have bombs fallen near the school?" Miss Wadley asked. Ken answered, "No," but was at once contradicted by the taxi-driver.

"What's that? I was rabbiting Sunday up there—three new cra-ters I saw. Not target-bombing, I reckon, just off-loading before crossing the Channel. Where you want to stop, miss?"

"Joe Lyons, if there is one. Is that what you'd like, Ken—a Joe Lyons?"

"No one's ever taken me out before. What is a Joe Lyons?"

The taxi pulled up in the main street opposite glass windows covered in strips of brown paper. Further along there was a road block with sentries on duty. The pavement outside the tea-shop windows was crowded with couples, most of them in naval uniform.

"Ask for crumpets, son," the taxi-driver said.

"Will you come back here for us in about forty minutes?" Miss Wadley asked. "Is that okay, Ken? Or would you like to stay out longer? My train's at five, but I could get a later one."

"I don't mind." Miss Wadley glanced at him standing against the glass window, shivering slightly, his thin brown legs looking unsightly under his mac.

"You look cold—let's go for a brisk walk, work up an appetite." She put her arm through his, gave it a squeeze but met with no response. It wasn't like her to try to make friends with the numerous young strangers entrusted to her care. It hardly seemed worth it for the hour or two spent with them. But this boy was different.

She plied him with questions without arousing interest or many answers beyond yes, no, I don't know.

"But you must know if you get enough to eat."

"Have they been saying I go hungry?"

It was an odd way to phrase it. Also, for the first time he sounded alert.

"No one's been saying anything, Ken. I just wanted to know."

"You've asked a lot of questions. Why are you pumping me?"

"Pumping you? It sounds like that? I'm sorry. I don't mean to be officious. All I'm doing is ask you the questions your parents have asked me to ask you."

"My parents! Dad and Ahme?" Perhaps no one ever spoke to him of his parents and that accounted for the astonished way he spoke, almost as if she had startled him by mentioning them.

"They want to know if you're happy, and well fed, and getting on well at school."

"Why?"

She was nonplussed and hesitated.

"Has the school been telling them about Butch?"

"Butch?"

"My dog. At least she's the milkman's really, but she's like my dog now. I'm allowed to take her for walks round the grounds, and after I went to the Head about it, I was allowed to give her my meat ration. I told them Buddhists weren't allowed to eat meat."

"Aren't they?"

"They are. It's the Hindus who aren't, but Matron didn't know."

"All the same, meat builds you up. Shouldn't you be eating your meat?"

He halted, faced her and almost shouted the words, "Wish I hadn't told you. Now you'll sneak. And if they take away her meat I'll—I'll—"

"You're being rude. I don't tell tales."

"I'm sorry. Please forgive me."

He had pulled away from her and now kept his distance, walking dejectedly along, scuffing the pavement with his shoes. Mist had congealed in a sprinkle of drops on his cap and hung from woollen tendrils of his scarf.

"Let's see if we can find the tea-shop."

This time he put his hand on her arm. "Listen." From ahead they could hear the muffled booming of waves pounding the pebbles.

"That was clever of you!" He smiled at her for the first time. His teeth were small, white, with a gap on one side of his mouth. "It's nice to be out of school, Miss Wadley. Gosh, I get fed up sometimes."

She put her arm through his but was careful to ask no more questions.

"Burbidge is my best friend, but I hate him too at times. Like Ko-Ni. He's my friend in Kaikun. Ko-Ni, Jemma, Hanif, Ja-Bo, they're members of my gang in Kaikun. Burbidge is the dorm prefect. He was the one who caught me when I was trying to run away."

"Run away!"

"I didn't in the end. Burbidge said 'where are you going?' And when I said 'home' he tried to be sarcy. 'You don't say! Home to Burma where the ladies smoke cigars!' He'd seen my snap album with a picture of my mother smoking a cheroot. He was laughing at her. I wasn't having that, so I let him have it"— he looked at Miss Wadley—"with my penknife."

They found a dark café and had taken their seats at a small table before he added, "There was a lot of blood but we mopped it up. The others said I'd be expelled and Burbidge would have to have stitches in hospital. But no one ever found out."

"I expect it was only a small cut."

"No, it wasn't. After that they left me alone. Burbidge tried to be decent. He still talks to me, but the others don't."

"Aren't you happy at school?"

"I'm not in England to be happy, Miss Wadley. I'm in England to be educated so one day I can become important. One day I've got to run my mother's sawmills and her rubber plantations."

"Your parents want you to be happy while you're here."

He shook his head. "They wouldn't have sent me away if they wanted me to be happy and not important. Do you think my mother loves me, Miss Wadley?"

The melancholy sound of a foghorn out at sea floated over the rooftops, and somewhere in the town a clock chimed four. From the station, not far away, they heard a train whistle, and on the opposite pavement, obscured by sea fog, they heard but could not see someone going by on roller skates.

Ken said, "If war had been declared in August instead of September, I would not have come to England. I left Rangoon on August the thirtieth, Miss Wadley. If they'd declared war before I sailed, my mother wouldn't have let me go, because she's afraid of bombs. I'll never forget leaving Kaikun. Father drove me to Bilin Station. We spent the night in the train, and I slept on the top bunk, and Dad slept on the bunk under me. I didn't sleep because I hadn't much time left to be with my father, so I kept awake so I could know I was with him. We had breakfast in Rangoon in my Aunt Hla Gyi's house in Tiger Alley Road. That's where my other aunt lives too, the one they think is mad, but she isn't mad. Afterwards we went to the docks and Dad found my cabin. We talked about Kaikun, about Ahme, and my elephant who's called 'Maung Khin,' and Hanif, Ja-Bo and Jemma and about my gang having a new leader once I'd gone. When Dad had to go, I lay on my bunk and looked out of the porthole. We didn't sail for hours. I saw the pilot taken off. When we passed Diamond Point, they told me that was the last bit of Burma I'd see, so I looked and looked till I couldn't see anything. I felt peculiar, with pains here." He held his stomach. "I get those pains whenever I think of Dad and Ahme and Kaikun."

It was time to stop him. "You haven't drunk your tea."

A sailor came into the café and started the jukebox playing "My Blue Heaven."

"It hasn't been nice here without my mother. I miss her. You won't laugh if I tell you something? I see her. Often. I know I don't really see her, but it's as if I do, and I feel much better when it happens. The first time was when we were going to church. There she was, coming towards the school crocodile. There's only one pavement on the road along there, the one on our side. She was walking on the wet road, on the opposite side. I saw her distinctly, her hair done up with a flower in one side. No one in England does their hair like that, so I thought it must be her. I ran out of line and across the road, but when I got near, it wasn't her. It was someone in a black shiny hat, that's all. After that I saw her lots of times but I never ran to her again. I just looked at her and felt better. Sometimes when there are air-raids, I pray and pray for a bomb to fall on me. It's a bit mean to pray for a bomb because all the others would die too, but gosh, how I'd like the bomb to fall on me."

Miss Wadley said abruptly, "Would you like to go back to Burma?"

"No. I told you why. Dad wouldn't like it, and I want to do as he says."

"Your father and mother have asked *me* to decide."

He had eaten very little after he started speaking of his home. As Miss Wadley sat looking at him she wanted to push back wisps of hair from his eyes, settle his coat more comfortably. She wanted to touch him, to pet him.

"I think I'll take you back to Burma," she said.

"Back to Burma?" He said this in a puzzled way. "But there's

Butch. If I leave her nobody'd feed her. She'd die. I'd only go back if I could take her."

This statement filled Miss Wadley with sudden anger. The cheek! She had been overwhelmed by his wretchedness, had made a fateful decision for him and for herself; and he had the gall to make conditions! "Are you telling me you want to stay in England because of a dog?" He leaned across the table, touched her hand and spoke cajolingly, as adults sometimes speak to children.

"It's not what I want, Miss Wadley. It's what I have to do because I love Butch."

He looked at her glumly. She did not know anything about his parents, or him. How could she be so sure?

"Have you had enough to eat?"

"I don't want to eat any more here." He gave her a quick, sly look. "But may I take cakes away in my handkerchief?"

"For Butch?"

He did not answer.

She picked up her gloves and bag, pushed back her chair and left to pay the bill. They were alike, far too much alike. "They don't want me . . ." Wasn't this the kind of remark she had made about her own parents when they had sent her to school? Out of perversity, out of a need to be reassured and also to punish them for the misery of separation, she had said it again and again, to herself and to others, so that in the end she behaved *as if* it were true. In her heart, however, she knew perfectly well it wasn't true. It was an ugly thing to say, and curiously enough, she gained an ugly kind of satisfaction from hurting them and hurting herself.

Sometimes Miss Wadley wondered if she hadn't started something within herself, a self-destroying mechanism, that was responsible for so much that had gone wrong in her life.

"It is possible to take a dog out of the country, you know."

They were out on the pavement when she said this. The taxi was there, looming through the mist like a strange animal feeding by the kerbside. Ken made no reply, politely opened the door for her, then sat down as far from her as possible. Without a word he started to stuff his handkerchief, full of cakes and crumpets, into his mac pocket. Miss Wadley noticed he was trying not to cry, but his mouth was trembling.

"What's the matter?"

"You shouldn't have said that."

"Why not?"

"It's not fair. It's mean—mean." Now the tears were flowing. "Me and Butch going to Burma together—it couldn't ever happen, and all you've done is put hopes in my head."

She took his hands and, finding them cold, started to rub them.

"When you get to know me, you'll realize I never say anything I don't mean."

"Don't you, Miss Wadley? Don't you? Oh gosh, I hope that's true."

4

"There's something about her," the milkman said. "Either you get it or you don't. It's the same with all bull-terriers. Myself, I wouldn't have any other breed. Mind, she's no beauty, but dogs that look pretty, like spaniels, mate, you can keep 'em. What Butch has is . . ." The milkman put his head on one side and tried to put into words what it was that struck him as unique about his dog. "Damned if I know . . . makes me laugh, I guess. She'll last till she's fifteen or sixteen like my others did, provided she has one good scrap a day, and one pound of raw meat—with brown bread and a little gravy, Ken, and not too wet. With a war on, where am I to get a pound of meat a day? You'd better take her, lad . . ."

And so it was settled. Butch went on board the *Circassia* to some obscure corner belowdecks in the care of the ship's cook. Twice a day Ken was allowed to see her and exercise her round the lower decks.

Each time Ken went below he always asked Miss Wadley, "Are you sure you don't mind?"

"Why should I mind?"

As if Ken were off to see her rival and needed to make his peace with her in advance!

"I like dogs, you know."

"Anyone who likes dogs and wants to take her for a walk, I charge sixpence. I'm saving for Christmas presents. But I wouldn't charge *you*."

"That's very kind of you."

"It's only fair, after all you've done."

"Not that speech again, Ken."

Despite what she said, he made the "speech" leaning against her arm, looking dreamily over the sea. "You can laugh, Waddy, but I'll never forget, and I'll always be your friend. Next to my parents, and after Ko-Ni, and Jemma and Ja-Bo, you are the person I like best."

"Thank you very much. Now buzz off."

"You do love me, don't you?"

When he first put this question Miss Wadley had been disconcerted, particularly as he asked it within hearing of a number of people.

"*Don't* you?"

"You know I do." This satisfied him and he went off happily.

When the *Circassia* took on the pilot and entered Rangoon River close to Diamond Point Fort, Ken went down to the galley and badgered the cook until he finally gained possession of Butch —for good. He immediately led her to the cabin, where Butch lost her head, jumped over the bunks, knocked off suitcases, worried towels, barked and thoroughly upset Miss Wadley.

"Take that creature out of here. I wish I'd never let you bring her . . . ," and so on. Ken and Butch made themselves scarce, clattering up companionways until they reached the boat deck. Ken propped her up with her forepaws on the rail, a most uncomfortable position that stretched her paunch and made her nipples stand out like organ stops. But she endured it, for his sake, throwing him melting glances and licking the back of his head.

"Look out for elephants, Butch."

But there was nothing much to see at first beyond the fort and its guns: two long low bands of khaki divided empty sky from empty land. The ship settled down for the uneventful sail of thirty miles on the floodtide, and the passengers who had left their bunks to see Diamond Point settled back for another nap. There was no hurry. It would take five hours at least to reach Rangoon, and there was nothing much to see. Stretches of sand,

kaing grass, a collection of huts with crops on either side, and a
country boat moored by a wooden jetty, a patch of mangrove or
the feathering of Dhani palms—that was the pattern repeated
mile after mile until a cone of gold appeared on the port bow,
ten miles distant. The early morning sunlight flashed off it, and
as passengers sighted it, there was a stir of interest.

"The Shwe Dagon, Butch. Now we'll see elephants."

The dull banks were transformed with gleaming cupolas of
storage tanks, brick ovens, factory chimneys, sheds, power cables
strung between pylons striding along beside the ship. And . . .
at last, sawmills!"

"There they are! Those dots are elephants aunging [pushing]
logs with their bony foreheads." Ken pointed his dog's muzzle
in their direction. "Wait till you see them close to, at Kaikun. But
they hate dogs. I saw a pi-dog crushed when Me Kyauk-Kyi put
her foot on it. She's Maung Khin's mother, and Dad says she's
a bitch on four legs. Maung Khin will probably hate you, Butch,
but he's got to stop it because we're all three going about together. First thing I'll do is to show you Maung Khin, the very
first morning in Kaikun, before the sun's up. We'll creep into the
jungle and fetch him. He's pretty dangerous still. Half-trained
elephants always are. But Ko-Ni will be there. Maung Khin, Ko-
Ni, and me, isn't it funny? we're all the same age—thirteen years
old. Maung Khin and I are practically twins. He was born an
hour after me, that's why they called him Maung Khin, "Ken's
brother." He's going to be the biggest tusker of our herd. I was
going to train him, Butch, but they sent me away, and now Ko-
Ni's his elephant boy. When we go into the jungle to bring him
in from grazing, I'll ride him back. Ko-Ni can have Me Kyauk-
Kyi. If Ko-Ni tries to stop me, I'll use my dah. I don't care, I'm
determined to ride Maung Khin. Just you wait, I'll be on his head,
my toes under his ears and . . ."

Ken had been kneeling behind his dog, his arms round her
back, but gradually settled into a more comfortable position,
squatting in the scuppers, his legs stretched out, his head against
his dog's side. It was lovely to feel the sun on his lids. He should
be feeling happy. They were nearly there. Nearly in Rangoon.

Then disembarkation, taxi to the station, the train, and at dawn they'd arrive at Bilin Station. Dad would have hired a bus. Seventy miles to Kaikun. Breakfast at home. Breakfast with his mother opposite him.

Yet . . . he was not happy—that is, not a hundred percent. Excited, yes, so that his heart thumped and his stomach felt as if a hand squeezed it.

If only he was eighteen years old instead of thirteen. If only he was coming home knowing everything, ready to run the mills, to become important, he wouldn't have this queer feeling inside him, a kind of dread, spoiling everything.

He decided not to dwell on it, instead to think how lucky he was to spend Christmas at home after two Christmases with the Formby-Smiths. Perhaps Dad had arranged a Christmas camp again. If so he would ask if he could be in his mother's tent, and for once Dad could have the small tent. Jemma would be there too, and Mrs Dowall, who was Jemma's granny. What would Mrs Dowall give him for Christmas? She gave the most wonderful presents. Next to his mother and father, Ko-Ni, Jemma, Ja-Bo and Miss Wadley, he liked Mrs Dowall.

Jemma and he would sit with the elephant men on one side of the Christmas campfire, and the grown-ups on the other. The grown-ups would drink whisky while he, Jemma and the elephant men would eat chapatties and baked potatoes, curried vermicelli, gnapi and rice. Jemma would be silly and singe the tips of her plaits. In the morning he would sit in the "thunderbox" with the flap back. This was a little cubicle attached to the tent, from where he could look up at the tremendous teak trees soaring above the camp. Shafts of light dappled their trunks, and leaf after leaf would fall languidly. He liked to watch the tumbling leaves, sometimes put out his hand to catch one. While on the thunderbox, he would think of Matron in Downderry, thousands of miles away, walking up and down the line of W.C.'s, her heels clicking over cold white tiles. "Hurry up, boys! You're not to sit there all day." As each boy emerged, she went in, inspected. Yes, she did! She looked at it. He never got used to that.

He did not want to waste time thinking of Matron. He wanted
to think of Kaikun, of his house, the dark-brown Forest Bungalow beside the Yunzalin. He recalled details, checking them as
one might an inventory of furniture: arrows and dah on the top
of the big cupboard in his bedroom; cane hamper under the
window full of strips of wood, saws, planes, nails; bed with mosquito net rolled up over the canopy; by the door the gunmetal
basin that fitted into the hole of the washstand. Under the legs
of his bed he recalled tops of Player's cigarette tins filled with
paraffin oil to stop white ants eating away the wood. In imagination he gazed out of the door that opened out of his bedroom
on the back. There he saw the vegetable garden, the servants' quarters, the stables and the river glinting through the
jackfruit trees. Beyond, he pictured the Dawna hills grey under
a monsoon sky, and seemed to hear distant thunder rolling up
and down the wet grey valleys. And now he could almost
feel the big raindrops of the first monsoon downpour, drops of
water that fell heavily, making holes in the river's silk, jumping
about on the gravel, bombarding the corrugated iron sheeting of
the roof. He saw himself rush out to join Ja-Bo, who came
cavorting down the kitchen garden, his dusty body streaked with
rain. Together they dashed about, across the lawn, in and out of
trees and flowerbeds, their skins tingling as the raindrops hit
them all over. Jemma joined them, wet through, her dress clinging to her bony chest, her black hair in rat tails . . . The day-
dream changed. Now the three raced round the house, down
the drive, into the kitchen-gardens, where irrigation channels rip-
pled through the pineapple patch. The race ended abruptly at
the parapet of the garden wall. In the blue-black well water, Ken
and Jemma and Ja-Bo gazed down at themselves, three black
blobs moving gently against a spring sky. Chunder-ji had once
called Ken a frog in a well. Chunder was his father's Indian
clerk—all the clerks were Indians. "You do not want to be a frog
in a well," Chunder-ji said when he found him crying because
they were sending him to England. "He who does not go out
and explore the earth is a frog in a well."

"I'm going to push you in!" Suddenly Ken caught Jemma's

shoulders, jerked her forward and held her body over the eye
of the well. She made no attempt to free herself, but hung limply,
teeth clenched, her eyes fixed on him. He pulled her back, screaming, "Why didn't you fight back?" He was furious with her,
and filled with terror at what he might have done. Jemma said,
"If you had pushed me in, you would have got me out." Ja-Bo
told him, "I knew you would not." But Ken was not so sure. He
liked Jemma and he didn't like her. She gave in to him. Even
Ja-Bo and Ko-Ni stood up to him more than Jemma.

He dreamed of Deer Hill Valley, where it formed a crescent
round Kaikun Hill. The monastery stood about halfway up, on a
ledge overlooking the valley.

It was cold, before dawn, and his cotton robes created little
warmth. The others, novices like himself, also shivering, were
telling him to hurry up. He picked up a wooden mallet, struck
the ground to summon earth as witness, then hit the big bronze
gong. The sound bayed across the valley, and must have surely
carried to his mother and father asleep in the Forest Bungalow.
As he crossed the terrace round the monastery, he gazed down
at the Yunzalin where the hill's dark knob was reflected on the
water. The reflection seemed to be playing a game. It shortened
itself as if preparing to leap, then leaped, extending itself in an
attempt to touch the opposite bank. There, on the other side of
the river, the lawns of his mother's garden came down to the
reeds. No one walked across the lawns just then where only
the tips of the poinsettia bushes showed through the layers of
river mist. The time to look for people on the lawn was around
four in the afternoon. That was the time his mother strolled
out to cut sweet-peas, and searched for him up there in the
monastery.

When the novices, laymen and monks arrived on the fore-
court, the procession started, three of the boys going in front,
two to hold the pole, a third to beat the gong hanging from it.
They walked down the hill, through the village, sounding the
gong, stopping at doors where the women stood ready to fill
their bowls. Everything was done to lend dignity to their collecting round. They looked at no one, and when their bowls

were filled the women bowed and thanked them for the privilege of feeding them. From the village they walked over the water meadows, then crossed the bridge to the officials' houses and the bazaar. It was their usual route, but Ken was not certain if they would stop at his mother's door. This was the first time he had been out on the round. He had been initiated the day before and his shorn head felt cold; his body was unaccustomed to clothing that did not fit him. He walked at the end of the line carrying his iron bowl, one hand under it, the other on the lid, concentrating on the back of the ko-yin ahead of him. He willed the leading monk to take the path skirting his father's guava trees. Miraculously, he did so. Eyes cast down, stepping out gravely, but unable to control his shivering, Ken waited for the pongyi's signal which would direct him through the guavas to his own door. When it came, two other ko-yins, novices like himself, also left the line, walking sedately beside him. Ken was the last to receive food, and while awaiting his turn dared not look up, but stared at his mother's skirt and her feet under the hem.

At last it was his turn. He stood in front of her, eyes down, saying not one word. He lifted the lid of his begging bowl and she filled it with rice and curry, each portion wrapped separately in a plantain leaf. Ken yearned to look up, to speak, but it was not allowed, and he had not the nerve to disobey. When his bowl was full he replaced the lid and would have turned away having seen nothing of his mother but the lower part of her skirt and her feet, but she touched his arm. "Would you cheat me of merit, ko-yin? I have more for you. Take off the lid." This time he looked up and met her laughing eyes. He gave her a swift, guilty look, grinned, but, almost instantly, assumed the gravity befitting those of the monkhood.

She stuffed another packet into his bowl. He guessed it was sugar. She whispered, "Be brave. Don't cry. It is only for a little while."

He did not reply but turned away, following the others back to the procession. He was exhilarated by this meeting, not merely because he had seen his mother, but because he had not spoken to her and he had not wept. He had showed no emotion, he had conducted himself well.

It was an achievement in self-discipline, only a minor victory to be sure, but the Abbot had been pleased with him. Afterwards the old man told Kyi Minh, "Refuse the lesser good for the greater—that is the vision of Buddhism, my son. But you must not think you are meant to torment yourself or others: neither self-indulgence nor self-mortification." Then he had quoted words which had stuck in Ken's mind because he couldn't make head or tail of them. "He who is indifferent but mindful dwells in happiness."

How was that possible? It didn't make sense, and so the words irritated him. You couldn't mind and not mind at the same time. And if you ever did feel like that, it could only make you wretched . . . as wretched as he felt at that moment, hidden with his dog behind the lifeboats on the *Circassia*.

He faced up to it at last: this homecoming filled him with happiness and misery, both together, and at the same time, as if the happiness made his heart thump and the misery buckled him up round the stomach.

It was difficult to understand why this should be so. He knew dimly that his feelings were bound up in his anxiety to please his mother, his father, Miss Wadley, and to gratify his own desires. He had wanted so desperately to come home, but it was Miss Wadley, not he, who had taken the decision. It wasn't his fault. Dad and Ahme would see that, wouldn't they?

5

Hamish was out of the trench, giving orders.

"Dil Tharpa!"

"Sir!"

"Get out—and get *them* out."

"Sir."

"Go to the Lakes—to my club."

"Sir." Dil Tharpa saluted and clicked his heels.

Miss Wadley got to her feet too, head and shoulders appearing above the trench where the orderly had scrambled out. She looked about in a daze, taking in details one by one, first the orderly's boots and puttees and then the man himself rearing above her against a background of flames and smoke rising from a big white building—the Law Courts, on the far side of the gardens. Nearer, in the precincts of the Sule Pagoda, a palm tree and part of the monastery roof were ablaze, and within yards of the trench flames enveloped the clothing of a man spread-eagled on the grass. The sight of the Gurkha police orderly standing to attention and saluting Hamish in the midst of this shambles, Hamish Waight himself taking charge so quickly, issuing orders, made a deep impression on Miss Wadley. Discipline, order, the faculty of responding instantly in an emergency, these were what was needed in crisis, and were qualities she believed she possessed.

She held out her hand to Dil Tharpa and was the first he pulled out. How strange it was—so quiet. The crackle of flames sounded louder, and now she could hear above the tree tops the tinkle of bells. In the gardens all was still save for a painted paper umbrella which somersaulted lazily down the main path, its spokes clicking over the concrete. No other people save for Hamish, Dil Tharpa and herself seemed to be upright and conscious. The group of Burmese men and women who had stood chattering by the trench now lay in a mound of tangled cloth, legs and arms in unnatural attitudes. It was impossible to judge how many sticks of anti-personnel bombs had fallen round them and in the streets round the Sule Pagoda.

"Why the Lakes? Send them to Hla Gyi." Tom had scrambled out and was speaking to Hamish.

"Right. Dil Tharpa—know the house of McNeil Thakin in Tiger Alley Road?"

"Know, sir."

"Go by the parade ground. Keep away from bazaar streets."

"Sir!"

The Englishwoman, her daughter and ayah were standing round Hamish looking at him as if waiting to be told what to do. "Shall I go back to my hotel?"

"Where is it?"

"Strand Road."

"Should be okay. Go quickly—that way—and run, get inside before the panic and looting start."

Everyone was out of the trench with the exception of Ken and his dog. The old white bull terrier knew all about air-raids and refused to leave, crouching against her earth, struggling when Ken attempted to lift her. Eventually Dil Tharpa clambered in again to heave her out. From the garden bench where Hamish and Tom were working among the dead, dying and wounded, the orderly heard a furious shout. "Dil Tharpa! What the hell are you doing there? I told you to clear out."

"It's the dog," Miss Wadley called to them.

"If that bloody dog won't follow, leave her."

Ken heard this and leaped out hauling at Butch's lead while Dil Tharpa shoved from behind.

"Leave Butch! I won't! I won't!" In his agitation he flung his arms round her and started to weep. Tom came over to his son, knelt beside him, patting his head and the dog's head too.

"There's a good boy. Take your dog, but you must be quick. You're to go at once with Dil Tharpa to your aunt's house in Tiger Alley Road."

"But I don't want to. I want to go to the station, to the train. I don't want to see Hla Gyi. I want to see Ahme."

"The trains aren't running."

"Then let's go by car."

"There'll be a stampede—the roads will be blocked."

"But Butch is trembling. She must go into the train or the car. She can't walk. It's miles and miles to Tiger Alley Road." Ken's sobs grew louder. "I don't want to go with Dil Tharpa."

"But Miss Wadley will be with you."

"I don't want her. I've had enough of her. I want *you*."

Tom looked at Miss Wadley. "He doesn't know what he's saying. I think I'd better come with you."

Hamish Waight shouted, "Tom." He was signalling to him to join him where he worked among the people lying round the bench. All round them wounded men, women and children were now emerging from shock, shrieking with pain, calling for help.

Miss Wadley said, "I've passed my St. John's Ambulance. If you like, I'll stay and help while you take Ken."

"Good of you. No." He looked round in alarm at the clanging of fire engines, the roar of a building collapsing, and down the street a mob of half-naked men, dock coolies, surging up from Strand Road. Tom bent over a dead man lying on the grass and removed his staff. "Dil Tharpa—here—" He put the staff in the policeman's hand. "If necessary—must use that too." Tom indicated the revolver in the orderly's holster. "Now, go." He did not look at his son again or speak to Miss Wadley.

"Thakin—hold belt, please?" Dil Tharpa lifted Ken's hand. "Pya, in belt, please." He also placed Miss Wadley's hand in his belt.

They set off, Dil Tharpa slightly ahead, Ken and Miss Wadley hanging on to him, the dog dodging between their legs.

Miss Wadley said, "For goodness' sake, keep your dog on the outside. If you can't—you heard what Mr Waight said. She'll be left."

Miss Wadley could feel Ken's gaze on her, but she kept her eyes fixed ahead. Dil Tharpa was trying to push their way across a road solid with frightened, fleeing pedestrians. Private cars, taxis, handcarts, bullock-carts were also trying to push their way along. He used his staff on backs and bullocks, and once, unintentionally, brought it down on Butch. Ken let go of the orderly's belt and flung himself over the yelping dog. "They're all against you!" he sobbed.

"Don't be silly. Get up." Miss Wadley yanked him upright and thrust his hand roughly back under the belt. He tried to wriggle away.

"Butch! Butch."

Miss Wadley picked up the dog in her arms.

"I'll carry her. But if you misbehave once more—just once more, Ken—I'll get rid of her."

The boy did not answer but his eyes betrayed his fear.

"I'll be good. Promise. If you look after Butch. I'll do anything."

When they crossed the road Dil Tharpa turned down a side road, and here Miss Wadley put the dog down. Ken sidled over to her.

"Waddy, please forgive me for what I said to Dad. I haven't had enough of you. Do you believe me? I do really love you, because you rescued me from rotten old England."

Rotten old England! England where after an air-raid people behaved like human beings and not like stampeding cattle, where it was not left to one or two men to succour the wounded and where the dead were not disposed of like cockroaches. As they were leaving Fytche Gardens Miss Wadley had heard Hamish tell Tom that at least a thousand had been killed. "If the sweepers have bunked we'll have to get gangs of convicts to remove and burn them," Hamish had said, and Tom had agreed.

"I'm not interested in what you think of me or England. Look where you're going, and hang on."

The street down which Dil Tharpa led them was some kind of

rice mart, flanked by rice storerooms where the warehouse owners were frantically heaving shutters into place. Three youths
came running down the street with a lighted torch, halted
before a locked and shuttered store and deliberately set the shutters alight. Behind them others raced along with a handcart, came
to a stop where a man was wedging an iron bar over shutters.
He was clubbed, the bar was lifted, shutters removed and the
youths rushed into the store. Dil Tharpa drew his revolver and
quickened the pace. As they passed, the youths were busy hauling sacks of rice onto the cart. One of them noticed the white
woman, said something in Burmese which made the others laugh.
Miss Wadley flushed. She had been about to stop, to help the
unconscious man lying on the road, but walked on. At the end
of the street they ran the gauntlet between several wooden
houses which had caught fire.

Out on a wide road with shops and offices Ken halted.

"Can I finish my Christmas shopping?"

Miss Wadley gaped at him.

"Are you trying to be funny?"

"No. Why?"

Was this why she avoided children? Their total self-interest
was incomprehensible and sometimes, as at that instant, aroused
her fury.

They had turned left to enter this road, and Miss Wadley was
beginning to understand why it was almost deserted. Each road
crossing it and going north was jammed with traffic. By turning
left, westwards, Dil Tharpa was leading them away from the
direction of the main exodus.

"You're not going the right way," Ken kept saying. "That's the
way." He pointed to the north.

"Quicker this way," Dil Tharpa said, but he did not sound too
sure. He looked worried, hesitating before taking them down
any more side streets.

"It isn't quicker. You're going miles round, and I'm dropping."
Dil Tharpa gave in, joining the flow of the main evacuation
traffic, where large buildings in spacious grounds were set well
back from the highway. One was a leper hospital, and not far

from it stood a convent where nuns could be seen walking serenely under the trees as if nothing unusual was happening. Were the good creatures so engrossed in the small black books they were studying that they failed to see the poor Indians hurrying by, all they owned tied in a bundle and carried on their heads? And their children, small naked boys, running beside their fathers, arms going like pistons, in the desperate effort not to be left behind. Outside a college a mob of students had surrounded a fire engine and were refusing to let it drive towards the stricken city. Hundreds of fellow students lined the college railing waving flags, singing, blowing and whistling, and jeering at the refugees.

"Why won't they let the fire engine pass?" Miss Wadley asked.

"Because it's an Indian city and they want it to burn," Ken told her.

The students excited him. He dashed to the railings, begged one for a flag and, when it was given him, joined with them singing "Doh Bama."

Dil Tharpa scowled at him. "No! No! Bad song. Give me that." He tried to take the flag, but Ken pranced away. "It's not a bad song. My aunt taught it to me. 'Doh Bama' means 'We the Burmese.' What's wrong with that? I'm not a beastly Indian anyway."

Miss Wadley said sharply, "That's enough." She met his defiant gaze and held it until he lowered his eyes. He tried to slip his hand into hers. "Sorry, Waddy." She shook him off.

Past a hospital where a number of ambulances stood in the yard. Where were the drivers? And if the drivers had fled, why didn't someone—anyone—drive them out? Perhaps they had tried and found it impossible to force a way through this multitude. Dil Tharpa ducked down a side road and started a jog-trot towards an open space, a parade ground. Many bombs had fallen here. A car lay burning on the road, and on one side of the parade ground a wooden pavilion had been burnt to the ground. Nearby, and for the first time that day, Miss Wadley saw an ambulance and stretcher bearers lifting casualties. Not far from the blazing car a strange noise could be heard, a kind of keening. Ken heard it, froze, shoved Butch's lead into Miss Wadley's

hands and, before the orderly knew what he was up to, had
snatched the revolver out of his holster. The boy ran to where a
cart had overturned and a horse or bullock lay trapped between
the shafts. Dil Tharpa went after Ken, caught him beside the
cart, where there was a scuffle. Miss Wadley couldn't see what
happened, but heard a shot and the anguished keening ceased.
Ken's face was white and he was trembling. He threw his arms
round her and tried to smother his cries against her skirt. She
wanted to scold him for snatching the revolver, but his distress
affected her and she said nothing. She held him tightly, murmuring anything that came into her head. "Good boy. Brave boy.
It was the only thing to do. Don't worry. I'm here. I'm looking
after you." After a while she said, "Now straighten up. We must
go on." As she said this she found herself questioning it. Must
we? Must I? Why couldn't she turn south, return to the docks?
The *Circassia* was returning to England in three days' time, and
England was where she wanted to be. Home. Where in an air-
raid traffic moved, ambulances found their way to the wounded,
and the dead were not carted off to be burnt like dead cockroaches. Did she really care for this boy sufficiently to live—even
for a week—in a place where everything seemed to grate on
her? Once with his mother, Ken would have no further use for
her: she had been a stopgap. Miss Wadley was determined to
regard their relationship dispassionately. She did not mean to
allow this show of affection from one small boy to affect her life.

Dil Tharpa was taking another short cut. The area was greener,
cooler, and though there were still crowds of Indians hurrying
by, there were also groups of Burmese among the crowds. Where
roads led into woods, the gilded pinnacles of monastery roofs
could be seen above treetops. It was to these sanctuaries that
the Burmese seemed to be making their way.

It was no longer necessary to hitch themselves to Dil Tharpa.
They walked one behind the other down a street of small shops,
all open and doing business. The Gurkha was in the lead, followed by Miss Wadley and, behind her, Ken and his dog, when
they overtook a Chinese family. The father and mother were
pulling a little cart heaped with brightly coloured tin boxes,

their baby wedged between two. After them they passed a stout middle-aged Indian woman whose saree was woven and bordered with gold thread. Over her wrists and arms she wore a number of gold and silver bracelets. For a time Miss Wadley walked beside her, conscious of the woman's sultry perfume. Overtaking her, Miss Wadley joined a knot of Indian clerks— willowy, boneless-looking youths in collarless shirts and floating sleeves who looked as if they were out for a picnic.

"Where are you going?"

"Everyone going Prome Road."

"Are you going back to Rangoon?"

"Not going back, madam. We will walk to India."

"It's a long way."

"Five hundred, six hundred miles. Not knowing."

"What about food and shelter?"

"God will provide."

Suddenly from behind them there came a sound of tearing cloth followed by a scream. Miss Wadley whipped round to see the Indian woman standing in the middle of the road, a red gash extending from the fleshy pad of her shoulder down the length of her arm. Blood from her wrist covered her saree and had fallen on the skin of a half-naked man, a Burmese who was grubbing up bracelets strewn about her feet.

Miss Wadley also saw something else—Ken, hands on his hips, laughing.

"I know she was an Indian," Ken said later, "because of her fat. Burmese women are never fat. As she walked I'd been watching a rolled-up pancake along her stomach. This one big roll changed into three small ones as she walked. Just then I looked up and saw a man with a dah in a doorway. He was also looking at her, and I knew at once what he was going to do—because I'd once seen a man in a fair do it. That man didn't make his lady squirt blood though. This one did. With one big swipe he cut all the bangles down her arm so that they fell off, and her blood went over everything. One gold bangle stuck, and the man lifted his dah to have another go when Dil Tharpa butted in. I told him she was only an Indian, but Dil Tharpa clouted the man with the butt of his revolver. He got away with every one of the bangles except the one that stuck."

Miss Wadley tore a strip off her petticoat to bind the woman's arm while the Chinese couple ran back to the shops for a cup of water. The Indian clerks offered to take care of her until they reached Prome.

When they left the woman, Ken walked close to Miss Wadley, scrutinizing her face and trying to hold her hand but did not know how to get round her. He said tentatively, "You didn't like me laughing and you didn't like him hitting her, did you? Well, he shouldn't have. And I'm sorry I laughed. It was only because it was so clever. Admit, it was clever. You couldn't swipe like that with a dah, could you? *I* could—almost, I think. When we get to Kaikun I'll show you."

Miss Wadley looked at Ken for a moment without speaking. "I am going to take you as far as your aunt's house, then I'm going back to the *Circassia*. I'm going back to England."

6

Up a slight rise the houses of Tiger Alley Road came into sight. Some of teak, some of masonry, nearly all were big bizarre buildings reflecting the taste of Chinese and Indian millionaires. The gardens, full of statuary, fountains, pergolas, were ablaze with flowers.

"Hollyhocks in December!" Miss Wadley exclaimed.

"We had hollyhocks in the beds below the classrooms, but they were black and broken. England's so sad." Ken poked his head round her side to peer at her face. "You don't mind me going on about England, do you, Waddy? It's so gorgeous to be away from England, I can't help kind of gloating."

"I miss England."

"You're only saying that to be quits."

"Nonsense."

"And if you did go back to England you'd miss Burma. Bet you. You didn't mean what you said about going back. It was only to shut me up. You wouldn't break your promise. You've promised to teach me so I won't fall behind, so I'll get through Common Entrance and get into Shrewsbury."

How much of what he said was part of a deliberate technique to acquire what he thought he wanted? How much was genuine?

But why should she assume his affection, gestures and persistence, his way of wearing down her opposition were part of a scheme? He did need her. In a muddled way he was trying to

convince her that he needed her as well as his mother, needed
Burma as well as England.

"This road goes on forever. Where's this house? Run ahead
with Butch and wait outside whichever it is."

But Ken was incapable of patience. When he reached the drive
turning into his aunt's red-brick mansion, he gave a whoop and
rushed forward, Butch at his heels. By the time Miss Wadley
and Dil Tharpa arrived, Ken was already at the entrance platform, the panat-choot, or "shoe-removing platform," where Butch
was drinking water from an enamel wash-basin and Ken was being fussed over by an elderly woman in Burmese dress. She wore
old-fashioned foot-bags, and was small, nondescript but with
the vivacity and bright-eyed glance of a sparrow. While hug-
ging the boy, patting his cheeks, she managed to help him off
with his shoes and socks and to shriek orders at servants.

"Pin Wa! My Pin Wa! Bring lemon squash! Bring sweets!"

She never stopped talking and took no notice of Miss Wadley
and Dil Tharpa staring at her from the drive.

"How tall you are, and how dirty! You must have a bath, food,
rest. You must take off those awful English trousers and put on a
green silk longyi I have bought specially for you."

"Can they come in?"

"First your strange animal, then these people! I suppose so.
But the man is an Indian! I will not have an Indian here."

"Don't play that game with me, Aunt!" Ken caught her face
between his hands and rubbed noses with her. "Pretending to
be daft when you know you're not. Anyway it isn't your house.
Where is Hla Gyi? And my uncle?"

His aunt Ma Hla Gyi and his uncle U Thet Nyein owned one
of Rangoon's best silk shops in Phayre Street. It wasn't his uncle
who ran it, but his aunt, and her name was placed first, "Hla Gyi
and Thet Nyein Silk Emporium." His uncle preferred to run
the house, look after the baby, and, when free, to enter chess
tournaments.

Daw Hla Palai flapped her hand in the direction of the city in
answer to Ken's question. "They're over there. They'll be all
right. The bombs aren't meant for the Burmese, only the people

who shouldn't be in our country. When I've bathed you and fed you, Pin Wa, you and I will go on the roof to watch Rangoon burning and Indians,—thousands of them—running away down the Prome Road. This is the happiest day of my life." In her glee she hugged him and covered his face with kisses.

"Do stop messing me about, Aunt. You know I don't like being kissed or kissing people. Dad says we're to stay here. We've walked all the way. We're hot and tired and hungry. Aren't you going to do anything for us?"

The old woman started to laugh. "Listen to him! Already the English milord!"

"That's rot. I only want you to treat us properly."

"Since when have I not treated you properly?"

"This English lady has to have a room, Aunt, and a bath and then some food. And so have I. And Mr Waight's orderly has got to be looked after too."

Far from being annoyed at the way Ken spoke, Daw Hla Palai cackled, wagged her head and, Miss Wadley decided, behaved, as if she really were daft.

"Wicked one! Ordering me about! But I am so pleased to see you, you can make me do anything." She gave Miss Wadley an indifferent glance. "Enter, madame. As for the Indian—he can go round the back, where the servants will give him something to eat."

Dil Tharpa listened with a stony expression, but instead of obeying marched off into the garden, where he sat down under a tree.

"You have offended him."

"Offend a plains Gurkha! That's good!"

A plains Gurkha was one who had settled in Burma, in one of the villages in the northern plains round Myitkyina.

Ken jumped off the panat-choot to help up Miss Wadley, and though she allowed him to take her arm—good manners in boys should be encouraged—she behaved stiffly, refusing to smile. She had been watching his wiles with his aunt. Impudence mixed with affection: a combination Ken had evidently discovered worked wonders with spinsters.

"There are lots of rooms. I'll make her give you one near me."

The cheek of it! As if she cared two pins where he was.

"A bath and a rest, then I'll get you something to eat. There's always lots of grub in this house—Coca-Cola too. Okay, Waddy?"

Half of her itched to put him in his place, to make it clear she wasn't to be cajoled by stratagems, but the other succumbed, yielding to his sweetness.

The old woman bobbed along like a pied wagtail, Butch behind her sniffing at her clothes. They passed a high green door where Ken stopped. "This is the room for Miss Wadley. I'll have the smaller one."

The bedroom was as big and airy as a barn, full of amber light which turned to green when Ken closed the shutters. The aunt had opened a door communicating with an adjoining room and stood, with obvious impatience for Ken to join her.

"Come, Pin Wa! I've so much to tell you."

But Ken was playing the host. "If you want to read while you rest, Uncle Thet Nyein puts old detective stories in this cupboard with his French, English and German books. I'll be next door."

He was about to join his aunt when he hesitated. Something was troubling him.

"Waddy?"

"Yes."

"Cheer up. It's nice here. Please, I want you to like Burma. I want you so much to stay with me."

After his bath Ken lay luxuriating against taut, cool sheets, wriggling his bare toes, feeling fresh and clean. He wore a green silk longyi, bunched in front with the customary knot, leaving his chest bare.

His aunt sat on a stool beside the bed, the flit gun in her hand with which she had been attacking mosquitoes behind a cupboard. Her eyes devoured him. "Why are you so thin, Pin Wa? Have they been starving you in that English school?"

Ken frowned. Pin Wa! Fat Bottom! What a nickname. It might

have suited him when he was two years old, but he was now thirteen and his aunt should have more tact than to treat him like a toddler.

"I wish you wouldn't call me by that name."

She put down the flit gun, bent over him. In the dim light her face hung above him like a moon. He had a good look at her two spots, one on her upper lip, the other on her chin. Later he'd ask permission to touch them. Touching warts made wishes come true.

"Not Pin Wa? He! He!" She had a way of blowing through her nose when she was indignant. "Such a tone of command! The commanding little Englishman already! What else have they taught you? What other infamy? Would you like Burmese women to take their husbands' names like English women? Would you like us to hand over our businesses to our husbands?"

She was baiting him. To get even with her Ken said. "I'll tell you what I'd like to do. I'd like to go back near Voyle Road where I saw a dacoit gash a Bengali woman's arm to get her bangles. Her blood went all over me. I'd like to use my dah on that Burmese. I'd like to kill him."

"Thou shalt not take any life at all." She quoted the first of the Five Great Precepts. "Did you learn nothing at the monastery school?"

Of course he had. For six months he had chanted aloud the Precepts morning, noon and night in the big hall with the statue of the Lord Buddha gazing down upon him. But his aunt wasn't being consistent: sometimes she said one thing, sometimes the other, and he suspected her of twisting the Noble Truths to suit her own ends. According to her, it was all right to take life if you were Saya San. Ken hadn't forgotten her stories about him and his rebels, how he stole silently through the jungles of the Yomas to the paddylands of Pegu and there, spreading out across the moonlit fields, Saya San and his men drew their dahs. One lit a bamboo torch, ran forward, set fire to the huts, and when the Indian cultivators rushed out, they used their dahs to kill men, women and children.

"Why can't I kill a dacoit if Saya San can kill people?"

"The Lord Buddha taught it is the motive that matters. If you kill, what counts is *why* you were forced to do it. Saya San wanted to give us back our spirit, and to do that he had to get rid of the Indians, the eaters of Burma—who have taken our jobs, our trade and our lands."

How his aunt hated the poor Indian! Ken did not. Hanif and Ja-Bo were Indians, the sons of his parents' Indian servants, the cook and sweeper. Old Fatima, the cook's mother, who had become his nurse, was also an Indian. Ken had never understood his aunt's hatred until his mother had told him something of Daw Hla Palai's story.

Daw Hla Palai was a gambler, as most Burmese are, and like hundreds and thousands of Burmese she had borrowed money from the Chettyars, a group of Indian money-lenders, giving as security the title deeds of her land.

"When you see a wicked dacoit trying to kill a poor fat woman walking along, it's natural to want to kill the dacoit. And you should," Ken said.

"It's not worth thinking about."

"But aren't you sorry for the Bengali woman?"

"Perhaps I am. But only because she was hurt, and not because she was running away from Rangoon. I want her to go. If she changed her mind and tried to come back, I would tell that man to hit her harder. The jewellery he took really belongs to you and me."

"Oh, Aunt, it doesn't!" She was so outrageous, he could only laugh. She started to laugh too, and slapped his buttocks. "What do you know of Burma and her troubles, Pin Wa? You are a puppy, not even a fat puppy with a pretty fat bottom, but a scraggy little fellow, all bones and opinions. If you want to learn the truth about this war, tune into Radio Tokyo. At least they don't insult us by relaying everything in English like the Rangoon Radio. They have the courtesy to speak our tongue. When you listen to Radio Tokyo you'll find out that the warriors of Saya San are still carrying his standard."

"Will you go and work for them? Will you put on nun's robes again?"

"I became a nun to redeem my self-respect." She referred to her bankruptcy and her subsequent divorce. She had shaved her head, put on the cream-coloured robes of the Buddhist nun and retired to a nunnery on the eastern slopes of the Yomas. She had lived as a penitent for a year. Had it not been for the advent of Saya San in 1930, she would have been then pensioned off in her sister's house, as eventually she was bound to be. But the advent of Saya San postponed her retirement and gave her one glorious year of revenge. In her nun's robes she travelled all over Chettyar lands, working for him as a spy. "But we were all spies for him," she used to tell Ken. Wherever a Burmese worked, there he established a listening post, as a servant in an English club, as a messenger in the High Court, as a waiter in the Strand Hotel.

At first his aunt had worked in the foothills, slipping through police cordons to secret rendezvous. Later she worked in Rangoon, where in nun's robes and walking barefoot she passed unnoticed.

"Tell me about Saya San." He tugged at her scarf. "Start like you used to, please: 'In the tractless forests of the Yomas there lived a magician called Saya San . . .'"

As English boys are brought up on the legends of King Arthur, so his aunt had brought him up on the legends of this Burmese hero. Not a hero like King Arthur of long ago, but one who had been fighting British soldiers in their lifetime, since 1930. Saya San was a Burmese peasant who declared war on the British after proclaiming himself King of the Galons, and King of Burma on Alaunstaung Hill in the Yomas in 1930.

Ken put his hands behind his head, gazed into the fold of the mosquito net and saw there the dappled light of deep forest, and the palace protected by a stockade of bamboo stakes. In Burma only palaces and monasteries may be gilded, and this secret palace of the King of the Galons was painted in gold inside and out, hung with silver paper and quantities of tinsel by the Burmese to honour the man they had crowned "King" of Burma. Ken saw in imagination the rebel armoury too, shotguns and rifles wrested from village headmen, and, most interesting of

all, home-made fire-arms made from waterpipes, guns and can-
nons constructed out of the steel casing of telegraph posts, oil
drums, and segments of the giant bamboo. These they had
thonged with leather and lashed with cane. His aunt told him
these makeshift weapons killed hundreds of Indians. Even better were the improvised mortars with shells made of nails and
broken glass. In Ken's opinion, the most ingenious weapon of all
—and one he would have loved to possess—were the Galons'
crossbows, whose arrows were tipped with snake venom.

Daw Hla Palai started: "In the tractless forest of the Yomas
there lived a magician called Saya San who could turn glass into
rubies, lead into gold and whose spells and charms were renowned throughout the kingdom. He enslaved with a magic
formula a cruel ogress called Nyo and pacified many nats°
of Tharrawaddy, Insein and Pyapon. Saya San diagnosed all ill-
nesses by consulting the Nat of Earth, the Nat of Water, the Nat
of Fire and the Nat of Wind, and with knowledge of healing
herbs, he cured the Ninety-Six Diseases.

"One day the Guardian Spirit of Rangoon† appeared to him.
U Shin Gyi was playing his harp and weeping amidst the leaves
of a peepul tree."

Ken interrupted: "Saya San was a good Buddhist, so he
couldn't believe in nats."

"If you interrupt again, I'll stop. Saya San, being a Buddhist
monk, as well as a magician, did not worship nats, but, because
he was polite he reverenced them, as the Buddhist reverences the
sacred beings of all religions. Also, Saya San had more sense
than to reject the beliefs of common people who believe in nats.
'What is troubling you? U Shin Gyi,' Saya San asked, and at this
question the Nat looked astonished. 'Don't you know who I am?'
he asked. Saya San replied, 'You are the Guardian Spirit of Rangoon.' 'Isn't that cause enough to weep? I have become the
Guardian Spirit of the unhappiest city in Burma. Rangoon is an

° Godlings of the old animist religion of Burma. These are spirits of
the dead who return to earth to inhabit trees, rivers, etc.
† A Talaing prince who was buried alive under the Sule Pagoda by
King Alaungpaya in the eighteenth century.

Indian city and milch cow, surrounded by foreigners who have stolen her self-respect, and her riches.' Saya San replied, 'This every Burman knows, U Shin Gyi. But no one can change these things.' Whereupon U Shin Gyi started to weep afresh. 'You are the most renowned magician in Burma. You can cure leprosy with chaulmoogra oil, you can induce or alleviate labour pains with the nigella plant; you have charms that can make a man invulnerable to bullets, and spells that can make him invisible. You have only to point your finger at an aeroplane to make it fall out of the sky. That is why I have come to you. Your alchemy can liberate Burma. You can become the successor to Mindon, and become the next King of Burma, live in a palace, use the white umbrella and possess a white elephant. Saya San, I command you to restore Burma to her people. Rid Burma of the foreigners who mine her rubies, fell her teak trees, and extract her oil.'"

Ken fidgeted. Teak implicated his father.

"Burmese sell the teak too."

For a moment Daw Hla Palai was silent, deliberating what course to take with Ken. He was no longer the wide-eyed, trusting little boy who once accepted everything she said. "Foreigners are the eaters of Burma. They eat our golden land with a hundred mouths. Should one admire the snake with a hundred heads or the hawk that destroys it?"

The Indian was symbolized by the hydra-headed snake, the Naga. According to Burmese mythology, only the Galon, the mythical hawk-griffin, could kill the Naga, and that was why Saya San had made it his emblem.

"Answer me. Which are you for, the Naga or the Galon?"

Ken would not answer her but demanded instead, "What did Saya San reply to the nat?"

"Saya San told U Shin Gyi, 'Our religion teaches us to desire neither riches nor power. Buddhism teaches us to want nothing.' At this the nat said in disgust, 'And that is what you have— nothing.'

"His answer made Saya San ponder, and he realized that what the nat said was true. Saya San decided to leave the forest, to go to the villages of Tharrawaddy and recruit young men to his standard. Anyone who joined him he decided to tattoo with his sacred emblem of the Galon, to make him invulnerable to bullets."

"May I feel your arm?"

His aunt held it out, and Ken felt bumps where her skin had grown over three pellets. Ten years ago, she had told Ken, Saya San himself had inserted these pellets under her skin to give her immunity to lethal weapons. On her right shoulder his aunt was also tattooed, not with the Galon, but with a magical formula, the letters ATK, which stood for the Galon, the Tiger and the Naga.

"Saya San's message spread quickly because it was one all Burmese wanted to hear. There had been countless portents—for instance, the earthquakes of Pegu, which the nat-kadaws [wives of spirit nats] interpreted as predicting a return of a king upon the Lion Throne. Every Burmese, rich or poor, some openly, others secretly, sympathized with Saya San's rebellion. Saya San issued a proclamation declaring war on the British, and telling the Burmese that he intended to overthrow the British Government."

"To overthrow the British Government!" A simple monk, defying a nation: David defying Goliath, Ken McNeil defying Mr Formby-Smith! Ken could not but admire Saya San.

"The Galon Army won victory after victory, the brave young Burmese fought the trained soldiers brought from India to shoot them down. But these Indian mercenaries could not kill the Galons because Saya San's magic made them invulnerable. Bullets passed through their bodies and out again leaving no mark."

"Really? Truly? Bullets didn't kill them?"

Daw Hla Palai looked at him levelly and repeated carefully, so that Ken would remember her words, "Bullets could not kill the Galons. No matter what people say, that's true. Saya San's men did not fight stupidly as British soldiers do, marching into the open and in broad daylight. The Galons never came out except at night, kept to the jungle, and used bird-calls to signal to one another. When the British patrols went after them they melted into the trees, and when the Indian soldier went into the forests the Burmese ambushed them. Our men won battle after battle, Insein, Yenatha, Mezali Ywana; one day those three names will be glorified in our history books. The Galon Army kept the British on the run month after month. The British took 10,000 Galons prisoner, but still Burmese flocked to join Saya San. The Galon Army grew so big that Saya San had to appoint generals under him—San Huta, Aung Myat, U Arthapa . . ."

Ken heard the sound of wheels on the gravel and ran to the window.

"It's Dad and Mr Waight." He peered through the shutters. "They're in a police van with a loudspeaker. What are they doing in a police van? And what's the loudspeaker for?"

His aunt's face twisted with a smile full of malice. "I think I can guess."

7

Miss Wadley felt so clean and fresh after her bath she could not bring herself to put on her soiled, sweat-soaked clothes. She would cool off for a bit in bed, she decided. Lying down naked between the sheets, she had fallen asleep almost at once.

How long had she slept? The room was full of shadowy colour, the ceiling dappled with globes of green and golden light, the marble floor with browns and amber, its surface so polished that the bed with its white linen and canopy of mosquito-netting lay mirrored above it like a ship in full sail.

She lay in the big bed savouring a delicious sensation of languor. It wasn't like her. She permitted herself the odd day in bed only when she had flu. Nor was it in character for her to lie between sheets with nothing on. In convent school she had worn a shift to prevent her looking at herself in her bath, but while she now recognized this as going too far, the inhibitions of early training remained with her and normally she simply did not look at her surprisingly young, firm body, nor indulge in the minor sensuality of enjoying the touch of sheets on her skin.

Holding the sheet up over her breasts, she got out of bed, wandered barefoot to the corner where she had dumped her clothes. She could not find them so went round the room taking a good look at everything: a small jade Buddha placed in a niche and evidently used as a shrine, for there was a lighted candle and flowers before it; glass-fronted bookcase with detec-

tive stories in French and German which, according to Ken, his
uncle liked to read; vases of flowers with an oversweet perfume;
and by her bed a curious basket padded with cotton in which a
teapot and a shallow bowl were embedded. Miss Wadley helped
herself to the green tea, enjoying it despite its bitterness, then
walked over to the window. Her clothes must be somewhere. She
needed more light to find them. When she had thrown back the
shutters she had stood quite still, too astounded to move or to
explain. How had it got there? Shouldn't it be miles away and
to the north. Was the house then so far from Rangoon, to the
north? Beyond the foreground of flower garden, dark-green
hedges of jasmine and an orchid house, she saw a green wooded
hill rising from a wooded area. On the summit a small citadel
of glimmering white and gold buildings, spires, fretted rooftops,
turrets and lesser pagodas formed a ring, spreading out like the
petals of a flower. From the centre rose a slender stalk, the fila-
ment of a stamen, crowned like a stamen with a lacy hood, as
it might be the pollen sac of a flower. The Shwe Dagon. She
couldn't be mistaken: hadn't she watched it for hours from the
deck of the *Circassia,* and later plodding behind Dil Tharpa
she had caught a glimpse of it rising at the end of an avenue.
What astounded her was the change in character and colour-
ing. No longer a harsh, brassy cone, winking and flashing in the
sunlight like a heliograph, it was now glowing, softly touched
with rosy streaks like the stem of a rose.

Someone had entered the room.

"Are you awake? I did knock. Ah—it's lovely, isn't it. But under
the full moon—that's the time to see it."

A Burmese woman entered the room holding some folded
silks in her arms. She was small and exquisite, her hair scraped
back surmounted by a black bun with an orchid tucked into it,
and she was barefoot.

"I am Hla Gyi, the aunt of your Ken. That's what he tells me
he is now called, and wants to be called."

Miss Wadley shook her hand. It was small but its grip was
surprisingly strong.

"My husband and I were caught in the raid, then had trouble

with looters. Mr Waight insisted on bringing us back in his police van. He's here. So is Mr McNeil. And as we're going to have some food soon, I thought I'd wake you."

Her English and her accent were so good as to be almost too good, giving the impression of someone mimicking upper-class English.

"I'm sorry I slept so long."

"Kyi Minh—Ken told me he woke you at dawn to see Diamond Point, and you walked here. You must be exhausted. I told them to bring you some tea and get your things washed. When I got back I felt smoky, tasted smoke and smelt smoke in everything I wore. In the meantime, would you like to wear these?"

She had laid the clothes on the bed where she now led Miss Wadley, first giving her a white cotton slip and a vest, the only underclothing worn by a Burmese woman. She spread out the Burmese skirt, the tamein, a circular piece of Bangkok silk with a waistband woven into the selvedge. There was also a long-sleeved, transparent blouse, the aingyi, and a scarf, the pawa, a length of soft lemon-coloured gauze.

"As you are thin and not as tall as some English ladies, everything should fit you. We just wrap our skirts round us—they aren't fitted like yours."

"They're prettier."

"More flattering to the woman's figures, yes. Why do Western women allow men to design their clothes?"

"Do we? I suppose we do. They are a bit masculine."

"They are for boys. Your clothes do not compliment the woman's body. They do not take into account this and this." She made a half-circle over her breasts and her buttocks.

"It's war. The First World War, now this one. Women have got to do men's jobs, so they've started to dress like them."

"But this is silly. It is so much nicer being a woman. Here we don't have men's jobs and women's jobs. Women can do what they like, and it is often what you would call men's work. Didn't you notice in the shops and bazaar—the traders are all women. My husband looks after our home and enters for bridge tournaments—and chess too. It is I who manage the shop. And my sister Hla Gale, Tom's wife—it is she who runs the mill, you know."

While she talked, Hla Gyi's small strong hands gripped the top of the skirt band, folded the material so that it fitted round Miss Wadley's waist, then tucked her vest under it. "We know how to keep our skirts up without belts, but you will feel nervous, so I have brought one." It was a black one, the colour of the skirt band, and was studded with semi-precious stones.

When Miss Wadley had put on the blouse, Hla Gyi arranged the scarf round her shoulders and surveyed its effect with head on one side.

"You look different. May I say—younger. Yes, you look well-dressed the Burmese way. There is only one thing. Our dress is simple and neat—we like it to be the background for beautiful jewellery. Will you let me lend you some necklaces and ear-rings? All Burmese women wear earrings."

"My ears aren't pierced, and on the whole I'd rather not wear necklaces."

"Then let me do your hair."

"It's too short. I'm afraid you can't do anything but just comb it. I'm not used to fussing over my appearance."

"Why not? Such a nice figure, such a nice face—you *should* fuss over yourself. Also, I'm told you are altogether a very nice person."

Hla Gyi looked slyly at her. "You can guess who's been talking to me."

Miss Wadley managed a smile. Where was the conversation leading? Experience had taught her when smart attractive women went out of their way to pay her this type of compliment, which did not please but embarrassed her, they had one end in view, and this was to make use of her.

"My nephew is very fond of you. He's a mischievous boy and he can be very naughty, I know. But I'm sure you like him. I'm sure you both get on very well. That's why I think it was such a good idea to persuade you to stay in Kaikun and coach him."

Miss Wadley said nothing and her silence was beginning to

disconcert Hla Gyi, who stopped, but after a slight pause came out with, "Such odd expressions he's collected. 'Bate.' What does 'bate' mean?"

Miss Wadley was looking down at her bare feet below the hem of her skirt. Hla Gyi was also barefoot, but whereas the Burmese woman's small, brown, bare feet looked in keeping with her general appearance, Miss Wadley felt odd, half-dressed, without shoes and stockings.

"Ken said I was in a bate with him?"

Now she knew where the conversation was leading and what they were after.

"He did use that word."

"Being in a bate means in a temper. But it was more than that. I was angry, very angry indeed with Ken, and his bad behaviour coming after the appalling experiences in those Rangoon gardens—it was the last straw."

"Ken is most upset."

And so, evidently, were the family. Ken must have repeated her words about returning to England, giving the impression that, soothed down, she would reconsider them. She had not been in a temper. She had not threatened. She had said what she meant, simply, that she had had enough and was no longer prepared to live in exile for him—or for anyone else. It was no good beating about the bush, so she told Hla Gyi,

"I've decided to return to England for a number of reasons, so Ken mustn't think he's to blame. I'm very fond of him."

"Couldn't you reconsider it?"

What was this to do with her? Curiously enough, if the subject hadn't been brought into the open, if Miss Wadley had been given time to mull over events, she might have hesitated. Miss Wadley's resolve hardened. However, she was not prepared to discuss a private arrangement with the McNeils or with anyone else. She said nothing.

"Your first impression of Burma has been most unfortunate. It must have been dreadful to see that dacoit hit the poor woman. And I heard how upset you were with the students stopping

ambulances and fire engines—but war makes people mad. It must
be like that in England too."

Miss Wadley had walked over to the window, where she
stood looking out—not at the palely glimmering pagoda but at
the dark bushes of jasmine alight with fireflies.

"Oddly enough, it *isn't* what's happening in England now.
And when it does, when people get excited, demonstrate, they
do it in a way I understand. Those dead people in Fytche
Gardens—on the steps of the City Hall—it wouldn't happen like
that in London. The Luftwaffe comes over every night, but
whatever it destroys, it can't destroy order—we're right behind
them, clearing up, restoring order. But even before the bombs
fell, Rangoon—the sight of all that disorder and poverty and
chaos got under my skin. It isn't my sort of life. I couldn't live
here—couldn't cope here. I must get back."

"Rangoon isn't Burma. Rangoon is like Lucknow, or Calcutta,
or Bombay—it's Indian. Indians live in filth and disorder. We
don't. Wait till you've seen Kaikun. It's like England—a line of
nice tidy bungalows. You'll love it, I'm sure you will. Why don't
you give it a chance?"

Miss Wadley was standing looking about at nothing in particular. To one side of the garden she could see the drive where a
van was standing in silhouette broken by two loudspeakers on the
roof. The lawns were sinking into darkness, and where darkness
enveloped the forests a few lights glimmered through the trees,
and where fires flickered in a line must be the Prome Road,
where the refugees had halted for the night.

"It's not a question of me giving anyone a chance. I'm not
sitting in judgement on Burma, you know. That would be cheek.
It's something that's happened to me, that hasn't happened before. I'm afraid. I don't want to stay here because I'm a funk. All
through the blitz I never turned a hair. But this morning . . .
those crowds . . . the . . . disorder. I just can't exist in mess, and
it's done something to me. Repelled me. I want to go back. It's
death to stay—for me. Eerie. But then, premonition is eerie."

Miss Wadley settled herself quietly at the table in the family's big dining-room. No pictures on the wall, no carpets, the table of black polished wood, the cutlery undistinguished. Only the candlesticks appealed to her: they were of pewter with tall glass holders to protect the wick from the fan's downdraft. The table was laid with an assortment of dishes, bowls of salad, plates of noodles, mincemeat, curried vegetables and in small salvers various delicacies—salted ginger, pickled tea-leaves and shrimps.

She had been placed on the right hand of U Thet Nyein, her host, on formal occasions the place of honour according to Western etiquette. It probably was not meant as a compliment to her, Miss Wadley decided. She attached little importance to this kind of convention. Well-bred people, her mother used to say, don't bother with trivialities. It had frequently happened to her while on duty as a Helping Hand that she had been sent to the kitchen to eat with cook, housekeeper and parlourmaid. She had always preferred this arrangement to eating with the very wealthy and the very high-born. On other occasions she was regarded as one in the anomalous category of the nannie. A tray was provided in the nursery.

Out of habit, also, she took no part in the conversation, assuming a manner which was self-effacing without appearing servile.

When she had first entered, her clothes had created a stir. Ken had rushed over to her and demanded loudly, "Waddy, why on earth are you dressed like that?" For fear of what he might next say, Tom had said hurriedly, "Miss Wadley's clothes are being washed—like yours. If you can wear a longyi, why can't she? And besides, I think she looks splendid."

She had been touched and amused by Tom's remark. After the unsuitable "splendid," he had in fact made an involuntary double-take, glancing quickly back at her for a second look. It was Hamish who, after frank scrutiny, announced loudly, "Burmese dress particularly suits slim people—that's why it looks well on you, Miss Wadley." He turned to Tom. "Why don't the Dowalls let Jemma wear an aingyi? That awful gym dress. You must speak to them, Tom. Or perhaps Miss Wadley can when she gets to Kaikun."

Miss Wadley felt Tom's and Hla Gyi's eyes fixed on her, but

she made no comment. Tom told Hamish, "Miss Wadley may not be coming back with us after all."

So, Ken had relayed her decision to his father, but not, evidently, to Hamish, who now demanded, "What's up? I understood you and Miss Wadley had agreed on a six-month arrangement to cram the boy."

Tom said uneasily, "It doesn't matter."

From his corner Ken piped up, "Will you coach me, Mr Waight? If someone doesn't, I'll never get my 'C.E.'* It's my maths and algebra. Latin's okay. I got sixty-two percent."

Since everyone was looking expectantly at her, Miss Wadley felt bound to say something. "I did give an undertaking, and if you feel I'm letting you down . . ."

Hamish grunted, "To say the least . . ."

Tom glared at him, daring him to say one more word. To Miss Wadley he said, "Don't worry. If you like, we'll discuss it later. After all, we weren't at war when you agreed to come out. I don't see why you should be involved in our mess."

There was a pause and they started to talk together of something else, mostly of the raid. While U Thet Nyein passed Miss Wadley a salad bowl of black lacquer, filled with strange leaves and white flowers ("coriander and lemon leaves, and the flower tastes like celery—try it, you'll like it"), Hla Gyi described her encounter with looters in her silk shop. They had been a poor lot, she said, shivering, cowardly boys whom she had frightened with a pair of cloth shears and chased into Phayre Street.

"And when Mr Waight and Tom turned up in the police van to see if we were all right," U Thet Nyein told Miss Wadley, "my wife refused to leave. She said she was going to sleep in the shop to protect her precious bales of silk."

"Don't be taken in by her fragile looks," Tom told Miss Wadley. "Hla Gyi's a tigress. Like her sister! A pair of tigresses who do what they like with husbands and looters."

"And police constables," Hamish said with an indulgent look at Hla Gyi. "God knows what Fairweather will do if he hears

* Common Entrance Examination for Public Schools in England.

what she made his men do"—which was, evidently, to shift her more precious bales into the police van.

"Is that the car in the drive, the one with the loudspeakers on the front?" Miss Wadley asked.

"Loudspeakers—yes," Tom replied but with an oddly changed manner. He did not look at her but across the table at Hamish Waight. There was a hush: both Hla Gyi and Thet Nyein looked up. Miss Wadley was aware of undercurrents, as if her words had revived a quarrel in progress before she had come in. Police van . . . loudspeakers? It couldn't be because Tom objected to the unauthorized use of the van to transport Hla Gyi's silks. It was Hamish Waight who was the policeman, not Tom. In any case, both Englishmen had been laughing at the escapade.

Suddenly Ken piped up, "Mr Waight promised I could go with him down the Prome Road, Dad."

"Did you?" Again that odd tone, not overtly hostile but a marked change from the bantering friendliness of a few moments ago.

Hamish shrugged. "I did—but if you'd rather not."

"Oh, Dad—please."

Tom said coldly, "I don't see the point."

"Good psychology. I've told Ken to wear his flannels and his school cap, so when they see him they'll think, that's an official's son. If he's not bolting—perhaps I shouldn't. Perhaps Rangoon's going to be safe enough!"

There was a cackle of laughter. "A fine role for a Burmese boy! A decoy! Our Pin Wa a decoy for Indian filth!" It was Daw Hla Palai, the shrivelled Burmese woman with a crooked face. She sat beside Ken picking at a plate of nuts like a monkey. Hla Gyi turned on her sharply, "Taw-bi," she said, which meant, "Enough."

Miss Wadley compared the sisters—one so pretty and sophisticated, the other an ugly little crone. Hla Gale, Ken's mother was the third sister; Miss Wadley wondered what she would look like.

"Aw, Aunt, do be quiet or you'll ruin everything. Dad—please

—I only want to go because of the A.V.G.* If we go down the Prome Road, we'll go past their airfield, past Mingaladon." When Tom ignored his pleading, Ken persisted, "But, Dad—the radio said the A.V.G. and R.A.F. shot down eleven enemy planes!"

The old woman rasped out, "Enemy? Whom do you mean by 'enemy,' Pin Wa?"

No one answered her, but Ken told her indignantly, "The Japs haven't lost that many planes in all the five years they've been fighting the Chinese. So there! It'll teach them a lesson."

"So, my son, now the Burmese must be grateful that the Japanese have bombed Rangoon so that foreign pilots can teach lessons!"

Since no one attempted to silence the creature, Miss Wadley decided to intervene. "Would you prefer our planes not to go up? Not to fight back? Surely, you don't want the Japanese to occupy your country."

Daw Hla Palai's monkey eyes rested on the English woman. "Our country is already occupied, miss. We Burmese don't differentiate between foreign overlords."

"Tha-di-Hta! Take care!" U Thet Nyein started scolding her in rapid Burmese. When he had finished, Hamish said gravely, "I'm glad U Thet Nyein doesn't share his sister-in-law's views. We've never regarded ourselves as overlords—and I hope never acted like them. Right from the start we've promised self-government."

Tom interrupted. "Must you, Hamish? You're ruining my appetite. After a day like this I don't feel up to political chit-chat."

"And I don't feel up to hypocrisy," Hamish retorted, "particularly after a day like this—when Burma's future hangs in the balance."

Tom's voice became sharp, "'Hangs in the balance!' That's dramatizing. We're talking about terrified Indian coolies on the run. If they can get away now, before the monsoon, they've a

* American Volunteer Group: airmen under command of General Chennault who were seconded by Generalissimo Chiang Kai-shek to the R.A.F. after war was declared with Japan.

chance of reaching India and their homes. If you stop them—
they'll die in Burma."

What was this argument about? Miss Wadley listened in bewilderment to the acrimonious exchanges between Hamish and
Tom. They had been talking good-humouredly about a police
van and enemy airplanes, then Tom had flared up suddenly at
the words "Indian coolies." Whatever the cause of their disagreement, Miss Wadley was astonished that neither made any
attempt to conceal their disagreement from their Burmese
friends. As Miss Wadley glanced at U Thet Nyein, and Hla Gyi,
she realized they knew what lay behind the dispute, but could
not tell from their expressions where their sympathies lay.

Hamish was saying, "They won't die if they come back. We'll
promise to protect them and look after them. But if they persist
in running away—then they've bought it. Six hundred miles over
mountains—on foot—no food or shelter and damn little water.
That Taungup tract's a wilderness. You know that. Hundreds and
thousands pushing down jungle tracts, you can see what'll happen—cholera, dysentery, epidemics. Their one chance of survival is to trust us, do as we say, get back to their jobs."

"To serve our ends."

"Why must you twist everything? We want them back to help
save the country."

The old woman exclaimed, "Save the country for whom? The
Indians? The British? Or the Burmese?" Hamish disregarded
her. He shifted his gaze from Tom to Hla Gyi and U Thet Nyein.

"No government in wartime can allow essential personnel to
leave. You agree, don't you? If this Indian exodus isn't stopped,
the docks will be paralyzed and Rangoon come to a standstill.
If all subordinate staffs bunk, who'll run the railways, river steamers, post offices? Without the Indians, Rangoon will pack up and
the Japs can walk in. If they walk into Rangoon, they'll walk into
the rest of Burma. I'm damned if I'm going to let that happen.
This is an emergency. Get 'em back. Make 'em do their jobs.
Make 'em do their duty. God's teeth, I'm going to do mine. Government's taking the right steps, and I personally will see these
bastards do what Government says."

"How?" Hla Gyi's voice was non-committal.

"Reason with them for a start. That's what the loudspeakers are for. We'll go down Prome Road with one of their own leading men—Sir Shama Rao has promised to come with me."

"And if persuasion doesn't work . . . ?" Hla Gyi was looking at her hands.

"There'll be various inducements," Hamish said.

At this, Tom pushed his plate aside, his hands trembling. "And these inducements, Hamish—you might as well tell everyone what they are."

"Certainly! Rice rations. Medical supplies. Inoculations against cholera. Free accommodation in camps out of the bombing zone with free transport to places of work."

"And?" Tom goaded him. Miss Wadley could tell Tom McNeil was not used to standing up to Hamish Waight. He looked the weaker character, and she was sure it was not only because he looked physically less robust but because he was by nature more amiable and far more tolerant than the massive, dominant Hamish. But though Tom's pugnacity had exhausted him, he persevered. Why? It seemed to Miss Wadley Hamish was right. People must do their duty, carry out what they were paid to do and what in wartime became essential service. Perhaps Hamish was a bully and had aroused Tom's antagonism by being too blunt. But Miss Wadley believed one had to bully and be blunt in an emergency.

Tom glared at Hamish. "Let's have the complete list of bribes. What about guaranteeing their safe passage back to India? Hasn't the Government promised that too?"

U Thet Nyein turned to Miss Wadley and explained quietly that this was the root cause of the panic exodus. There was not a single road between India and Burma. All these Indians—indeed, everyone entering or leaving the country—were forced to use the single combined entrance and exit: Rangoon. Burma, he said, was a vast cul-de-sac, shaped like a horseshoe with mountain ranges cutting it off on three sides from India, Tibet and China.

"Isn't the Government offering the bribe of evacuation, if necessary? You know that's a promise that can't be fulfilled. It's nothing but a dirty trick on wretched, illiterate people."

Hamish surveyed Tom calmly.

"A massive airlift could be arranged."

"That's impossible—and you know it. How many planes do you think the R.A.F. scraped up today against seventy Jap bombers? Twelve! Twelve obsolete Buffalo fighters!"

There was a long silence which Miss Wadley was tempted to break by saying everyone should remain at their posts, but she said nothing because she felt much more was going on below the surface than she understood.

In an altered voice, spent of passion, Tom went on flatly, "Say you get them back tomorrow—what's going to happen?"

"What do you mean?"

"If Rangoon falls—that's what I mean. What's going to happen to these Indian coolies, municipal sweepers, clerks, shopkeepers and their thousands of dependents—women, children, old people?"

At the far end of the table the small monkey face of Hla Palai was thrust forward.

"We will take care of them! The Burmese will know what to do with Indians once the British can't protect them." She drew her finger across her throat.

Miss Wadley could no longer contain herself. "Disgraceful!"

"What's disgraceful, Waddy?"

"That's enough, Ken."

Daw Hla Palai's malicious eyes rested on Miss Wadley. "Let the boy speak. He is not in school. He is with his family."

But Ken decided to shut up.

Daw Hla Palai looked triumphantly at each in turn. "Why does the Police Thakin bother to take his loudspeaker down the Prome Road? It is only for face—the Government has already done what is necessary to stop the Indians. He knows very well the road to the Tagup Pass has been closed by police, and police are also stopping river-craft taking refugees across the Irrawaddy."

There was silence. All looked at Hamish, who had listened to Daw Hla Palai with a bored expression.

"Is it true?" Tom asked.

"How the hell should I know? I was asked to go down to the Prome Road with Rao and reason with them, and I'll do just that."

Miss Wadley found herself suddenly speaking up for Hamish, not because she wanted to defend him—Hamish was quite capable of defending himself—but because she disliked the old aunt so much.

"Running away from danger is understandable, especially in wartime. But threatening defenceless people is despicable."

"It isn't, Waddy. Threatening is only silly, but running away is despicable. You only say that because you aren't threatening Indians, but you do happen to be running away."

"Running away!" An ugly flush spread over Miss Wadley's neck.

Tom McNeil told his son to be quiet.

"But she is, Dad. If going back on the *Circassia* isn't running away—what is?"

"Where did you get that?" Hamish snapped. "She's doing no such thing. She said she wasn't going to let you down—and she won't." He looked across at Miss Wadley. "Correct?"

There was nothing Miss Wadley could say except, "Yes."

8

For various reasons Miss Wadley had not kept a diary since she became the Chairman's secretary: too busy for one reason, and for another, keeping a record of clandestine meetings would have been indiscreet. She was very glad also she had resisted the temptation to commit to paper her emotional turmoil. When that reckless, stupid intrigue was over, it made it easier to pretend it had never taken place.

It was about three weeks after her arrival in Kaikun, when she and Ken had gone into the bazaar to buy exercise books for his lessons, that she had seen a thick day-by-day diary and on impulse bought it.

"But what's there for you to write about? Us children have adventures, but not grown-ups."

"Burma is an adventure for me. Besides, it's January. I always buy a diary every January, though I admit I don't keep it up after the middle of February."

When they returned to the Forest Bungalow, Miss Wadley had set Ken two pages of sums, leaving him to work in the schoolroom while she returned to her bedroom to change out of her riding clothes—jodhpurs and shirt borrowed from Tom McNeil —and to decide whether or not she would use the diary or chuck it on the gardener's smouldering heap.

Her room was at the back of the house, looking over the kitchen-garden. She had stood at the window staring out at the untidy crown of dark-green leaves and unripe fruit of a papaya tree growing just outside in a patch of gourds. She caught herself thinking the papayas looked like plump, pendulous, dark-green breasts, and recalling what Tom had told her. "If you start talking to yourself by this window, no one here will think you're mad but cheering up the papaya tree. The Burmese think the papaya only grows within the sound of human voices. Every village has its papaya trees, and if the village is abandoned, it's true, these trees do die." Dear Tom! What a charming creature he was. He seemed to enjoy having to entertain a stranger to Burma so that he could impart some of the freakish facts he had collected about the country.

So much was happening to her. She needed spells of solitude in which to take a look at herself. In England she may have broken her private code of behaviour, but there it had been a gradual process and whatever risks existed had been taken knowingly, after weighing the advantages. She had misjudged, and she had suffered for it.

What was now taking place in her, around her, was not to be compared with the plodding, routine misdemeanour of her time at Burnett's. The combined impact of the new exhilarating country, the people, the way of life was becoming too much for her. She was getting out of her depth and was searching for help, for someone to guide her. There was only Mrs Dowall, and Mrs Dowall in a way was her enemy.

Then why not keep this diary? If she could write down what was happening to her, wouldn't facts confronted coldly serve as checks? She could keep the book locked up, and could always burn it.

She carried the diary to the writing-table and sat still for a few minutes to let her thoughts settle. Her room was large and shadowy; its timber walls of teak had been treated with earth oil so that they had darkened to the colour of old saddle-leather. There was only one picture, a sepia reproduction of Frans Hals's "Laughing Cavalier." Behind it two Tuck-too lizards lived, making occasional forays after insects. Two small, flat snakelike heads and brilliant black eyes peered out from a corner of the frame. Should she make a bet on them? Tom had told her how everyone in Burma liked to bet—on anything. He had pointed to a group standing round a tea-stall betting on two flies crawling across a saucer. It was silly, of course: If the near lizard snapped up a fly she'd keep the diary; if the other one darted out she'd throw the thing away.

There was movement, so quick it wasn't possible to say what happened. However, the fly had vanished. She'd have to keep the diary.

This was ridiculous. She had never behaved like this in her life. Betting on lizards! She was going backwards, becoming as callow as those two girls, Mibs and Jemma.

Despite the protest, Miss Wadley's eyes remained fixed on the frame and on the Tuck-too, which hadn't yet moved. If it does, then what I want I'll get, whether it's right or wrong, wise or unwise. The lizard remained fixed to the wall as if glued there. Was that another omen signifying that—she frowned, banged the diary on the desk. What was the matter with her? She had taken to behaving and thinking along such strange lines she hardly recognized herself. The notion that she needed to keep a diary, as if to keep tabs on herself, was nonsense. Her self-control was perfectly adequate. An old woman with a wagging tongue had upset her—that was all. Nothing on earth would persuade her to keep a diary—she wasn't a romantic, immature, lovesick schoolgirl. She pitched the irritating book into the waste-paper basket.

She returned to the window. It must be nearing midday, for there was Mohammed Khan, the cook, in solitary prayer before the door of his room. Eyes closed, chin tucked into his neck, was he reciting from the Koran, or praying for favours? She watched him kneel, stand up, kneel again to knock his head on his prayer mat. Did he sometimes pray for something he knew he hadn't any business to pray for, as she did? And then she remembered something Ken had said to her—Ken, so stupid and irritating during lessons, and so oddly mature at other times: "We aren't like you lot." He meant Christians. "We aren't allowed to pray for anything, not even for forgiveness." Hla Gale had explained

that Buddhists, Muslims also, repudiated intercession and atone-
ment. "Both the Lord Buddha and Mahomet taught no one
could save you but yourself," she said.

Miss Wadley considered this for a moment, then walked back
into the room to pick the diary out of the basket. Eight years
of wretchedness believing, hoping, trusting someone to do right
by you, in a way to "save you" when the truth should have
been obvious to her, that he had no intention of bothering about
her. She did not want to make a similar mistake. Who was there
in Kaikun in whom she could confide? Garrulous old Mrs Dowall? God forbid! The sensible course was to put it down on
paper, and put down only the truth. Miss Wadley shook her
head. The truth! There were truths she knew she could not,
would not, face: nevertheless, it would be better to have a stab
at half-truths, she decided, than to drift into self-delusion as in
the past.

Bought this diary today, January 15th, but will start keeping
it as if from date of arrival Kaikun, December 25th. Reached end
of train journey from Rangoon at 1.30 A.M. on Xmas Day, at
station called Bilin. Went to Rest House to sleep till dawn, but
could not: brain overactive, also strangeness of surroundings.
An old bus turned up at about 5 A.M. and we drove seventy
miles to Kaikun. McNeils have no car, Tom says, use only pony
trap, and in jungles, horses and elephants. First impression Kaikun nothing like as Hla Gyi gave me to expect, no resemblance
whatever to England as she seemed to think. River makes lovely
crescent round cliff and here officials have houses, bungalows,
yes, but nothing like ours: some on stilts, others spread out, all
enclosed in large gardens, lawns to the river, big fleshy-looking
red flowers bordering drive, flowerbeds everywhere, also or-
chards of strange fruits. One outside my bedroom is papaya.
McNeil's Forest Bungalow at far end from Club, which has best
position on riverside—also has swimming pool, tennis courts, and
for such a small place, surprisingly luxurious lounges with all
English newspaper and magazines, dining-room, bars, and deep
verandah where everyone meets at least once a day. Another

surprise—Hla Gale. Pronounced La-Gerlay, accent on "lay." Not at all pretty, and looks at least five years older than her husband. Tom's good looks—he's quite an Adonis—makes La Gale look all the plainer. Tom has dark hair, with those red lights that make one say it's "chestnut." He has a bony, ascetic face. The fineness of his bone structure is most obvious when you see him side by side with Hamish. Hamish—now, there's a bully! See a little of myself in Hamish, no wonder we don't get on. Hamish is definitely coarse compared to Tom, a beefy bully who fancies himself as a he-man. Not that Tom is effeminate. La Gale is very vivacious. Is that what attracted Tom to her? Tom's so English, I would have thought only a typically English girl would have suited him. But you can never tell which kind men will marry.

After bath, breakfast etc., La Gale dragged Ken up to pagoda on top of hill opposite. Servants set off with them carrying offerings, flowers, baskets of fruit and, of all things, two aluminium saucepans and an aluminium kettle and some cotton curtains for the Abbot. I was about to stroll down riverside path to have a look round Kaikun when Tom came into my room with jodhpurs and shirt—for me. Hadn't they told me, he said? They were leaving for the Xmas camp in the jungle almost at once, and as I'd have to ride he had brought me riding things. From the first Tom has struck me by his thoughtfulness, unusual in a man.

Xmas Camp Dec. 25th–30th.

These five days have made the most impact. From moment I landed this whole business has jolted me, didn't know if it was good or bad for me to be so thoroughly shaken up. At first recoiled—that appalling air-raid, then the row between Tom and Hamish in Hla Gyi's house. All I wanted was to escape to England and get back to familiar faces, the old routine, and my normal surroundings. Now I'm not so sure. This fantastic camp has made me turn a somersault. And now I find Burma agrees with me. Suddenly I've fallen in love—with the country—and shed years. Frown lines gone and lines round my mouth gone. Being out-of-

doors all day has given me one of those tans that bring up red
along cheekbones and end of one's nose. Even Ken noticed the
change in me—and didn't approve. "I don't like you always laughing, Waddy," he said.

From being a humdrum woman who made her own bed,
dined off cornflakes and brown sugar, and was interminably
washing up—I've become someone who ate peacock instead of
turkey for Christmas dinner, whose clothes are put out on a
bed—admitted, a camp bed—for whom four-course meals are
prepared, served, washed up, without having to give any help
whatever. And the strangest part of all is that this life of ease
and luxury is experienced, not in a hotel, but in the jungles.
Goodness knows where the camp was, somewhere in the heart
of one of Tom's Reserves in the Dawna Hills. The camp was
all ready for us, put up in a clearing on a ridge overlooking the
wooded valley along a dried riverbed. And this camp had no
resemblance to the camps I'd known as a girl guide on the
banks of the Severn during those drenching fortnights of Easter
holidays. Tom's Rangers, with the help of local villagers, had
built it, small bamboo and thatch huts on stilts, one for each of
us, with two long huts, one for meals, the other as the cook-
house. Mostly we ate out-of-doors at night under the stars beside
the log fire, watching the sparks shoot into branches and creepers. Ken's hut was next to mine. The first night I was awakened
by him. "I came in to see if you were afraid, but it's miles away,
in the valley, I think. And anyway, he won't come near with a
fire." I asked, "Who?" All Ken said, "Can't you hear? Only a tiger
makes that sawing noise." Two nights later Jemma Dowall, old
Mrs Dowall's granddaughter, who is fourteen or fifteen, woke
me up. She was frightened and had come to me for comfort because she thought she heard the trumpeting of a herd of wild
elephants. I wasn't alarmed by tiger or wild elephants and assume it's because everything is unreal to me still. But this soon
wore off. These five days in camp were so glorious I wanted them
to go on forever. Misty mornings, dazzling afternoons, and with
evening the orange hour of the setting sun and the blue hour of
dusk . . . nothing in my life has filled me with such happiness.

But gradually this life has lost its dreamlike quality: as it became reality, so my old life became remote, irrelevant. The change troubles me. I seem to be losing touch not only with the old ways, but with old values. This struck me forcibly the night Hamish Waight and Hugh Chapman, Kaikun's District Commissioner, joined our party. Hamish had loaded an elephant with his huge battery-driven wireless set so that we could hear the war bulletins. That evening Butch strayed, and as night fell Ken became frantic because there are leopards about and they are evidently partial to dogs. Hamish put on the radio full-blast so that Butch would hear it and find her way back. Hamish's dodges, I'm discovering, usually work. Those poor Rangoon Indians, for instance, whom Hamish meant to stop escaping to India. He made them come back, all of them, he boasted, and seemed quite proud of himself. At the time I agreed with him; now I don't. I'm on Tom's side.

Hamish's blasting radio brought Butch back in about twenty minutes plus a crowd of about twenty odd-looking individuals. They didn't wear the long skirt affair, the longyis, of the Burmese, but loose black trousers, native-weave coats and enormous swords slung on bands across their chests. The women clinked along with heavy bead jewellery over long robes, nearly all of them with big cigars stuck in their mouths. By the way, a little scene here between Tom and Hugh Chapman gave me a silent laugh. Hugh Chapman is Number One of the District, Head of Civil Law, Excise, Land Revenue etc. Even Hamish, I'm glad to say, has to knuckle down to him. This was the first time I'd met Hugh and we liked each other at once. He's about my age (though I say now I'm 30), and though he isn't good-looking like Tom—and in his rough way, Hamish—Hugh Chapman, taken as a whole, certainly is nice in the way those tall, lean, physically wiry cowboy heroes are. But there's something sad about him. It's in his eyes. He lost his wife, but it's not that. According to Mrs Dowall (who enlightens everyone about everyone), Mrs C. was no loss but an absolute B——. When these wild forest people walked into the camp I said, "They don't look Burmese." Tom immediately started telling me who they

were (he regards himself as my guide to Burma), when Hugh
leaned across him to give me *his* version! Tom's face was a study!
Almost as if he was jealous, though I don't suppose he was.

According to Hugh these are Karens, not the same race as
Burmese, though their flat faces and slant eyes look the same to
me. His butler, Saw Hardy, he said, was a Karen (everyone calls
him "Kiss-Me Hardy"). Karens are tough people but are kicked
around by the Burmese. The Burma Rifles are mostly Karens,
plus Chins, Kachins and all kinds of other Burmese races—"all
except true Burmese," Hugh said. "Burmese are rotten soldiers
because they love freedom, and simply won't put up with discipline."

Hamish behaved as you'd expect him to—he's really funny,
though he doesn't know it. The Karens said they had come to
listen to the "magic box," and asked him to switch on to Burmese music or a pwe. A pwe is a Burmese fair, at which old
Burmese plays are performed. Strolling players perform these
plays all over the country, and most Burmese know them by
heart. Hamish agreed but said first they must listen to the war
news. He gave them a pep talk about the war, and when the
news came on, in English, he translated it. Ken told me afterwards Hamish's "translation" made it sound as if the British had
swept every German out of Europe and every Jap out of the
Pacific! Even the kids (all three are here—Ken, Jemma Dowall
and Hugh Chapman's daughter, Mibs) don't take Hamish's bom-
bast too seriously.

I was so happy this evening, watching those Karens sitting
round the campfire, their faces lit up with an orange glow, with
Ken's hand in mine, and Tom on the other side of me. Some
of the Karens wore turbans, which I swear were made out of ordinary coloured hand-towels, the ones we use on the beach. One
of the Karen boys had a crossbow. Ken got one of his arrows to
show me. Its tip had been dipped in "deadly Datura poison,"
he said, but I expect he was dramatizing. Another funny incident occurred between Tom and Hugh Chapman. I asked about
the cheroots the Karens were smoking. Tom started to tell me,
but Hugh leaned across him and corrected him: "No, they're

called *Se*—tobacco, *baw*—large, *leik*—rolled! *Se-baw-leik*. That's the correct name, and the shield of bamboo is inside the white paper, Tom—the bamboo is the casing, not the paper. The stuff inside is pure tobacco." Tom looked furious! Is there rivalry? Or is it that I'm the only woman available—except for Hla Gale? Incidentally, both men laughed, though it made me embarrassed when one of the Karen women, suckling a baby, found the brat refused her breast and so put her cheroot in the baby's mouth. The baby took it! After the war news Hla Gale handed out little packets to the Karens. I thought they were sweets but Hugh said, "Not sweets. Something far more valuable to Karens —they're as thrilled to have it as you'd be to have a diamond. Salt!"

It was strange, but sitting there, watching these people, I had the feeling I'd known them from some other time. As that's impossible, I suppose I'm sentimentalizing. I hate sentimentality in others; it's surprising to find myself guilty of it. It's the effect of these magical days, cold clear nights, stars so bright, the mysteriousness of the jungle with white-faced baboons calling across the valley in early morning, and those rather sinister explorations with Ken—who likes to take me off on his own—following game trails that lead to eerie pools of water where, Ken says, tigers, mithan, elephants and deer come to drink in the evenings. I expect this fantastic Christmas has been too much for a spinster from South Ken. I frequently remind myself that "a spinster from South Ken" is what I am, and so I mustn't let my thoughts run away with me. At other times I ask myself, "Why shouldn't I let my thoughts run away with me?" I'm human. Is it wrong for a woman to want love and a mate? I know people laugh (particularly the women who've found love and a mate) if they suspect your secret thoughts. So I must be careful—outwardly. To myself, to this diary, however, I'm going to admit that there have been moments recently when happiness filled me in a way that was almost unbearable, and made me want to weep! I seem to be waiting for something, I can't think what. Perhaps it's what a child feels the day before a birthday, wondering what the birthday presents will be.

As I listened to Hamish booming away at those forest people, it struck me how unreal it was to hear about Hitler invading Russia, Japanese landing in Manila and southern parts of Burma. I couldn't make myself believe any of it. Reality for me was that jungle camp.

Jan. 1st–4th.

The day after we returned from the Xmas camp, Hla Gale left for Moulmein. She'll be away a week. Ken says his mother seldom remains long at home; her sawmills—one lot five miles down river, the main ones in Moulmein—keep her busy. In both places she has a house, the Moulmein one being the family mansion where Ken and his father sometimes join her. Ken takes it for granted that he may not see his mother for days, and as his father is often out of the house before he's up, and not back till he's in bed, his attachment to me is understandable. Tom is very busy just now opening up a new forest, the Me Ping, and goes off early with his Rangers and clerks: soon he says he'll be besieged by contractors. At the moment he returns home about tea-time, when I officiate. At dinner again I sit in Hla Gale's place. It seems strange to me to assume the social duties of his wife, but Tom's so vague he doesn't notice anything. One night the Hodges, the Baptist missionaries, called here; on another, Hugh Chapman and Hamish. Each time I acted as hostess, and Tom took it for granted. Admit I rather enjoyed it. Daily routine: Ken starts lessons after he has returned from pagoda (mother is a strict Buddhist). I teach him till lunchtime. Afternoons we go off on our ponies (I can "trot" at last, and Ken threatens to teach me how to jump), or Ken goes off with his gang—Jemma, Mibs, and two or three Indian boys and one Burmese boy. Bath at 7 P.M. My Indian bearer Hanif, the cook's son, puts out my evening clothes. What would they say in the office if they saw me now—a manservant putting out my undies—which, incidentally, Hanif washes and mends too!

Jan. 5th.

Have so little to do, suggested to Tom that I order meals, check the cook's "bazaar" (I'm sure he cheats them) and generally supervise household. Tom said, "I shouldn't bother. They're used to managing on their own while my wife's away. She believes Mohammed Khan would die rather than cheat her."

I told Tom my impression was different. Also, I'd noticed from my bedroom window (looks out on kitchen-garden) how the gardener slacked. Tom refused to take this seriously. All he said was, "I'd better have a word with Hla Gale." He wasn't trying to snub me, I'm sure of that. Don't know whether to speak to Hla Gale or not. Don't want to get wrong side of her, but she may not object to my help. After all, why should she? She should be pleased someone can find time for her home, as she cannot.

Jan. 5th–10th.

How far away the war is—and London—and my old self. Ken took me to the bazaar, and yesterday up Deer Hill to the pagoda. The Abbot, a nice old man, very fond of Ken. Several times to Club for tennis, a bit rusty, but improving, partnered by Tom, Hugh and Hamish in turn. Also to Club or one of officials' houses most evenings, for drinks and chatter. Hla Gale still not back. Hugh invited us, Tom and me, over to dinner. Strange going out with Tom to dine at someone's house—as if his wife—but Tom completely oblivious. D.C.'s house more luxurious than Forest Bungalow. Strolled on lawn with Hugh after dinner, and was certain I saw Mibs, his daughter, eavesdropping behind some bushes, but said nothing. Hugh gave us Chateau Lafite at dinner—and revived hateful memories of Guy Burnett. Strange, though—this is first time since arriving in Kaikun that I've given a thought to that person.

Jan. 15th.

First disconcerting experience, first fly in ointment, the talk of evacuating Kaikun. Perhaps I'm being unduly upset. I *am* upset, though. It's because of Mrs Dowall, I know, and what she said to me and tried to put into my head. Oh, why can't people leave one alone—why can't the war stay in Europe and Manila— why has it got to come here?

I've met "Doc" Dowall and his wife, old Mrs Dowall, several times. I noticed she eyed me, but thought it was only because I was new. She's old, over seventy, limps, uses a stick, but in spite of it gives an impression of vigour, and of being a very strong character. "Doc" Dowall is always sniping at her in public because, Tom says, he'd get hell if he tried it in private. But in spite of that they seem to be devoted. "She's a domineering old woman who prides herself on being blunt," Tom told me. "She upsets a lot of people, but we think her a bit of a joke—and a harmless old eccentric."

Eccentric certainly. After lunch yesterday Ken offered to show me Mrs Dowall's grave. "She always said she was going to die in Kaikun and be buried under the mimosa tree in the Club grounds. Now the Japs might come, she says it won't make any difference to her. She won't budge even if Mr Waight threatens to shoot her. So we asked if we could dig her grave. She said no because the Club gardener would object, but if we liked to decorate the top, we could. She's given us two knitting needles."

Talk of evacuation had started at breakfast after news broadcast from Tokyo (Tom and everyone else tune in to Tokyo— you learn nothing from Rangoon and All-India Radio), and we heard Japanese were invading Tavoy, a port in the south, also bombing of Rangoon had started again and there's been another exodus of Indian labour.

Went with Ken to Club, and sitting in a deck-chair under a mimosa tree was Mrs Dowall. The ground round the chair had been marked out the size and shape of a grave with bits of broken brick and the glass bottoms of whisky bottles. Those two girls, Mibs and Jemma, were fighting over the knitting needles and Mrs Dowall was shouting at them, "Stop it, stop it! I won't have you fighting. Give me back my needles. Who told you to make a cross? I'm a Buddhist, didn't you know that, you horrid children? Go away—all of you. You too, Ken. I want to talk to Miss Wadley."

She didn't take long to come to the point with me too, starting off rather darkly about having a lot of relatives in England to whom she wrote regularly. "And they send me all the gossip about the family, when someone dies, or has a baby or gets married. And if there's a scandal or a bit of gossip, it all comes back to me." She stopped dramatically and looked hard at me. She has piercing, hooded, hazel eyes, which make the upper part of her face look like a buzzard's, but the lower part, round her jowly neck, reminded me of a turkey.

"My niece is Millicent Youell."

The name seemed vaguely familiar, and though I knew she was getting at something, I couldn't make out what it was.

"She married Guy Burnett." That was all she said. She didn't add, "Wasn't Burnett's the firm you worked for?" or, "Weren't you secretary to the Chairman of Burnett's?"

At once I realized this old termagent knew all about me and Guy and why I had left Burnett's six months after Lady Burnett died. She knew, so all Kaikun would soon know, I left because Guy did not marry me, as he led me to suppose he would. He married someone else, a girl of twenty-two called, I remembered now, Millicent Youell.

There must have been a few generalities after this: if there were I don't remember them. I was too stunned to think or to listen. When Mrs Dowall's voice at last managed to get through my dopey state, I could hardly believe my ears. She was saying, ". . . babies. You want babies, don't you? You're the youngest woman in the station, and that's a great advantage. Really, you are the only marriageable girl here. I wouldn't have called you a girl when I first saw you. You looked fifty. But this climate has done wonders. You're no more than thirty. Young enough. I'll help all I can. But no more mistakes. Change direction. Hamish Waight. Hugh Chapman. Both free, both make good husbands. Hugh's wife was no good at all. Refused to come East, and when war was declared said she was evacuating Mibs to Canada. But she was running off with a man. They were torpedoed and

serves them right. Mibs was saved—and Hugh got her out here—
yes, Hugh's the likely one. You're a sensible woman, and you
want a husband and all the sensible things a woman should
want, a nice home, babies, and a man who's free to marry you."

When I could escape from her I ran back to the bungalow and
wept. I hadn't realized what was happening between Tom and
me until this old woman told me.

9

Ken was home. He should be whooping with joy, and in a way he was, but there were undercurrents to his happiness which he did not understand and which he found troubling. In some subtle way his home had changed.

On the morning of his arrival, that is, on Christmas Day, there had been far too much going on for him to look at his house properly. The verandah and porch were crammed with the customary Christmas dalis [gifts], garlands, enormous iced cakes, presentation baskets of fruits the Indian merchants always brought to his parents on Christmas morning. Also, there had been the excitement of undoing all his own presents—he had never received so many in his life—and the scramble to pack up and get ready for the camp.

There hadn't been time then, but now he was back and Miss Wadley wasn't starting lessons for two days, he scanned his old home with the attention of someone verifying items on an inventory.

Heavy brown teak walls had been newly treated with that smelly oil: he wondered if this had been done in honour of his homecoming. Probably. Nothing really looked changed, yet it *was* changed. Perhaps Mohammed Khan and Saw Peter and Hanif had put it all carefully back to please him, because he'd told them before he left they must not alter anything.

Ken had taken up his stand for inspection on the mounting

steps facing the house on the lawn. The steps, his father had told him long ago, had been built by a "fat predecessor" who had had difficulty heaving himself on his horse. The words "fat predecessor" had stuck in Ken's mind because he could not make out what they meant.

"You're probably a 'fat predecessor,'" he told Butch as he shifted her from the top step to a lower one. "Sit still, then I'll take you up Deer Hill like I promised."

At first his gaze took in the house as a whole—the roof of teak shingles, the upper storey with its balcony and line of shutters, and below, the covered-in verandah and the big front porch where a ray of sunlight glinted off the sides of his favourite lamp, the big brass "elephant lamp." He used to pour paraffin oil through a hole at the top into the elephant's belly, screw in the wick-holder and push down the glass funnel which fitted into the howdah.

All the other lamps were taken out each morning to the lamp room at the back and, after being filled with oil and having their wicks cleaned, were brought in by Saw Peter at dusk. The "elephant lamp" was different. It never left the round table in the porch.

By leaning this way and that he could catch glimpses of the verandah furnished with cane chairs, each with a glass-topped peg-table beside it, the dark-brown bamboo hat-stand with his father's old pith helmets and his mother's coloured umbrellas, and the cloth frill of the hand-punkah which poor old Maung Tin, an assistant elephant man, had to pull whenever they sat in the verandah in the hot months. What a lot of flowerpots there were, on four sides of the porch, on a bench along the back of the verandah and banked down the steps. He had forgotten about them and the way his mother was always telling the gardener to water them and replace them. But she wouldn't let him touch her hanging baskets with orchids growing out of cork and moss, suspended from eaves: all eight at that moment swaying gently together in a breeze.

His "best" tree, the gul mohur, he noticed, was breaking into flower, and where it spread over the balcony of the upper storey

Ken noticed something different—one branch had grown out and was knocking against the shutters of his bedroom. Well, he'd grown two inches. Why shouldn't the gul mohur? Looking across the garden Ken noticed flowers and flowerbeds exactly as he remembered them. The hedge of sweet-peas, round which his mother never allowed them to play hide-and-seek, was still there, bulging with flowers and planted in the same spot, this side of the canna beds with the river glinting through trees on the right.

He couldn't get away from the fact that, though nothing seemed changed, everything was different. Was it that the house looked as if it had shrunk a bit? The roof wasn't miles up, and the balcony outside his bedroom looked as if he had only to grip a couple of branches of the gul mohur to land on the top verandah. Also, everything seemed dustier. He was going to use the word "scruffier," but loyalty forbade it. Just dustier. It shocked him that he should find his home less perfect than it had once appeared to him. He wanted peace and privacy to consider this, but Jemma appeared and started to jump up and down the mounting steps.

"It really is a wonderful secret. Why don't you want to hear it?"

"I do, but later."

"But I want to tell you now."

"And I want to think now."

"Think? What about?"

"Kaikun."

"What's there to think about? Kaikun's same as usual except for Mibs Chapman. And my secret's about her."

"Your secrets are always stupid."

"This one isn't. It's disgusting. It'll make you spit blood."

"Spit blood" was one of Hamish's expressions.

"I don't want to spit blood for an hour. Go away for an hour, please, Jemma."

But she would not. Girls! They could never leave a man alone. In a way he had been looking forward to seeing Jemma again, but now he only wanted to kick her. What she was really after, he suspected, was the present he was saving for Ko-Ni. He could tell by the way she had eyed the catamaran that she was determined to have it. "Where did you get it?" she demanded, and when he had told her, "Colombo," she rolled her eyes in an idiotic way. "Romantic!"

"Durban's romantic too. I got your present in Durban, and I chose it especially for you because Miss Wadley said that was what you'd like." Ken had bought all kinds of presents at different ports during the long voyage round the Cape. The small carved rickshaw, pulled by a zulu with real hair, had been bought for Jemma or his mother or Mrs Dowall or Fatima, depending . . . It was because Jemma had taken the trouble to go to Bilin to meet him that he had decided to give it to her. Ken had likewise changed his mind about Hanif's present. Originally Hanif was to have had a penknife bought in the ship's shop with a picture of the *Circassia* on the handle, but since Hanif had not even tried to wangle a seat on the bus to Bilin, as Jemma had done, Ken was going to give him the compass from Madras. Ja-Bo was to have the penknife.

Jemma had offered to swap her rickshaw for the catamaran, and had said something before the rest of the gang which had hurt and embarrassed Ken.

"Why should Ko-Ni have the best present? He couldn't even be bothered to come and stand at the welcome arch for your arrival."

Ja-Bo was only the sweeper's son, but it was he who had erected the bamboo arch by the gate with "Welcome Honoured Ken" in letters of silver paper. Here all Ken's friends had gathered to cheer him when the bus arrived from Bilin. Ko-Ni, the eldest Galon, the one whom Ken liked best, just hadn't bothered to turn up, as Jemma said. In a way Ken expected it. He and Ko-Ni could never behave towards each other in an ordinary way. It was either sulks or ardent loyalty. The trouble, of course, arose over Maung Khin.

Jemma's sharp eyes detected the change in Ken's expression. "You know Ko-Ni doesn't really like you. And I do. Why can't I have the catamaran?"

"If I don't give it to Ko-Ni I'll keep it for myself. Catamarans are for boys. Girls don't sail catamarans."

"Girls don't pull rickshaws."

Later Ja-Bo put things right by telling Ken Ko-Ni was not up to his usual tricks, sulking and slighting Ken. It just happened he had been sent off on Maung Khin and could not get back in time. Moreover, he had sent a message to say that the moment he returned he would go to Ken's house, even if at dead of night.

Ko-Ni, Maung Khin—two more problems Ken wanted to think about in peace.

"About that catamaran, Jemma. I'm not saying I'll give it you and I'm not saying I'll give it to Ko-Ni. But as I did get another penknife from the ship's shop, and as I might give that to Ko-Ni, if I do, then . . ."

"Then I can have the darling boat."

"Provided you don't bother me."

"You want me to scram? Okay. But you're being stupid. Part of my secret's about your Miss Wadley."

"You said it was about Mibs Chapman."

"It's about Mibs Chapman *and* Miss Wadley."

"What?"

At last Jemma had succeeded in arousing his curiosity. "Miss Wadley's trying to marry someone."

"Why shouldn't she—if she wants to? Anyway, all women can think of is getting married. Your secret's a swiz." He gave Jemma a push, and Butch at once joined in by snarling at the girl.

Jemma's small pointed face assumed an expression of fury. "Don't push me, Mr High-and-Mighty. And if you don't look out, I'll kick that hideous dog. There's plenty more to my secret, but now I shan't tell you."

"And I don't want to hear."

Ken plugged his ears with his fingers and ran to the river's edge, where he threw himself down. She had spoilt his mood. He was stung by "Mr High-and-Mighty." It was the kind of reproach he had been anticipating and had therefore taken pains to avoid. When Jemma did not follow him, his resentment gradually evaporated. He rolled over, watched clouds pass over Deer

Hill where they enveloped the pagoda, blotting out the whole of the gleaming shaft save the finial. Watching the small gold finger sticking out of the clouds, it seemed to Ken that it, and not the woolly mass, was moving over the hill.

Downderry was a miserable hole; he'd hated it, but it was going to feel funny sleeping under a mosquito-net, using a tin tub, and reading by oil-lamps. In April and May it would be hot too, and Maung Tin would be hauling at the punkah rope all through mealtimes. They didn't have one electric fan in Kaikun, as they did on the ship.

Electric light, pull-and-let-go's, a proper bath, were all jolly good, but didn't he prefer to be home with Ahme? Ken asked himself. Yes, he did. He loved her. There was no one in the world like his mother. She had grown a bit fatter, but still smelled marvellous and was prettier than other boys' mothers. She wore much prettier clothes too than the English mothers who came to Downderry on Speech Day.

As soon as it was safe to get up—that is, when he was sure Jemma had gone—Ken planned to explore his home from top to bottom, starting with his bedroom upstairs and ending in the saddle-room. Then he'd run down the towpath as far as the Club to see if any of the bungalows had been altered. In his mind he passed Jemma's house, where her grandfather, Dr Dowall, the Civil Surgeon, had given him his inoculations. Next door stood Mr Waight's bungalow, adjoining the Police Lines. A stretch of wasteland covered by the ramshackle huts of Madrassi agricultural labourers lay between the S.P.'s house and the two biggest and best-sited houses of Kaikun—those of the D.C. [District Commissioner] and the Club. The houses stood on the tip of the crescent of the Yunzalin, where the river emerged from the gorge to round the bluff of Deer Hill. Ken decided to sign for a lemonade and soda at the Club, return down the towpath, cross the bridge and make for the village on the ridge. He'd find out there exactly where Ko-Ni was, and where he could find Maung Khin. Most of all he wanted to see Maung Khin. Would he recognize him? Would he obey? Elephants were supposed to have long memories, so Ken was sure

all he would have to say was "Hmit" and in a second he would
be on Maung Khin's back with his toes under the tusker's big
ears.

Butch had got up and was sniffing about behind the canna
beds. Jemma suddenly jumped up from behind the big leaves.

"Sucks—I'm still here. Come on, be friends. Fatima's been making sweets for you all week. Rasagoolahs, jellabis, sandesh. Piles
of them. If I can share them with you I'll tell you all about Mibs
Chapman."

He'd forgotten all about his old nurse. At the thought of her
jellabis his mouth began to water. He might as well go: there
would be no peace with Jemma around.

"You're always thinking about food," he said, but started
down the towpath with Butch frisking ahead at the prospect of
a walk. "Just like a girl. Girls are greedier than us boys."

Jemma pattered after him. "'Just like a girl'! I like that! As
if girls were inferior. Is that the way boys talk in England?"

It was. It had at first surprised Ken too.

"Well, they *are*."

"Maybe in England. Not in Burma."

Fatima's hut clung to the edge of the ridge in the Muslim
settlement, which had been built at some distance from the
village. To reach it they crossed the Yunzalin by the wooden
bridge, traversed the water meadow, then went up Deer Hill,
skirting the village by one of the numerous tracks leading to
the bluff. As they climbed the hill Ken saw the wooden roofs of
the monastery showing above trees. He'd been up every day to
the pagoda, as his mother made him go, but soon he'd like to pay
the Abbot a visit—not on duty, but on his own as he did in the
old days. Staring upwards, a patch of scarlet caught his eye, and
he looked puzzled. Before he fell asleep at night in England he
used to conjure up places in Kaikun, his house, the river, the
whirlpool, the monastery, the pagoda. Never once had he recalled the carmine cherry where he used to sit for hours talking
to the Abbot.

"Where is the Abbot?"

"Dunno. Don't care. But Balu Pun's coming." Balu Pun ran a gambling stall at fairs.

Ken whooped. "Why didn't you tell me before! A pwe! When? When?"

"They asked Mr Waight for permission and he said yes when there's a full moon, and there will be a full moon next week."

A full moon made it easier for Hamish Waight's constables to keep an eye on the bad hats who arrived at pwes, which were a special type of Burmese fair with strolling players, stallkeepers, gambling booths and all kinds of sideshows.

From the top of the hill they could see the Bilin Road with the courthouse and jail, the bazaar, and the river with the line of officials' houses. Ken could see someone coming out of the back of his house and crossing the kitchen-garden. In the D.C.'s house he could just make out a small figure racing about with a butterfly net.

"Is that Mibs?"

"Yes."

"Why don't you wave to her?"

"Wave to that—that snooper!" With a sudden change from fury to pleading, Jemma added, "Promise you'll come to the pwe with me. Only me. No one else."

"But I always do go with you."

"And promise you won't have Mibs in our gang. She creeps below verandahs and listens to what grown-ups are saying."

"Is that what your secret's about?"

"As a matter of fact, it is."

"Snooping is bad enough, but snooping on snoopers—that's bottoms, Jemma."

"Don't pretend you don't want to know what Mibs found out."

Ken did not bother to reply. He would be told all because Jemma couldn't stop herself telling him.

"Mibs says she went to get some iodine from the dispensary when she heard Mrs Dowall. *I* think she was creeping along under the verandah as usual . . ."

Ken said nothing.

"Mrs Dowall said about sin and Miss Wadley. Terrible things. All true too."

"How do you know?"

"Because she looks sinful. She's got a bit of moustache."

"So have you."

"I'm young yet, so it doesn't matter. Later I'll pull mine out, hair by hair, like Tibetans do."

A pause.

"Miss Wadley looks sinful because that's what she's been doing in London. Sin. At week-ends. For years, Mibs says Mrs Dowall says. She only stopped because she couldn't go on when the man married someone else. Mrs Dowall says now Miss Wadley's got the habit, she'll go on. And that's the point. Who?"

"I don't know what you're driving at."

"Yes you do. Sin."

"It's drivel. I don't want to hear any more."

"Only because it's Miss Wadley and you like her."

"Yes I do like her."

"Then you shouldn't. You wait. You don't know where she'll strike. Didn't you see her at the camp talking to your dad?"

"*And* Mr Chapman, *and* Mr Waight! What are you hinting at? If you're saying my dad . . ."

Ken was wearing his dah, the long-handled Burmese sword carried in a wooden scabbard and slung over one shoulder by a red cord. Jemma's words so infuriated him he was on the point of drawing it, but changed his mind and, holding the hilt like a cricket bat, hit her across the haunches.

Jemma said nothing, did nothing, but sat there, eyes fixed on him until tears started down her cheeks.

"It's me who should cry. Not you. Shut up, Jemma. Miss Wadley's my friend. Miss Wadley's good. She didn't want to come. She came to help me. If she hears what you're saying she'll go, and I'll fail my 'C.E.' Then they'll hate me. For ever and ever."

"Who?"

"My parents." At this, Ken turned his head away, suddenly stricken, ready to weep. Jemma peered round his shoulder and, seeing his crumpled face, put her arms round his shoulders and touched foreheads.

"Don't cry, Ken darling. I'll help you. I'm always on your side. Promise I won't make Miss Wadley leave. And I'll see Mibs doesn't either. I'll tell Mibs to fry all her beastly secrets."

"Mibs made it up, didn't she?"

For the fraction of a second Jemma hesitated, then said firmly, "Yes, she made it all up, because Mibs is wicked. So let's punish her. You and me will join forces and be against Mibs from now on."

They were within sight of Fatima's hut and could see the old woman squatting before her door pounding spices. She had not yet caught sight of them, so Ken led Jemma down a sidetrack. "Butch is puffed. Let's sit down for a second."

He looked thoughtfully at Jemma, at her small face, black hair, black brows, and her bright eyes. If anyone looked wicked, she did.

"When I tell lies it's because I've got to—to get out of a fix. But why does Mibs tell lies? She isn't in a fix and she doesn't even know Miss Wadley."

"Mibs thinks spying's exciting, that's why. Sometimes she spies and doesn't hear anything interesting, so she makes up things."

"I don't believe that."

"Don't let's talk of her anymore," Jemma said.

When Fatima saw Ken she dropped the pestle, shook out her baggy pantaloons and came forward, bobbing and grimacing, her arms out to embrace him. Ken hugged her and at the same time glanced over her shoulder into the hut. It was true —mounds of sweets had been laid out, arranged in patterns on a big brass tray. The earth floor was scattered with marigolds.

"Eat! Eat!"

It was all Fatima had ever demanded of him. She squatted beside them as they guzzled, her eyes on Ken, now and again touching his head and stroking his arm. When they were gorged, Ken and Jemma prepared a betel-chew for the old woman. Ken fetched the betel-box from a niche in the wall, selected a glossy green betel-vine leaf and spread slaked lime over it. Jemma cut slivers of areca nut with special clippers and added tobacco, cutch and other spices. It fell to Ken, as her "butcha," her "child," to fold the leaf into a three-cornered packet and pop it down the betel-stained cavern of Fatima's jowl. She pressed it with her teeth, not chewing it, for fifteen minutes, which is the period of a "betel-chew." Fatima loved these attentions from Ken and Jemma. Her heart became so full, tears trickled down her cheeks. She mopped them up unself-consciously with the edge of her scarf.

It was Butch lying on her back, four feet in the air, who gave the alarm. Without warning she rolled over, hackles up, growling ferociously. "Must be Hanif!" Hanif was Fatima's grandson. Ken grabbed the dog's collar. But it wasn't the boy, but a girl who appeared, silhouetted in the doorway.

"What do *you* want?" Jemma had recognized her at once.

"Miss Sahib! Enter! Eat! Eat!"

Fatima scrambled to her feet, grabbed the big tray and offered it to a pretty, round-faced, fair-haired girl. "Take! Take!" She thrust the tray at her, pressing it against her dress. Mibs backed away.

"Who's this filthy old woman? What's she want? I don't eat bazaar sweets."

Fatima, her eyes on Mibs, did not understand the words, but was hurt by the contemptuous tone.

"Don't speak like that." Ken tried to place himself between Mibs and the old woman, but Jemma was too quick for him. Head thrust forward, body swaying like a mongoose striking a cobra, Jemma pounced on Mibs, struck so swiftly no one was sure what happened except that Mibs reeled backwards, fell in the dust, and once down, Jemma kicked her and tore her clothes.

Ken pulled them apart. At first the violence of Jemma's attack stupefied him, and he had been too dazed to move.

"She's bleeding. You've cut her mouth and her legs. Why did you do that?" He held Jemma by the wrists, digging into her skin with his nails.

"Because I hate her."

Mibs did not look at either of them, nor did she sob or tremble. She found a handkerchief, dabbed at her cuts and methodically dusted herself. Then she left the hut. Ken looked from Jemma to Fatima, and made his decision. He hugged the old woman good-bye, whistled to his dog and left.

After a moment Jemma followed him. She heard him shout after Mibs, "Wait for me," and watched him catch up with her as she strolled down the hill. Jemma trailed after them, keeping close enough to catch snatches of their conversation. She heard Ken speak of Colombo and his catamaran. As they were crossing the bridge she heard him tell Mibs, "You can have it, if you like."

10

Butch growled, awakening Ken, who turned over and lay for a moment half-awake. Against the rectangle of faint light from the doorway he saw someone move stealthily across the room.

His dog growled again. Ken put his hand over her muzzle.

"Kwe-ma-tha!" A Burmese swear word. It was Ko-Ni.

Ken fumbled with matches, trying to light the oil lamp by his bed.

"Don't! They'll hear you. Why aren't you ready?"

"What for?"

"What do you think! Didn't you get my message?"

Ja-Bo, the sweeper's son, had said something about fetching Maung Khin from the jungle with Ko-Ni, but Ken had not taken him seriously.

"But it's still pitch-dark!"

"Won't be for long. We should have left an hour before dawn. His feeding grounds are miles away and it doesn't matter how far he roams—I've got to go after him and bring him back by eight. Remember I'm not a Thakin like you. I'm just an ordinary u-zi."

An ordinary u-zi! Oh dear, Ken thought, Ko-Ni is out to pick a quarrel. The boys had known one another all their lives, and they had always agreed there was a no more desirable and honourable calling than that of the u-zi. The word, which means "ride at the front," is used in Burmese to describe the elephant rider.

It was their first meeting since Ken had returned from England. To be greeted by his dearest friend with these sarcastic, hateful words made Ken miserable. He searched for some way to humour him although he felt Ko-Ni was taking an unfair advantage of him, as he always did. Even as quite a small boy Ken had become aware that Ko-Ni's sudden, perverse and wayward hostility was rooted in envy. At first Ken had been puzzled. To him, he and Ko-Ni were the most important boys in Kaikun—well, if not in all Kaikun, certainly in the elephant camp, where they spent most of their time. This was because Ken's father was the Forest Officer and Ko-Ni's father was Saw Chaw Hlaw, Head Elephant Man. As time went on, Ken became aware which father in this hierarchy possessed the greater authority, but whereas he was careful never to allude to it, Ko-Ni could never let the subject alone. "Just because your father's the boss."

"You don't know how I've missed you, Ko-Ni, and the camp, and Maung Khin and Kyauk-Kyi. I haven't forgotten anything we ever did together."

Kyauk-Kyi (Big Rock) was the "schoolmaster" elephant, or koonkie, who had helped to train Maung Khin.

"Haven't you?" Ko-Ni's voice was still harsh, but Ken recognized the words as an invitation to cajole a little more.

"Didn't you get my letters? You know I missed you more than anyone. You are my best friend."

Ken had got out of bed, changed from his English night pyjamas into longyi and, because Ko-Ni chose to sit on the floor, diplomatically sat down beside him. On the bed, in the place Ken had vacated, Butch lay stretched out luxuriously, her head on Ken's pillow.

"All the same, you don't want to be a u-zi anymore."

How was he to get out of that one?

"It's not up to me. It's my father and mother who decide."

Ko-Ni grunted. He was not taken in, but Ken's placating manner had appeased him a little.

"We'll go the way I came in—down the tree." Ko-Ni ordered and Ken stood up, ready to be ordered about if that was how peace could be restored between them.

"What about my dog? She's too heavy to carry down trees."

"Are you mad? Dogs and elephants! Have you forgotten already! Tie her to the foot of your bed."

The boys were standing up, and in an effort to re-establish their old affectionate bond, Ken had put his arm over Ko-Ni's shoulder. At these words he withdrew his arm. "I want my dog and my elephant to get used to each other. They must get together right away."

"*Your* elephant," Ko-Ni said.

"Well he *is* mine, isn't he?"

Never before had the anomalous and thorny question of Maung Khin's ownership come into the open like this. But Ken had had enough, and Ko-Ni's scornful "*Your* elephant" was the last straw. Maung Khin, or Mister Ken, had been named after Ken. One of Tom's elderly female elephants, Miss Firefly, had escaped and joined a wild herd. After being recaptured she had given birth to a male calf on the day that Tom's wife, Hla Gale, had given birth to Ken. Hla Gale asked if she could buy the calf from the Forest Department for her son. After some difficulty Tom arranged it. The calf was to be registered in Ken's English name, Kenneth, and was known thereafter as Maung Khin. The boy was given technical ownership, but the calf remained with the Forest Department. Hla Gale agreed to pay for its keep and training. As an elephant is not a trained "traveller" until he is over thirteen, Hla Gale must have already paid out nearly seven thousand rupees, about seven hundred pounds, for Maung Khin. But since her son had learned all about "breaking," training, and riding elephants through this arrangement, the practical Hla Gale did not mind. She was prepared to continue paying for Maung Khin, for his feed, harness, and u-zi's wages because she calculated that as he graduated to teak extraction—the next step in his training—he would be worth about a thousand pounds by the age of twenty. She earned plenty of money from her sawmills: expense was not the point. A fully trained elephant for teak extraction, she hoped, would prove the nucleus of the herd she hoped Ken would want to create. For, one day, when Ken assumed the management of her sawmills, Hla Gale was going to persuade him to cut out intermediaries and to undertake teak extraction himself. Ken was more likely to fall for the idea—a difficult, troublesome venture—if he retained his boyhood love of elephants and friendship with elephant men.

The arrangement whereby the Forest Officer's son owned an elephant but another boy trained it could never have worked satisfactorily because of human rivalry.

The young boy who at the age of about eight is lowered onto the head of the young calf fenced into a "crush" becomes, in time, almost a part of his animal. It is the boy who gives the calf its first order, "Hmit" (sit), and first bribe, a bit of tamarind and salt, or a banana. It is the boy who "breaks" the calf, and then trains him, first as a baggage-elephant or traveller, and finally for the more exciting task of moving teak logs. The training of the elephant and apprenticeship of the rider take ten to twelve years during which man and beast develop a unique understanding of one another.

It was natural that Ko-Ni should have become possessive over Maung Khin—what u-zi isn't possessive over his animal? The jealousy between Ko-Ni and Ken had become apparent when they were no more than five and seven years old. As time went on it had increased alarmingly. Ken's departure for England had been opportune.

Ko-Ni was speaking with exaggerated politeness.

"Since Maung Khin is technically your property, you can choose another rider, Thakin. First I have to take him out on a little trip—but after that . . ."

Slow to temper, but once aroused, Ken could speak as sharply as Ko-Ni.

"I want Maung Khin to remain in Kaikun. I want to ride him. He's not to go away."

"Very well. It was nothing anyway. I'll tell my father."

"As for my dog—she's coming with me wherever I go. She's very obedient and she knows all the commands."

Ken turned to his dog, a white blur in the dark room. "'Hmit.' See? She knows that's to sit. 'Tah,' Butch, 'Tah.'" This

was the command for "stand up," and the white blur seemed to
be obeying it.

Ko-Ni started to laugh. "A dog obeying elephant talk!" Ken
had expected to impress him and found his amusement infuriat-
ing. "You're laughing because you're jealous. You're not even
glad I'm back. You're afraid I shall take Maung Khin away from
you. And perhaps I will."

There was silence. Then Ko-Ni said, "Truly, you speak like
an English Thakin. They said you'd learn to, and you have." There
was a movement in the dark and Ken became aware of Ko-Ni
bending up and down before him. He was wai-ing, making an
obeisance reserved for important people.

Ken grew hot with shame; of all the defects of foreigners, ar-
rogance most jarred on the Burmese, who were a nation without an aristocracy, a true community of equals.

Ken said, "Please don't quarrel on my first day. I'll tie up my
dog."

"Take her, if you want to."

In the end it was Butch herself who settled the matter. Under
cover of darkness she had gained the heaven of her species, a
human's bed, a human's pillow. When daylight came she would
make a bid to remain where she was, but at night, when she felt
entitled to enjoy this captured territory, there was no question
at all in her mind of being dislodged. Through some inexplicable
agency she was able to make herself heavier and heavier. When
the boys shifted her an inch or so, she wriggled back. In the end
they gave in and left her.

They scaled down the trunk of the gul mohur tree, crossed
the drive and ran through the garden, where the sweet-peas
were glimmering faintly in the moonlight. Ken, watching the
moon through a bank of soft cloud, recalled his mother's saying
that a peepul tree grew there. If he stared at it until his eyes
watered, she said, he would see monkeys climbing about its
branches.

Dimly through the river-mist Ken could make out various
garden landmarks, beds of cannas bordering the river, a sweet-

pea hedge planted at right angles to the water, and three old lemon trees.

"What was England like?" Ko-Ni asked.

Ken made no reply. It was the question everyone was asking him. Even his mother hadn't the tact to leave it alone.

In the water meadows, bullfrogs croaked so loudly that Ko-Ni raised his voice to shout above their din.

"Tell the truth, Khin. You hated England and the English school. We know more than you think." Did he? How? But Ken said nothing because school had taught him the best way of extracting secrets was by pretending not to be interested.

"It cost us five rupees," Ko-Ni said. "We each paid a rupee."

"You went to Hanuman Lall? All right—since you know all about me, why ask?"

Ken was mortified to think that his gang had spied on him. It was no good being indignant with Ko-Ni and the other members of the Galon gang because they had bribed the Postmaster. In the past Ken himself had paid the old man to steam open letters—four annas for inland, eight annas for airmail.

With a torch lit and held over their heads, the boys jogged down the river-path.

In the darkness, high above their heads, a wind stirred, bringing down the valley the tinkling sound of monastery bells. A jackal howled and from the hill a village pi-dog barked, setting off jackal choruses in all directions. They climbed up from the valley and Ken, looking towards the village, imagined the quivering leaves of banana trees and the small dusty pomegranates in yards between the houses. Skirting the village, they climbed a path that was really a dried monsoon watercourse. It took them behind the monastery up to Wild Bee Cliff, where hives hung from the rocky ledges. Once on the clifftop, Ken noticed an eerie phosphorescent glow, the first gleams of dawn. In the valley colours appeared, soft warm reds and golds, and above the hills the sky was dappled with pale lavenders, creamy white, blue and rose, the colours in his mother's hedge of sweet-peas.

With his back to the glowing sky, Ko-Ni spoke wistfully. "Did you see a fire-engine in England? A red one with ladders and brass bells and hoses? How I wish I'd been you. How I wish I'd had the chance to go to England. Why don't you speak about England?"

Because I don't want you to hate me! Aloud he said, "Because England is so ordinary."

"If I'd been to school in England I'd get a job in a factory. A factory!" Ko-Ni's face was transformed; he looked upwards, made extravagant gestures, drawing with his arm the factory of his dreams over the dawn sky. "Wheels, pulleys, pistons! Hiss-whoo-whee-hiss-hoo. Up and down and then siz-zas-siz. That's where I'd like to go, a factory, watching the big wheels and the pistons."

Ken looked astonished. "You'd leave Kaikun? You'd leave your mother and the jungle?"

"Why not?" Ko-Ni came alongside Ken, caught his arm and pulled him round to face him.

"If I went to England I wouldn't be bad, like you. Why did you knife that boy? He was ten, you were thirteen."

"Shut up!"

"It was cowardly."

"It was not. He tried to stop me. I did it without thinking."

"You were trying to run away. That's cowardly. Then you tried to knife someone weaker than yourself. That's what the letter said."

"It didn't."

"Hanuman Lall knows perfect English, and that's what he read out. 'Coward!' 'Coward!' Your teacher wrote it."

Ken felt the tears rise. "Running away isn't cowardly. Sometimes you have to. If you saw a tiger, you'd run too."

Ko-Ni considered this. "Even from a tiger there's more merit in *not* running away."

"Fat lot of good if a tiger eats you."

"Sometimes common sense and courage are one. Two weeks ago Ma Than Min heard a tiger roar near the waterfall. It was coming down the same track, so she got behind a tree a few feet away. The tiger passed without seeing her."

"But what happened to your uncle when he tried to be brave?"

It was an instance quoted in the village to illustrate foolhardiness. U Pon See, Ko-Ni's uncle, had ridden his elephant for thirty years. One hot season it went musth and killed a woman, so the Forest Manager went out to shoot it. U Pon See begged him for a chance to save his beloved beast. He said that, as the elephant had been his lifelong companion, he would obey him even in musth. The Forest Manager agreed, so U Pon See tracked it to a clearing in the jungle and started to walk across the open space, talking and cajoling his beast, as he always did. The elephant did not charge him but waited quietly until U Pon See was within reach of his trunk, then it caught him round the waist and trampled him to death.

"You think I don't like you, Khin. But I've been telling them the letter is all lies, and that you are not a coward. I told everyone, 'No one knows Khin like I do, and I tell you all he is brave.' Now I want you to prove it. Go alone and get Maung Khin and ride him back. If you do that, no one can say you are afraid."

"Why should I be afraid of bringing back my own elephant?"

Ko-Ni shrugged. "He's much bigger now, and he's fierce. Other u-zis are frightened of him. If you could catch him and bring him in, they'll soon change their minds about you."

Ken wanted to make sure of this challenge. "You want me to track him, mount him, ride him back here?" Ken touched the ground with his bare foot. "Right here?"

"Yes . . . here. I'll stay here and wait for you."

"Done!"

"I won't stay more than an hour. If you haven't returned by then I'll know something has gone wrong and I'll go for help."

"What could go wrong?" Was Ko-Ni holding something back?

"Perhaps you've forgotten how to track, or the sound of his bell, or the words of command. He might even hurt you. He's fierce. If you startle him by appearing suddenly he may even charge you!"

His friend was deliberately trying to make him feel uneasy. Ken had carved his elephant's bell, the kalouk, with his own hands and had tipped one clapper with a copper disc to distinguish its note from others in the herd. As for forgetting the words of command, hadn't Ko-Ni just heard him say "Hmit!" "Tah!" "Digo-la!" to his dog. As for being charged by his elephant— that was only possible in musth. Maung Khin's glands were not yet developed enough to discharge the fluid which trickled into the eyes of elephants, irritating them to a point of madness.

"You're trying to frighten me, but it won't work."

"I'm putting you on your guard, that's all." Ko-Ni handed him a segment of bamboo cut in the form of a whistle. "If you do get lost, blow it, and the search party will know where to look." He unwrapped three bananas from the cloth slung over his shoulder. "I don't expect you remembered his favourite titbit, so you can take what I brought."

"It's you who don't remember what he likes." From his pocket Ken produced balls of tamarind pulp filled with crystals of salt.

Ken went off to the point where the game trails entered the forest. Just as he was about to follow one of them, Ko-Ni shouted, "Wrong way! Look left. Look by the bawdi-bin."

Ken hesitated, then retraced his steps. Now he was sure Ko-Ni was trying to deceive him.

11

Ken hesitated before the bawdi-bin. Everyone hesitated on its threshold. It was an evil tree, if you could call it a tree, with roots in the ground and foliage like any other, but it was a parasite, his father said, a creeper whose roots and branches, coming in contact with other plants, wound round them to suck in their sap and in the process hugged them to death. To Ken it resembled a python constricting its prey, because, like the python, it swallowed whole, leaving no trace of its victim.

There were only a few slivers of bark wedged in the coils to tell what kind of victim this bawdi-bin had destroyed. Ken scrutinized these slivers and recognized them for the padauk, one of the kings of the forest. Take that! He used his dah on the bawdi-bin before entering the ranky-smelling husk, as hollow as a chimney. When its host was dead the bawdi-bin grew a cage of ribs to support itself. Spreading outwards like flying buttresses, these ribs formed curious partitions in which Ken had often found snakes. To give himself courage, he started to sing:

> The bawdi-bin, the bawdi-bin,
> The nats live here so don't go in:
> Not only nats but snakes an' bats,
> Lizards, an' toads, an' slimy rats . . .

Conscious of Ko-Ni's eyes upon him, Ken went boldly into the bawdi-bin, crawled over exposed roots and through one sinister compartment after the other until he found his way out on the far side. There, sure enough, he found marks showing where Maung Khin had rubbed himself against the tree before following a game-trail down a slope. Ken followed the tracks, which led to a place where Maung Khin had stopped to graze on bamboo. Here Ken paused to listen to the sad groaning noises of culms rubbing against one another. The bamboo had been violently pulled about: in places where succulent shoots grew, entire clumps had been devastated.

It occurred to Ken that Maung Khin alone could not have done this; examining the ground, he saw that the tracks of many other elephants covered the earth. So Maung Khin must have got wind of a wild herd and joined it here.

It wasn't difficult to track Maung Khin, because his footprint was distinctive. When young, the flesh under one of the toes of his right forefoot had been lanced to relieve an abscess, and a small, clear "V" scar had remained. Over the disturbed ground Ken could see Maung Khin's "V" and those of a much larger animal. Had there been a fight? Had Maung Khin made himself unpopular by showing interest in a female? It looked like it. Two sets of tracks veered off—Maung Khin's ahead, and those of a full-grown elephant in pursuit. The young tusker had taken to his heels! Serve him right. He had no business to be courting at the age of thirteen. Ken followed the tracks until they ended on a steep slope, down which there was nothing but a muddy slide. What had happened? Ken guessed Maung Khin's legs had not proved fast enough, so he had tobogganed to safety on his backside.

Ken gave himself up to the jungle, watchful, mistrustful, yet at the same time delighted to be back in known and loved surroundings. Looped vines, liana creepers and dangling aerial roots reminded him of the patterns made by the masts and rigging of fishing boats in Moulmein Harbour. And as the boats heaved gently in the swell, so these lines and loops above his head seemed to be moving in rhythm.

There was nothing much to fear from above except red ants' nests, which were sometimes suspended from a branch, or the mad-dog creeper. This was "Dry Forest" land where the tall trees grew—sal, ironwood, teak—whose leaf canopy was usually dense enough to prevent a secondary growth, that rank sprawl of cane-brake, tree-fern, screw-pine and Kythaung bamboo which made "Wet Forest" areas so difficult to traverse. Ken looked up at the "clean" boles of trees, which in his father's terms meant "clean" of branches. The boles of all the trees were in fact covered with epiphytic ferns and orchids, and acid-green wart-like moulds.

He paused under a tree with a gouty-looking trunk, where he watched a swarm of purple sunbirds feeding on yellow blossom. Their wings vibrated so fast he could not really see them, but as each one hovered over a corolla it seemed pinned there by a piece of fine black wire—its long, extensile, tubular tongue. A similar tree grew on the Deer Hill, in the shoemaker's yard. In spring the village boys, Ken with them, swarmed up its trunk when the owner wasn't looking, yanked down handfuls of blossom and, like the sunbirds, sucked the nectar out of tiny yellow tubes.

The name of the tree? It was on the tip of his tongue! Champa? No, the champa's flowers were white.

"No other boy forgets things like you do, McNeil! You can't remember one single history date. And look at you! You've forgotten to tie your laces and your tie. Don't you *want* to remember? Or are you plain stupid?"

Something bit him on the nape of the neck. He slapped his hand on the spot, catching an insect between thumbnail and finger. It was a springing-plant lice, the kind his father told him lived on the garuga tree.

Garuga! That was the forgotten name. He shouted it aloud. Garuga! Garuga! Garuga! He leaped, executed a mad dance, swinging his dah round so that it sliced through nettles and seedlings.

They were wrong about him at school. He wasn't plain stupid. One day he'd go back to Downderry in a car, or perhaps when he was a fighter-pilot fly over the beastly place in his Spitfire. He might even bomb it. Drop an H.E. on Matron's sitting room.

What other jungle names could he remember? He heard a

bird. "Tonk-tonk-tonk." The barbet! He then mimicked the tree pie, filling the forest with its ugly screech. Catching sight of the scarlet flash of a flock of minivets, he screamed, "whee-whee-ri-ri." The small birds dived and banked through tree-trunks, spiralling upwards towards a ridge. Maung Khin's tracks led him there too. The minivets alighted on a great teak growing on the edge of an escarpment. Hadn't he been here before? The place was so familiar Ken seemed to recognize the lay of the land and many details about the tree whose boughs spread like wings over the valley.

The Hill of the White Elephant—that was the name of the place! Long ago, he remembered, his father had stood before this tree, taken off his hat, and bowed before it, saying, "Reprieved T. Grandis Esquire."

That was when Dad had taken him on tour to open up this compartment of the forest which had been closed for thirty years. Dad had said, "Keep your eyes open: we're walking on the highways of the tiger and the mithan and the bear. You can learn so much from the beasts; they are wiser and nobler than men."

The snag of the trip had been Mr Poole; Mr Poole, the Welsh manager of a timber firm. Dad had been opening up the compartment for Mr Poole's firm, who were contracting for the teak.

There were seldom more than two or three teak trees in an acre, and each one had to be mapped, logged and measured at chest level. The mature trees—those whose girth was over seven foot six inches—were blazed and hammer-marked in two places. It was his father who decided which tree should be girdled, and it was about girdling that Mr Poole made a nuisance of himself. All big trees were girdled, that is, killed, so that Mr Poole's timber firm could extract them. It usually took three years for them to die, and when dead the firm was free to fell and haul them away. Timber firms were only allowed to fell the trees Dad selected and killed. Mr Poole had inflicted himself on them in the hope that he could persuade Dad to girdle all the big trees. But his father wanted to keep some of the big ones for seed-dispersal, particularly those whose seeds would be scattered over a wide area.

The tree growing on the Hill of the White Elephant was just the kind both Dad and Mr Poole wanted—Dad for seed-dispersal, Mr Poole to sell.

Before Dad could make up his mind about the tree, Mr Poole started prancing about under it.

"Look at its bole—clean as a whistle and it's a hundred feet at least. Biggest I ever saw. I want it. Who's got the hammer? Hey you—" He shouted at Ken. "Pyat it."

Ken, like his father—indeed, like all Forest Officers—had his own "pyat," or logging hammer. This was a square-faced, double-sided hammer embossed on one side with "rej," short for "reject," and on the other, "pyat," the Burmese word for "cut." Trees destined to be "killed" or girdled for the contractor would be marked "pyat," those spared for seed, or for any other reason, "rej."

If Mr Poole was keen to have the tree, it was unwise of him to give the orders concerning it. It was not the way to get things out of Dad. When Ahme wanted anything, Ken had noticed, she stopped talking and watched his father in a silent, stealthy way.

"Wait a minute, Ken," Dad had said, and Ken could tell from his voice which way the wind was blowing.

"Look here, McNeil, I want that tree. I'll have it, whatever you say."

What a way to speak to the Head Forest Officer! If Mr Poole had tried taking teak trees without permission in King Thibaw's time, he would have had his head chopped off.

Dad did not reply, but turned his back on Mr Poole so that he faced the tree. Then he removed his hat and bowed low to the teak.

"Reprieved, Tectona Grandis, Esquire," he said, and without a word Ken had walked up to the tree and given it a hard knock with the "rej" side of his hammer.

After all that time, after sailing away in a ship, after the Blitz and Burbidge and Matron, here he was, Kenneth McNeil, Kyi Minh, looking at the blaze he had cut and hammered in a forest tree.

Maung Khin's tracks led down from the ridge to the Valley of the Water Buffalo and there, on the far side, Ken came upon

the orange-coloured mound of the tusker's droppings. To discover when the elephant had passed that way Ken broke it apart
with his toe—as elephant boys were taught to do—and tested the
temperature. Maung Khin must have passed that way not more
than twenty minutes before.

Slashing through bamboos, he found himself on the edge of a
clearing where, on the far side, a movement caught his eye.

"Easy! Easy! Don't startle him. First accustom him to your
presence: talk to him, let him take his time to recognize you
by your voice, and tell him it's time to stop grazing and come
back to work." That was what Saw Chaw Hlaw used to tell
the elephant boys.

Ken stood still, and started softly, "Lah! Lah! Lah!"

Maung Khin had been pulling up kaing grass but now turned
about and busied himself with something else, as if to say, I don't
know who you are, and I'm not interested.

"Lah! Lah! Digho Lah!"

At last intelligent eyes looked up to examine Ken, but they
seemed filled with suspicion.

"Don't you know me? I went away, but I've come back to you.
I had to. Aren't you my brother? My twin? Weren't we born on
the same day? Come! Come! Come here!"

For an instant the young bull stopped swaying his trunk and
shaking the kalouk, his wooden bell.

"I'm not going to stand here all day. If you hurry I'll give you
something." Ken held out the lump of tamarind and salt. "I
haven't forgotten what you like."

Ken was watching and listening intently, waiting for Maung
Khin to suck in his cheeks and to make the slobbering, suckling,
jubilant noises which meant he was giving in and was about to
acknowledge his kinship, and his affection for Ken, his master.
But there was no sign that Maung Khin recognized him. Disappointment turned to irritation and Ken called out sharply,
"Digho Lah! You fat brute! Come here!"

When this also met with no response, Ken left the cover of
jungle and walked boldly out into the clearing. It wasn't wise to

do this, and Ken knew it, wondering what he should do if Maung Khin attacked him. Attack him? Charge him? Ridiculous!

Maung Khin hauled down more creepers, trampled them underfoot, then stood swaying his trunk, head slightly bent, glaring at Ken across the sandy strip. Something about his attitude bothered Ken. It was as if the elephant were biding his time, enticing him to approach. Without warning, Maung Khin trumpeted. He is challenging me. Why? What's up? Once more Maung Khin savaged the creepers, taking up some lying before him to lash them across his knees. Abruptly he dropped them, curled up his trunk. Ken knew what that meant. He was going to charge.

Run, run, get back under cover, but he could not move, stood rooted, not feeling fear, but unable to move or control his trembling.

Sand spurted under Maung Khin's feet, the kalouk clanged, the grey hulk swelled, filled the sky, shouldered the clouds.

"Hmit!"

Ken shouted the command but Maung Khin did not pull up. Ken closed his eyes, waiting for the trunk that would snatch him up and crash him to the earth.

Abruptly the clanging bell became silent. All was quiet save for a sound of brushing, as if someone were sweeping the grass. Through half-closed lids Ken watched the tip of Maung Khin's trunk pass gently over marsh herbs and, glancing up, noticed the big domed head was lowered, the body relaxed, the attitude one of docility. Ken stood shivering, unable to take the initiative, too stunned to know what to do next. The moist pink tip of the trunk felt its way to his neck, nuzzled the back of his head, then crept down his shirt, along his arm, and probed inquisitively round the opening of his pocket.

"Here you are!"

Maung Khin only wanted his titbit, and Ken was so relieved tears started to pour down his cheeks. He did not mean to blub, he couldn't help it.

Maung Khin nuzzled his other pocket. "Sorry, no more! Besides, it's time to go."

Time to go! Could he mount Maung Khin? The elephant stood quietly swaying his trunk, waiting. Ken had only to say "Hmit" and Maung Khin would drop on his haunches, his four legs extended. But fear crawled over Ken. He was still so shocked he was incapable of touching the beast. He wavered, half-turned to go and there, grinning at him, not a yard away, was Ko-Ni. He had been watching him.

"Well done! It's the first time my trick hasn't worked."

"Trick?"

"I trained him to charge. To scare people."

"You *knew* he'd charge me?"

Ko-Ni said triumphantly, "He'd charge anyone, even Hit-ta-la! I've played this trick on lots of elephant boys. They scream with terror—but when Maung Khin pulls up just in time they start to cry, and then how I laugh." Ko-Ni took Ken's arm. "But you didn't flinch—you're not a coward, after all. So—you can ride his head. 'Hmit!'"

Ken climbed up and dug his bare toes against the rough folds of skin under his elephant's ears.

"Thwa!" "Go!"

Maung Khin stood up and with the familiar, rolling walk started through the jungle.

Ken couldn't get over what Ko-Ni had just admitted. All the time he had been in England this so-called friend, this member of the Galon gang had been busy training Maung Khin to play a trick calculated to terrify him. Oddly enough, Ken really did not mind Ko-Ni's prank because quite suddenly he felt differently, as if the last half-hour had changed him.

There were other things to do in the world besides wandering through jungles, testing dung with his toe and saying "Hmit" to elephants. And Ko-Ni evidently thought so too! Didn't he want to work in a factory? There wasn't much chance of Ko-Ni becoming anything but a u-zi of course. However, if Ken became important it would be in his power to help poor old Ko-Ni! The question was, should he? Ken pondered over this and in the end decided it would be unwise. Once someone plays a mean trick on you, he is never to be trusted again. From now on, Ken resolved, he would avoid Ko-Ni.

12

Jan. 16th.

Vibrating with nerves after that extraordinary talk with Mrs Dowall. That expression, "Opening your eyes to . . ." That's what she did to me. Realize how happy I was before she spoke, floating along in a state of bliss without realizing precisely what caused it. Now I know I cannot act naturally when Tom comes into the room, become rigid, can't look at him. My emotions have always affected me like this. Outwardly I may appear cool, but I know I have only a limited control over the demands of my hidden nature. I know I want to marry, want a husband, a man— but not primarily for sex, for children, for security, but because I fear loneliness, as some people have a neurotic fear of death or disease. At times I believed I could not bear one time more to return to the empty rooms of my Elsham Road home. Not *one* time more. Night after night, without anyone to talk to and be with.

But am I genuinely in love? "In love," yes, I think so. But falling in love is a trick of Nature. That other state, deeply loving someone for life with all the love and loyalty of one's nature —what about that kind of love? If the first love fails, as mine did for Guy Burnett, is one capable of really loving deeply again? Or does one merely live in the hope of intervention by fate?

To add to a churning of my inside over Tom (love isn't centred in one's heart, but in the pit of one's stomach), the war news is alarming. No bombing of Rangoon for a fortnight. Everyone's been sitting back and congratulating R.A.F. and American A.V.G. for "winning supremacy of air over Rangoon." At the time thought this a bit complacent. Now the bombing has started in earnest. Rangoon caught it yesterday and again today. Can't help comparing this to days before blitz in England. Exactly same kind of lull. Is this the start of a big offensive on Rangoon with widespread bombing over Burma? Kaikun next perhaps? Tokyo Radio jubilant. "Tokyo Rose" announced exodus of Indian labour again from Rangoon, and this time authorities unable to bring it back, and had to open Taungap Pass. Indians in thousands pouring over desolate Arakan, "Where they'll die in thousands," Tokyo Rose cooed, and adding that Rangoon had now a gigantic refugee problem, as cholera had broken out in camps and there was a hopeless shortage of doctors. Tom and Hugh believe flight of labour will bring Rangoon port to a standstill with Lend-Lease piling up. If Indian traders have left there'll be chaos over food, as Indians run nearly all food shops.

Hugh Chapman called meeting of all district officers, to which Tom asked if he could bring me—because of my first-hand experience in the London blitz.

Meeting a waste of time. They were unable to come to a decision over the most urgent problems, whether to evacuate Indian population or not, also the European families. War intelligence is nil, here as well as in Rangoon. Hamish spoke of finding a subaltern wandering about Kaikun in the early hours looking for a post office. He was brought to S.P.'s office, where he told Hamish he was trying to get his Field Commander's messages back to H.Q., and the only way to do it was by telegraph to Pegu post office, from where they'd relay it to Rangoon. "Imagine if the Japs were here," Hamish shouted at us. "Generals depending on old idiots like Hanuman Lall in our post office before they could contact base!" The subaltern's General, incidentally, was sitting in a car some miles away on the Bilin Road. They had no wireless, no proper maps of the area, no interpreter. The young man asked Hamish where, in the S.P.'s opinion, the Japs would invade. According to Hamish, "the poor young devil admitted he'd had no jungle training, nor had his troops. The Regiment was on its way to the Western Desert when it was diverted to Rangoon. So I hadn't the heart to tell him the Japs were bound to come through jungle, as there wasn't anything else this end of Burma." During the meeting Hamish and Dr Dowall announced their decision to leave immediately for Rangoon, to which both Hugh and Tom objected. The Doctor said he wanted to help with the cholera epidemic in the refugee camps, and Hamish because he wanted to vent his wrath on the Military Secretary over some top-secret and (I agree) very stupid orders that have just arrived. These instructed all district officers to remain at their posts if the country is overrun by the enemy and to hand over records, Treasury funds, etc. to Japanese commanders; furthermore, all D.O.'s must be prepared to remain and administer under the Japs if so desired. "Utter drivel! We wouldn't last two minutes with the Japs. They'd shoot us. I refuse to comply. I'm going to Rangoon to tell Willie I'm resigning." Most of the meeting was taken up with listening to Hamish rage. Hugh Chapman tried, in his dispassionate way, to explain and calm him down. He suggested some lunatic in Whitehall must have found these orders, which originally applied to Dutch burgomasters, and thought they would come in handy for officials in Burma. A Whitehall official, Hugh said, was incapable of seeing any difference between Germans dealing with the Dutch Government and Japanese dealing with the British Government in Burma. All they had to do was to point this out to Willie and the orders would be withdrawn. But Hamish raged on, until I got fed up and said, "Aren't we wasting time? Mr Waight is determined to go to Rangoon. Okay—let him go. But after he has dealt with the Military Secretary, perhaps he could help us by finding out about official evacuation schemes. In the U.K. the Government was marvellous, got everyone away who wanted to get away, and I'm sure the Burma Government has ships, special trains, coaches and river-steamers all ready to do the same. All we've got to do is to find out."

My interruption pulled them up and I could see by Hugh's expression he was surprised, but impressed too. And, thanks to me, this was the agreement reached. Hamish is leaving at dawn tomorrow, Dr Dowall going with him. No one seemed to be bothered that Kaikun would then be left without a doctor. Gather Doc's past it and people here prefer to be treated by his Indian dispenser, who knows just as much and doesn't smell of scotch.

It's past midnight as I sit entering up my diary by the light of an oil-lamp. Table crawling with moths, greenfly, and insects of all kinds. I am worried. If there's an evacuation, what's going to happen to me? What I want to do—that I know, but it's lunacy. Common sense tells me I should get out at once, sail back to England while there's still time. I'll sleep on it.

Jan. 17th.

More alarming news. Invasion of South Burma confirmed. Don't like sound of an official broadcast telling everyone to keep calm, and essential workers to stick to their posts because "Rangoon will be absolutely held. Rumours that the Governor and officials are evacuating are false and pernicious." That's a statement typical of a government about to run.

Children very irritating. Do dislike Ken when he's with Jemma and Mibs, shows off, tries to cheek me. All they care about is the fair, the pwe (pronounced pway), which is to be held on flat stretches of the river-bank in about three days' time when the moon's full. As these fairs attract opium smugglers and other bad hats, the S.P., according to Ken, won't give permission for a fair unless there's plenty of moonlight.

War scares have unsettled everyone. Hla Gale announced her intention of inspecting her Kadbingti sawmills, five miles down river, and possibly going on from there for a few days in Moulmein. When Tom heard she was off he decided he would have to go off on a trip too. Flap on about tent-poles, he said. The Army, which had till now relied on Japanese bamboo, wanted him to find other suppliers. The Army was also demanding walnut for rifle-factories and teak for ammo boxes. When Tom is worried —and he was today—his grey eyes turn a paler colour and he doesn't seem able to focus. I long to help. When he told me some of his clerical staff had run away, I offered to take dictation and to type, but he didn't seem to hear me. He's at his wits' end over his elephants too because the Army are asking him to let them have fifteen for some road-building project south of Bilin . . . but don't believe these are true cause of his anxiety. During past few days I've noticed a change in Tom, and I'm beginning to wonder—is it possible that he is wretched over the problems that are also upsetting me? This is not wishful thinking. Tom said something which caused me to think deeply.

We were left alone to spend the evening. Ken had gone to the fair-ground, and Hla Gale had left by launch at midday. Tom suggested walking over to the Club for a drink before dinner. I agreed because I like to get away from the house. You never know with children: Ken wouldn't spy on me, but I'm not so sure about those girls.

As we walked along the river-path with Hanif ahead holding the lantern, I thought how wonderful it would be if . . . if I could always be sure of going for a stroll with Tom on warm twilight evenings like that one, the air soft, and the river shimmering with lights of the fair-ground. Tom started to tell me about a village headman who was going to help him over the tentpoles—at least that was Tom's ostensible reason for introducing this subject. I soon discovered his real motive! Last time he'd visited this village, Tom said, he found the headman conducting a divorce case. When I heard the word "divorce" my heart started to thump loudly. Tom went on in a matter-of-fact way to explain that divorce wasn't common in Burma and this was his first experience of listening to a case. Evidently there was no legal formalities, and the headman had been approached by the couple on the division of property. What was Tom's motive for dragging in this topic? There can only be one—the obvious one.

I asked him, "Is it just as easy for two people to get married in Burma?"

"In the villages—yes," he said. "It's not like India, with involved contracts and ceremonies. If a Burmese village boy falls for a girl he elopes with her, and if they're not caught by nightfall the

parents accept them as married. If the boy is *persona grata*
with future in-laws, they don't chase him. If *not*, he's chased
with spears, and the girl, if caught, is brought back at the point
of a spear!"

I asked about the middle-class Burmese. At that Tom smiled.
"Middle-class! Thank God—there isn't one in Burma." He went
on to tell me about the democratic Burmese who dressed alike
whatever their background, but I wasn't really interested. I
wanted an answer to my question, and it struck me he was hedg-
ing. So I repeated it, "Surely all young Burmese couples don't
just elope?" "Well—no. There's the 'Mingala-Soung,' a marriage ceremony for the better-off. But don't get me wrong. In
Burma if a man lives with a woman, then he becomes her *yauk-
ya*, her man. You never hear her refer to him as her *husband*, only
as her *man*. I don't even know the word for 'husband' in Burmese. There may not be one."

Interesting! I thought I was beginning to see where this little
lecture on Burmese marital customs was leading us. Wasn't it
Tom's timid way of informing me that he was Hla Gale's
"man" and not her *"husband"*?

As I put two and two together, I recalled what I overheard
Mrs Dowall telling someone in the Club, that when an Englishman in Burma contracts a liaison with a native woman, there
are no hard feelings when he decides to break it off to marry a
white woman. The Burmese is sent back to her village with a
lump sum for herself and so much for each child, whom the Englishman usually agrees to educate in one of the hill schools especially founded for this kind of offspring. There's no shame attached to the *affaire*, and the woman soon finds herself a new
husband.

Tom is preparing the ground. I think he will soon tell me something I long to hear. His mood was very strange this evening. I
could see that all the time we were together his mind was
occupied by other, worrying ideas—about us? about the war?
Probably both. He started speaking suddenly of Burmese fifth
columnists. It isn't the first time I've heard of them: I heard

Hamish Waight speak of a gang in the neighbourhood he was trying to catch. Tom said, "We call them fifth columnists and traitors, but are they? After all, we've no business in Burma, or rather, we came to Burma on business—and have no other excuse to be here," and then, after a pause, "I'm worried about Hla Gale. She's getting involved, she can't help it." I asked, "You mean your wife's a fifth columnist?"

At that Tom's eyes seemed to focus on me in a different way. "Fifth columnist? Hla Gale!" He put his hand over mine and gave it a squeeze. "Heavens! I hope not." I didn't know what to make of this and waited for him to explain, but the vague Ken-ish look returned and he spent the rest of the evening wondering about the best evacuation plans—if necessary. Whose did I consider most practical? Hamish's plan, to send convoys of In-dians and Europeans away by train to hill stations, or if that wasn't possible, by road to Rangoon and on to India by steamer; or Hugh Chapman's idea, to send only Indians to India and the European and Anglo-Indian subordinates to Maymyo? I already know all about Maymyo, a hill station said to be "Just like England" with delightful villas, gardens, golf-course, race-course, etc. The Governor would go there, Tom said, and Hugh had hinted at a big house he might rent . . . in which case wouldn't I like to go there with Ken and Mibs, and run it for them?

Naturally, the first question I asked was, "Run it? Me! But what about your wife? Isn't Hla Gale coming with us?"

Tom wrinkled his forehead and hesitated. "That's the prob-lem. I'd like to get her away, but frankly—I don't know. She may refuse to leave her sawmills. The Japs won't touch her—at least, that's what she firmly believes."

"You mean, if there's an evacuation you, I and Ken go off to-gether without Hla Gale?"

He nodded. "We three will stick together, yes. The problem is —do I send you and Ken off to India, or do I keep you in Burma, say in Maymyo, where I can keep an eye on you and occasionally join you?"

To that there could only be one answer, and it took all my control to conceal my elation.

"Remain in Burma," I told Tom.

Jan. 18th.

As Tom was about to set off this morning on the tent-poles trip a messenger arrived from Hla Gale. She was in Moulmein, but was safe and well. He was not to worry and she would be back in a few days. He questioned the messenger because it wasn't like her to send this kind of message. The man rolled his eyes and made the kind of noises and gestures Ken does when imitating a bomber. So—I was right. The Japs are starting a big attack. Moulmein was bombed. And Moulmein's only sixty miles from us!

Tom said, "I'll have to postpone my contractor. I'm going to Moulmein."

"But she says she's okay," I said and then jokingly quoted the wartime slogan at home, "Is your journey really necessary?"

Tom gave me a queer look, distant, hard. "My journey *is* necessary, Miss Wadley. Hla Gale's my wife."

When he had gone I took Ken for his lessons but couldn't concentrate. Ken asked for the rest of the day off to see how the pwe was coming along. Pwe—pwe—that's all he can think of. I let him go. I felt very lonely. For something to do, I put on a pair of white gloves and brushed my hand over the surfaces of all the furniture, as mother used to, checking if Hanif had dusted thoroughly. Made him do every piece again. What's the use? The moment Hla Gale arrives back the house will be back to normal, dusty, untidy, with Hla Gale chattering all day and the servants doing as they please. In early January when Hla Gale was in Moulmein I really did turn this bungalow into a real home for Tom. I insisted on quiet and order and cleanliness, and I personally did the flowers. *She* may be great on growing them but never cuts them to brighten the place indoors. What are flowers for? While she was away last time I cut armfuls of cannas, roses, sweet peas, and the rooms came to life. It happened that on the day Hla Gale returned, I was in the garden and saw her enter the porch and stand by the big table. She saw my bowl of sweet-peas and I watched her pass her hands over them, as if distracted. So she didn't approve of me cutting her flowers! I felt guilty, but as I'm not afraid of her I promptly went in, ready to be ticked off, and to apologize. But she never said a word. She seemed to be watching me, though, and I noticed she removed a small vase of violets I had placed on Tom's desk.

I have been going over every word said between Tom and me last night. Could I be mistaken? Doesn't he care for me? If only I could be sure. He might have given me a sign—I'm sure he did —but I missed it. When one is in love it is inconceivable that the other person does not return one's love. You feel he does, he must! Soon he'll tell you that he does. I wonder.

Jan. 18th., evening.

Falling in love is a wretched business. One day you are yourself, free, the next you're someone else, trapped, with your mind concentrated on one person.

After dinner Hugh Chapman called round, saying he was worried when he heard from Ken I'd refused to go to the pwe. He tried to persuade me to go with his party (Mrs Dowall and the Baptist missionaries) to watch the play, but though I wanted to go, I refused, saying I'd already inspected the fair with Ken in the afternoon. I also said I was tired—and tired I am, sick and tired of myself.

I am a fool. I'm in Burma. I should be enjoying this strange country, strange people where our customs are arranged differently, sometimes upside-down. This afternoon I saw the village girls rehearsing the Paddle Dance, the big attraction of the evening according to Ken. They didn't dance, merely waved their arms and remained in the same spot. Then the orchestras . . . three rival ones, each with a man sitting in what looked like a circular tub, just his head appearing over the rim. Inside there were sets of drums, sixteen in one, with cymbals, gongs and wooden clappers. The drummer had the time of his life whacking them from the middle. I can hear their din as I write. The loudest is a police band. I recognize "Colonel Bogey" on bugles, pipes and cornets.

All evening I've struggled to keep my thoughts away from Tom, but it's no good and I may as well give in. Falling in love with a married man for the second time! Really, I have no luck. But whatever the consequences, I refuse to play the hypocrite.

That gambit of the Other Woman, "We couldn't help ourselves. We fell in love and so he had to leave his wife"—that's humbug. It's the woman who makes the running, not the man—and there comes a point where she makes the decision. Will she go ahead and grab him for herself, or let him go back to his wife? During the Guy Burnett episode I obeyed my conscience—partly. I told Guy I'd no intention of breaking up his home, and though that's another gambit of the O.W., I really meant it. The fact that Guy himself had no intention of leaving his wife, but of using me and my Woolworth wedding-ring for week-ends in quiet hotels, makes no difference. It was my decision and I stuck to it, but behaving reasonably well got me nowhere. This time it's to be different. This time I've no intention of obeying my conscience, only my yearning. I want Tom. I want him for my husband. Perhaps he may not yet be as deeply in love with me as I am with him—but he will be, and I can wait. Whatever happens, this time I am prepared to do everything, anything, to get what I want.

Jan. 20th.

Hugh Chapman round here again, just before lunch. His excuse for calling was that Hamish Waight had returned from Rangoon with alarming news which he—Hugh—wanted to tell me, so would I care to have lunch with him! As if he couldn't have told me then! Well, well, so that's how the wind is blowing!

I changed my dress, did my hair a different way and told Ken he could have the afternoon off to go again to the pwe. Incidentally, Ken didn't get to bed until after 3 A.M. Hugh said nobody does because the plays go on and on and most people stay till

6 A.M. Gave Ken five rupees to spend at the fair and set off with Hugh.

All the way to the D.C.'s bungalow I listened with almost total apathy to Hugh relaying Hamish's news about the appalling state of Rangoon, of Burma, the Army, the Government. For what it's worth, Hamish says morale in Rangoon amongst Europeans couldn't be worse: the Civil and Military are at loggerheads, each blaming the other for Burma's total unpreparedness for war. "The Civil have no faith in the Military, and the Military none in themselves." Army is short of everything, equipment, planes, guns—there isn't one bomb, and not one bomber-plane in Burma. There isn't even enough telegraph wire or wireless sets or maps. The maps were all bought up, openly, by Japanese agents in Rangoon a few weeks before Pearl Harbour.

Because of the exodus of Indians, shops are shut, banks too, you can't get bread except one day a week, and then only "between air-raid times." (There are two air-raids a day, morning and afternoon.) Docks are paralyzed with unloaded ships stacked with Lend-Lease equipment. At night, looters are everywhere and some are British Tommies. (Don't believe this.) Hamish said he saw a dozen Tommies who had been unloading a ship, staggering round drunk after opening crates of whisky. Hamish also said he saw a troopship returning to Madras almost empty though thousands were milling around the steamship offices—clamouring for passages to India. And this was where I *did* start listening. Hamish was convinced Rangoon would fall within a month or six weeks, and the immediate evacuation of all Indians and Europeans from Kaikun was essential. He had therefore arranged for accommodating about two hundred people on the next troopship to leave for Madras, probably in a week's time.

"Hamish asked me to ask you if you'd agree to go too in charge of the children—Mibs, Jemma, Ken, and any Indian and Anglo-Indian child whose father had to remain behind?"

"Wouldn't you be going?"

"No. I'd have to wait for orders."

"Hamish and Tom too?"

"It applies to all district officers and essential personnel."

Why had Hamish suggested the plan? To get me out of the way because he had guessed about Tom and me? That was my first suspicion, but since then I've worked out another one. I tried to be calm and said, "India—isn't that a bit drastic? The war's hardly started and we've only Mr Waight's word that things are so bad. Isn't he always inclined to rush things?"

That made Hugh smile, though he wouldn't agree openly. I then asked him about Maymyo, and his manner altered immediately.

"I was coming to that. Maymyo's my suggestion—but I didn't want to say anything if—well, if you preferred to get right away from Burma."

"But I don't," I said. "It's the last thing I want."

"Oh, good." He immediately started to tell me about Windermere Lodge, a house he had rented in anticipation of my agreement. "I'm hoping you'll take complete charge of Mibs."

"But I'm working for the McNeils!"

He did not answer and I noticed his gaze was fixed straight ahead. We had arrived at his house and I too saw Mibs, partly hidden by a cane screen. She was standing behind it, watching us approach. "We'll have to discuss this later," Hugh said.

The District Commissioner's house, I gather, is usually the largest and best sited amongst officials' houses wherever one goes. Hugh's bungalow was twice the size of Tom's, and whereas the Forest Officer's house with its verandah facing the drive looked as if it had been dumped down without thought, the D.C.'s had been carefully built so that verandahs looked out on the river on two sides. There was also a tennis-court and a much larger garden.

Mibs came out to meet her father and greeted me fairly politely but couldn't or wouldn't conceal her hostility. She doesn't like me, and I don't like her.

The verandah table was laid for two, and I assumed the places were meant for Mibs and her father. However, the moment I walked in Mibs told the houseboy, "I've changed my mind. I don't want those sandwiches, I'm going to lunch at home."

"No, you're not," Hugh said. "You've a date with Ken, so off you go. Bring the sandwiches, Saw Hardy." I tactfully ignored this little comedy, and when Mibs eventually flounced off, packet under her arm, I cut short Hugh's apologies with, "At her age I was just as possessive over my father and suspected all females of designs on him."

"Oh, I don't believe she thinks that!"

Either he's naïve or refuses to see what he doesn't want to see.

Lunch was spoiled by more war talk; Hamish's report has thoroughly upset Hugh, and he seemed determined to unbosom himself on me. In the end I became so irritated I said, "I don't believe it. No country could be so utterly unprepared. It sounds more as if Hamish were making a case for evacuating. Is he a bit of a coward and is he the one who wants to bolt?"

Hugh looked shocked, then laughed. "You don't like him, do you?"

"He lays down the law so."

Hugh seemed to agree. "Perhaps, but he's no coward. There's some talk of forming a guerrilla unit to remain in the Dawnas if the Japs come. Hamish was the first to volunteer, and because he has, half his constables have too. He's an excellent police superintendent, and his men worship him."

The Karen Christian houseboy, Saw Hardy, carried the coffee-tray to a summerhouse in the garden. Though it looked a bit ramshackle with holes in the flooring from which snakes might pop out, it had been built in a delightful spot, embowered in bamboos and within a few feet of the river. We sat drinking our coffee in companionable silence for quite a time, gazing across at the opposite bank where u-zis were giving their elephants a bath, scrubbing hides with switches of the mad dog creeper. Ken once brought me some of it to demonstrate the pith which really does lather. As I sat there, pleasantly replete, mind soggy, taking in the river smell, listening to the croak of frogs and the sound of distant hammering from the fair-ground, I was aware of feeling completely at ease with Hugh. It's strange. Provided I am not emotionally entangled with a man, I get on so much better. Once I'm "interested," I become wooden and incapable of being an amusing companion.

I brought him back to our earlier conversation. "Would you join those guerrillas?"

Hugh seemed to hesitate. "I wouldn't be allowed to. If Rangoon falls I'll be sent to Maymyo. That's why I've taken that house. That's why I'm hoping . . . look, I'm not doing this very well, but you've guessed what I'm trying to say."

I must have looked blank. "I want you to marry me. Don't say anything now. Think about it for a day or two—then tell me."

"But you don't know anything about me," I said and found myself telling him the story, not the version I give to old school friends, but the true one, or at least the one I recognize as the truth now—the sordid story of the "office wife," starting with Guy's offer of a lift home to Elsham Road, next the drink in a pub on the way, and eventually the drink in the flat and so on until I was buying a Woolworth wedding-ring and sneaking off with him to Trust Houses in Hertfordshire.

Hugh kept pressing my arm in sympathy, and oddly enough, this irritated me. I didn't want his sympathy, and I didn't want his affection. I told him about the death of Guy's wife and how I expected to become the next Lady B., and how I felt when on the way home from the office one evening I opened the Late Night Final to find a picture of Guy and a woman standing on the steps of Marylebone Register Office after their marriage. Hugh started stroking my fingers, but again a wave of unreasoning irritation swept over me and I snatched my hand away.

"Are you sorry for me because you think I was turned down for someone younger and prettier and better connected? I wish it had been like that. But Guy married someone older than me, plainer, and from a very ordinary background. I used to think I had lots of useful and attractive qualities—I ran his office perfectly, and I could have run his home perfectly, and we got on well—but when he did this to me he destroyed all the reasons I had for believing I was worth marrying."

Hugh said, "Even if you hadn't all those splendid qualities of the perfect Chairman's secretary, I would still want to marry you!"

He was joking, but instead of treating it lightly I heard myself say, "May I give you my answer straightaway? If we can keep it to ourselves for a bit—well—my answer is yes, Hugh."

He didn't speak at first but sat quietly looking at me.

"You're not in love with anyone else?"

"Who else *is* there? You know how I feel about Hamish."

"I meant in England."

"There has only ever been Guy Burnett, and I made a fool of myself over him and I'm glad that's finished."

We must have stayed talking in that summerhouse for hours, not like two people who had suddenly confessed they were in love, but like people who had struck up an acquaintance in a bus-shelter and found they had much in common. I was happy in a way, but under our friendliness I was all too conscious of guilt. Tom had only to crook his little finger at me—and I'd drop Hugh without any compunction at all.

At least I am honest with myself. It is the only way to be if you intend to do what you *want* to do, and not what you *should* do. Hypocrisy makes it very difficult to live with yourself. And that's why I refuse to go in for the humbug of the "Other Woman." When Guy first fell for me perhaps I could have broken up his marriage. I didn't even try to. And it didn't pay off. One should benefit from experience, and I intend to. If anyone's to be left in the lurch this time, it's not going to be me.

Evening colours glowed on the river, gold of the sand-spit and from the setting sun orange ripples shot with acid-green. I saw a flock of about a hundred jade-coloured parakeets flash out the gorge, skim over the shallows then rise together and settle on a tree. I was watching them when Hugh said it was time to leave. He wanted to kiss me, but I suppose was too shy and only managed to turn my palm over and kiss me there and on my arm. Poor man. I should have helped him, but it's no good, I can't. I am grateful to him, of course. I feel different since he asked me to marry him. If I can't have the man I really want, then it is comforting to know there is someone—and Hugh is really quite nice —for me to fall back on.

13

Ken's invitation to Mibs was to join him at the bridge, bringing her own sandwiches (he would bring some too), and together they would climb to the Ridge, taking the path past the Muslim village to the Look-out Point. From there, Ken said, they would be the first to spot the Posein launch and to broadcast the good news of its arrival. That's what he and Jemma always did. At the first blast of his whistle—a police whistle called "The Thunderer" given him by Mr Waight—children and grown-ups from all over Deer Hill and Kaikun would start running towards the river to escort the launch to the jetty. After all, said Ken, the Poseins were famous; they went all over Burma to act at pwes; they were probably "the most famous travelling troupe in the world," Ken added, but catching sight of Mibs's supercilious look, added, "well, anyway, in Burma."

Really, Ken was a wet, Mibs decided. Fancy making a fuss of Burmese actors—so-called—who wandered round fairs and didn't even put up a proper stage with dressing-rooms and a marquee for the audience. Ken had pointed out where they were going to perform, and Mibs had stared incredulously at a dusty square of the fair-ground where an area had been marked out by pegs, the footlights by storm-lanterns. There were only two seats, chairs brought in honour of her father's expected visit; everyone else was supposed to use the ground. "We bring blankets," Ken said, as if that was part of the treat. "The play starts at about

ten but goes on till after dawn. When we want to sleep we roll
ourselves up and go to sleep. It's lovely!" So—no stage, no seats,
and no box-office because the show was free. "Some play!" Mibs
exclaimed. The cost of the Poseins' performances during
the three-day pwe was met by various rich patrons in Kaikun,
amongst them Hla Gale, Ken's mother. Since Ken had said
nothing about this, Mibs assumed the entertainment was a form
of charity and her contempt was complete. The best plays in her
experience—and she had been to the Palladium, Drury Lane
and The Palace—were those whose seats cost the earth and were
sold out for months ahead. In England you always paid to see
professional players, even when they appeared in Shakespeare in
Regents Park, and that was boring enough.

Boring! That was Kaikun in a nutshell. No cinema, no shops,
no dance-hall or skating-rink, nothing to do except go to the Club
and have a swim in the pool. She would never have agreed to
meet Ken that day save to spite Jemma. Jemma was a mug.
Fancy having a crush on a weed like Ken, a mere boy, when
there was a man, a proper grown-up, keen on her. She was such
a clot she hadn't even noticed it. If Mibs had been in Jemma's
place, she'd have soon got him to buy her orange squash in the
Club every evening and glass bangles in the bazaar. She might
even have got round him to take her into Bilin—hire that old
bus—or even to Rangoon or Moulmein or wherever one went
for treats in this dreary country.

Despite Mibs's disillusionment she had, during a recent session
of eavesdropping, learned some cheering news.

If conditions grew worse in Rangoon there was a chance the
Japs might take the port and then—wh-ee-ee—Europeans in Kaikun would have to be evacuated. It didn't matter to Mibs where,
since she was sure no dump on earth could be as deadly as
Kaikun.

This particular eavesdropping occurred two days before Miss
Wadley arrived to lunch with her father. Mibs was not at her
home but at the Club, where she had gone to replenish her powder compact from the bowls of powder provided for members
in the ladies' cloakroom. While helping herself, Mibs had heard

voices. Peering through the window which looked out upon the Club verandah, Mibs saw Miss Wadley and Ken's father, Mr McNeil, sitting with their backs to her, looking towards the river. It was six-thirty, so Mibs assumed they'd come over for a drink before dinner and would soon leave.

She settled herself by the window. There was nothing to do, so she might as well listen and watch. It was growing dark, the Club was deserted, and with luck, those two might start snogging.

Apart from the hint from Mr McNeil of the possibility of evacuation, this snoop, Mibs felt, had been a waste of time. They never once held hands, or swore, or told blue stories, just hammered on about the war and a lot of dim old customs. Who cared how the natives got married or divorced?

Mibs had started eavesdropping as a game. It was so exciting it gave her cramp in her stomach and made her sweat all over. As at the Club that evening, she rarely heard anything that interested her, but this at first was not the point. The point was to listen, to feel her skin crawl with fear, also not to be caught. As time went on, however, Mibs did occasionally acquire snippets of surprising information of which she made good use.

When her parents' marriage started breaking up, that is, when her mother refused to go out to the East, Mibs's favourite game assumed a desperate and guilty character. There was nothing else she could do if she wanted to keep up-to-date on her parents' plans and plots, for to ask blunt questions was to unite them against her in a conspiracy of silence.

By the time her father had left for Burma, leaving the field clear for the Canadian, Francis Fletcher, Mibs's feelings of guilt had vanished, her spying had become more expert and her attitude businesslike.

Mibs walked away from the D.C.'s house leaving her father and Miss Wadley at lunch in a resentful mood. She was stung because her father, whom she adored, had not only sent her away when she wanted to stay with him, but also because he had ticked her off in front of a stranger. And Miss Wadley was nothing more than that—a stranger. They scarcely knew her in spite of the way she had taken to calling Mr McNeil, Mr Waight and her father by their Christian names. Poor thing! She was old, twenty at least, probably much more. She might even be thirty or sixty. Pathetic really, particularly when she caught you watching her when she put on lipstick and powder. A woman that old should give it up, or did Miss Wadley still hope someone would fall passionately in love with her? Some hope!

On her way to meet Ken, Mibs kept pushing away certain other ideas about Miss Wadley that lurked at the back of her mind. Finally they rose to the surface, and Mibs came to a halt, her hands turning clammy as she confronted them. Say, if Miss Wadley really was after her father! Of course, her father couldn't be interested in an old bag like that . . . or could he? What were they saying to each other?

Mibs did not give Ken a second thought as she returned home, skulking through shrubberies to avoid being seen, and, having reconnoitred, taken up her position in the poinsettia hedge to scrutinize them during the meal.

When Saw Hardy crossed the lawn to the summerhouse carrying the coffee-tray, she couldn't help smiling. The summerhouse was a dilapidated place with matting walls conveniently thin. The matting against which she leaned couldn't have been more than a foot or so from the bench where her father was sitting beside Miss Wadley. She could hear the rustle of Miss Wadley's dress, the chink of a coffee-spoon stirring sugar, the wheeze of her father's pipe, and every word said.

Cramp in her stomach started when she heard her father say, out of the blue, "I want you to marry me. Don't say anything now. Think about it for a day or two—then tell me." At first she could not believe she'd heard it, but imagined it. But as she listened, sweating, cramp doubling her up, she realized it was true. She could think of no way to escape because the slightest noise would reveal her presence. So she sat there listening to the hateful woman talking about herself, on and on, and finally heard her say yes, she would marry her father.

When the time had come at last for her to creep away, Mib's dress was saturated with sweat so that the cloth stuck to her

body like an extra skin. Her teeth chattered, and the uncon-
trollable shivering that shook her body frightened her. She wasn't
going to let anyone see her like that, not even her own father,
so she returned home, ordered a cup of hot cocoa and a bath.
While kerosene tins filled with the bath-water were being
heated, Mibs lay in bed, her mind busy with schemes of defeating
Miss Wadley. There were dozens of ways. Which was best? She
decided on one while soaking herself in her tin tub, then in clean
clothes and feeling more like herself set out for the fair-ground.

As she approached the river, trees and bushes stood out in
silhouette against the blaze of light from the far bank. The dazzle
stretched towards the right, following the river. Above it rose
the mass of the hill, its bulk blacking out the sky. Where the
river flowed out of the gorge, silvery light poured across the water from the moon hanging low between the cliffs. Soon the
moon would climb over the Ridge, and like a cut-out in black
velvet the flat roofs and squat chimneys of the Muslim hamlet
would stand silhouetted against the brilliant light.

Dark woods climbed to the summit of Deer Hill where the
pagoda stood, blazing with the only electric lights in Kaikun.
Mibs gazed at them, a fuzz of yellow where garlands of coloured
bulbs had been wound round the pagoda's fringe of bells. Below,
arc lamps lit the gilded stem so that the pagoda looked like a
naked sword flashing on the hilltop. What a waste, she thought.
Only one electric-power plant in all Kaikun, and they have to
use it to charge lights for the pagoda. Ken told her his mother
had donated the plant. Why on earth hadn't she kept it for her
own house, Mibs wondered. Fancy putting up with oil-lamps
in your home and giving a pagoda, where no one even lives, the
benefit of proper lighting! The stairway from the monastery had
been illuminated, not with electric bulbs, but myriads of oil-
cruses, one or two placed on each of the thousand steps. The
flicker of wicks through foliage gave the impression of thousands
of fireflies crawling up the mountain.

Mibs paused for a moment beside the Yunzalin. The night
before, the river had glided by in oily darkness, now it was
covered in threads of orange, scarlet, acid-green, white, colours

reflected from the raft shrines floating by. Even Mibs, so determined to feel superior to her surroundings, found pleasure in the sight of the little shrines, each with votive candles, and each built to resemble a small house with an altar. Some were quite elaborate with gables and balconies, others were constructed as miniature replicas of the Deer Hill Pagoda; all were heaped with flowers. Most of them had been placed on rafts of bamboo and launched from a barge moored amidstream. Nearly all of them sailed steadily, reflecting candle-flames on the dark water. One small shrine zigzagged over the streaks of moonlight spilled from the gorge.

When Mibs reached the bridge she found the crowds denser, smellier and more rowdy than the night before. Buses from Bilin which had brought people to the pwe were parked anyhow and not as they would have been in England, in lines; there were also bullock-carts and pony-traps to add to the clutter. Mibs also noticed an enclosure where a constable was standing guard over several men lying on the ground—drunks. As for the bridge, Mibs nearly turned back in disgust when she was hit in the back by a food-vendor's tray. The stuff on it was that foul-smelling fish paste everyone in Burma gobbled up as if it was chocolate.

"Mibs! Where have you been? You've missed the jugglers and the boxing, but you're in time for Kiss-the-Cobra."

Ken grabbed Mibs's right hand, Jemma the left.

"I'm not going near those snakes!"

But they were too excited to listen. They pulled her, protesting, to a crowded tent where Chockalingam sat on a central mat surrounded by a dozen or so dirty-looking cane baskets. All save one were covered by battered lids. Out of the open basket a hamadryad reared its head, hood spread and about thirty inches of glistening yellow body banded with black. The rest of it—

"Could be fifteen feet," said Ken—flowed in plump, horrifying loops and coils over basket and mat.

"Who'll kiss this sweet old fellow? He's as gentle as a dove, a nice fat dove with a neck as thick as my arm."

About a foot from the snake's head Chockalingam moved his closed fist with a mechanical movement. The cobra's sinister little eyes were fixed on the flashing lights of a ruby sticking above one of Chockalingam's knuckles.

"No one want to kiss my beauty? My king cobra! Fancy, all the trouble I went to, climbing up Mount Popa after him, and no one will kiss him. Then I will. Watch!"

Never for a moment was the ruby still, and as Chockalingam moved his hand, so the cobra, with expanded head and shining body, swayed in time.

Mibs watched with revulsion. She managed a smile, all the same, as she said, "Let's dare Miss Wadley to kiss it!"

"Why poor Waddy? She might get bitten, and I'd hate that," Ken said.

"Would you die if it bit you?" Jemma asked.

"They're all milked beforehand, but you never know. I heard someone was struck once, not here but at the Pegu pwe, but they didn't die."

"Let's go," Mibs said, but Jemma was all for staying. "Everyone is much more warmed up this evening," she said. "They'll all start kissing it, and if they do, I'm sure there'll be an accident. I'd like to see it."

"Don't you want to find out about Balu Pun's raffle? Jemma's taken tickets for your father's grand piano."

"What are you talking about?" Mibs demanded.

This convulsed Ken and Jemma. "Shall we tell her? Might as well. It's only a joke. Balu Pun and the Chinese who helps him, Pauk-paw, have got out books of tickets for important people in Kaikun like my dad and yours. They think the Japs are winning. They do, really! And they think we'll soon start burying our precious things. Whoever wins a ticket can dig up the treasure!"

Mibs gaped at them.

"And you're laughing!"

"Don't *you* think it's funny? I'm going to take a ticket for Mrs Dowall's silver teapot. Balu Pun's saying she's buried it already."

"It's true," Mibs said. The way she spoke startled them and they stood still, staring at her. "The Japs *are* winning and Mrs Dowall *has* buried her silver teapot. Dad won't bury his grand piano because that would ruin it—he'll have to leave it for the Japs."

Ken retorted, "We're not being beaten by a lot of silly Japs."

"Yes we are. I heard my dad tell—tell someone."

"Snooping again?"

Mibs turned savagely on Jemma. "All right, I *was* snooping. And just as well I was—they don't tell us anything until they've decided. I've heard two terrible things. One's about the Japs taking Rangoon and then we'll be evacuated. The other is . . ."

Ken was looking wildly round. "But I've only just *been* evacuated! I refuse to be done again. I won't go. I'll refuse to leave Kaikun."

Mibs took a step nearer to him. "Yes you will, and you'll want to when your father marries Miss Wadley."

"W-what?"

Ken gave her a bemused look. He hadn't understood. Mibs was about to explain fully when she felt a jab in her side. It was Jemma, who had understood and was slashing at her with sharp-pointed elbows.

"Snooping, fibbing, beast!"

Mibs screamed, "Stop her, Ken. If you don't I'll shout out what I heard. I'll tell everyone about your father and Miss Wadley."

Jemma immediately ended her physical attack to mount a verbal one. "Don't listen to her. She's lying. It's tripe. No one can marry your dad if he's already married."

Ken seemed incapable of words. He stood still, staring about him with a vague, slightly daft look.

Mibs shouted at Jemma, "Married people try to marry someone else all the time. They find someone and fix it up. My mother did. His name was Francis. And it was because of him my mother drowned. He made her go to Canada. If he hadn't made her get on that ship . . ." Mibs's eyes filled with tears.

"Boo-hoo! Pretending to cry! You're putting it on."

At last Ken spoke, "Let's find somewhere quiet behind the tent." He looked sternly at Jemma, as if she were to blame. "Mibs doesn't always tell lies, you know."

Jemma followed them, keeping herself sufficiently apart to

show Ken he had hurt her. Why did he hold Mibs's hand when
he never held hers, and why say loudly, "Mibs doesn't always
tell lies," when he knew she did all the time. Why did he side
with Mibs just as he sided with Ko-Ni? People who, like Mibs
and Ko-Ni, were nasty to him, those were the very ones to
whom Ken was nicest. Why? It must be Ken's English blood,
Jemma decided. According to bazaar talk, English people had
a curious characteristic. Even the clowns who came on during
the intervals of plays were known to make up riddles about it.
One clown would ask, "Why is it better to be an Englishman's
enemy than his friend?" The other would answer, "Because if
you're an Englishman's enemy you will be bought, but if you're
his friend you will be sold up."

When Ken and Mibs sat down behind the tent, Jemma too
squatted close by, near enough to hear what was said.

"I just happened to be passing the summerhouse when I
heard them."

"But we haven't got a summerhouse," Ken told her.

"Don't be silly. *Our* summerhouse. This evening. Just before
I came here. My father was there with Miss Wadley."

"Did he want to marry her too?"

Mibs gave a high-pitched laugh. "No, he did not!" she snorted.
"My father loathes her, thank goodness. He asked her to lunch
and was nice to her because he wants to make use of her. We've
got this posh villa in Maymyo near Government House, and my
father wants Miss Wadley to be his Cook General, that's why he
was being polite to her."

"I'm not interested in all that. I want to know what Miss Wadley and my dad said."

"I was in the Club, in the ladies' cloakroom the night before
last, and I heard them on the verandah."

"Night before last?"

"If you don't believe me, if you're going to interrupt . . ."

"I only wanted to be sure. That was the night before Moulmein
was bombed, so Dad *was* here. Okay."

"First they yakked about the war, then your father got on to
Burmese village customs and how they get divorces. He said it

was easy. They just went to the headman and he fixed it because people in Burma weren't properly married."

"Dad said that?" Ken sounded as if he didn't believe her.

"How could I make it up? I don't know anything about your stupid country. After the divorce bit he asked her to marry him. She said she would, and they decided to keep it a secret. They'd have to, wouldn't they? Your mother will be furious."

There was silence. Jemma craned forward to see why Ken made no reply. A slit of light shining through a rent in the tent's canvas revealed Ken's fingers twisting up a lock of hair on the top of his head. Whenever Fatima saw Ken do that, she slapped his hand. The old woman said it was a nervous tic and she must cure him of it, because "it is unwise to let the world see when you are frightened."

If Ken was too frightened to tackle Mibs, Jemma resolved she would do it for him. It was time to debunk the fibber, for Jemma was sure Mibs must be telling lies. From what she knew of the grown-up world, talk of love and marriage was always accompanied by snogging. Not once had Mibs mentioned any. Jemma sidled forward until she sat in front of Mibs, their knees almost touching. She asked Mibs, "Did they kiss?"

Mibs pulled a face and spoke reluctantly, as if embarrassed. "Yes. Mr McNeil kissed Miss Wadley all up her arm."

At that, Ken was finally stung to reply, "Dad wouldn't! He doesn't slop over anyone."

Jemma stretched out her hand to Ken. "Don't worry. It proves Mibs is lying. No one kisses like that. It would be too ticklish."

Mibs regarded them superciliously. "You're babies. It's not worth arguing about. Mr McNeil *did* kiss Miss Wadley and that's that. If you had any sense you'd be asking important questions."

"Like what?"

"Don't you see?"

"No, I don't," Ken answered.

"Well, like how to stop your father marrying her."

"All right—how?"

"I've been hours trying to work it out. I'm in this too, you know. Miss Wadley has picked on your father, Ken, but she could have picked on mine. All she wants is a husband, and as there are so few here, we two will go on being in danger until she can find someone else, or we can find someone for her. But I can't think of anyone but Mr Waight, and he hates her. There's nothing we can do. Except one thing." She paused to gaze at them solemnly. The light from the slit seemed to shine inside her pale-blue irises reminding Jemma of an animal's eyes. Which animal? Was it a ferret or one of those parakeets?

"Kill her."

"Don't be silly!" Jemma said. "You aren't allowed to. Besides, children haven't got the strength."

Ken compressed his lips and regarded Mibs with hostility. "Miss Wadley is my friend. I like her. I'm going home right away to find out if you made this up."

"Sneak!" But Mibs looked frightened.

Ken stood up. "I'm not a sneak, so don't panic."

"But you're going to Miss Wadley!"

"I'm not. Someone else. And I'll tell what's happened without giving you away, or anyone. It won't be difficult, because this person is nice and never asks questions."

Both girls were staring at him.

Jemma said, "He means his mother."

14

Hla Gale sat at her dressing-table, long black hair down her back, so long its ends touched the floor. Ken watched his mother from a stool placed behind her, sometimes leaning sideways to catch her reflection in a panel of her three-leaved mirror.

A shake of the bottle filled with amber-coloured oil, two or three drops spread over the palms of her hands, then rub, rub, rub over the crown of her head, and scratch, scratch, scratch as she massaged it into her scalp. Now and again her long nails tangled with oily strands and there was a sound that set Ken's teeth on edge. After the oiling and massaging his mother combed her hair. Ken's eyes followed the sweep of her arm as she drew the wooden comb from the crown of her head to the ends flapping over the back of her chair. When her comb hit a knot he shuddered, feeling the tug and jab in his own scalp.

While in prep school he had come to acquiesce in a numb sort of way to the idea of life as lived in Downderry and the idea of woman as personified in Mrs Formby-Smith. He came to the conclusion that, as it was painful to dwell on his former happy life, he must try to forget it. He bullied himself so successfully that when he returned to his home he was at times racked by a feeling of unreality. Was he really home? Was he truly sitting on the same old stool waiting for his mother to finish the tricky part of her hair before attracting her attention?

After hearing Mibs's tale, he had run weeping into the house.

His mother could not have seen his tears, as her eyes were fixed on her mirror. One hand held the small black drum in place on the crown of her head, the other wound a long wisp of black hair round and round it. Comforted by her presence, Ken sat down quietly, moving a little to see if . . . ah yes, the tip of her tongue, small, pale pink like a cat's, protruded between her lips.

This detail delighted him. Just like before. Really, nothing had changed. Every piece of furniture stood where he had left it: two big cupboards against the wall; small black table cluttered with bottles of oils and perfumes; his parents' bed, mosquito-net furled, still covered by the yellow cloth made by Daw Daung Gyi on the loom under her house. In the mirror he could see the flickering tips of candles reflected from the shrine behind him, where his mother kept her pet Buddha, the green jade one he'd never liked. If all these objects were the same as ever, why should anything else alter? His father, for instance. His father's love was for keeps, just as his home was. Within reach stood the black lacquer box with a dragon in gold-leaf, where his mother kept her pins, clips, combs and spare supports for her elaborate head-dress. At the other end of the dressing-table there used to be the pair to this box, its interior lined with red velvet. In it his mother kept her jewellery.

"Ahme, where's your jewel box?"

He caught a glimpse of her face in the mirror. Her tongue went in and her lips pressed tight. "It was always on the dressing-table, Ahme. I remember. Why isn't it . . . ?"

She became aware of his eyes on her in the mirror, and her expression altered. "There, wrapped up, on the chest. Something's wrong with the hinge, so I'm sending it to the mender's."

Ken jumped up from the stool, picked up the parcel and shook it. He could tell by its shape, its weight and the muffled clink of jewellery that it was the box he'd missed.

"Don't! Do you want to break my things?"

He put it down and said to her reflection, "But, Ahme . . . all your precious jewels will be stolen if you leave them there. Before it goes to the mender's you must take them out."

His eyes held hers. She didn't smile, at least not for a moment, but when she swung round to face him, she put her arms round him. This was her old self, looking mischievous and refusing to take him seriously. Normally he enjoyed being teased; today, however, he wasn't in the mood.

"Is that why you've come rushing up here, eyes all red, to see if my jewel-box is safe?"

So she had seen his tears, but all she could do was laugh! It needed very little to set him weeping again, so he said rudely, "My eyes aren't red and I didn't come about anything. I just came to see if you were ready so I could take you to the play. But if you don't want me . . ."

For answer, she held out a spray of jasmine and a hairpin. Reluctantly, sulkily, he took the flower. "I don't need that," he said and deliberately dropped the pin, using his little finger to push in the stem until the flowers stood up against the bun. There! Now he felt better, and to show he had forgiven her said, "Your hair is nice, Ahme. I like black hair when it's shiny and on top, not when it hangs down like Jemma's. Sometimes I like fair hair, too. Mibs's hair is fair."

"Have you been fighting again with Jemma? One day she'll grow into a beauty. You'll see, Jemma will be more beautiful than the English girl."

"I don't care if she is. Mibs is the one I like."

"Ah—so!" The way his mother said this nettled him.

"Mibs tells me things."

His mother made no comment and his sense of grievance flared up once more. Why didn't she ask, "What things?" That would give him a chance to start about Dad. But his mother was only interested in herself. Look at her now, standing in front of the mirror arranging her scarf, taking no notice of him. Once more their eyes met, and this time her merriment disarmed him. He grinned shamefacedly and butted his head against her.

"Run along and see if your father's ready."

He lingered, looking at her with admiration, proud that he was to lead her across the fair-ground in such a beautiful tamein —white, with blue and purple sequins embroidered along the hem in a pattern of peacock's tails. The girls would stare, and when they took their places the actors would be sure to pay her compliments. They'd better! Hadn't she paid for it all!

"And you might see if Miss Wadley's ready too."

For once he lied without hesitation. "Miss Wadley isn't coming." Why shouldn't he, just once, have his mother and father to himself?

"Are you sure?"

"She's got a headache. Every night of the pwe she's had a headache. I don't think she wants to be bothered with our plays."

Burmese plays were usually about Burmese kings, of which there were 587,000. Though most of these monarchs were obscure, almost all provided promising material dramatically—murder, elopement and court-intrigue.

His mother shrugged. "English plays about Tudors and Plantagenets don't appeal to me much."

"Do you mean Shakespeare? Oh, Ahme, you mustn't say you don't like Shakespeare. That's wrong."

"Stop lecturing me and find your dad."

Ken had taken her hands and stood looking at her strangely.

"Just tell me something."

"Yes?"

"Do you love Dad?"

"What a funny question!"

"Please don't laugh. Tell me, do you?"

"In Burma husband and wife accept one another as destiny, as Karma, and such questions are not asked—and by children, never!"

"But I want to know."

"Very well. I do, and he me, and because our marriage was made by brow-writing* it was inevitable and will always be happy. Now are you satisfied?"

"Does that mean we three will be together for ever and ever?"

She took his face in her hands. "What is all this about? Is it

* Lines or signs on the brow, Burmese believe, predict marriage to a foreordained person.

the D.C. and the S.P. who have started it with their talk of evacuation? Mibs has been listening and repeating it to you?"

"About the evacuation, yes. But that's nothing. That's the
start. It's . . ." Ken stopped. The words he had ready were, "Dad
and Miss Wadley." But they would not be said. It was as if someone inside him, stronger than himself, placed a hand over his
mouth.

He felt himself grow hot round his neck, then ice-cold down his
back. He started to shiver. Suddenly it became too much for him,
and the tears he had fought back refused to be withheld any
longer. He flung himself into her arms.

"Don't send me away again, Ahme. Dad, you and me. We must
stay together."

"Send you away! How can I? I am part of you. If you go, I go
with you. But if you want to remain by my side, then you shall.
But do you really want this? If you had to live at home forever, you would itch to be gone. And that's right; you are not
a paddy-bird who stands in a puddle all day waiting for a min-
now to swim between his legs. You want to go out to learn from
the best teachers so that you can come back and run my mills
when I'm an old lady."

"You'll never be old. I want to die before you."

"That's not the way to speak. Be moderate. If you show your
affection too openly you know what happens—people will take
advantage of you. Now, smile. Give me a kiss."

He hugged her tightly. "But I want to be a paddy-bird and I
hate good teachers."

She laughed, refusing to take him seriously.

"Why can't we remain together, Ahme?"

"Because we are grass over which big buffaloes are fighting."

"But even if the Japs and everyone are fighting we can remain
together. Let other people run away to India or Maymyo. We
don't have to. I've got a plan how we can all stay together in
Kaikun."

"Running away? Who is?"

"Everyone. Mr Chapman, Mr Waight, the Doctor, the Padre,
everyone. But I know you're not. You aren't digging holes in

the compound like they are. You aren't hiding things like everyone else." He went on to give her details about the lottery devised by Balu Pun. Hla Gale listened, sitting very still on the chair by her dressing-table. Ken added, "As you are sticking it out in Kaikun, I'm going to stay by you and so must Dad."

"You don't know what you're talking about. The Japanese may not harm me, but they'd put you and your father in a prisoner-of-war camp."

"Let's hide in the hills. That's my scheme. You and I can go to a distant village, and if Dad wanted to fight he could join the Plunties. Mr Waight's joined them, so has Wazier Singh and Pannu Ram."

These were police constables who had joined the Volunteer Reserve, the guerrilla unit of which Hugh Chapman had spoken to Miss Wadley. "Plunties" was as near as an Indian or a Burmese could get to the pronunciation of "Volunteers."

As he was talking, Ken saw his mother's expression alter. When the light went out of her eyes and her mouth became firm she lost her prettiness and looked strict, like Matron.

". . . and if you're worrying about Miss Wadley, I've got an idea about Miss Wadley too. Mibs says Mr Chapman's got a posh villa in Maymyo for when the Japs come. Mr Chapman wants Miss Wadley to run it for him and Mibs and Jemma and for me too, if I want to go, but I don't."

His mother's attitude had become wary. "Where did you learn about the Plunties?"

"Mibs."

She took his hand. "A time is coming when one imprudent word might endanger our lives."

"But, Ahme . . ."

"I've taught you to be cautious. Be so. When you hear Mibs talk like this, tell her to be quiet."

"You've got to be practical, Ahme. The Japs are coming, so why pretend? They nearly destroyed our mills at Moulmein when you were there, didn't they? I know it was only a fluke, because of the crash but . . ."

She said sharply, "Where did you learn this?"

"The overseer told me. But it's all right, Ahme. Everyone knows. I even know what kind of planes, Mitsubishu G4M, the ones they used at Pearl Harbour. The pilots in Mingaladon call them "Flying Cigars" and they're medium bombers with . . ."

"What else did you hear about the raids?"

"All the English people who live on the Ridge rushed out to watch in their pyjamas, but you didn't, he said. The Japs bombed the aerodrome and the river quays. There were nineteen bombers and an escort of five fighters the first time, and only two R.A.F. planes took off, but as they hadn't any warning they couldn't get up before the Jap fighters shot them down. The one that crashed near your mills started the fire. Apart from a fluke like that, the overseer said, we've got nothing to worry about because the Japs know which are our mills and won't touch them."

He was standing with his back to the door so did not notice his father enter. "What does that mean?" Tom asked Hla Gale, not Ken. His wife was silent as she walked to the window and remained there with her back to them. Tom went up to Ken. "Well?"

The boy looked uncertainly from one to the other. "Can I tell him, Ahme? I mean—you haven't got secrets from him, have you?"

His father said nothing but stood looking down on him, waiting for him to answer his question.

"It's only the fifth columnists, Dad. *You* know. They signal. They signal where to bomb and where not to bomb, everyone knows that."

There was silence in the room—one of those menacing silences only grown people were able to create.

"Dad, please, I only . . ."

His father walked over to his mother and, to Ken's relief, put his arms round her shoulders. "What about the pwe?" Going out at the door he shook his head at Ken in mock despair.

> *All things that are seen or heard*
> *In science or the sacred word*
> *All things in interstellar space*
> *Are known among the populace.*

So great was Ken's relief, he skipped joyously along the river-path, keeping a few paces ahead of them, sometimes walking backwards so that he could chatter to them and make sure his father was still holding his mother's hand. This was how Ken wished their lives to be lived. When they reached the theatre he rolled himself up in his blanket between their chairs. The play was about the deportation of the last Burmese King to India in 1885. Some of the audience were in tears, but Ken was too exhausted from his own recent emotional storms to care. Soon he was asleep.

The pressure of a hand squeezing his side awoke him. One of his parents, perhaps? Though half-awake, he discerned a mark on the back of a small brown fist, the hawk-griffin, symbol of a Galon! Ken sat upright with a jerk but someone whispered, "Careful! She has sent for you. Come on, I'll take you to her."

It was Ko-Ni, already wriggling away like a snake among the sleeping people. Ken followed him.

Daw Hla Palai, said Ko-Ni, was in hiding in a charcoal-burner's hut. Ken could make nothing of such strange behavior. When his aunt visited Kaikun in the normal way, she stayed with his family in the Forest Bungalow, sleeping in the room that had now become the schoolroom for himself and Miss Wadley. Surely this could not be her reason to go elsewhere. His aunt could have had his dad's dressing-room. And what had Ko-Ni to do with her? Ken would have liked to question the elephant boy but would not risk a snub. Ko-Ni had become too fond of scoring off Ken, particularly when other boys were present. Ken regretted the falling off of their friendship, putting it down to the way Ko-Ni had grown up much faster than himself. Why, since Ken had been in England Ko-Ni had grown hairs on his upper lip! Ken was prepared to defer to him because of this, but Ko-Ni seemed to think Ken felt superior because of his trip to England, and so seized every opportunity to make him feel small.

It took them over half an hour to climb up from the fair-ground to the Ridge, thence round the flank of Deer Hill by goat-paths to the charcoal-burners' pits and shelters. From this ledge in the forest above Wild Bee Cliff, they could see nothing of the Kaikun Plain, only fold upon fold of hills ranging to the borders of Yunnan. In the moonlight the hills looked flattened out, without shadows to indicate the ravines, resembling ripples of water rather than the savage hill country of the Dawnas. It was quiet too. Eerie. Once they had rounded the shoulder they no longer heard the pwe's hubbub; the position of the fair-ground, however, could still be judged by a glow rising fan-shaped and pink in the valley.

Where the hillside was pock-marked by stumps of trees, earth-mounds and pits, the silver light gave it the appearance of a graveyard rather than that of a charcoal-burner's clearing. The huts scattered under tall, ghostly looking trees looked uninhab-ited, and it wasn't until Ko-Ni led him deeper into the forest that Ken saw lights in about six of them. At the door of one Ko-Ni halted, saluted, and stood aside for Ken to pass. Ken was puzzled. What was the saluting about? Within, there was at first too much smoke and too dim a light to make out where his aunt could be. He saw a man crouching over an earth-stove fan-ning smoking twigs with a peaked cap. Beams from a lantern on the floor struck upwards revealing a wattle of skin and two warts on the cheek.

"Aunt?"

"Enter! Enter!"

"But—you're dressed like a man! Like a soldier!"

"Shouldn't I be? Is your male highness the only one permitted to wear trousers and shirts, epaulettes, leather belts and a pistol holster?"

Flaring up already! It was the same old Daw Hla Palai, all right, but with something added, a truculent, swaggering boy-ishness. She was showing off too and Ken was tempted to laugh when she jumped up, preened herself, unclipping her cartridge-belt to dangle temptingly in front of him.

"Is it for me?"

"We'll see."

"What's it all about, Aunt?"

"It is for me to ask *you* questions. Are you still my comrade, my Han Tha? Will you let me train you to be head of Free Burma? If you have changed your allegiance I will tell the Monk U Arthapa to tattoo you with the Galon upside-down . . ." She chuckled. She had taken the pan off the stove and was eating from it, stuffing rice into her mouth with her fingers. "Upside-down! Think of it! The Naga on top of the Galon, the snake killing the sacred bird."

His aunt talked like no one else he knew, a high-flown language he normally enjoyed, but not at that moment when he was impatient to find out what she was up to. But she was going to take her time before telling him anything. She started her old, old story about Saya San and the Galons, about her love of country and how she proposed to save Burma with his help and, that done, make him its king or president. Ken stopped listening. He picked up the peak cap lying on the ground, tried it on, peak in front, then peak behind, hanging down his neck. He wandered across the hut to where he saw a pile of clothing. Turning it over with his foot, he found bundles of different uniforms, naval, air force, army. He was about to investigate more carefully when a blow on his ear sent him reeling.

"Show respect!" His aunt whipped her cap off his head, pushed him down on the ground, glaring at him with such malignance that, for the first time in his life, she scared him. "Am I some old nat-kadaw that you turn your back on me and don't listen to me?"

A nat-kadaw was the equivalent of a witch, the wife of a nat, or spirit, and was about as insulting a term for a woman as could be found.

"I—I'm sorry."

"I've banked on you. Told them about you! My nephew this —my nephew that. You're the kind who'll free us, I said—and listen to you! Acting the Englishman. Being lofty with me!"

"I said I was sorry. I didn't ask to come here. I only came because you . . ."

"Silence!" She was pacing up and down and frightening him by her savage tone and the sudden transformation of her personality. There was nothing of the dotty old woman about her now: she looked more like a fierce, hungry old jackal. Something about her feet made him stare. When last he'd seen her slopping along the verandah of the house in Tiger Alley Lane she'd been wearing shoebags, mark of the granny, of the pensioner. Now she was sporting canvas shoes with a split toe. Ken had studied posters in the Police Lines and recognized the shoe—that of the Japanese soldier. She came to a halt in front of him, the light behind her so he could not see her expression.

"I've risked a lot coming here. And I've come because of you. I've come to take you."

Take him! He was becoming alarmed, wondering if his aunt planned to take him by force, and if other people weren't right about her and she was a bit dotty.

"And I'd love to go with you, Aunt, wherever you're going. But I'm only a boy. I'd have to ask permission first. Why don't you go down to Kaikun and ask my dad?"

This speech made her laugh. "Diplomacy at this age! Perhaps I'm not mistaken in my Han Tha, after all. And what shall I ask that simpleton Tom McNeil? 'May I have your son to teach him how to blow up bridges, sabotage railway lines, snipe at men from trees?' You know what your father would say, 'But my dear old girl, certainly, only the boy has first got to go back to England.' Tom's a diplomat too. Do you want to go back to England?"

"I've got to learn."

"Learn what?"

Now she was laying traps for him.

"Oh, Aunt—I don't know. You just sit at your desk and learn whatever they say."

His woebegone expression touched her and she gave him a hug. "Enough! I am bullying you. You are like a poor little dog who has rolled in filth to get rid of his true scent. Try to remember what you learned down there in the pongyi-kyaung." She pointed towards the door, indicating the monastery school somewhere below. "Being happy, being contented, having just enough—that's the Burmese aim. A small house, plain food, one suit of cotton clothes and a silk one for festivals—that is enough for happiness, Burmese believe, so don't be tricked by the English into believing you need more, like all poor sad Westerners."

She lit a cheroot and stretched out her legs. "Now, boy, press my feet. Am I weary! Do you know how many miles I've walked today and yesterday, every day for the past three weeks? Twenty-five, sometimes thirty!"

"You haven't!"

"By all the nats in Popa! It's nothing. I'm as wiry and strong as the hair of a yak. It is for Sona Paranta.° Why should I complain even though my company was told to sweat it out on foot over the hills to Raheng, and back on foot, while others went by train to Ye? Still I swear my platoon guided our allies to Misty Hollow before these train-travellers got theirs over the Three Pagodas."

Misty Hollow, that is, Kawkareik Pass! That was where Mr Waight said British soldiers had been sent.

". . . and then back over the hills to collect—certain things!" She looked at him in an impudent, knowing way as if to say, "I have important secrets!" Ken saw her glance at the corner of the hut. "Certain things! I know they're British uniforms. What are you doing with them?"

"Ah—ha!"

"You could get into trouble stealing army and navy gear. It's nothing to joke about."

"If I want to joke, joke I shall! People don't joke if they are afraid and weak. But from now on you and I can afford to joke. It is we Burmese who are strong, and foreigners who are weak." She thrust her face close to his. "Soon the Burmese will be free and their rulers will be on the run . . . run!" She made a face and dumped a foot in his lap for massage. "What are you waiting for! Start pressing my toes! One by one. Pull them gently. That's better! Kamamaung to Hlaingbew, up over by Dawlan to Ban Ma Sot, where there's an air-strip, Han Tha, but I had no time to look round. Marching, marching, sometimes through bamboo jungle, sometimes indaing. What keeps me going is will power, and that's another word for courage, Han Tha. Keep ahead of our allies, I told my guerrillas. It is the soldiers of the Burma

° The Golden Land, Burma.

National Army who are setting the country free, and not the Japanese. Therefore, Burmese Nationalists must enter villages first. The people must be in no doubt who are their liberators. If we let our Japanese friends outmarch us, what will our people think? They will tell each other, these Thakins and Galons are no better than the old, cowardly, pacifist Buddhists. But we are the new, fighting Buddhists of Co-Prosperity!"

Ken shouted, "You've been guiding in Japanese! Our enemies!"

His aunt gave him a contemptuous look and did not bother to justify herself.

"Courage is will power, Han Tha, and this is what we Burmese lack. We've degenerated into a nation of cowards because the monks have preached courage doesn't matter, only peace and kindness matter. So we did not fire one shot, and the British marched in and occupied our country and sent away our King and Queen. Then Saya San formed the Galon Army, but there were not enough men like him to fight for Burma. That's why we failed. We need not have failed, Han Tha. We could have defeated the British ten years ago. Now we have the ignominy of seeing the Japanese doing it for us. There are no greater cowards than the British and Chinese and Indians and all the other foreigners who swarm here, battening on our country. They are cowards like ourselves, but . . ."

"The R.A.F. and A.V.G. *aren't* cowards! I saw them in Rangoon. They chased the Japs . . . uurrump, zing . . . they shot them down . . . gummp!"

"Don't interrupt. You know nothing. Listen and you will learn what is really happening. Our allies are about to sweep out the armies of the Raj as a broom removes chaff, and I am helping to hold that broom, and so will you. What can the British do? Nothing. They are demoralized, Han Tha. They have not the men or the equipment or the courage. They have 3000 men by Misty Hollow, and we have 22,000! What can a brigade of frightened Tommies do against two crack divisions of Imperial troops? And wherever the British fight in Burma they will find the Japanese in front and the Burmese behind. Out! Out by the monsoon, that's the schedule." A spot of orange lamplight shone in her excited eyes. "And when the Japanese have helped us chuck out the British, Indians, Chinese, we'll chuck *them* out!" She giggled, nursing one bare foot in her hand.

She didn't know what she was saying. Did she really think she could chuck out an invading army when she chose? Poor Aunt Hla Palai really was dotty. Ken put one foot down and started to massage the other one, her skin was as gritty as an elephant's hide.

He said gently, "Now, Aunt, you're wrong about these Nips. Before they'll let you push them out they'll kill you and me."

She beamed at him. "They are great killers, true, but they won't kill me. I'm an important person now, Han Tha! A guer-rilla leader. I have influence. I can protect you and your mother and whoever else I like. And I'll prove it. Why do you think they've been pounding Moulmein every day but not one brick of our property has been touched? For the moment I act as a guide, but that's only because I know these jungles. When they set up their government, you'll see . . . I'll end up in the English history books."

She preened herself. "Here, eat a little—overcooked but it fills the stomach." She pushed the blackened saucepan against him.

"I'd be sick. It looks like frogs' spawn."

"About to be killed, but the chick is particular about his din-ner!" She chuckled, thrusting her warty cheeks near him in an unexpected gesture of affection. "Don't worry, little chicken, our soldier friends are a hundred miles away and won't arrive in Kaikun just yet." She sat back on her hunkers, claw hands clamped on her knees, a gnome in uniform.

"You know the auntie elephant, the one who protects and nourishes a calf when the cow refuses to—well, I'm that one. And usually, as you know well, the auntie elephant is more devoted than the best mother."

What was all *this* about? Ken watched her warily.

"Why do you think I've suddenly appeared here? To amuse myself at the pwe? To take a dip in the Club swimming-pool?" Ken refused to be baited, but gazed at her, teeth clenched. He knew what was coming and must not show panic.

Small strong fingers snapped round his wrist.

"I've come for you."

"I thought you'd come to collect those uniforms."

"Yes. But also for you. If I don't look after you no one else will. Your mother cares only for her mills." Then the old woman quoted well-known Burmese sayings: "'With the world afire a mother will lay her son down and stand on his body . . .' 'When in agony a mother will even deny being related to her son . . .' 'A heifer is not attracted to its calf.'" Ken had no words to answer her but hated her for trying to make mischief between him and his mother. "As for your father, he is off on Friday."

"Friday?"

"Didn't you know?" Kaikun is to be evacuated. Indians, Anglo-Indians, Europeans, all the rubbish."

"To Maymyo?"

"Who cares where: Maymyo, Mandalay, Myitkyina, India! Wherever they run, you can be sure the Japanese will follow and cut them down. But you, Han Tha, you shall remain with me."

"I'd like to, Aunt." This he said to soothe her. "But I've got to be loyal. If I wasn't loyal I'd be no good to you either. So I must look after my parents. I'll take them to Maymyo. When they're safe, I'll come to you."

"And if you go to Maymyo, foolish chick, don't you know what will happen? They'll post you to India and from India to England. Put you on a plane and post you off, as they've done before. You are nothing to Hla Gale and Tom but a parcel to be posted here and there as it suits them."

It wasn't true! It wasn't true! He struggled against tears, knowing that to weep in the presence of this old hyena was to arouse her contempt and invite more bullying.

"If that happens I'll run away to you."

"Ha! When it's convenient you'll come to me! I don't make bargains with little boys. You'll come on my terms."

"Oh, Aunt, don't be an old goat. You're not Napoleon and Churchill and Tojo rolled into one."

"That's how I like to hear you! Stand up to me! Answer back. I was beginning to wonder if you'd any spunk."

"Let's have a secret signal so you'll know when I want to come to you."

"It's the British who need secret signals these days, not us. Go into any bazaar, hold up your fist with our symbol of invulnerability [she meant the Galon] inked on your skin, and dozens of Nationalists will gather round . . ." She was staring at him, or rather, a little behind him, her mouth open with the butt of her cheroot sticking to her lower lip. "Fool that I am! That's the best prize! That's the goal! What does it matter who blows the bridge and puts booms across the river! Any village boy can become a saboteur. But my Han Tha must play for bigger stakes. Ah, son! Pin Wa, beloved! To think I nearly missed the chance, and it is you who put it in my head. Sit closer!" She caught him round the neck and pulled his head against hers. "You are right. It is to Maymyo that you must go, because it is in Maymyo that you will serve me best. Have you eyes and ears?"

"Eyes and ears?"

"Ah, you think you have. But I watch you. You are in a dream. You observe nothing, you hear nothing. From today, Han Tha, you will look at the person who speaks so that, should I need to ask you, you will be able to tell me what he said, who he is, and anything else I want to know about him."

"Whatever for?"

"That's *my* business. When I turn up in Maymyo—as I shall, sitting on a bench overlooking the lake between four and five in the evening—you, my Pin Wa, must be able to answer all my questions. And if you do, then I well rescue you, or do whatever you require of me."

15

Jemma sat with legs astride a railing post on the Kaikun bridge, cotton dress tucked into bloomers, legs bare and wet. She was watching the Posein launch pass downriver—for the second time in ten days. The bridge was built over six old barges, poled aside at intervals by Maung Maung and his son to allow river-craft to pass. From a barge slewed by the far bank Ken and Mibs also watched. Those two were now always together. Didn't matter. Jemma too had someone. And Mibs could try as hard as she liked, but he was one person who had no use for her. He was, would always be, Jemma's property.

The Posein launch was preparing to weigh anchor, and while crew and captain screeched and ran about, Posein's relatives exchanged gossip with locals on the bank.

"Heh! Dacoity at Ingwe. Po Se's head slit and all his opium stolen."

". . . and at Kutlong, arson, fights and five arrests."

Mibs hoped the others were listening hard, as she was, despite blasts from the captain's whistle. So far not a word had been said worth hearing. Jemma cupped her hands over her mouth, directing her voice at fat May Mayoo, stage manager and the troupe's gossip. "Big mouth, heh you! What's the news?"

"At Wingla, U Ba Nyunt eloped with the watchman's daughter."

"Owl! Tittle tattle! Give news. Big news. The war." Mibs gave

Ken's imitation of a dive-bomber "Gr-r-r-ump! Banzai! Japs! Bombs. What about them?"

May Mayoo rolled his eyes. "Heh! Heh! The war! Oh mother! No! We don't go near it. We went no farther than Kamamaung."

"Didn't you go to Moulmein? You said you would!"

As they suspected! It was Ken's mad aunt who'd spread the rumour of fighting in the hills, and the moment the Poseins got wind of it they struck tents, packed, upped anchor and scuttled off, saying they were due at the Moulmein pwe. Their panic affected others, and within hours stalls, sideshows and other showmen, including their favourites Balu Pun and Chockalin-gam also took to their heels. Scary-cat Poseins, the children agreed, had deprived them of two days of pwe, all to no purpose. If there'd been fighting it had been too far away to matter—even to the Poseins themselves, for they were soon scuttling back to Kaikun to collect money owed them.

Another member of the troupe joined May Mayoo at the ship's rails. "Thakin-ma, come with us! Flee! It's not safe here. We will give you passage to the Great Rapid."

That meant they were scuttling down to Kamamaung again, the river-port on the confluence of Yunzalin and Salween, and would be sailing north to Dagwin.

"Don't believe you!" Jemma shouted. "You run before every silly rumour, and that's bad because you make others run too! Look what you did to our pwe! Ended it! Spreading alarm is punishable in wartime. I've a mind to get you all locked up."

This delighted them so that they hit their sides with merri-ment. "Thakin-ma, we speak the truth! It is you who will get locked up—in a prisoner-of-war camp."

"Tell me the truth, then. If you can't, God's teeth, I'll scupper your old tub with a left and right from my grandad's duck gun!"

"Ghosts, Thakin-ma. Moulmein is besieged by a host of ghosts. That's what we heard. Here, there, everywhere. When English soldiers go out to fight them, they cannot find them. But all the while they are closing in on Moulmein from all directions. Moulmein is doomed. The City of the Beautiful Pagoda will be captured today or tomorrow."

"So you say! But you'd believe anything."

"Already the General Lord and Commissioner Lord have pulled out of Maymyo and gone to Kyaikto, where they sit in the gaol directing the battle."

"Battle?"

"Have you not heard? A big battle goes on in Moulmein. An English Lord from Mergui told us—we brought him from Kamamaung—he'd run away from Mergui, and he was running away from Moulmein. And so must you, Thakin-ma, if you don't want the Nipponese to grab you."

When the launch sailed away and Maung Maung and his son had clumped the bridge section back across the barge, the children sauntered off together walking aimlessly along the riverbank as they compared notes. Ken heard one of the players quote a saying that when Moulmein falls Rangoon falls, "And he said this signifies Rangoon will fall in ten days' time."

"How did he make that out?" Jemma asked. Ken didn't know. "But I've got a feeling in my stomach that it's true."

"And so have I," Jemma said. "But I'm not going to moan like you two. Look at you! If you could only see your faces. Cheer up!"

"We're going to be conquered, and you say 'Cheer up'!"

"*I'm* cheerful." Jemma turned handstands on a ledge. "It's an advantage being an orphan."

"Don't gloat."

"Why shouldn't I? For once it's better to have no parents telling lies. For once it's better not to have a proper home you want to stay in."

Ken could not bear to have his parents criticized, even by inference. "My parents haven't told me lies."

Jemma had given up hope of winning Ken's allegiance from Mibs, and no longer bothered to be tactful. "Your father told us to clear off that time we were listening to them discussing things on the verandah. He said, 'There's nothing to worry about.' There is. We know there is. Why don't they tell us, then?"

Surprisingly, Mibs sided with her against Ken. "And that ramble—remember! Your father must think we're nits. I know what that ramble was for." After barking at them Tom had offered to take them on a jungle ramble, and Ken had assured them it would be fun. Later, however, Ken agreed this one hadn't been fun at all, nothing but a botany lesson. His father had taken them into the forest, picked berries, leaves, dug up roots and lectured them. A certain root, boiled sufficiently, tasted like potatoes, he said; the tops of ferns made good salad, certain leaves were excellent for headaches, others for stomach trouble. He had also drummed at them, "Human beings were originally plant-eaters, so if you know what to eat in the jungle you'll never starve."

Mibs added, "They all know what's going to happen but they can't make up their minds."

"You and Ken can't either," Jemma retorted. "But *I* can. I don't mind if they send me to Maymyo or India or Timbuktoo."

Ken was thoughtful. "Even if Mibs and I did know which plan was best, it wouldn't make any difference. They wouldn't let us choose."

"Sometimes they do," Jemma said. She was thoughtful too. "Sometimes they're in a certain kind of mood, and if you can find the proper way to put it, you can make them do exactly as you want. *I* can. With a Certain Person I nearly always get my way."

"Certain Person! My, we *are* mysterious! As if we didn't know. Your Certain Person's not so hot. He couldn't stand up to my father. That day my father got back from Bilin he fairly tore strips off your marvellous Certain Person!"

"Tore strips off Hamish! Can't imagine that!" Ken retorted and Jemma gloated. It was reassuring to find Ken turn against Mibs. "Even Ken, who's always on your side, thinks you're lying—as usual."

"I didn't mean . . ." Ken tried to part the girls, who were hissing and spitting across him like jealous geese.

Jemma pointed a grubby forefinger with black-rimmed nail at Mibs. "It's *your* father who's a wet. The Almighty D.C. is a ditherer, everyone says so! It's because he can't make up his stupid mind that my—my Hamish had to make it up for him. You know why? Your father's scared."

"Scared!"

"Of everything and everyone—of the Chief Secretary, of the Japs, of losing his pension, of Miss Wadley—I could go on forever!"

Ken pushed them apart, shoving Jemma harder than he did Mibs. "Stop it! Everyone's exploding. Even grown-ups! What's the use. Let's not. Let's think. Let's make a plan. If we don't, what'll happen to us?"

Since bad news started circulating in Kaikun, it was noticeable that everyone, even good-tempered old souls like Fatima, snapped, worked themselves up, taking it out on the children and anyone else handy. That adults were snarling at each other openly disturbed the children above all. Yesterday at a Club committee meeting the Hodges, the missionary couple, had brought up the question of poor Mrs Dowall's ground under the mimosa, and members had been asked to veto any claim the Civil Surgeon's wife imagined she possessed. In retaliation, Mrs Dowall had backed out of the bridge four. The children, while sympathizing with poor Mrs Dowall—deprived of her grave and her bridge—were startled by invective expressed in their hearing by people who in normal times embodied the virtues they were expected to admire: self-control, charity and good manners.

The bad news, of course, had started on the night Daw Hla Palai and her gang of fifth columnists (partisans, terrorists, Galons, according to the individual's view) had been surprised by Mr Waight and his constables lurking in charcoal-burners' huts along Wild Bee Cliff. Daw Hla Palai had vanished, but five of her confederates—among them Ko-Ni—had been caught, handcuffed and marched to the cells in the Police Lines, together with a sackful of bogus British military uniforms. Followed rumours of a battle in which a brigade of ill-trained, ill-equipped British troops had been annihilated on Kawkareik Pass by two divisions of seasoned Japanese troops. Eight hundred men against twenty thousand! No wonder the British were routed. Thousands upon thousands of Japanese, according to bazaar talk, were now surrounding Moulmein. Allah Karim! It was but a matter of days before launches full of Japanese soldiers would come steaming up the Yunzalin! Ram! Ram! Not a moment to lose. Harness the bullocks, tie up bundles, collect children, goats. Is it true the S.P. Lord and the D.C. Lord are issuing rations of rice? Ar-re! Run! Run! To Rangoon. To Hind! There is no time to collect rice. No time! No time!

"Even if the rumours aren't true, it would stop panic if we put up notices announcing a firm date for evacuation." This was Hamish.

"Get them out to India," Mrs Dowall boomed. "Poor frightened crows! Give them a police escort so these devils (she meant Burmese) can't start settling old scores."

But Hugh Chapman hesitated. He could not act without orders. He must wait for orders. This was only rumour. If the telegraph lines were down between Kaikun and Pegu, urgent messages could get through by runners, so . . . let's do nothing for a bit. Hamish started shouting, summoned the My-ok, the township officer, for his views. Useless to set up road-blocks: even if the police could be spared they would not stop the flight of this terrified multitude, the My-ok said. Hamish asked, Hadn't Hugh learned anything from the lesson of the Rangoon exodus? Let them go, Hamish persisted. Let them go—and make arrangements to evacuate them to India. Hamish spoke of empty troop-ships returning to Madras. He volunteered to accompany the Kaikun refugees to Rangoon and there see to it that they were given passages on the troop-ships. Hugh wavered. On the face of it, it did seem the most humane thing to do, but . . . but he had still to keep Kaikun ticking over, hadn't he? Eventually he agreed to appeal to the skinny Ooriyas, known to Burmese as mye-du-kala, earth-digging Indians, the oily bazaar-traders and the fat Babus, to wait until preparations for a properly organized exodus could be made—points to be set up along the route to Rangoon for rice dumps, and clerks to dole out rations (which must be paid for). As a veteran of the blitz and one most recently arrived from Belat, Miss Wadley volunteered to speak (through Ken as an interpreter) of British steadiness under worse threat and to press all to remain in Burma. She spoke well and with passion about the bastions of Singapore and Rangoon: before Burma fell both these great fortress towns, she said, must fall to the Japanese, and that was impossible.

To some degree this propaganda worked. Subordinates of many of the essential services—Public Works, Forest and Post Office—unpacked their tin boxes and pulled protesting womenfolk from the Bilin bus, pony-traps and bullock-carts. The next day one of them, old Hanuman Lall, the Postmaster, was found drowned, his body bobbing among the reeds below Kaikun whirlpool, not two hundred yards from the house of the Superintendent of Police. He had been murdered. The work of dacoits (armed robbers), fifth columnists or Burmese with grudges against Indians? From the Bilin Road came reports of other murders, these unquestionably the work of vindictive Burmese villagers. In some cases violence was linked with robbery, cattle had been unyoked and led away, cash and jewellery had been stripped off corpses, but in more instances gain was not the motive but the settling of old scores. And this decided the Indians. Without the firm control of the Raj, they did not stand a chance in Burma, and their terror of the Burmese kept lamps alight all night in back alleys of Kaikun as Indians loaded on carts their pots and pans, bedding and old people and started off, ignorant and uncaring about the most elementary facts of their journey. They set off in a mass with the steadfastness of those strange processions of ants so often seen moving across the baked earth of the tropics.

"Everyone's exploding," Ken had said. In prosaic times the explosion between Hugh Chapman and Hamish Waight over the evacuation would, at least, have occurred in private. It was part of the disagreeableness of these days of crisis that the differences between the two senior district officials should have become common knowledge.

With the murder of Hanuman Lall and the second exodus, the only way Hugh Chapman could stall was by leaving for Rangoon to obtain official sanction. Hamish, left in charge, made no bones about his determination to push through his own plans once the District Commissioner's back was turned. Up went the

notices on the walls of gaol, post office and law courts, summoning all Indians to register names, number in family, etc., if they
wanted to secure passages to India. A special marquee was
erected on the old pwe-ground, where Hamish himself ha-
rangued frightened people. "If you do as I say you've got a
chance of getting to your homes. I'll see there's a police escort to
each bullock-cart convoy. I'll see there's rice and water and a
vaccinating Babu at certain stopping places. But if you run like
goats before a charging tiger, what hope is there for you?"

It was a pity Hamish was not to have the opportunity to be
proved right—or wrong. Hugh Chapman's trip to Rangoon ended
at Bilin, where he discovered Kaikun was not the only place in
chaos. The military had taken over the railways: troop trains
stood in sidings or shunted in and out of the station, some
bound south, others, with coaches converted into dressing-
stations, screamed by without stopping. Several refugee trains,
coaches crammed inside and out, also chugged through. After
forty-eight hours in a waiting-room filled with clamouring Indians, Hugh returned to Kaikun. It was then, according to Mibs,
"strips were torn off" Hamish. The marquee came down and
fresh notices went up, these announcing (over the D.C.'s signa-
ture) that no official evacuation was scheduled since there was
no emergency, but should need arise, all necessary steps would
be taken. In the meantime essential personnel were expected to
remain at their posts, etc.

Those who bothered to stop and read these pieces of paper—
and these were now only the Burmese—looked amused. "While
being troubled by snakes, he is harassed by centipedes," one of
them quoted, but whether out of sympathy for the D.C. or S.P.
he did not say.

". . . what'll happen to us? At least nothing'll happen to you."
Ken bent down to rub behind Butch's ears. "You'll be with your
master, and your master will take care of you. It's only when you
go to England that they part dogs from their masters."

"Because of rabies," Mibs said. "You don't have to run England down, even to a dog. Do they let dogs into India?"

"There's loads of rabies in India, so they're bound to."

Jemma looked thoughtfully at them. "Hands up who hopes they'll send us to India." Only Mibs held up hers.

"Why not, Ken?"

"Because Burma's my country."

"Even if the Japs take it?"

"Ahme isn't going."

"Your father'll have to."

"I know. That makes it so miserable. I don't know what I want. If you both go, they'll send me too. I wouldn't mind but . . ."

"It's because of Miss Wadley," Mibs said.

"I didn't say anything about Miss Wadley." Ken had stiffened. "Please, Mibs, don't start about Miss Wadley again."

"She's got Miss Wadley on the brain," Jemma said.

"Ken has—not me. And he jolly well should."

"I only said I wanted to be with my dad . . ." Ken hesitated so Mibs finished his sentence for him, "But if you are, that's if you don't go to India, and have to go to our house in Maymyo, you'll have to put up with Miss Wadley as well. She'll be there—bossing everyone about. What do you think I feel, having her there, being told what to do in my own house? Jemma won't like it either. But it'll be worse for you, poor old Ken. You'll have to sit there and watch Miss Wadley and your dad . . ."

"Shut up!"

"I won't! I've warned you and warned you! Who's caused all the trouble? Miss Wadley! Who's pinching your dad from your mother? Miss Wadley! And you've done nothing! You haven't even told your mother!"

"I couldn't!"

"Because you're a coward. If you'd told your mother she'd have fired Miss Wadley. But you're scared of Miss Wadley, so you're doing nothing, letting everything happen as she wants. She's got round my father too, because he won't stand up to her either. She's told him to send us to Maymyo with her in charge, and that's what's going to happen—thanks to you. Miss

Wadley's going to run my house and me, and you and Jemma and my father and your father."

"You're a beast and a liar!" Ken stuffed his fingers in his ears and ran back towards the bridge, trying in distracted, shambling manoeuvres to avoid falling over Butch.

Mibs cupped her hands to screech after him. "Run, rabbit, run!" To Jemma she said angrily, "Don't smirk. They're all the same. Weak. Now we're alone, you'll find we'll fix up something and get on better too."

"Are you trying to make up to me?"

"Yes, I am. I'm fed up with boys."

"So am I. Okay, friends. But you shouldn't hurt people. Ken's not bad, but he's not like us English. Ever felt his fingers? No bones. That's Ken. That's Burmese. They're soft, but soft in a nice way. Gentle. And the things you said just now will worry him. If he goes up to the Abbot it means he is very worried."

Jemma halted to watch two small running shapes cross the bridge—one greyish-white, small as a grub, the other in school-grey shirt and bazaar-green longyi. On the far side they started up Thieves Path, the short cut to the monastery school.

"You *did* upset him. He's off to the old man."

"What am I supposed to do—weep? Let's forget him and be friends."

The girls fell into step, walking along the riverside towards the officials' houses, Mibs self-absorbed, Jemma darting sly glances at her. Friends with Mibs! A trick? Was it possible that she actually meant it? Having quarrelled for so long and venomously, the prospect of friendship was disconcerting. On the whole, Jemma would have felt more at ease with the old-established enmity.

"Let's go and see your Mr Waight."

"He's not 'my' Mr Waight."

"He is. Girls can tell. But he won't be for long if you don't clean your nails and your ears. And another thing, when you do handstands you should tuck your dress into your bloomers."

"You *are* rude."

"That shows you're stupid. It's me who's stupid to tell you. If I let you go on putting Mr Waight off, he'd soon be saying, 'Fancy! Showing her navel button *and* dirty nails.' Then he'd see my nails are clean and I didn't stand on my head, and go for me."

"I'm not like you, always thinking of men."

"You've got to if you want to get married."

"I don't want to get married."

"I don't *want* to; got to, that's all. And I wouldn't marry Mr Waight, so don't worry!" She was silent for a minute, but added thoughtfully, "Might do, though, for a start. Doesn't matter who you marry for a start, provided you keep on the lookout for something better and end up with a duke."

"If that's how you feel, why do you want to see Mr Waight?"

"Gosh! Don't you know? The evacuation. We've got to find a way ourselves. It's no good hoping *they'll* help."

By "they" Mibs presumably meant her father and Ken's parents.

"My plan is to tell Mr Waight about Miss Wadley and throw ourselves on his mercy. We'll say—no, *you* say, please, please, Mr Waight, get her sent to India, or us to India, we don't mind which, so long as our parents and us go to one place and Miss Wadley goes somewhere else."

"I thought you didn't like Ken anymore. Why are you going to all this trouble for him?"

Mibs kept her head turned away, picked up a stone and aimed it at the vortex of the great whirlpool boiling in the stretch of river opposite the S.P.'s house.

"Ken's all right. It's not him, it's her. You wouldn't understand."

"Why not?"

"Because you're an orphan. No one suddenly butted into your family and took your mother away and then let her get drowned. I'm not going to let a second person butt into my life and this time take my father. That's why. My father's all I've got, so Miss Wadley can't just . . ." She shut up.

They had arrived at the garden gate of the S.P.'s compound. Footsteps had beaten a path that zigzagged across the lawn to the verandah.

"This place isn't a patch on ours." Mibs firmly changed the topic. "Garden's half the size of ours, so's the verandah. But that's only fair. My father's Number One in Kaikun, Mr Waight's Number Two. Naturally this is the nastier house."

"Mibs, you're a fool. Honestly. You don't know what you're talking about. Mr Waight's house is the best in Kaikun. Ken thinks so, so do I, so does Ko-Ni, Hanif and Ja-Bo. All the gang think so. Because of the whirlpool. You can see it from his verandah, and from his lawn you can chuck things into the vortex. What's any other house in Kaikun got compared to the whirlpool? In the rains its noise is so loud you can't hear anyone on the verandah—you've got to go inside to talk. Mind, it's not a patch on the Teng whirlpool on the Salween. That's a hundred feet across and Mr Waight's is only twenty. If a country-boat got sucked into the Teng vortex it would . . ."

"I know. What do we say to Mr Waight? We've got to work out everything beforehand. If you've got your plan pat it's easier to make them give in."

Give in to taking her away from Kaikun. She was beginning to think she didn't want that, after all. It was all very well for Mibs, with her London and posh ideas, but some people really really liked Kaikun.

Mr Waight's police orderly, Dil Tharpa, was watching them cross the lawn. Jemma waved to him. "Is the Master in?"

Dil Tharpa put his finger to his lips. "Gaung-gaik!" Jemma translated for Mibs, "We've got to be quiet. Hamish has a headache."

"I'm going in, all the same."

"No, Thakina! No go in. Eik-thi!" (Sleeping!)

Spread-eagled on a bed in an attitude of exhaustion lay a stranger—a bony, dirty man, his mouth open, grimy arms and legs covered with a tattered bush-shirt and khaki slacks. His feet were bare and streaked with dried clay, the bright orangey-red clay of river-banks below Kamamaung. Kamamaung? That was it! The man the Poseins had brought up on the launch.

"He's from Mergui, Dil Tharpa?"

"Yes, yes, Thakina, and the Police Superintendent has

ordered me to see that Etheridge Thakin is left undisturbed to sleep. He has not slept for four days. He has not eaten for three, and, you can see, he has not had a bath for a long time. Come away, please. I will bring you two young ladies lemon squash and biscuits as long as you leave here and sit quietly on the verandah."

"We've got to go." Jemma pulled Mibs out of the room.

"Tell him we'll be good, provided he tells us everything—who this is, when he came and what he said to Mr Waight. And don't look like that, Jemma. He's only a servant. He's got to do as we say."

"I'll ask him, but nicely. And, if you'll excuse me, Mibs, I'd rather not have a pax. I don't want to be friends with you."

"Do what you like, but get on and ask him."

Dil Tharpa wasn't saying much. Yes, the Thakin was from Mergui and had arrived about forty minutes ago. He had suffered many tribulations, having escaped from the Japanese. His news had greatly disturbed the Superintendent of Police, who had gone to the District Commissioner's main offices to report it. Wouldn't it be best if the young Thakinas themselves went to the D.C.'s bungalow?

"Ask him about the Japs." But clearly, Dil Tharpa felt, he had said too much.

"It's all your fault, Mibs. If you hadn't taken that tone he'd have told me everything."

"If he won't help tell him I'll wake up that old tramp on the bed. I'm not budging until Mr Waight comes."

Footsteps clicked over tiled flooring. Jemma, who recognized them, gave a yelp, rushed into the living-room and came out with Hamish, one hand hooked into his leather belt.

"All right, Dil Tharpa—I'll cope. Bring out drinks, please, and tell the water-man to heat up Etheridge Thakin's bath-water. So, young woman, you refuse to budge from my house!"

"I didn't mean to be rude . . ."

"No? All right, child." Hamish threw himself on a long cane chair where Jemma perched on the arm. "But I can't help you if you've come to pump me about the evacuation."

"How did you know?"

"Because two thousand people have already tried it this morning. All I can say is—*you* tell *me*."

Jemma said, "Fibs, Hamish. We know about everything. Moulmein might be taken."

"Might be? Is. And how did you find out about Moulmein? You didn't waken . . ."

"The Poseins' launch brought Mr Etheridge here—and the bo'sun told us."

"I didn't want to frighten you but we're getting out within forty-eight hours. Run home, both of you, and see how you can help."

"Not me." Mibs said, coming over to Hamish. "Not while Miss Wadley's in my house. That's where she is, Mr Waight. She's always there, pretending she's come to help my father. But that's not the reason. She's afraid of Mrs McNeil. She's afraid Mrs McNeil might find out about her and Mr McNeil. You see, she's trying to get Mr McNeil for herself. Didn't you know? Please be on our side and send her away. If we go to Maymyo, send her to India, please, Mr Waight, or if we go to India, buzz her off to Maymyo, but keep her away from our fathers."

Hamish straightened up, glowering at Mibs in the way he normally reserved for lying dacoits.

"Where did you get these ridiculous ideas?"

"They're not ridiculous. Aren't you going to help?"

"You mustn't repeat this nonsense to anyone."

Because Mibs had left her perch on the rail, she had failed to observe the arrival of one more person. Miss Wadley's head and shoulders suddenly appeared above the verandah plinth.

"What nonsense must Mibs not repeat to anyone?" Her voice was meant to sound gay.

Hamish did not answer but asked her what she'd like to drink. Tea? Beer?

"I'm looking for Ken. Do either of you girls know where he is?"

"No," Jemma said.

"He was with you."

"We said we don't know." Mibs's look and tone were openly rude.

Miss Wadley replied pleasantly.

"Very well. If you see him, tell him to go straight home. No need to ask if you've heard the news, Mr Waight?"

"Evacuation within forty-eight hours with or without orders from Rangoon."

"I hear Maymyo's a delightful hill-station."

"Evacuation's not to Maymyo but India. Disappointing for you, but in the long run—safest."

"I think you've made a mistake."

"I've just returned from Hugh's office. It's all settled. Best news is we've fixed passages for Indians on a returning troop-ship."

Mibs's attitude was rigid and her eyes were fixed on Hamish. "Please, Mr Waight . . . what I've been telling you is true."

Miss Wadley asked brightly, "And what did Mibs tell you that was true, Mr Waight?"

"I'm sorry to break this up, but I've got to talk to a man here who's been through a lot. Run along as Miss Wadley told you to." He looked at Jemma, who at once slipped off the arm of his chair. As she did so he said, "Good girl," and caught her hand affectionately. This time Miss Wadley's voice was louder. "Mr Waight, I asked you what Mibs had been saying?"

Hamish shrugged. "I really wasn't listening. I was thinking of the story this planter—Etheridge—told me this morning. Appalling business. Tavoy fell on the nineteenth, Mergui on the twentieth. Nearly everyone in Tavoy was captured. The D.C. was hanging on for orders, as Hugh has been, but his orders never came, as Hugh's won't either. When Rangoon heard about Tavoy, they had to act—Mergui was cut off completely. So they sent a boat to rescue the Europeans. An ill wind, I suppose, where Mergui was concerned. Etheridge got his wife and kids on board but stayed behind to help with the demolitions. The D.C. had his steam-launch standing by to take him off. Etheridge told me he thoroughly enjoyed blowing up everything, including crores of his own rubber and latex, and setting on fire lines and lines of his own rubber trees. But the trees wouldn't burn, so he made them useless for tapping by slashing them with a dah. They'd finished and the D.C. was just about to shove off when he remembered his dog. The D.C. refused to wait and said Etheridge would have to get out on the A.S.P.'s [Assistant Superintendent of Police's] motorboat."

"Did he find his dog?" Jemma asked.

"I'm afraid not."

"He should have shot it. It's the humane thing to do," Miss Wadley said. "Have you been trying to lead me off the point with Mr Etheridge's adventures, Mr Waight? If so, you don't know me. May I ask—again—what was Mibs saying as I came in?"

"The kids want to go to India, that's all. In a way, they'd be much better off. There's a big co-ed school opening in Naini on English lines for U.K. evacuees. They could all go there together."

"And you and Mr McNeil and Mr Chapman would take them there?"

Again a non-committal look from Hamish.

Miss Wadley went on evenly: "If this is true—and I refuse to believe it until I hear it from the D.C. himself—I think your reason for encouraging these girls to go to India is very questionable, Mr Waight. It is certainly not for academic reasons you are talking Jemma into it!" Miss Wadley said no more but stared at Hamish's fingers loosely linked with Jemma's grubby ones. At first none of the three understood what she meant, but the fixity of her gaze soon made it plain. Jemma started, pulled her hand away, a frightened look in her eyes. Hamish's reactions were slower. It was only when he saw Miss Wadley smiling in an unpleasant way, the corners of her mouth pulled down, that he jumped to his feet and joined Jemma, this time putting his arm round her shoulders and drawing her close to his side. To Miss Wadley he said, "That's enough. Now I'm inclined to agree with the kids. They should go to India—with Tom and Hugh and me."

16

The Buddha required his monks to live at the foot of a tree, preferably in the heart of forests because Arannasanni, the "forest sense of things," calms the mind and helps to produce that sense of detachment in which the Buddhist may achieve liberation by seeing things as they really and truly are.

Ken rushed across the water meadows—where the fairground's tents had stood—and up Deer Hill, taking the "Thieves Path," a rocky short cut he used when he attended the monastery school.

The gloom of dense forest might help bhikkhus towards Enlightenment, but Ken, diving into green silence, sought the forest like an animal desperate for cover.

Everyone had turned against him. "Run, rabbit, run!" Mibs was right, and so was Ko-Ni—he was nothing but a coward. "They'd post you off . . . you are nothing but a parcel to them!" Even the old hyena insulted him—worse, she was probably right too. Dad and Ahme didn't care for him anymore. The burden hardest to bear was his conviction that his father preferred someone else to his mother.

Butch scrambled ahead, ungainly as a toad climbing out of a pond, as she flattened her pink belly against rocks while her hind legs fumbled for footholds. Now and again she rested on a ledge, tongue lolling out, waiting for him to catch up. Her baleful glance seemed to ask, "Better now?" Ken's sobs while crossing the bridge had bothered her. Arannasanni was restoring him, but he still felt drained and pervaded by a feeling of hopelessness. He was thinking: I really was better off in Deer Hill Monastery. I wish I was back there. At the time he had found it boring, nothing but ceremonies, lessons, homework and only one meal a day. Also rising before dawn and setting off on the collecting round on bare feet and cotton tchingen before the mist was off the river, was a misery. He used to marvel at the self-discipline of men like the Abbot and senior monks who could voluntarily give up all fun in life. It wasn't so bad for boys like himself, who were only low-grade temporary monks. He had only to bow three times before the Abbot and ask permission to leave the monastery, to be free once more. His period of initiation had lasted three months, though his mother would have liked it longer. She had given in so that he could spend one month at home before leaving for England. Now Ken wished he had never left the pongyi-kyang, remained a ko-yin for months and months. Like his uncle U Thet Nyein, who had returned five times to his monastery in the woods below the Shwe Dagon, he too could have made the pongyi-kyang his headquarters, so to speak, issuing from it only for a spell of school, marriage, having kids and possibly starting a business. When things became too awful, as they were now, he could have presented himself before dear old U Naind Da and asked for permission to put on his yellow robes once more.

Mulling this over, Ken convinced himself the life of a monk had much to recommend it. He started to chant verses of a sutta of great antiquity which extolled the monk's life as manifested in the lonely wanderings of the rhinoceros:

> Play, pleasures, mirth and worldly joys,
> Be done with these and heed them not,
> Aloof from pomp and speaking truth,
> Fare lonely as rhinoceros.

> Son, wife and father, mother, wealth,
> The things wealth brings, the ties of kin:
> Leaving these pleasure one and all,
> Fare lonely as rhinoceros.

He was not so sure about the mother bit. He loved his mother, and had never approved of the prohibitions laid down for all monks, even for the low-grade ko-yin he had been. Not to touch a woman's hand, not to look at her, not to sit with her in the open, not to preach the Dharma in more than five or six words "except in the presence of an intelligent man." It seemed a very rude way to behave to women. It astonished Ken that when he reported these vows to his mother she did not take offence. All she said was, "But you enjoyed being home with me all the more, didn't you?"

Ken and Butch rested when they reached Half-Way Point, a grassy spur where only a few trees grew and the breeze was markedly colder. Air eddies swirling out into the void carried the faint rippling of bells from monastery eaves, and fainter, the distant jingle from the pagoda's hti [finial]. Ken heard a jungle cock calling, and then no more as he propped his head against Butch's coarse coat and slept. He dreamed too, a dream which presented him with a solution, of a kind, to his most pressing problem. He sat up, eyes wide. Gosh! Plain as plain! Why hadn't he thought of it earlier? To make sure, he consulted Butch. Was it practical? The old dog looked at him adoringly. She seemed to think so.

The Pagoda of Deer Hill shot out of the forest like a rocket on its way to the moon, which was not as the Buddhist would see it, but as Ken did. (The Buddhist would see its base, cupola, stem and finial as symbols: circular base—symbol of concentration; cupola—symbol of the sky; stem—symbol of the tree of life; jingling golden cap—symbol of sanctuary of Nibbana, enthroned above the world.) About a hundred feet below the pagoda, the domes of foliage of the forest-covered hillside were pierced by a miscellany of wooden roofs, some with fussy seven-tiered turrets, others with gold-tipped pinnacles and fretted gables. Approached through trees, the timber walls, timber staircase, timber pavilions appeared like a part of the woodland.

Ken removed his shoes, curling his toes as he skirted the courtyard: monks wore sandals, but someone like himself, a ta-byi, which means a very low pupil, had to put up with the flints.

Under the carmine cherry, Ken knelt and bumped his head three times against the ground.

"Holy Father, I have come to pay my respects."

U Naind Da, the Abbot, small and wracked with rheumatism, sat bundled up in his orange cloak on a red mat. Saffron robes, red mat and the flaming tree of magenta, scarlet and puce blossom created clashes of colours to gladden the heart. It must be almost three years Ken calculated, since he and his father had called on the Abbot, ostensibly for a chat but in truth to see the tree. Dad had said, "The cherry starts off the spring. This *Primus cerasoides* is like a shot from a starting pistol."

"I've been meaning to come ever since I got back from England, Holy One, but circumstances made it impossible."

"Ah—circumstances! When need be, I have found circumstances can make water flow uphill. No matter. I am glad to see you, ta-byi, and with a strange animal. What is it?"

"A dog, Paya, my only friend and my sole source of happiness."

This statement brought a gleam to the Abbot's eyes. He said nothing but waved his hand at the attendants who had brought out his mat and helped him to sit down. The monks left, but unwillingly, and with disapproving glances in Ken's direction. No person of sensibility should present himself when the odours of cooking rice waft out of a monastery kitchen. No nourishment had been taken since dawn, then only a cup of tea, but the hour was approaching, eleven o'clock, when the monks hoped to sit down punctually to their only meal of the day—which had to be finished by noon.

"I have arrived at an inauspicious hour, Paya. May I have your permission to withdraw? I will climb to the pagoda and return at two o'clock."

The Abbot, always calm and with children so polite and gentle as to appear almost courtly, disconcerted Ken by speaking severely. "By two o'clock you will have returned to your Forest Bungalow with your troubles. I prefer you to sit here. Collect your thoughts. Release the elephant."

Ken smiled. It was comforting to hear again one of the Abbot's favourite quotations from scripture. "Question not with hesitation: release this elephant which is your mind."

"Paya, it's not my elephant. It's someone else's. But I'm so miserable about it I want to die—truly. The mind of this Someone is upside-down. He's about to make a terrible mistake and do something really bad. I've got to help."

"You suffer? Good! Sufferings develop spiritual sinews."

"Are you laughing at me?"

"Laughing? No. I peck at you."

Crouching under the folds of his robes, the Abbot looked like a bird, a small, inquisitive weaver-bird about to peck at a seed— or Ken. He added, "To be a pilgrim in the Four Paths, ta-byi, seek out only your failings. The failings of others do not concern you. Self-knowledge, self-reverence, self-control, these are your tasks."

"But if what this person does hurts my mother as well as me, I must stop him."

"If someone does evil, all the worse for him. How many times I have tried to drum into you, ta-byi, he who suffers most is the evil-doer. It is Karma, the universal law of cause and effect. Do good, and you will be rewarded; do evil and you will be punished."

"Sorry, Holy Father, the Law of Karma doesn't work for me!"

"The natural order of the universe does not work for you, my son?"

"I can prove it. When I was here, being a ko-yin, eating one meal a day, trying not to think of my mother even, I was good, wasn't I? I should have been rewarded. What followed? I was punished, sent to hell, sent to England, made miserable. In school I wasn't good. I did bad things all the time, and once I stabbed a boy with a penknife. What followed? I was rewarded. War came and I was sent back to my parents and made happy again. I've been ever so good since I got home, but now it's Karma in reverse all over again. I'm being punished. Everything's going phut. My friends say I'm a coward—Mibs says so, and Ko-Ni, and I *am*. And I don't think my parents care for me; otherwise they wouldn't have sent me away—like a parcel—and now, and now, my dad . . ."

The Abbot gripped Ken's shoulder. "Calm yourself. The surface of Minbu [a mud volcano] is less agitated."

"I'm sorry. But I do love Dad."

"Both your father and mother are my friends, both good people who love you and would not harm you. Whatever they do, they do for your good. They act according to their truth."

"Truth!" Ken's voice rose. "You're always saying this is truth and that is truth. There can't be hundreds of truths. What Dad might do is miles from truth."

"There is not *one* truth. Truth is all truths, and what is the truth for your father and mother may not be the truth for you. Your father is a man who loves nature, so he sees a different face of truth to the one seen by Dr Dowall, or Mr Waight. The forester, the doctor and the policeman live by different truths."

"I give up! Next you'll be saying a Buddhist can kill if he's a soldier."

Ken was speaking wildly, as no ta-byi should speak to a holy man. U Naind Da put up with Ken's hysteria because there was something he wanted to plant in his mind, and something he wanted to eradicate. The Abbot found the boy changed. Formerly the old man never hesitated when he spoke to him; on this occasion he picked his words and watched for their effect.

"For the Buddhist all war is wrong, all killing forbidden."

"I wasn't going to kill anyone. I came here to ask a favour, like my mother did before she sent me here. Anyone can ask it—anyone can become a novice, provided he's instructed first, can't he?"

"Who is this person?"

Ken tried to bring out the words he had prepared, but though his mind spoke them he was mute. But he did find himself saying, "He'd only need to be a monk of the first grade. So long as he made the vows about ladies—that's all that counts, and nobody here can have anything to do with ladies, can they? Not touch them, or talk to them or teach them the Dharma in more than five or six words unless an intelligent man is present."

"Is it your father?"

Ken's finger went up to the crown of his head, where he pulled at wisps of hair. The Abbot watched him in silence, then, "Do not try to shoulder the problems of others, my son. Perfect yourself— that is all that matters; for if you do wrong, no one can redeem you but yourself. No one can set you free but yourself. Our scriptures tell us there was not one being whom the Tathagata set free. So, Khin McNeil, I tell you now as I have told you a hundred times, your father's deeds are not your concern."

He reached forward to pull Ken's nervous fingers from his head, taking the clammy hand in his own dry one. "It is hard for you. Relatives are no more closely united than travellers who meet and part . . . no one really belongs to anyone else."

Ken did not realize at the time that these words were a quotation from the Suttas. For the first time he rejected the Abbot's teaching. People *did* belong. His parents belonged to each other, and he belonged to them. Butch belonged to him. How could anyone say Butch did not belong to him. There was no one else in the world she loved as she loved him. Without him she would die.

The old man was saying sadly, "Nibbana is not to be won by retaliation, or interference, or telling others what to do. Nibbana is won by ridding oneself of wanting anything at all, even wanting to love and be loved."

The attendants reappeared, helped the Abbot to his feet and ushered him, willy-nilly, towards the smell of cooked rice and curried vegetables.

17

Newspapers no longer arrived, radio reports were so contradic-
tory they could not be trusted, telegraphic communication with
Pegu, and thence Rangoon, was disrupted after the murder of
Hanuman Lall. All the same, the report brought to Kaikun by
the Mergui rubber planter, Etheridge, was confirmed by Burmese traders, farmers and fishermen. War or no war, they went
about their business as usual. Several of them, amongst them Hla
Gale, visited Moulmein, and their stories tallied. The battle had
lasted three days, the Indian troops retreating yard by yard, fighting every inch down to the quays, where they took to river-
steamers with Indian sappers at the controls. The Japanese
machine-gunned them across the Gulf of Martaban, but as far as
could be judged, most of the troops escaped. The Japanese—
who were never referred to as "the enemy" by the Burmese—
were now spreading northwards in the direction of Paan, so the
next battle, these Kaikun observers believed, would be for the
Lower Salween.

The front, in other words, had moved nearer to Kaikun, and
with enemy patrols in the Paan area, the war zone was no more
than seventy or eighty miles distant. Despite this, no evacuation
was ordered by officials. By mid-February, Kaikun's European
community were asking, "What on earth's going on? Do we pull
out, or don't we?" Mr Chapman replied that, as Government
had sent no orders, the existing orders must be carried out, and

these were to stay put. There was no need to worry, he said. If there was danger the Government would find ways and means of letting him know in plenty of time what action to take.

"A most trusting attitude," was the comment of Mrs Hodge, wife of the Baptist missionary. "The same trusting attitude of officials in Victoria Point and Tavoy, Mr Chapman? Weren't they all taken prisoners? Do you think that's going to happen to us too?"

If the D.C. had no reply to this, he continued to look bland and to pretend he did not know what Hamish Waight was saying. "Beat it. Don't wait to be evacuated. Pack up and go. If I know parties of six or more are going out, I'll send a police escort as far as Bilin."

A party of about sixteen Anglo-Indians and Anglo-Burmese set off, were given the promised escort, but got no further than Bilin before changing their minds and returning home. They had listened to a broadcast by the Governor of Burma, who said, "Rangoon will be absolutely held," and had also met the C.O. of a road-building party who assured them there was no need for panic: Churchill, he said, had promised reinforcements, and Chiang Kai-shek was pouring in Chinese troops to defend the Eastern Sector.

If people in Kaikun did not know what to do or whom to believe, neither did anyone else in Burma. Everyone was waiting. For what? Some, like the sixteen Eurasians, answered, "For news, for something to happen—not something awful, but just some kind of sign, which will tell us what to do." In other words, a sign which would work intuitively on confused minds.

Dithering ended in Kaikun with the arrival of a middle-aged Burmese lugale, Gaung Tu, Dr Dowall's houseboy. He had been sent back by his master, he said, because cholera had broken out in the camp near Mingaladon airfield, where the Doctor worked. At first Gaung Tu had refused to leave his master, but threatened with a beating, he had at last fought his way into a refugee-train—he had a pass, as a medical orderly—and here he was, with a letter and parcel for Mrs Dowall.

Halfway through the letter Mrs Dowall had stumbled to the edge of her verandah and shouted, "Singapore's gone!" Since no one was passing along the river-path at that time, she sent her gardener to fetch Jemma.

"Off you go, child!"

"Off? Off where, Granny?"

"Hallet war school, Naini Tal. There's an old Gladstone bag on top of the surgery cupboard. Get it. Pack it."

"Is Ken going too?"

"There'll be room in the bullock-cart, I expect."

"Bullock-cart? Not a proper evacuation? Mr Waight's convoy? Okay, but only if Ken goes too. I'm not leaving unless he does."

"Please yourself. I'm too old to make anyone obey me—but I warn you, if they tie you up for bayonet practice, I'm not going to rescue you. That's what they do, tie you to a tree alive and wriggling, for bayonet drill." She gave the girl a whack across the calves with her stick. "And it'll hurt more than that. Before you make up your mind, read what your grandfather says. When you've finished, wash your face, put the letter into its envelope and run round to each verandah as far as the McNeils."

Apart from the news of the fall of Singapore—three days before—nothing in the letter was sensational, considering the times. Nevertheless, after reading it almost everyone came to the decision that the time had come to leave. Hearing this, Mrs Dowall speculated which incident influenced each individual. That of the nun, she decided, must have unnerved the bossy spinster, the Wadley woman. Hugh Chapman's faith in official omniscience must have also been considerably shaken after reading about the cable to the Secretary of State in London. On one person only, the letter produced no effect—that was herself. Her husband could please himself, die of cholera, blow up Syriam, jump aboard the last ship, but she wasn't leaving her verandah until they deposited her in the Club compound under the mimosa.

Dr Dowall's letter was dated February 16, the day following the Japanese capture of Singapore.

The Gymkhana Club, Rangoon.

Feb. 16, 1942.

Dearest Mary,

I gave Gaung Tu a bag of silver coins for his journey. Tell everyone to take plenty of small silver, nothing else is accepted, ten-rupee notes sell for a few annas. I'd like you to give him three months' wages and send him to his village. There's no need for him to remain in Kaikun because, dearest, I want you and Jemma to leave immediately. Listen to me for once. You can both get transport to Bilin. When a hospital-train comes in, show the enclosed pass. You shouldn't have any trouble getting to Rangoon. Come straight to the Club—there are always army lorries at the station, and with the pass you'll have no trouble getting someone to give you a lift. Each pack a small bag, food for three days, mepachrine, salt tablets and pinky-pani crystals [permanganate of potash]. There'll be no difficulty in getting you on board a steamer, provided you leave at once.

Gaung Tu will probably exaggerate the cholera scare, but though worrying—six deaths a day—it hasn't got a grip yet. We must stop it before the rains break; otherwise it may rise from fifty to a hundred deaths a day.

Life's not too bad, and though I've lost two stone, I feel fit. Made friends with an American who takes me out to Mingaladon in his jeep—in return, I've fixed him up in the Club. He's one of the last of the A.V.G. When he's patched up his ship he'll be off to China. The R.A.F. packed up some days ago, a wing to Magwe, but the rest are back in India. As far as Burma's concerned and the troops are concerned, there ain't no R.A.F. in Burma! Japs have air to themselves and bomb Rangoon at leisure, day and night, mostly the docks. The Yank has promised me his jeep when he leaves, so I'll be able to get you to the docks, and myself in due course, when the last ship leaves. I've been promised a berth on her. She'll be standing by for the demolition gangs working in the refineries, so don't worry about me—you pretend you never do, but I know you do. I've asked for news of your area each time I call in at the airport, but the pilots I meet—they come down to refuel—have no idea of the country—couldn't tell Kaikun from Snowdonia. One of them brought Wavell down in Moulmein, thinking it was Rangoon. They're not the only ones who're fogged; we all are. Communications gone, generals fighting the war from Java, Delhi, Calcutta, Chungking, Rangoon, military at loggerheads with civilians, civilians blaming military. No one knows what's happening, not even the Governor. I heard in the Club he'd cabled Amery asking for an appreciation of the situation in Burma!

Apart from raids, twice daily, Rangoon is peaceful. It's another story at night, when it's only safe if you stay indoors. I'm called out frequently and go out with an armed guard. It's no joke with looters working in gangs and the dock area —where there's always someone with a broken head—stiff with drunks. One night I did not see a sober British soldier —our Club cellars have been looted too, we haven't a drop of Scotch. I stop my men shooting even if we're attacked— usually with dahs—because you can't tell if it's a lunatic on the loose or a dacoit. The asylums have been opened and there are about 1500 lunatics at large, some harmless, some criminally insane, all wandering about the streets, looking for food and shelter. There are also gangs of dacoits from the Delta terrorizing the few shopkeepers who haven't skipped. This riff-raff have looted all the big shops, set fires to hundreds of private houses, and sleep where they like. When I was called out a few nights ago I passed my bank in Sule Pagoda Road and saw a crowd of them inside making merry behind the grilles. The case I attended was one of rape—an old woman, a nun, one of the good creatures who work in the Leper Asylum. She had been attacked by one of the lunatics: he was still hanging about, watching, no idea what he'd done. Poor H. is being blamed for the hooliganism. As Judicial Secretary he gave the order to open the Asylum. What else could he do? The warders left some days ago on the big Government-sponsored evacuation scheme.

Staffs of hospitals, schools, jails, all went off together in an enormous train to Mandalay while patients, schoolchildren and convicts were sent off earlier in I.F.C. [Irrawaddy Flotilla Company] steamers—the convicts in a barge, packed like sardines. H. was in the Club looking yellow and pulled down. I tried to cheer him up, pointed out he couldn't have left them locked up without food or water. But he was too upset to listen.

Last night I was called out to a big house in Millionaires' Row [Tiger Alley Road], and, as I was coming away, heard yelps from next door. My driver and I broke into the house, which had been deserted and looted—broken crockery, curtains on the floor, part of a carpet set on fire. We found three spaniels shut up in a bathroom, food and water enough for a few days left out for them. I let them out. Best I could do. Rangoon is overrun with good pedigree English dogs, deserted by their owners. Some of these animals have been adopted by B.O.R.'s [British Other Ranks].

I don't know what Chapman's doing and hope I'm worrying unduly and he has already got you out. If he hasn't, tell him from me with Singapore gone, time is running out. They'll be hoisting the "E" [Evacuation] signal here in a few days, which means only the demolition squads—and one or two doctors—will be left. If Chapman is thinking of evacuating you to Maymyo, where most of the Government departments have already set up shop, try to persuade him to change his plans. Tell him from me that, from what I've seen and heard, the prognosis is not good. Tell him to look at a map and work out what's going to happen if we can't stop them. This damned country's a cul-de-sac. People who've bolted to Mandalay, Maymyo, Monywa and so on, will be pushed further and further north, ending up in God-forsaken spots like Mansi and Myitkyina. Where do they go from there? They don't. Once under those pestilential mountains —most malarious place on earth—they've two alternatives: wait for the Japs to lock 'em up in P.O.W. camps or attempt the Hukong and die of malignant malaria. Personally, I'd opt for a P.O.W. camp.

My dearest, I am relying on your good sense and your concern for Jemma and for me, to leave Kaikun as I advise —at once. How relieved and happy I will be when I see you in the Club—and can get you off on a ship. Don't let me down.

Your loving Rob

P.S. Have just heard H., who left for Maymyo this morning, got out of his car somewhere along the Prome Road, went behind a tree and shot himself.

Dr Dowall's letter lay on the office table between District Commissioner and Superintendent of Police.

Hamish Waight looked glumly at Hugh Chapman. "When" had been decided, thanks to the Doctor's letter. It remained to give battle over "where." Hugh had agreed to fix the evacuation for the following day, but over its destination Hugh was being stubborn.

Hugh also looked glum. "I know your views, but I don't agree, and you can argue till doomsday but I won't come round. Let's drop it." Pause, fingers drumming on the table. "I really must be going. Someone's coming to lunch."

"Miss Wadley?"

"I really don't see . . ."

"That it's my business? It isn't, but I think she may be influencing you."

"Nonsense. I'm carrying out Government policy."

"I think you're also carrying out Miss Wadley's. Hill station, gay social life, G.H. next door. If she wants to risk it, let her, but why take everyone else?"

"Are you trying to pick a quarrel?"

"I'm trying to fathom your mind."

"I might say the same. What's behind this pig-headed insistence on India?"

"This . . ." Hamish flicked the letter. "Dowall's no fool. He's on the spot where he can judge and he's told us the prognosis is bad. It's his way of saying he thinks we'll be run out of Burma."

"He's talking rubbish."

". . . and by the monsoon. Have you thought of that? When the mosquitoes are hatched out. Walking out through forests infested with malarious mosquitoes without shelter, food, medical attention, medicines."

"This is sheer panic. The monsoon's months away and . . ."

"Eight weeks."

"And there's no question of Rangoon's capitulation. You heard H.E.'s broadcast: Rangoon's going to be defended. We can take it that's official, that's Whitehall."

"It may be Whitehall's idea—but is it Tokyo's?"

"All this fuss over Maymyo! What have you against the place, Hamish? It's perfectly normal for Government to go up there every summer."

"I'm not worrying about a lot of Government officials going up, or Miss Wadley and your daughter. I'm sure they'll be looked after. What I'm worrying about are hundreds and thousands of poor devils being sent north. Those convict barges, for instance, and the sort of feckless crowd we've got here, coolies, clerks, each with a host of dependents. They'd be useless in a crisis of this kind. And with the best will in the world, we'd be incapable of helping a great mass."

Hugh Chapman sighed. "I know all that. Now I really must go."

"Then I'll walk with you as far as your bungalow."

Another sigh. "Can't we finish it here? I really don't think there's much more to say."

"The point of Dowall's letter is that this is really our last chance to get our people out to India, and I agree. If you send them north you are merely postponing the exodus and taking an enormous risk. The Japs have control of the air and sea, on land we haven't held them up for two minutes anywhere. What makes you so sure we will . . . ?"

"Churchill. Wavell."

"Okay, but if they don't? And you find you've sent hundreds of coolies and clerks and old women and children into a trap? As Dowall says, it's a bloody cul-de-sac, mountains whichever way they try to escape. What chance has a fellow like Gupta Babu [Hugh's Bengali clerk] of surviving a five-hundred-mile trek without food and shelter? And Gupta's got about ten children. You'd never forgive yourself if they got caught—and thousands like them. It might prey on your mind as it did on the Judicial Secretary's. We don't want that."

Hugh said nothing; his silence tempted Hamish to believe he was persuading him to his point of view. The D.C. was not a bad fellow. People liked him. Perhaps his refusal in this instance to see beyond the end of his nose wasn't wholly his fault. It was strange how a man's obsession in one direction could warp him in another. Hamish said softly, "It would be just as easy for us to get them over the hills to Rangoon as up to Toungoo . . . what do you say?"

"I say, for reasons best known to yourself you are trying to unnerve me."

"I'm not thinking about you at all, but the people in your charge—and mine. I've heard about places like the Hukong from my brother. He had to go in there occasionally when he was in the Frontier Service—but only did it in the dry season. During the monsoon he wouldn't have gone far because the rivers can rise twenty feet in an hour, the hillsides run with mud, making clay slides and potholes impossible to get across. A few primitive tribes live out of the malaria belt on mountaintops with a patch of hill rice and a few pigs. Bob had a string of mules carrying everything he needed. How are people like Gupta Babu and family going to cross this kind of country without shelter or food?"

"Do shut up about Gupta Babu! It's all supposition. If—if—if. Very well, I'll contribute an 'if' too: 'if' any of these situations do arise, the Government would do something about it. A mass airlift."

"With what? Magic carpets? You've read Dowall's letter. We haven't enough planes to support our Army. Where are we going to get the armada to lift a million people? Or were you thinking only of yourself—and your daughter and Miss Wadley? I'm sure there'd be no difficulty in getting them flown out. After all, Windermere Lodge is bang up against G.H., and you can be sure the Governor . . ."

But Hugh Chapman had snatched up the Doctor's letter and walked out of the office. He was very angry.

Near the small brick-and-steel building in the Police Grounds a table, chair and account books were carried out for Hamish. When the heavy steel door of the vault was opened, Dil Tharpa stacked bags of silver rupees on the table, opened the ledgers, and the normal procedure for payday started, with this exception—each man was to receive wages for six months.

"Because I'm going away for six months," Hamish said. "So please stop blubbering Havildar Bhim Singh."

All constables who asked for leave to join their families were given leave. Those who volunteered to escort the evacuation convoys were told to go into the vault, select a rifle and as much ammunition as each could carry. These orders were also given to the "Plunties," the Burma Volunteer Army, a guerrilla organization under the command of two white men, a British officer whom Hamish knew only as "Daddy Long Legs," and the other, a Roman Catholic priest. The "Plunties" were to remain in Kaikun as long as Hamish needed help with demolitions. After that they were to join their new commanders in the hills.

Some of the men looked guilty, unable to believe they were really free to help themselves to rifles and ammunition. "Carry on —as much as you like," Hamish shouted. "Only get a move on."

"And me, sir? Can I take some bullets? And a rifle too?" a young voice sounded behind Hamish.

"What for, Ken?"

"Just to have, sir. Please."

"Certainly not, but you can help me. Let me feel your muscles. Not bad." Hamish pinched his arm. "When they've finished in there, you and I are going to throw the rest into the whirlpool."

"Not rifles, sir!"

"Rifles and ammo. And we're going to burn bundles and bundles of rupee notes. Denial to the Japs. We're Kaikun's last-ditchers."

"A last-ditcher! This is the most wonderful day in my life, sir."

One of the police lorries was loaded up with the vault's remaining stores, driven to Hamish's bungalow and backed across his lawn. Together Hamish and Ken ripped open the boxes of ammunition before tipping the bullets into the water. Then, one by one they chucked in the rifles, seeing who could throw his the furthest.

"You know our law of cause and effect, sir?"

Hamish picked up a spotless, gleaming mechanism and spun it over the reeds into the whirlpool.

"Yes, Karma."

"You can't escape from Karma, sir, even if it's in reverse like mine. There's a war on, and what's my Karma? Not grabbing rifles but throwing them away."

Hamish gave him some matches. "Start on the bank-notes." Before the first wad caught fire a breeze whipped notes from the rubber bands and blew them over the treetops. Hamish brought out a tin wash-basin, told Ken to saturate the notes in petrol and then burn them in a slit trench. While they worked Hamish questioned him.

"Hla Gale isn't leaving Kaikun?"

Ken gave him a stricken look. His job was to press each bundle of notes into the petrol. When it was thoroughly saturated he passed it to Hamish.

"Dad and I and Miss Wadley have to go tomorrow in the D.C.'s party with Mibs and Jemma and the Hodges and the Botibols. Dad doesn't want to go. He wants to stay and look after Ahme. So do I. It's Ahme who's making us go. She says she'll be all right. Will she, Mr Waight, sir?"

Hamish did not answer this question immediately but pushed the boy away from the trench where arcs of burning petrol flame were shooting upwards.

"I don't know what to say, Ken. We men like women to depend on us, don't we? They usually do, then suddenly they decide they won't anymore—and we're upset. Now, let's concen-

trate—and enjoy ourselves. Forty lakhs of rupees up in smoke
in a few minutes!"

Ken stared at him and repeated his question. "Is Ahme going
to be all right by herself, without me and Dad?"

Hamish threw in another five wads of petrol-soaked notes.
"I'll speak to your dad. I think your mother should go out with
you."

Tears trickled down Ken's cheeks into the petrol.

"I'll tell you my secret. Dad can't stay because he has promised to look after someone else: someone he's going to marry
next. But what'll happen to Ahme when we're gone and there's
no one to protect her? They think I don't understand, but I do.
It's nothing to do with her mills. She's got to stay because Dad
doesn't want her. And there's another reason, Fatima told me.
Fatima says my mother's going to have a baby."

Hamish climbed out of the trench, kicked earth into it. "I
don't know about the baby—but if your mother's hanging on
here it's because of that, and no other reason. The rest is piffle.
Your dad dotes on her. Your dad is not going to marry anyone.
I know him, and he wouldn't leave your mother when she's going
to have a baby . . ."

"But he *is*."

"Because of the Japs—but later when the baby has arrived,
you'll see, your mother will get herself smuggled out to a remote
hill village and she'll hide there until everything's normal again."

"Or until Dad can get back to fetch her?"

"Perhaps."

"Wouldn't it be simpler to smuggle Dad back?"

"He'll work out something, you don't have to worry. To help
them best you must keep quiet and hide your feelings. Don't let
them see you crying."

"But you think it's okay to have feelings? The Abbot says
it's best not to love or want to be loved."

"I don't think he meant quite that. After all, the Abbot has
affection for you and your mother."

"I know he has for Ahme. When I was in the monastery a
funny thing happened. I saw a brown paper parcel by one of

the big vases in the Great Hall. The last time I saw the parcel
was in my mother's bedroom. Just as I was leaving, one of the
lay brothers came out to me with it and asked me to return it
to my mother, with the message that the Abbot was sorry but
by the rules of his order he was not allowed to dig holes and
bury things. Then the lay brother gave me a wink and said the
Abbot had no objection if my dog dug a hole for the parcel, and
the best place was one the Japs, being Buddhists, would not
desecrate, and that was under the sacred cherry tree. So you see,
he must have affection for Ahme."

"What was in the parcel?"

"Her jewels."

Hamish beamed as he gripped Ken's arm. "There's the proof.
If she's burying her jewels it can mean only one thing. She's
thinking of leaving too—as soon as she can."

"Do you really think so?"

"Burying her precious possessions before leaving is instinctive.
It's what we're all doing. Now I'm convinced your mother in-
tends to get out but in her own good time. If a woman decides
to do something her own way, it's no good arguing or grieving.
Just don't worry, that's all. Your mother is small and looks frail,
but she's tough, and she'll look after herself and the new baby."

"Thank you, sir, but I still wish I could only reverse it, like my
Karma reverses me. If I could only smuggle Dad back to
Ahme . . ."

Hamish linked his arm through the boy's and led him away
from the smell of petrol and charred paper.

"Don't dwell on this anymore. Let's be practical instead. You
know what I'm going to do now?—show you how to build a
basha."

Hamish led him into the verandah, called for lemon squash
and water biscuits, then sketched circles and lines to represent
posts and crossbeams, writing directions over them.

"This is where you tie the roof bamboos with rattan. Four
or five janput leaves—tie them to the crossbeams—and that's your
roof. Here's the flooring—remember how you split bamboos to
make the planks? And last, the cooking platform at the back."

"No bogs because you use the jungle."

Hamish drew a "v" over a circle. "I'm sure Miss Wadley will never let you use the jungle with red ants about. Here's the hole. Two bamboos tied with rattan. Put them across the top of the hole—a loo fit for a general."

Ken took up the pieces of paper and studied them. After a moment he looked up. "Why are you telling me all this, sir? I mean, sir, are you telling me it all *because* we're going away tomorrow?"

"Yes, in a way, and also because there's just a chance that things might be tougher later on. And it's because of someone else too. I want you to look after someone for me. Not only while you're in Maymyo but after that, wherever you go."

Ken nodded. "I promise. It's Jemma, isn't it, sir? I don't know why you bother with her. But as you've asked me, I'll do it. For your sake, sir, not for Jemma's."

18

"Hamish! Hamish! It's started. Get up or we'll be gone. *And* she's trying to swipe Maung Taw and Kyauk-Kyi."

Hamish gazed, still half-asleep, through the mosquito-netting. How could anyone swipe an elephant? And these two, Maung Taw (Mister Jungle) and Kyauk-Kyi (Big Rock) were the biggest in his herd. What was Jemma doing there, hopping about, poking the net, a marigold garden round her neck?

"And she's making people cry! Do get up. Don't you want to say good-bye to us?"

Marigolds suggested farewell deputations, and the crumbs round Jemma's lips, coconut sweets which were usually part of the presentation baskets.

"Dil Tharpa!"

"Sir!"

"Get her out of here and bring me my dressing-gown."

"Sir!"

Jemma snatched the threadbare gown from the orderly, threw it over Hamish's face, then herself upon him. When the rough and tumble was over, she pushed Hamish onto the verandah.

"Look! Hundreds and thousands! They've been collecting all night. We're leaving at eight, in two batches—the hoi-poloi by the cart track, and the high-and-mighty, that's us, by the upper road."

Hamish's expression hardened. Whose decision was that? It did not sound like Hugh. Were there still Britishers who even in flight insisted on first-class and steerage? No one he knew in Kaikun could be so silly, then . . . who?

"Who's been making who cry?" Hamish asked Jemma—not that he expected much sense from her that morning. The girl was overwrought, throwing out her arms, jumping on and off things, and in a spontaneous effort to release tension, whirling down the verandah in a series of handstands.

"Don't be silly! You know who. Mr Chapman's put her in charge of all of us refugees. There she is! Yakking to him, telling tales, I bet. She's complaining about your Head Elephant Man, I heard her. I've got my own name for her now. Mar Nat [Devil]. *And* another one "Mi-Aung" [Miss-Driver], and it goes beautifully in our theme song. We're going to sing it marching out. Ken too. But Ken's such a wet, and he *likes* her; when he sings it, he means it nicely.

> *Lead kindly light, amid encircling gl-ooo-om!*
> *Lead thou Mi-Aung!*

Hamish put his arm round her thin, bony shoulders. "Come and sit down and calm down. You're to have some breakfast."

"I've been eating ludoos from the good-bye basket the My-ok sent Granny."

"I guessed as much."

"It's a swiz for the My-ok. Granny isn't going."

"We'll see about that! Drink that tea, or would you like cocoa?"

"She won't listen to you. She won't listen to anyone. As we've all got to walk, how can Granny go?"

"Who says you've all got to walk?"

"Your darling Miss Wadley."

"You're not to start abusing Miss Wadley like Mibs. I don't like to hear you being rude."

Jemma pushed away her cup, plumped her arms on the table and hid her face. "You're against me too. Our last morning and you're being mean to me."

"I'm not against you, silly. I love you best, you know that.

You were up too early and you're overexcited. Come along." He put his hand over hers. "Let's go and see what's happening."

She rose unwillingly, sniffing. "Promise you're not sticking up for her. Promise you're on our side."

"Silly child."

He dried her tears with a table-napkin and tried to tidy her hair by pushing sticky black strands behind her ears. "Who's looking after you?"

"I'm looking after myself."

Hamish sighed. "I wish you'd do as I say. I wish you'd let me send you to Rangoon with Dil Tharpa. He'd put you on a boat to Calcutta, and in Calcutta I've got friends who'd take you up to Naini—your grandmother agreed to my plan. I've got plenty of money and no one to spend it on, and I'd like to spend it on you, pay for you in this grand school they've started for . . ."

"I know, I know, Granny told me. But I won't go."

"Prefer Maymyo, Windermere Lodge and, and . . ." It slipped out—"Miss Wadley?"

"It isn't that, and you know it. It's because Ken's such a nit. Someone's got to look after him."

And someone had to look after poor little Jemma. The only person Hamish could think of was Ken.

As they were leaving the bungalow, Jemma dashed back into the verandah, reappearing with Hamish's riding-crop. "Please can I take it—to remember you?" She knotted the plaited leather thong round her waist, leaving the bone-handle hanging behind to flap against her buttocks. When Hamish tried to belt it more comfortably round her she flared at him. "Don't! I hate people touching me. Old people, that is. They've got scaly skin."

"Really! How old do you think I am?"

"You're old, Hamish. I'm sorry, but you are. Admit, you're twice my age. When I'll be twenty you'll be forty, and when I'm forty you'll be eighty. So I can never marry you."

"Too bad! I'll have to marry someone else, won't I, and scrub your name from my little book."

It was still very early. The river smoked, iridescent veils wreathed over grey water to drift over the heads of evacuees gathering on the river-side clearing—where, not long ago, the pwe had been held. As Hamish and Jemma crossed the lawn, Jemma's cold hand in Hamish's warm one, a line of saffron dots descended Deer Hill, novices and monks on the collecting round. So, it couldn't be much after seven, and Hugh's timetable for an eight-o'clock start was well in hand. The first tentative rays of orange light coloured the puffs of dust kicked by bullocks along the cart-track. The mass of evacuees was grouping along the earth-road that would take them through hot moist valleys, while Jemma's "high-and-mighty" travelled by cooler hill paths. Nothing could be seen of them but countless black heads and heads covered by drab grey-white headcloths, or the coarse blanket-cloth which hooded the humblest, the earth-digging Ooriyas. A group of these labourers crouched by the river-bank passing a waterpipe from hand to hand. Nearby Hamish observed some of Kaikun's Europeans, sitting on camp-stools, servants standing respectfully behind, grooms holding their ponies. At a little distance from them, clustering round a cigarette seller, stood some Indian youths in shimmering white-lawn dhotis and bazaar-cut Western suits. One or two were chaffing a group of Anglo-Indian girls, dressed in flimsy dresses, high heels and wide-brimmed straw hats, as if off to a garden-party.

"What's the best way of getting off leeches?" Hamish suddenly asked Jemma.

"Leeches? There won't be any leeches. You only get leeches in the monsoon."

"Must you always argue? If you happen to walk in the jungle in the monsoon you are to tie a string round your waist, and to the string you are to tie another string with a bag of moist salt on the end. Never pull off a leech. Dab it with the salt bag. And you are to take three tablets of mepachrine a day. I will send the mepachrine to Maymyo."

Jemma gave him a puzzled look. "It's only February. We're supposed to get to Maymyo in a few days. When we get to Maymyo we're going to stay for the duration, Miss Wadley says. Aren't we?"

He did not answer her, his gaze directed across the river, where

he followed the movements of Ma Roi, a Burmese trader who
with cheroot stuck in her mouth was staring at the tent—Hamish's
tent—commandeered by Hugh as the centre for evacuation business. Along the foreshore many Burmese women had arrived like
Ma Roi to erect umbrellas, set up brass scales and heap produce
on palm mats. The only gaudy display of the scene was exhibited
in the line of stalls where sunlight filtered through different-
coloured oiled silk, shedding rose and cinnamon tints on scarlet
chillis, green bananas and small hill oranges.

"What's Ma Roi so interested in?"

"Those people, snogging under the tent."

Canvas roofing obscured head and shoulders of two people—
no, three. Hamish perceived the third presence in skinny arms
that hugged silk skirt and khaki slacks.

Jemma said, "It's Mr McNeil, Hla Gale and Ken. Poor Ken!
I'm glad I'm not him. I've only got Grandpa and Grandma . . .
and you, but that's different."

How was it different? He would have liked to ask her, but
this was not the time. Jemma's hand had become hot in his
own. He wiped the palm against her dress and let it drop to
her side, but she refused to release him. "Please, it's our last
morning. Don't you want to hold my hand? I want to hold yours
till the last moment, and I'm going to."

As they crossed the bridge Hamish repeated an earlier question. "What was that about making people cry?"

"Mi-Aung. She's opening people's bundles. Poor old things like
Fatima. She pokes into them and throws away what she says
isn't necessary."

Hamish had seen refugees carrying half a bicycle, others a bag
of car-tools, broken sewing-machines, a heavy steel charcoal-
burning dhobi's iron. He had himself tried, but usually failed, to
persuade these people to replace useless articles with food or
clothing.

"You can't walk two hundred miles cluttered up with rubbish."

"There you go again, siding with her."

He patted her hand. "Be a good girl, and don't be jealous of
anyone Ken likes. That's it, isn't it? You can't bear Ken liking

Mibs—or Miss Wadley. Why can't you try getting on with Miss Wadley too? No point getting on bad terms with someone you've got to live with for months."

On the far side of the river Hamish's lecturing ended because it was all he could do to thrust a way for them through the crowd.

"Sahib! Sahib, help me! I am Mohammed Khan, Sahib, the cook of McNeil, Sahib. I cannot find my master."

A small man with lined monkey face, black teeth and wearing a Muslim cap pushed himself in front of Hamish.

"What am I to do, Lord? My mother is seventy and cannot walk. The Memsahib says if my mother cannot walk I must find people to carry her or she will have to be left behind."

"There! What did I tell you?" Jemma exclaimed.

"How can I leave my mother behind, she who . . ."

"I am not responsible for arrangements, Mohammed Khan, but I'll speak to the Deputy Commissioner. Both of you remain here. Don't move until I return to this spot."

Like well-trained gun-dogs, noses pointing after him, cook and mother stood rooted where he'd left them.

They found Miss Wadley in the grove where the elephants had been assembled, at a little distance from the main clearing. Dressed in khaki bush-shirt and slacks, sleeves rolled up, an army knapsack and shoulder-bag slung about her, she looked businesslike and considerably changed to the Miss Wadley of the Christmas camp. She was thinner, yet her cheeks and arms appeared more rounded; she looked prettier and younger. When Hamish had last taken stock of her, an evening at the Club during the first week of her arrival, her manner barely dissembled a hoydenish, truculent bravado he had noticed in other spinsters —as if to say, I can manage better without a man. It occurred to him that she looked more at ease, more truly self-assured.

Some kind of argument was taking place between her and Saw Chaw Hlaw, the Head Elephant Man, their differences aggravated by Saw Hardy, the Chapman's houseboy acting as interpreter. Of the eleven elephants Hugh had requisitioned from the police herd, all save two, Maung Taw, the big tusker, and

Kyauk-Kyi, the big cow elephant, were loaded and ready to start.

"So glad you've turned up, Mr Waight. I'm in trouble. Can't get it into this man's head Hugh's frig is to go on the smaller elephant, and the tent"—she indicated the one used as the evacuation's H.Q.—"on the big one."

A frig? Hamish looked round and saw that there was indeed a small white enamel Kelvinator, a frigidaire run by oil, lying on the ground. What possible use was it? Impossible to use en route, and in Maymyo, the rented "Windermere Lodge" would almost certainly have one.

"Madame not understanding"—Saw Hardy addressed Hamish, but got no further. Saw Chaw Hlaw stepped forward, scowling, and in rapid Burmese told Hamish, "The tent has been up all night and is soaking. A wet tent, Thakin!—you know how much that weighs. As for the white box"—the u-zi glared at the Kelvinator—"Kyauk-Kyi cannot carry it. She cannot carry anything. That is the Dr Babu's orders. Kyauk-Kyi is to carry the sick, not white boxes."

Miss Wadley was watching Hamish closely. "For the sake of appearances you should back me up."

"There's no question of backing up anyone. The Elephant Man is being quite reasonable. I don't think you could have understood. What he's saying is the frig cannot go because the elephant has been reserved for sick people. As for the tent—Maung Taw's our prize beast, and even he couldn't carry a tent saturated with dew. No elephant's supposed to be loaded over six hundred pounds, and a wet tent weighs about a thousand. If you want Maung Taw to carry it, he'll have to wait for at least three hours till it dries out."

Miss Wadley answered without heat, "Oh do you think so? I'm afraid I disagree. That great brute can carry a tent, wet or dry, and as Hugh has asked me to supervise loading, I want them to strike the tent, pack it up, wet or dry, and get it up on him at once. So sorry, Mr Waight."

"He won't do it, you know."

"Won't he? I wonder if it's because he's been bribed to load other baggage?"

Though Saw Chaw Hlaw did not understand Miss Wadley's words, he had grasped her meaning and gave Hamish a cool, judicial look. Was the white woman now trying to browbeat the white man? Their prestige, as men, appeared to be at stake.

"I'm sorry the tent can't go. It happens to be *my* tent, and I need it."

"*Your* tent?"

It was Hamish's turn to be forbearing, to smile gently. "As for bribery, I wouldn't put it past Dr Babu to bribe anyone, but if he wants Kyauk-Kyi as his ambulance, he's got to have her."

"Are you telling me I can't have either of these elephants?"

"You can't have Kyauk-Kyi for your frig, I'm afraid. As for the other one—I daresay we can stretch a point to preserve 'face.' If you really insist on taking this frig out it can be strapped on one side of Maung Taw's pad, provided I can hoist an old lady, a friend of mine, on the other."

Miss Wadley accepted the compromise coolly. "Very well. Do as you like. I'm going to have a word with Hugh."

Saw Chaw Hlaw made no effort to conceal his disgruntled feelings. "The box on Maung Taw! I refuse! What good is it? I could load six old dotards in its place."

Hamish told him sharply, "That's enough. Old people are to be carried on the cow. Load up the frig at once, and in the other the mother of the Forest Officer's cook. Jemma, run and fetch them." Hamish's voice became less authoritative, "After all, Saw Chaw Hlaw, it is up to you. You are the u-zi, and if you want to take on more aged people, it is up to you, and if the box is knocked off by an overhanging rock, who is to blame you?" Saw Chaw Hlaw avoided the eyes of the Superintendent of Police. Anyone who had watched him and Maung Taw disperse a log jam could not but be aware of their uncanny communion. Were she present, Miss Wadley would perceive no signal, hear no word of command, but the frig would strike the rock and mysteriously topple off down the hillside.

"Hmit!" Maung Taw spread her feet on the ground while Jemma shouted instructions at Fatima.

Saw Chaw Hlaw strapped two balancing wicker panniers on either side of Maung Taw's pad. Into one of these Jemma and Hamish heaved Fatima. Jingling anklets, bracelets, clutching bundles, and calling on Allah, the old woman was finally settled, a hen trussed on its way to market.

There was a stir, the watching crowd parted as Hugh and Miss Wadley appeared together.

"Get down from there!" Jemma obediently slid down the elephant's flank.

"I didn't mean you—her." Hugh pointed to Fatima.

"Just a moment," Hamish said.

"I'm still in charge of my herd. Also, I'm in charge of denial —right?"

The Deputy Commissioner looked puzzled. "What are you doing here?"

"Came to see you off," Hamish answered. "I'm a bit worried about the animals. You remember the directive: u-zis to take elephants and hide them in the hills, ponies to be shot. I don't want you to take any of the elephants to Toungoo. I want them sent with the u-zis into hiding straightaway."

With Hugh present, Miss Wadley's manner underwent a change. She spoke emphatically. Hamish was also amused by the new proprietary air which, he had noticed, usually became evident in women after six months of marriage. In Miss Wadley it had developed since the Christmas camp. She said, "We haven't enough elephants. I really need six more. I'd be grateful if Mr Waight found other transport for that old creature. I'd like her off at once."

Hugh heard her but made no comment and did not take his eyes from Hamish. He spoke evenly, as if making a conscious effort to sound neutral.

"On second thoughts, the old bird can stay there."

Hamish nodded. "Good! On second thoughts, I won't insist on denial until Toungoo, but at Toungoo they must all be turned over to Saw Chaw Hlaw, who knows what to do. Now about the

ponies. I don't want them falling into Jap hands either. I'll deal
with the ones left here, but I've a soft spot for Tostig. You'll
get polo in Maymyo, Hugh, so what about it?"

"Polo!" Miss Wadley exclaimed. "Is this the moment to discuss
polo, Mr Waight?"

"We're not discussing polo—as such. Mr Waight is telling me
he doesn't want to shoot his favourite polo pony and is offering him to me. Thanks, Hamish. I'll take you up on that."

Hugh started pushing his way towards the cart-track, where
constables were barring the mass of refugees from taking the
upper road out of Kaikun, the road reserved for the elite. Here,
under trees, Europeans with horses, dogs, servants; family groups
of Anglo-Indians and Anglo-Burmese, as well as a group of subordinates of Government offices were awaiting last-minute instructions from the Deputy Commissioner. The McNeils were
there, Hla Gale's neat black bun and sprig of white flowers leaning against Tom's shoulder. Hla Gale and Tom were trying to
look cheerful for Ken's sake, but Hamish could tell that the parting was proving a strain for them. Ken's lids were so swollen
with weeping, there was nothing to be seen of his eyes. The boy
looked so wretched, Hamish told Jemma, "Go and cheer him
up," but Jemma refused. "I'm going to hold your hand till the last
moment."

Miss Wadley, however, had seen Ken's misery and walked
briskly towards him. Hamish watched her with misgiving:
this wasn't the time to offer sympathy or to interfere in any
way with those three wracked people. Hamish watched her approach Hla Gale, whisper to her and then disengage Ken's hand
from his mother. Unlike Jemma, Ken limply let go, turning his
face into his father's coat. Hla Gale kissed her son, kissed Tom
and, as if performing a conjuring trick, vanished into the mob.
Hamish was overwhelmed by a disagreeable sensation, the kind
of sensation that overtakes someone who has unwittingly wit-
nessed an act of cruelty. It was irrational, he told himself. Miss
Wadley had really acted very sensibly. Ken had to be parted from
his mother, Tom from his wife—to get the business over quickly
was only common sense. And yet . . . the impression persisted

that Miss Wadley's motives had not been disinterested, that Miss Wadley had acted officiously for reasons best known to herself.

"Is there anything I can stand on?" Hugh was asking. "I've got to speak to everybody."

Hamish pointed to a bullock-cart. "Before you start, do you mind if I say my piece about denial?"

When he had climbed on the cart, Hamish blew his police whistle. "May I have your attention, please. Before the Deputy Commissioner tells you about arrangements for the trek to Toungoo, I'd like to show you how to deal with your animals in case you are forced to abandon them. You don't want your pets to fall into enemy hands; nor do we. In the case of horses the Government is particularly anxious that denial is carried out. No one wants to botch this kind of job, so please watch me carefully."

Hamish drew his revolver, pointing the muzzle downwards. He had not allowed Jemma to climb on the cart with him, and noticed she was standing near Mibs. Miss Wadley between Ken and Tom, her arms linked possessively through theirs, stood immediately below him.

"If you have to shoot your horse or your dog, mark a spot on the forehead, get well above it, and aim like this . . ." Hamish sighted down the barrel of his revolver, and as he did so, found himself aiming at Miss Wadley's head. It was unintentional.

"Brace yourself. You've got to do it! Let her have it."

Her have it? or *him* have it? What had he said? Months afterwards Hamish turned over in his mind this phrase, wondering what on earth he'd really said.

19

Sayo Forest Bungalow,
March 1.

Ten days since we left Kaikun, trekking and camping through
hills along the Siamese frontier. Expected to record privations
and excitements of a wartime exodus, but this hasn't been anything but a kind of royal progress in great comfort, through
wonderful scenery and in the most wonderful climate. Nothing
in my life has approached this—the happiest time I believe
I've ever known.

We're camping in a forest bungalow, made of teak and built
on stilts, on the top of a hill overlooking a lake. The sun's setting,
turning the hills a dark velvety purple, and the lake's surface
into copper with an acid-green sheen. I can smell chapatties
being cooked and the faint tang of curried prawns and rice being kept warm. We're waiting for Tom and Hugh to return from
the jungle, where they've gone to shoot something "for the pot,"
probably jungle fowl. Butch goes with them to retrieve, and Ken
is torn between pride in the discovery of Butch's usefulness, and
anguish over killing birds. The night they brought back a peacock Ken refused to look at it, and when it arrived roasted for
dinner the next night, wouldn't touch it.

The mass of refugees followed the main valley of the Yun-zalin, but our contingent went into the hills. After two days we divided into small groups, ours going first so that those behind can have the advantage of the camps built for us. Yes built *for* us! Although we have two lots of tenting (one lot remaining to dry out), the orderlies sent ahead usually get villagers to build huts in readiness for us. They choose sites on hilltops, our highest camp was at Hpajawpu, 5000 feet up, where it was so cold the orderlies and servants had to sleep between fires. Our camps are always built at some distance from a village, for fear villagers are harbouring Burmese nationalists. By the time we arrive, at the camps, in the late afternoon, everything is ready, a circle of freshly made little huts or bashas put up, one hut with a bucket, as a Heath-Robinson shower, another as W.C. Within half an hour of arrival these marvellous Indian servants have a three-course meal ready. Afterwards villagers arrive with gifts of bananas, rice, vegetables, a chicken, and once a pig. Tom sometimes turns the radio on for them—most of them have never heard a radio, and a good many have not even been as far as Kaikun.

Both Tom and Hugh most attentive, summoning a horse for me to ride across streams, asking me if I'm tired and so on. I've never been so fussed over in my life. They politely ask me to choose which basha or tent I want. At first Jemma and Mibs came in with me, but when Tom heard me going for them for giggling he gave them a hut to themselves. We start early, stopping for ten minutes in every hour and at midday for half an hour for a light picnic meal.

We are all so fit after ten days we can now do ten to twelve miles without feeling tired. Our trek depends on the elephants who start at dawn. They are very capricious and, I'm told, sometimes refuse to walk further; then there's nothing to be done but find a suitable hilltop camping-place. Everything in the hills delights me. The flowering tree, the creepers—also in bloom the yellow flowers of Paduk, which Tom says is the Burmese rosewood. It smells sweetly and showers us with pollen. We also catch occasional glimpses of animals I've never before seen, like the mithan, a type of bison, grazing on a slope above us, and draped over a village wall a transparent emerald-green snake. A nat shrine usually signals the approach to a village. A pig's head stuck in the fork of a tree was the offering on one nat altar. The tips of the ears had been cut off "for the nats to eat," Tom said.

As for Tom, darling Tom! I wonder if he is aware of my endless stratagems to walk beside him. He and Ken seem to have got over their parting with Hla Gale; at all events, they never speak of her to me, and seem happy with me. Passing a monastery school on the outskirts of a village, Ken made me halt on the path outside while he listened to the monk intoning a verse of scripture. When the class repeated it in unison, Ken joined in. Later on he told me when he comes down from Oxford (which was news! I thought he never wanted to see England again!) he would return to Deer Hill Monastery as a u-pa-zin for three months: this, I gather is a higher-grade novice. I never know whether he tells me these things to get a rise out of me. He looks at me mischievously out of the corner of those slit eyes, waiting for my reaction. I usually give him a hug. He always responds to my affection. I think he needs to be loved, and is devoted to me because he knows I do truly love him. How happy he and I and Tom could be together. Because Ken and Tom are so gentle, they bring out the best in me. I could never harm either and would always be loyal and devoted. If only two people were out of the way—Hla Gale and Hugh—how perfect life would be! Luckily, Hla Gale is temporarily missing. Wish Hugh was too. What a nuisance he is becoming with his devotion and furtive love-making, stealing kisses, holding my hand in the dark, tickling the back of my neck. He gives me goose-flesh, but I can't very well snub him. When I catch him watching me with Tom, I sometimes wonder whether he's suspicious of Tom. I must be careful. I do love Tom, but so far I have had no sign from him. And if I'm wrong about him, if he doesn't really care for me, I am determined to make the best of Hugh. Whatever happens, I'm quite determined not to go back to England to earn my own living, queueing for rations, cooking little messes over gas jets, "enjoying" rainy holidays in Cornwall and being someone's part-time second-best week-end companion.

Here's Tom and Hugh, with the huntsmen carrying their bag—looks like jungle fowl. But—something's up, they look upset.

Later.

The first near-disaster. Tom and Hugh lost Butch. They were making their way back when Butch heard something—they think it was only a squirrel—and rushed downhill. They called and called but she did not come back. At the last camp a tiger had roared all night and kept us awake, and that morning we had passed eight men armed with spears who said they were after the tiger because it had taken a bullock. Ken was frantic, rushed into the jungle and had to be forcibly brought back. He was trembling and weeping, trying to call, "Butch! Butch!" between gulps. Tom sent men with torches and rifles to search round the lake, but after two hours they returned without having seen anything of her. It was then it occurred to me to use the radio. I got Hugh to get it going. It is a big powerful set run by batteries and has been carried in the pannier on Maung Taw, which originally carried the frig (which unfortunately met with an accident and fell off). I asked Hugh to turn it up full-blast so that if Butch had strayed—and not been eaten—she would hear it and find her own way back. It worked! After barely twenty minutes a grey object appeared out of the scrub-jungle and barked. All we could see of her after that was her tail, and its thump-thump on the ground, as she lay in Ken's arms. Then Ken ran to me. "Oh Waddy, you've saved me again!" He buried his face in my lap. Over the top of his head I saw Tom watching me.

Windermere Lodge, Maymyo,
March 15.

After nineteen days in the hills we arrived in Toungoo, spent two nights in the furnace of the plains and then came up to the hills again, to this wonderful place.

We had a bad two days on the road. Almost immediately after

parting from the elephants—that impudent Saw Chaw Hlaw dumped our stuff in a field and left for the hills—we saw Burmese dacoits at work. We were some miles out of Toungoo, passing a convoy of bullock-carts from a big Indian settlement in the town, when we noticed one of the carts lagging behind. Quick as lightning, two Burmese nipped out of the jungle and took away the cattle, while two others appeared to pounce on the drivers. Hugh ordered our constables to open fire, and the dacoits were sprayed with Bren guns.

Some miles further on we caught up with a platoon of Gloucesters who gave us grim news. They said the Japs had captured Rangoon on March 7th but the garrison had been evacuated, and last ditchers (was Hamish Waight among them?) completed demolition of oil-refineries, docks, harbour in five hours and were taken off to Calcutta by steamers standing by. They also told us Lower Burma was under martial law and there'd been a change of commands—Wavell back as C-in-C, and Alexander taken over from Hutton. One added, "What a way to fight a war! No planes, no wireless, no transport and no confidence!" Another said he couldn't tell a Chinese or Burmese from a Jap. They told us fighting was going on about a hundred miles south of Toungoo, and the Japs, they said, were advancing seven miles a day. We also heard the full story of the Sittang disaster, which took place the day we left Kaikun—Feb. 19. The bridge was blown up with most of our troops stranded on the enemy bank. The Gloucesters looked all in—their necks were covered with prickly heat and their cheeks with sandfly bites. Their only cheerful news was of the Chinese Army, said to be moving into Burma under the command of an American general.

At Toungoo we tried to get on a train, but the crush and heat made it impossible. Hugh and Tom got hold of two ancient cars and an even more battered bus, to take our gear. God knows how much money it cost them. We drove north up the Sittang Valley through Burmese villages where all looked peaceful—refugees crowding round wells or washing themselves and drying their clothes, and Burmese selling food, and where the road left the river, selling water! We drank quantities of coconut milk and bael fruit-juice, also horrible fizzy locally made drinks at roadside stalls. Distant blue hills appearing on our right made the plains seem all the more unbearable.

Contrived to get into Tom's car with Ken, Jemma and dog, Hugh driving the other with Mibs and servants. Our car broke down, so Tom and I spent the night in Meiktila in the Circuit House, which Tom said, was usually the best place to stay because it was reserved for "distinguished visitors." But it was very dim, and fans weren't working. Joined Hugh and party by lunchtime next day at Mandalay Club, where he and Mibs had spent night in far greater comfort than we had. Mibs looking one up and in a fresh dress, but Hugh was creating an "atmosphere." Knowing all I wanted was to get on up into the hills again and settle into Windermere Lodge, Hugh deliberately branched into romanticized description of life of old Mandalay kings and queens. The children naturally clamoured to be taken to see Mandalay's old royal citadel. Mibs especially insistent. She always pulls one way if she knows I am pulling the other. She resents my influence over Hugh and is stupid enough to think she can win. Hugh was being contrary, to teach me a lesson (because of my night, spent innocently, with Tom in Meiktila), so he agreed to take the children to the fort. I went with them but felt so itchy and headachy with the heat, refused to go inside but sat on the wall of the moat watching the gul mohur flowers reflected in the water.

Hugh, Tom and children back after an hour, and this time I decided to be diplomatic and went in Hugh's car. But I must be a Jonah. About eight miles out of Mandalay radiator boiled over. We left the car to cool down. Ken, who had come with me, very amused when I said I was ready to enjoy scenery above us— every hillock topped by a white, pink or gold pagoda, but refused to look down at the appalling plains. In the end he made me turn round to look at his "Mount Popa," a minute purple cone about a hundred miles away where live, according to Ken, the Mahagiri nats, the most powerful nats of Burma. He told me their story for the fourth time. It's a myth from start to finish. What a funny boy he is. He believes every word of it and assures me he once heard the nats in the mimosa tree on the mountain.

And so at last to Maymyo, where we arrived on March 10. Maymyo is my idea of heaven. Strange all my luck should come together. To be in a place like this with Tom and Ken! The climate is like a perfect English summer's day, but not as in England, once in a summer, but day after day. There is sunshine all the year round with small clouds and a blue sky. At the moment there are also strawberries for tea, and no washing up or weeding to do. What more can anyone want? As for the flowers—it's the first thing one notices after that ghastly "Dry Zone." All the English flowers, roses, hollyhocks, about fifty varieties of sweet-peas, as well as the exotic ones. Along the verandah of houses people hang baskets of orchids and train brilliant orange and purple Bougainvillia over trellises. The houses are very consciously "English style" with lawns, hedges, lavender paths and kitchen-gardens. Windermere Lodge might be a big rambling Victorian vicarage anywhere in the home counties, but with this difference: No poor curate's wife attempts to run it, but a person with ten servants and all too anxious to please her. These poor Indians know that their one hope of getting safely back to their own country is to stick to an English family—and ingratiate themselves with the Memsahib! Consequently, I don't lift a finger, and have all the day to enjoy Maymyo social life. There's plenty of it with a race-course, polo-field, wonderful parkland round a lake full of fish, and pine forests where bridle-paths are just right for my kind of horsemanship. We each have a pony—and each have a groom! I don't even have to fetch the children from school, for to school they all go—I insisted on it—Ken to St. Joseph's, and the girls to St. Michael's. It gets them out of my way—how I'm growing to dislike young Mibs—and leaves me free for social welfare and all the other activities of the Government House set. For I'm definitely *of* it, as Hugh is now on the Governor's staff as an adviser and I think has let it be known I'm no mere "housekeeper" but the person he'll soon be marrying. People receive me in a very friendly way and I must admit that this rather grand, official, privileged life suits me. Tom too has gone up in the world. He is in some kind of important liaison job with the Army and has offices in a big building on the Lashio Road. Windermere Lodge, like Government House, has quite a stream of distinguished comings and goings—ministers, generals, A.D.C.'s, liveried servants, and so on. I get the feeling, almost, of being royalty. It has gone to my head a little. I wouldn't mind being Mrs Hugh Chapman, if this is the way we'd live. Hugh's stock has gone up with me tremendously, but this is only while he's closeted with His Excellency next door. When he himself comes home to tea, sits down with that devoted look, and acts possessively, all I feel is irritation. Hugh is pressing me to fix the date of our wedding because, says he, it's "not too good" for his career to be living with "a single female." I told him he was being oversensitive. In wartime everyone is doubling up, and not even G.H. [Government House] stuffiness could object to me keeping house for him with our horde of chaperones. When I said this he asked, "What's the matter? Don't you want to get married? Don't you love me? If you don't, say so. And if you want to leave Maymyo and return home I could arrange to have you flown out."

What he was really saying was, "Unless you give in, I can turn nasty . . ."

Hugh doesn't take me in, and I don't suppose I take him in either. In a way we're well matched. He has guessed what I'm after, and he's ready to provide it even though he realizes I may not be in love with him. I am presentable, practical and fairly intelligent, and would make him a more suitable wife than most of the other females he meets here. He may suspect about Tom but discounts it, as Tom is a married man and therefore can't be seriously considered a rival. But Hugh doesn't know me. I'll put up with being bored and bullied by him because I am waiting for a sign from Tom, and when he gives it I won't waste another minute on Hugh. But first of all, I must be sure of Tom. It would be silly to sacrifice the very satisfactory life Hugh has to offer if Tom is not interested (or pretends not to be).

I'm getting to know Tom and Hugh far better since we trekked out together and since I've kept house for them. Tom is even

more woolly-minded than I imagined, but his sweet, vague,
unworldly way makes me love him more, not less. As for
Hugh—he's not as pliable as I believed and there's a streak of
niggardliness in him I never suspected. While Tom generously
continues to pay me a salary as Ken's governess, although Ken
now goes daily to St. Joseph's, Hugh makes Tom ante up for
my board and keep. I know there is some private arrangement
between the two over the running of Windermere Lodge, but
as it's probably discreditable to one of them—obviously Hugh—
both keep quiet about it! How men stick together! Hugh hands
over cash to me for the cook's daily bazaar. When I proposed
a round sum per week or month to cover all household bills he
remained silent. This is Hugh's way of saying "no" without actually saying it. I believe he feels the daily handing out of cash gives
him some kind of hold over me. Whenever an incident occurs
that annoys him—for instance, he wanted me to go to the races
with him, but I refused because I had already promised to go to
the Botanical Gardens with Tom—he carps over accounts, throwing me suspicious looks as if he suspected me of being in cahoots
with Mohammed Khan! Nice thought! The ex-secretary of Sir
Guy Burnett embezzling petty cash from a District Commissioner in Burma! However, a man as interested in money
as Hugh is promises to be a safer bet than someone as vague
about it as Tom. As Hugh's wife I'd never starve. Hugh's always
talking about his pension, his Provident Fund, his claim against
Government for furniture left behind at Kaikun, and all the
insurance policies I should have taken out before coming to
Burma!

The outcome of the veiled threat about flying me out of Maymyo is my capitulation over the wedding. I have agreed to let
Hugh announce the date anytime after the rains break. Everyone
agrees that the arrival of the monsoon will determine the course
of the war. The Japs have to throw us out of Burma before May
10–15, when the rains come—or call off the campaign. If we can
hang on till then—and everyone is certain we can—we'll have
virtually defeated the Nips. So that's settled. The month of May
will decide Burma's fate—and mine.

Having made this promise, I was plunged into one of my fits of depression. I've had ghastly dreams every night. In each I've lost something, my handbag or a train ticket, and I'm stranded in London without a penny. My feeling of loss is so intolerable I have to force myself awake, and sit up in bed sweating. Now I find myself almost hoping the war will go badly for us. If we are suddenly chucked out of Burma, the turmoil would be unspeakable, and in the chaos I'd shake Hugh off and somehow manage to get away with Tom and Ken for keeps.

March 20.

Hugh has played into my hands. He is off with H.E. on a wonderful trip and has been telling me how much I am going to miss because I delayed our wedding till May. If I had agreed to marry him the moment we arrived here, as he wanted, he says I would have been able to accompany him. H.E. has decided to make a tour of the Shan States to find out how the Sawbwas, Shan ruling princes, feel about the war. He wants to find out if they're going to back us, stay neutral or, like the Siamese, go over to the Japs. Since arriving in Maymyo I've heard a lot about the Shan States, which are fabulous mountain kingdoms inhabited by wild tribesmen and ruled in Wizard-of-Oz style. I must say I would have liked to go on a gubernatorial tour for its luxe as much as for the oriental ceremonial laid on. Hugh rubbed in all I shall miss—lake galas with dragon-shaped barges floating about, hillmen dancing with two-handed swords and women in turbans draped in silver and turquoise jewellery. I pretended to be disappointed but was silently having a laugh. Really I don't care how many sword-dances I miss. When Hugh goes off with the Governor for five days I'll have Tom to myself, and I'm already planning a few pleasant trips of our own and hoping we need not take those children. I do resent having the girls around. I've tried hard to win Mibs over, but she continues to glower at me and to act in a silly, possessive way over her father. I only wish she *would* keep him away from me! As for Jemma, she's an inscrutable child, but doesn't like me any more than Mibs does. Jemma's a fool. She should try to keep the right side of me, as the servants do.

The war news has taken a turn for the better—hence the Shan trip. Everyone got safely out of Rangoon, including General Alexander, who told us at dinner how he was trapped in a road-block and was allowed to escape by one of those stupidities that happen on both sides in wartime. General Slim is regrouping along the western front, south of the oil-fields, while above the eastern sector Chinese troops are already in the Toungoo area. Morale everywhere high.

March 21.

Governor's party set off early to the Goteik Gorge, and then they'll go to Hsipaw. H.E. and Lady D. in Rolls, bodyguard ahead, Hugh following with other officials. Felt so light-hearted wore new sharkskin suit (made by Anglo-Indian dressmaker, refugee from Rangoon) and ordered all Tom and Ken's favourite dishes, doctoring cream for strawberries with liqueur sold me, as a favour, by Club Secretary. Persuaded Tom to leave office early for a jungle-ride with me. On our way back I caught sight of Ken, also with his pony, on his way back from school. He wasn't riding but sitting on a bench, holding the reins, and talking to an old woman in Burmese dress. Daw Hla Palai! Tom also recognized her, but at my insistence, did not let her see us. Then I told Tom of my suspicions—during the trek I was sure I had seen her on two different occasions, once hanging about the camp, another time whispering to Ken. I had said nothing because I wasn't sure and didn't want to be alarmist. I persuaded Tom to test Ken. If at tea-time he openly spoke of meeting his aunt, there was nothing to worry about, but if he did not and appeared to be hiding something, then we should find out what was going on. As usual, Ken baffled us. He is so sweet, so honest, you wonder if he's acting the innocent, or if he is truly incapable of deception. Oh yes, said Ken, he'd often seen Daw Hla Palai since leaving Kaikun. It was part of their pact. He had promised to keep his eyes and ears open so that he could answer her questions. At this, Tom and I exchanged glances (just as parents do over their child!). Tom asked him, "Did you tell her the Governor left this morning?" Ken said she already knew this, also the names of the different Sawbwas H.E. was visiting. All she didn't know was which way the party was returning to Maymyo. "The way they went, I suppose," Tom said, but Ken knew better. One of the bodyguards had told him they were going down to the plains, completing the circle by returning through Thazi and Meiktila to Mandalay, and then up the hill to Maymyo. It seemed to us the kind of gossipy information enjoyed in the bazaar, so we let it go at that. Later Tom and I went to the Club and danced on the lawn, where fairy lamps had been strung between shrubs.

March 23.

Yesterday I suggested a picnic to one of the forest bungalows (as a Forest Officer Tom is free to make use of them) and Tom was all for it. The kids accompanied us, but mercifully went off to explore, leaving Tom and me in peace. We sat in companionable silence side by side on the narrow whitewashed verandah. These forest bungalows are beautifully sited with a watchman who usually plants a garden and keeps the place spotless. I'd often daydreamed about spending a honeymoon in one of them —with Tom! I was probably thinking along these lines when I heard myself say, "Hugh has asked me to marry him."

Tom didn't look up. "Yes, well, why don't you?"

"You know why."

"Yes." What was I to make of that? He put his hand over mine and kept it there until our skins seemed to melt into one. We must have sat like that, quite still, for some time. A slight noise made us both look up. It was Ken standing on the terrace and staring at us, his eyes fixed on our hands. Nothing was said. I walked to the end of the verandah to call the grooms. When the two girls arrived, we mounted our ponies and rode back to Windermere Lodge.

March 24.

Appalling news ended these peaceful days. The R.A.F. and A.V.G. have been destroyed. There wasn't much left of either after Rangoon, but we all hoped the forward wing at Magwe would be reinforced. Three days ago Jap bombers tore the place apart, destroyed thirty A.V.G. aircraft on the ground, and all but two or three Hurricanes. What's left of the R.A.F. has returned to India, and the Americans have gone off to China. So that's that! The Japs can bomb us and our troops whenever they like, as much as they like.

Everyone at Club, where Tom and I go every night for the whisky ration, is bothered by H.E.'s absence. The rumours from the Toungoo area are disturbing. Japanese are believed to be infiltrating. If they get up to their old tactics of turning our flank, it's a bleak outlook for Maymyo. The Japs could cut us off, and if they got to Lashio, where the Burma Road starts, they could cut off the Chinese from their supplies—and that would be the end of our Chinese allies. Very worrying. Shouldn't we go to India? Tom and Hugh are both anxious that I should fly out with the children, but I don't want to go—in fact, I refused to go—without Tom, and he can't leave yet.

March 25.

Just before dawn screeching tyres and honking woke me up. I ran to the window and caught sight of a jeep tearing by with unmistakable flappy hat and specs of the American General. *Now* what's happening? Top brass arriving like that at dawn made me thoroughly alarmed, and I didn't sleep anymore. By breakfast the news was all over the town. Toungoo has fallen. Does this mean it's only a question of time before Maymyo is attacked? Does this mean we'll have to pack up and leave Windermere Lodge? Can't bear to listen to this news—want to run away, put my hands over my ears. Tom and I were discussing it after breakfast when Ken appeared, looking green. I think he must have overheard us because he started off by saying, as there was a crisis, he had decided to tell us something which he knew, but had forgotten "to mention." It concerned the Governor's tour in the Shan States. When he last met Daw Hla Palai, he said, she told him she proposed to hold up the Governor's cavalcade on its way back from the Shan States, when it passed down the road near Thazi. There they were going to tie up poor H.E. and carry him off for sale to the Japanese Commander of Rangoon. I collapsed in laughter, but Tom took the story seriously. This was the raving of a dotty old woman, I told him, and implored him to do nothing about it. But Tom wouldn't listen and went haring off to Government House. A patrol was sent down, but just before tea the Rolls bowled sedately in. There'd been no ambush and Tom looked no end of a fool. Still, it provided something to laugh over during a gloomy evening. Tom and I went over to G.H. for drinks to hear all their depressing news. This concerned the refugees, a problem that gets worse daily and for which no one has any solution. With the fall of Rangoon the Prome Road-Taungap Pass exit to India was closed. The rumour went round that the Army was building a road to India from Tamu. It was more of a rosy dream than reality, though coolies were at work (but not one bulldozer in all Burma!). This was sufficient to start a stampede of refugees towards Tamu. Thousands upon thousands have arrived in Mandalay and Sagaing, where they've been told there is little hope of getting out via Tamu. When the road's finished it will be the Army's one route for supplies from India, and the Army's one escape route to India too. Naturally, the Army can't let refugees block it. Only five hundred are allowed through daily. For hundreds and thousands camped round Mandalay there's nowhere else to go. H.E. and Hugh passed these camps. No sanitation, no organization, and the few officials trying to cope are overwhelmed by the formidable numbers. Hugh said one doctor told him five hundred were dying daily of cholera in these camps. As the party's cars passed through Amarapura, the stench from unburied corpses lying just off the roadside followed them for miles. When Tom heard this he volunteered to go down to the plains to help. If he's allowed to go, I'm going with him.

April 4.

War's catching up with us so fast, what you decide to do one day isn't possible the next because that bit of earth has gone. Tom and I were going down to Mandalay to the refugee camps yesterday when he heard Mandalay had been bombed and was in flames with fire encircling the old Palace (how I regret not seeing it that day—now I never will), railway-station destroyed and direct hit on the fire-brigade garage. Tom went down the hill, but begged me to stay and look after the children. He returned home at midnight. He said as much damage had been done by fifth columnists, fire-raisers and looters as bombs. Hundreds had been killed, and there was no one to cart away the dead. He went back this morning. I now have the children on my hands all day, as St. Joseph's and St. Michael's are packing up to be evacuated to Bhamo. I suggested that the children went with them (by lorry to Mandalay and then I.F.C. steamer), but Mibs and Ken kicked up such a fuss at parting from their fathers, I gave in. Took children down the hill and saw black columns of smoke billowing up from Mandalay. On way back noticed three Buddhist priests lying under a tree. They were all dead, shot as spies by Chinese soldiers. Ken very shocked. It's doubtful that these men were spies, but Chinese soldiers suspect all Burmese pongyis and shoot them on sight. Saw several deserters, Chinese mostly. Club full of rumours; one is that the Governor's wife may fly to India. Villas emptying: most people going to Shwebo, where they hope to be flown out; others going by car filled with luggage, optimistically believing there's a road at Tamu and they'll get to India (plus possessions) that way.

April 5.

No papers. No soap. No ink. Tinned food scarce and very expensive. Cook afraid to go into bazaar because of Burmese ter-

rorists, so sent armed orderly with him. Rumours confirmed—
new Civil and Military H.Q. to be Myitkyina, and all Government departments packing up; files, desks, chairs stacked on bullock-carts going down to I.F.C. barges at Mandalay. Everyone
else off too. Club empty, everyone tense, waiting, even light
seems to be yellowing as before a storm. The Governor's wife
not flying to India but will go to Myitkyina in a few days. Alexander is to make a stand in North Upper Burma with 17 Div. to
look after us in the East and the Burma Div. guarding the Tamu
exit.

April 6.

It's getting me down. Try not to show it, but it is. Sometimes
wish I could get back to England and have done. Filled with
presentiment. Other times, with Tom, I feel it's going to be all
right. I've just got to stick it out and then . . . Children are adapt-
ing themselves better than me. Ken greets father, "What's the
bad news today, Dad?" Each kid has taken the name of a Chinese
general. Ken is "Ho," Jemma "Lo," and Mibs "Tu."

Chiang Kai-shek and Madame are in Maymyo, and their
visit also brought twenty-seven Japanese bombers! Our first air-
raid! For me a weird one after blitz. No proper siren warning,
only a whistle-blast. No ack-ack fire, no blackout. Jap planes
circled round leisurely to select targets (but didn't get Issimo
and Madame, if that's what they were after), dropped their
bombs in one big "crump" and flew off, one Zero cheekily lagging
behind to do a few aerobatics. Railway-station hit, also bazaar a
mess, and casualties mostly poor Indian traders. Stalls now
erected along roads. Dined at G.H. on 8th: strained atmosphere
because Madame Chiang Kai-shek had returned from visit to
Mandalay and was accusing stretcher-bearers (that includes
Tom) of tipping corpses into Palace moat. She cabled Churchill
about it, Hugh says. (Corpses were blown there after April 3
raid.)

April 13.

The Governor's wife off today to Myitkyina. She drives by car as far as Shwebo, then takes the metre-gauge railway and its one train a day to Myitkyina. Seeing her go off into the blue like this makes me depressed, and mood not improved by Ken, who has been hobnobbing again with that mad old woman. This time his story is Daw Hla Palai and her Thakins (it's "Thakins" now, not "Galons") are plotting to ambush the Governor's train. "Who is she going to sell this time? Lady D.? To Japs? Shans? I made fun of him and refused to listen to him anymore. Ken was most aggrieved. "You don't understand, Waddy." "What don't I understand?" "One day she might really do one of these plots. If she does you'll go for me. You'll say, 'If you knew, why didn't you tell me?'" I told him to talk it over with his father, from whom I guessed he wouldn't get much change—not after the last hare he'd raised. Nor did he. Tom made it clear if Daw Hla Palai pestered him, Ken was to bring the old lady back to have a word with him. "You should have forbidden Ken to speak to her and threatened him with a good beating if he did," I told Tom. He said weakly, "Beat Ken? I couldn't do that." I didn't pursue it. It's none of my business—yet.

April 16.

More disaster. Japs so near Yenangyaung oil-fields, they've been blown up. Without petrol and oil this war can't last much longer. They've started an airlift to India from Myitkyina—two American planes a day—but we can't leave Maymyo now, Tom and Hugh both say, until they can leave with us. At least this means we'll be going with the G.H. party, who'll have everything laid on, armed guards and a special coach on the train.

April 17.

Jemma announced she was off to Shwebo on her own to get on a plane to Calcutta. "Mr Waight promised to look after me.

He's going to pay for me to go to school in Naini." When Hugh told her it was too late she burst into tears. Strain telling on us all. As for Ken and Mibs, I could have whipped them when I found what they'd packed in rucksacks (all I'm letting them take). Ken's was full of tins of dog-meat, Mibs's of dancing-shoes, party-frocks and rubbishy jewellery. Strangely enough, Jemma's was full of bottles of mepachrine, three small bags of salt, and two pairs of canvas shoes and sensible clothes. When I asked where she'd got the mepachrine and what the salt bags were for, she refused to answer.

April 24.

Jap motorized columns said to be only eighty miles south of Mandalay, and Military are going to blow Ava Bridge. Let's hope this time they'll do it after their troops—and our party—are across. As predicted, Japs sweeping through Shan States to cut off Maymyo. The Chinese 6th Army, which is supposed to be fighting them, has vanished. Children put back into their rucksacks all the things I chucked out. Too tired to fight them anymore. If they're going to defy me, let them discover for themselves who was right.

We leave with H.E.'s party first thing tomorrow. Tom, Hugh, self, three children in one car; Mohammed Khan (cook) with Hanif (son), Fatima (mother), and the sweeper Nidhi Singh plus Ja-Bo (son) in another. Like the Chinese 6th Army, our Burmese and Karen staff vanished some days ago.

April 26.

This is noted in a deserted bungalow in Sagaing. We left Maymyo this morning, following the G.H. convoy down the hairpins. Every type of vehicle on the move—ambulances evacuating patients, bicycles with a baby strapped on handlebar, and every kind of refugee too with a percentage of Chinese deserters, in gangs, and with rifles. The Chinese were the only ones going up the road—towards Lashio and the Burma Road. The Maymyo Road was nothing compared to chaos in Mandalay, where streets were festooned in hanging telegraph wires, deep in rubble, burnt-out trucks and the dead.

Felt better once over the Ava Bridge. H.E. accommodated in D.C.'s bungalow—nothing for us but the pews in a mission church until an orderly found this empty bungalow. Children surprisingly helpful, but Butch is going to be a trial. Jemma put her hand over Ken's eyes when we passed the carcass of a horse lying between shafts of an overturned cart. It must have been trapped when the cart caught fire.

20

There was a last-minute switch in the travelling arrangements of H.E. in the Shwebo-Myitkyina train. Instead of using the special coach with its distinctive colour, coat of arms, and rear-observation window, he was asked to use, for security reasons, the standard first-class carriage which had been reserved for a member of his staff. Hugh Chapman and his party were given the special coach.

Ken, Jemma and Mibs entered this luxurious carriage with squeals of glee, but when Hugh told old Fatima, the cook, sweeper and Indian boys to climb in after them, they obeyed reluctantly. In the normal way the servants would have travelled third-class or in a special servants' cubicle attached to their master's first-class carriage. To travel with the Europeans was bad enough, but to enter the Lat Sahib's glory, this was too much for them. They squeezed themselves into as little space as possible, squatting humbly round the door of the W.C., their bundles in their laps.

"Why can't they go next door?" Miss Wadley demanded. Tom answered gently, "Because, my dear, there are already about thirty people there. We'll be lucky if we've only eleven in here by the time we reach Myitkyina."

Even a mild reproof from Tom upset Miss Wadley, who looked away and said no more. As the train drew out there was a stampede: brown arms and legs swarmed up the sides of the

Governor's special coach, using handrails, sills, anything, for hand- and foothold to reach the roof. Two youths ran alongside the carriage and at the last moment flung themselves against the door, clutching the handle and pressing frightened faces against the pane.

"I see what you mean," Miss Wadley said. When Tom let down the window, she helped to haul them in.

Japanese bombers had already breached the line in many places and there were continual stops, sometimes because the line was up, sometimes because of air-raid alarms. In fact, the train was strafed twice without casualties. Anxiety over bombing, however, was negligible compared to the suffering caused by heat. As more and more people fought their way into the "special," there must have been close on thirty people (plus two goats and Butch) packed into space suited to five or six. The heat thus generated must have been over a hundred degrees.

In days preceding the monsoon the Dry Zone of Burma exhales what feels like liquid fire to breathe. When the train was in motion faint breezes helped to cool the sweating travellers, but when it stopped, cold clammy patches formed wherever skin came in contact with the carriage.

Myitkyina should have been reached after a journey of about twelve hours, that is, by eight o'clock in the evening. But by midnight the train had not passed Kawlin, the station about half-way to Myitkyina.

When the train stopped yet again between stations, Miss Wadley noticed it had halted on an embankment approaching a bridge. Through low scrub she could see a river glinting in faint starlight. She could also hear voices and strange sounds. The voices were not those of driver and fireman, nor were the sounds those of clanking buckets, which usually signalled a halt near a river and the need to fill up the engine.

"Lots of pople are getting out. Can I?" Jemma asked.

"No."

Ken's excited voice proclaimed, "They're not getting out, they're getting in. And they're not our people. They're soldiers. They've got rifles."

Hugh and Tom leaned out. What they saw alarmed them, for they started pulling up shutters. "Dacoits! Lock the door. Keep your heads down."

Something hit the steel plating—there were more shouts. Miss Wadley was fumbling with a latch, trying to lock the compartment when the door swung open and she was grabbed round the legs and pulled out. She landed on her back on the track. It had happened so suddenly she lay dazed staring up at the night sky. Trying to roll over, she was hit, not by an assailant, but by something or someone else pushed out of the carriage.

"Jemma? I'm here. Don't worry. You're winded. It'll take a few moments." The girl lay gasping for breath, uttering high, frightened cries. "Lie still. I'll see if I can get you back into the coach."

But the door was locked. From inside someone was chucking out luggage, suitcases, bundles, tin trunks which were falling round Jemma. Miss Wadley helped her to her feet and propped her against a boulder. "Wait here. I'll be back. I must find the others."

In the darkness it was impossible to tell who were train passengers and who were train robbers. She heard Ken shout, "Butch! Butch!" and from inside the carriage the bleat of the goats. A few paces away a high-pitched hysterical voice shouted "Mohammed Khan! Mohammed Khan!" At first Miss Wadley thought it was a woman, but when she realized it was Hugh she ran towards him. "Hugh?"

"Shut up! What's the good of that? *Do* something!"

"Do what?"

She caught his hand and started up the track; then changing her mind, dived between two carriages, and, coming out on the far side, she halted.

"Uncouple his carriage. I'll go to the engine-driver. What do I say?"

"Say?"

"Don't be crass! Don't be stupid! Don't you yet understand what we're trying to do?" Miss Wadley stopped. As if speaking to a child, she added slowly, "How do I say in Burmese, 'Go—at once'?"

"You don't have to speak in Burmese. The Military are running the trains. And you don't have to speak to me like that."

"Sorry, but you're hopeless in a crisis."

"Thanks. I expect the driver knows how to behave in a crisis even if *I* don't, so leave it to him. Help me sort out this confounded thing."

But she refused to help him, preferring to run on to give directions to the engine-driver. When she had shouted her orders, a round blur appeared at the cab-window. Through the hiss of steam she heard a cockney voice, "Wot the blazes do you think we're doin' in this 'ell 'ole? Playin' marbles!" There was a pause. "'Ere we go, missus. Mind my bike!" With unbearable sluggishness, pistons started to work, arrows of light gleamed along the boiler, and wheels rolled. Four carriages passed, the last one the coach in which the Governor was travelling. As the train drummed away, black shapes ran down the line after it and there was the crack of rifle-fire. Miss Wadley dropped down the embankment and waited there for a few minutes before crawling back to the place where she had left Hugh.

"Congratulations! They'll give you an M.B.E. for this. Seriously —you really were splendid, darling."

Darling! She wasn't his darling, and his assumed nonchalance now that the crisis was partly over irritated her. "What's happening now?"

"They've arrested Tom."

"Whatever for?"

"They think he's H.E."

Passengers from the stranded coaches stood in a group, as sheep do when frightened. Their captors, like sheepdogs, circled round them, now and again hitting out with the flat of their dahs. One of these blows caught Ken.

"You dare strike me—jackal! Pig! Kala!" Ken swore in Burmese. "That's not the way for Liberators of Burma to behave!"

As Hugh approached, he exclaimed in English, "Liberators of Burma! They're a gang of hooligans." He raised his voice to

address the men guarding Tom. "Release the Thakin. He is a
Government official. You are going to get into serious trouble stopping a train."

"You cannot order us about anymore. We are soldiers of the
Burmese Nationalist Army. This man is the Governor of Burma.
We are going to hand him over to our Commander."

Ken called out, "Who is your Commander?" He used the
word "Boh." When the partisans heard the word, one asked, "Who
spoke then?"

"I did." Ken came forward. "You'd better let my father go.
I'm a Galon, and I know all about you, and I know your Boh.
Look!" He thrust out his hand. "Go on, take a look at what I've
drawn on my hand! Now do you believe me? I'm a follower of
Saya San too."

The insurgents clearly didn't know what to make of Ken. Others
joined them.

"I am Han Tha," Ken persisted, speaking excitedly. He walked
boldly between his father and one of his guards. "I'm not *the*
Han Tha, not the real one, but *she* calls me Han Tha. I am Han
Tha to the Old One." He stopped abruptly. His father was grip-
ping his shoulder. He told Ken in English, "That's enough," and
in Burmese to his captors, "Take no notice of my son, he is only
showing off. If you held up the train to kidnap the Governor,
you've wasted your time. I speak to you in Burmese. You know
well the Governor has only just come out from England and
does not speak your language. I'm an official—that's why I can
speak Burmese. Just an unimportant official, a Forest Officer,
so you'd better let me go. If you try to palm me off as the Governor of Burma you'll make yourselves a laughing-stock."

The youth who appeared to be the Leader answered, "We
don't mind being laughed at, and we are not fools. You are lying.
You are the Governor of Burma. You are also lying when you
say this boy is your son. He is Burmese and he says he is one of
us. We can soon find out if that's true." He spoke to one of his
lieutenants, who grabbed Ken. Tom tried to intervene.

"We won't hurt him."

"May I go with him?"

The Leader shrugged. "If you wish."

Ken showed no fear, whistled to his dog and walked along cockily. Nor did Tom seem unduly alarmed as he followed the young men into the scrub of the riverside.

"I know who's down there," Mibs said.

"Who?" Miss Wadley asked the question too sharply. Mibs retorted, "Nobody."

"Please tell us anything you know," her father said.

"All right, Daddy. I think it's Ken's aunt. The one with warts."

This was Hugh's guess and Miss Wadley's too. They waited without speaking again, while the hubbub among the passengers of the stranded coaches went on around them. After about quarter of an hour Ken reappeared with his dog but without his father.

"It's okay, everyone. I've fixed it. We can go."

"*You've* fixed it!"

"I know the Boh. That's what we call the Leader of the Galons."

"Not so fast." Miss Wadley confronted Ken. "Where's your father?"

Ken pointed down the hillside but said nothing.

"Why aren't you upset? What are they doing to him?"

"They aren't doing anything to him." Then he addressed Hugh: "Dad says to tell you—and Waddy—not to worry. He's okay. That's true. I know he is."

"What *do you* know?" In trying to suppress her emotion, Miss Wadley's voice sounded strange. "Tell me what you know, at once."

"But I don't have to, Waddy. You know already. And if you don't, you can guess."

Beside herself, Miss Wadley shook Ken. "What have you done?"

"I haven't done a thing."

"You told her which train."

"I did, but she didn't want it for Dad. She wanted it for the Governor. It's just sort of happened they got Dad. It's Karma."

Miss Wadley stared at him so wildly, Ken tried to wriggle towards Hugh.

"Dad doesn't mind, Waddy. He's glad. You see, they've promised to smuggle him back to Ahme."

"You and your father planned it." Her voice was flat.

"No, Waddy, we did not. It was an accident. But now it's happened I'm glad for Dad and . . ."

She turned her back on him. "If we are free, why don't we get back into the coach?" she asked Hugh.

"Please, Waddy, forgive me."

She kept her eyes on Hugh, waiting for his answer. With his long experience of the capricious Burmese, Hugh decided to get away before the rebels changed their minds. To return to the coach in the hope of being rescued by another train was unwise. "We'll have the bombers over by dawn, and every dacoit for miles will be turning up to loot what's left."

He called the passengers together. "I am the Lat Sahib's adviser. I want you to listen to me and do as I suggest. Start walking down the railway-line. The next station can't be far, and the Lat Sahib will probably have made arrangements for you to travel on to Myitkyina by other means. I don't promise this, but it may be so. If you remain here you may be bombed."

When he finished there were the inevitable counter-arguments, protests, discord, but he did not try to persuade them. "Do what you like. We're off."

He led the party down the cinder track, the children immediately behind him, the servants following, and Miss Wadley last of all. After a while Ken dropped out of line to wait for Miss Wadley. He tried to hold her hand but she shook him off. "It's too hot."

"Won't you ever be nice to me again?"

"Don't be silly and go back to your place."

"I did come back, Waddy."

She refused to comment.

"Dad said it was too dangerous both of us going back, but I could have persuaded him, I think. But I didn't try. I did come back."

She made an impatient gesture.

"I came back because I was sorry for you, Waddy."

This remark infuriated her. He did not mean to sound pitying, she knew that, but she could not control her burst of anger and hit him across the mouth.

21

April 27.

How could he do this to me? He has made a fool of me before Hugh—and the children. They all must know because Ken
must have told them. Tom's a coward. He ran back to the Burmese woman—who isn't even pretty—because he hadn't the courage to face up to her. Ken engineered it, and Tom weakly gave
in. But he *did* love me. He didn't have to put it into words. I
knew that day on the picnic, and that's when Ken knew it too.
Now Ken's laughing at me—they all are. And in a way I'm laughing at myself. Deserted—and for the second time. If a woman
allows that to happen twice, she's a fool. I'm sick of myself, of
Tom, of Ken, of this wretched Burma. Why did I ever come
here? Inveigled by romantic notions. It serves me right. I'm lying
on a towel in a bamboo lean-to put up by Ken and Hanif and
thatched by my own hands with bundles of bamboo leaves.
It's off a dusty road but not far enough off because I can taste
dust on my lips and feel it on my forehead and itching round
the roots of my hair. So much for the romantic East! But compared to other refugees I'm in clover. At least I'm not crammed
into a shed, or railway-carriage with ten thousand others, and
have plenty to eat and drink.

It took us four hours slogging down the line to reach the station. Platforms at first looked like a mortuary with corpses laid out in rows, but it turned out to be only Indians sleeping with heads and bodies swathed against flies. Children exhausted and fretful. Fatima's legs gave out and she had to be carried in turns by cook and grandson. Begged Hugh to find somewhere to rest in village—Ken suggested monastery courtyard—but Hugh refused. He had had a fright. We'd passed a family of Indians sheltering under a goods-wagon. They must have been there for days, place littered with rubbish and excrement. The man, doubled up, skin drawn taut over cheek-bones, appeared to be dead or dying. The woman was rocking to and fro, keening over baby, which was certainly dead. Certain signs (prolapsed entrails) convinced Hugh it was cholera. Two children, still fit, were also there, peering out pathetically at us. I suggested helping them, either taking them with us or finding a doctor, but Hugh would not hear of it, forbade any of us to go near them. Station refreshment-room full of Chinese soldiers cooking on the floor, and three B.O.R.'s who had been sleeping across tables and were polishing off "the last bottle of Scotch in Burma." They said they'd lost their "mates" and asked Hugh how to get to 'Omalin. Hugh said, "But Homalin's west. Aren't you supposed to be going north—to Myitkyina?" One replied, "Army's getting out. They should have blown the bridge by now." The other added, "If they got any matches. But 'ave they? No planes, no guns, no bombs. Wot makes you think they 'ave a box of matches?" Hugh's face was a study. He thought they were deserters and walked off, but I told them everything was going to be all right and they'd better join their unit in Myitkyina, where Army and Civil administration were all going. They were too drunk to take it in. Hugh made us walk four miles beyond the station before making camp. Ken silent, but insisted on making this shelter for me. Wanted to say I was sorry for hitting him, but could not. At the moment too hot to care what he thinks and too miserable and exhausted to sleep, even though Fatima is shampooing my feet.

April 30.

The first station after ambush was Kawlin; the next we reached was Wuntho. Hugh was sure something would have been arranged for us at Kawlin, but station-master said telegraph lines were down and there must have also been a derailment, as no trains were coming down. Two nights camping along line, buying eggs, bananas, green tea and rice from these sharp Burmese women traders who set up stalls along the refugee trails. Heat killing. Hugh very much in command, made us walk through midday heat of the first and second day. On third, we caught sight of stream running through a mango grove and I insisted we all stop for a bathe. Hugh refused, but we left him, myself in the lead. Fatima walked in fully dressed, silver anklets and all, and changed into dry clothes while standing in the water. Eventually Hugh joined us but giving me furious glances. "We've got to make Wuntho tonight." I said, "What does it matter? What does anything matter?" After a bit he relaxed and became gentle, asked if I'd like to camp there. I consulted Ken, the best I could do by way of a conciliatory gesture, and when he said yes, I asked him to help build the shelters. That evening we had a sing-song. It was the first time since we left Maymyo that anyone sang. Ja-Bo, the sweeper's son, made himself a flute from a bit of bamboo and accompanied Hanif's Indian songs. We lay on the ground beside the stream watching the cook's fire reflected in the water and the moon coming up over the thick black domes of the mango trees. None of those furtive attempts at love-making from Hugh. When I propped my back against his he gave a grunt. He'll come round, I daresay. If he does not, if he prefers it over between us, I don't care. Since Tom left I seem to have grown numb about everything.

May 1.

G.H. party did do something for us, after all. Station-master of Wuntho expecting us with rail-trolley, and news H.E. arrived safely in Myitkyina on the Tuesday—April 28. We are to go on the trolley, a kind of raft on wheels manually propelled, to Indaw and then by car to Katha on the Irrawaddy and up to Myitkyina by river-steamer, as no trains are getting through.

An odd sort of pang leaving the dusty road, wondering what was going to happen to some of the groups I'd been watching. There's the blind man being led by a girl—his daughter, I think. Mohammed Khan gave them cooked rice on two evenings. Another family for whom I was continually on the lookout was being led by an Anglo-Indian boy of about sixteen. He was responsible for two very elderly people, his grandparents, I imagine, and four children younger than himself, obviously his brothers and sisters. This boy used to help the decrepit old ones up the road, dump them, and return for the young ones, carrying the baby in his arms. In this way he walked twice the distance we did each day, which was never less than ten miles. I must look out for him in Myitkyina, and if possible help him into a job and see he has somewhere to live.

May 2.

After days of trudging through heat the trolley-ride cheered us all. To sit on this moving platform, usually trundling along a high embankment where delicious breezes billowed out our clothes, was such a treat we sang like people on a Sunday outing. The three men—Hugh, Mohammed Khan and Nidhi Singh —took it in turns with the three boys—Ken, Hanif and Ja-Bo—to work the handle while the rest of us—Fatima, Mibs, Jemma and I—slithered about on the pile of luggage to keep it from falling off. We travelled from dawn to dusk, stopping for snacks. At night, Nidhi Singh and Hugh slept on the trolley while the rest bivouacked nearby. Mohammed Khan should have shared this sentry duty with Nidhi Singh, but though he is a Muslim and supposed to be without caste prejudice, he nevertheless refused to lie down beside the sweeper. The first trolley-ride finished at sunset on the far side of a small town. As the trolley sung along the embankment we could look down on cattle coming in from the fields, kicking up a cloud of dust tinged with the sun's last rays. The buffaloes plodded through the village street as lamps were lit in all the small tea-shops. We caught glimpses of people sitting round tables sipping from shallow china bowls. We could also see the refugee road running parallel to the railway-line, and I couldn't help feeling a bit mean travelling so quickly and in such comfort with all those people—and the Anglo-Indian boy and his family—sweating away below.

May 3.

Got into Indaw at sunset, and at first thought the red glow was the sunset—but it was Indaw in flames. Bazaar, railway-station, hospital, school, shops, barracks, all blazing. And that wasn't all. Knew after one day's peace hell was sure to come—it has, in Hamish Waight. He was here, in the Indaw Club, where Hugh said we were to spend the night. We had to make a wide circuit of the smoking town to reach the Club and arrived dirty, dusty, tired and thoroughly bad-tempered. The Club itself was immaculate. Servants in white coats, drinks on the lawn, a gramophone playing, it did not seem possible that Indaw had just been bombed. (There hadn't been many casualties, I was told, because Chinese troops entering it three days before had looted warehouses and shops, and so frightened Burmese and Indian traders, most had fled.) When we arrived we were immediately shown into the changing-rooms and baths were filled. I told Mibs and Jemma to have theirs first, as I preferred to have the place to myself. When they were finished, in clean dresses, they went off to the Club rooms in search of Hugh. When I joined them Hamish was at the table, Jemma on his lap, her arms round his neck and weeping down it, presumably from joy. Hamish's first words were, "I hear Tom has sprinted home to Hla Gale. I thought he would. I'm glad." He gave me a meaning look and I felt my neck and chest flush. Under the tablecloth I felt Hugh groping for my hand. He held it tightly, even though there wasn't any danger of me losing my temper with Hamish. When I hate someone I'm in full control. I said nothing. It was Jemma who piped up, "And don't *you* leave me, Hamish, or I'll sprint back to you." He told her to shut up, but as he gave her an affectionate pat at the same time it encouraged her. She started pleading with Hugh, "Please let me go with Hamish. Why can't I go with him? Please, please, Mr Chapman."

Hugh said, "Mr Waight's joking. He's going to Myitkyina as he's been ordered, as we all have."

Hamish shook his head. "It's a muck-up. I'm off. We've lost the initiative, our morale's gone."

I said, "Didn't you know the Governor's gone to Myitkyina and Alexander's going to defend the North? A division's going to Myitkyina."

"Don't believe it. The Army's pulling out. So am I."

Hugh banged his glass on the table, but Hamish wouldn't let him speak. "You will never make a good civil servant of me. I don't care who signs the orders, I won't obey them if it means putting my head in a noose. I told the Military Secretary what he could do with his directive about officials staying to hand over to the Japs. He can do the same with this. The thing's crazy. The Commissioner of my division appointed me to close up the last districts of Burma—Shwebo, Meiktila, Thazi—and I've been telling people to get out and helping them burn their treasuries. And you tell me now—when we're all off—to go on to Myitkyina. Ridiculous! I'm getting out, everyone is with any sense."

Jemma continued to hug him. "I can walk fast. I'm coming with you, Hamish, darling. Which way are we going?"

He looked at her and smiled and then said to Hugh, "Why not? Shall I take her? I don't see why she shouldn't come with me. I'll take the car as far as Pinbone where the road ends, then we'll have to walk. Can you swim, child? We've got to get over the Chindwin—but provided we get over the hills before the monsoon, it won't be too bad. A month to get to Irrakpore, I reckon. From there, they say, trucks are lifting people to Dimapur, where you get the train to Calcutta. I'll take care of her, Hugh."

Hugh looked at me. Hamish seemed to assume Hugh had given his consent, because he pushed Jemma off his lap. "Go and pack your things. We're leaving in a few minutes in my car."

Jemma started whooping and dancing round the table, stopping to give Hugh a hug. I think she was about to hug me too when I said, "I won't have it."

Jemma said rudely, "It's nothing to do with you. Mr Chapman says I can go."

"It may not be anything to do with me, but I'm not going to allow this. There's a law about minors, Mr Waight. If you take her, I'll have you run in."

Hugh tried to shut me up, and my own sense of propriety told me to hold my tongue, but the devil got into me. I hated Hamish for his "I'm glad." Which was as good as saying straight out he was "glad" Tom had left me, "glad" Tom had gone back to his wife. I was out to hurt him as he had hurt me, even though I knew perfectly well Hamish is not the kind to touch a young girl. I went on and on, insinuating, threatening, while the two men looked at me in a horrified way. When Jemma started to weep I dragged her from the room. Everyone stared. I shoved her in the ladies room and said I'd have her food sent in. Between sobs she asked, "Please, Miss Wadley, can I come back if I stop crying?" I said, "No," and loathed myself.

I went back through the Club dining-room and was still so het up I remember quite enjoying the loathing I'd aroused. "Coming, Hugh?" Where I wanted him to go, I'd no idea, all I knew was there must be a showdown to establish whom he sided with, Hamish or me. Hugh gave me a slight nod, said something to Hamish, and I led him towards the lawn.

May 4.

Awake all night, revolted with myself. To have one kid less would have been a blessing—what I did was against my own interests. Hugh and I didn't have much to say when we walked on the lawn. I was trembling and he held my arm as if to say I wasn't wholly to blame. What he did say was Hamish wasn't the only one convinced that Civil and Military were packing up. I guessed Hugh wanted me to reassure him that he was doing the right thing by going on to Myitkyina. He was standing by me, so I decided to stand by him. I said people like Hamish were making panic decisions. The Governor would not have gone north unless the Army meant to hold on to North Burma. "We're not going into the blue, as Hamish seems to think," I said. "We're following H.E. and his Ministers and all the Heads of Departments. Myitkyina is where Burma is now being governed, so whatever's left of law and order and military protection is there and not down the road at Pinbone. I don't see how skedaddling west helps anyone."

It was what Hugh wanted to hear. He said, "Even if the Japs take Lashio and go up to Myitkyina they've only got an earthroad from Bhamo and they'd arrive in Myitkyina on the wrong side the river. Myitkyina is headquarters of the Frontier Force and there's an airfield."

Worried over this conversation all night, wondering if I'd advised the right course. Before last night's showdown, Hamish had offered to drive our party to Katha on the Irrawaddy, where Hugh heard that one hundred I.F.C. steamers had arrived on their way to Bhamo, where they were probably going to be scuttled. Hugh's plan was to travel as far as Bhamo on one, there find a small river-boat with an engine—failing that, a country-boat—and get to Myitkyina by water. As it would save walking, I was all for it.

Hamish couldn't very well get out of this arrangement, so early next morning I found myself in his lorry sitting with Jemma between us, the rest of the crowd behind with several drums of petrol Hamish said he had "found." We drove eighteen miles to Katha in silence punctuated by Jemma's sniffs. When we arrived at the I.F.C. landing-stage, all we could see were decks, gangways, funnels sticking at crazy angles out of the water while Burmese men, women and children swam around searching for loot. We learned that during the night parties of R.E.'s with explosives had been busy "denying" the fleet. There was nothing for it but to go back—this time to Naba Junction, where Hamish thought we might find another rail-trolley. No luck. So back we went to Katha again to see if there was some sort of

craft to take us up the river. While Hamish and Hugh were looking for it, I tried to make it up with Jemma, but she's a bundle
of nerves, wouldn't listen, and when Hamish suddenly appeared,
threw herself into his arms and started wailing again. Hamish
threw me a look of hatred, assuming I'd been bullying her. Let
him think what he likes, but being disliked bothers me even when
I don't care a damn for the individual concerned. A boat with
an engine of sorts was found. A party of Bush Warfare men with
some Anglo-Burmese refugees had brought this small river-boat
up from below Mandalay but had run out of petrol. In exchange
for the drums in Hamish's lorry, they agreed to take us to Myitkyina. This involved putting off the Anglo-Burmese, all men of
Burma Railways who had stayed to the last at their posts. It was
a most distasteful job for Hugh. Boat turned out much smaller
than I had hoped and we could each take only one small case.
We repacked for the hundredth time. No room for my new Maymyo dresses—including the sharkskin suit. So upset I chucked
them at dockside pilferers, and regretted it when I saw some
Burmese women-traders barter eggs, fruit and those useful,
pretty Shan bags with Hugh for what he was bound to discard
—riding-boots, a crocodile-skin suitcase, dinner-jacket and so on.
A week ago this scene would have struck me as typical of
Hugh, of his money-grabbing, niggling, penny-pinching character. It's strange I don't see it in that light now but a perfectly
sensible thing to do. Hugh seems to be much more sure of himself since Tom left. He no longer irritates me. Is it because he
is less apologetic and more dominant, that I respect him more?
Perhaps I'm the one who is changing.

Mibs pounced on those Shan bags, grabbed the prettiest for
herself, and threw the others towards me. Hugh made her pick
them up and asked me to choose the one I preferred. I deliberately took Mibs's one to teach that young woman who, from now
on, is boss.

Shwegu, May 4.

Left Katha at 3 P.M. and managed to sail about forty miles up
Irrawaddy before the light failed. I'm now entering up my diary

on the verandah of a deserted bungalow perched on the bank overlooking the river. As we tied up, the sun was setting, and the river-craft lining the shore stretched for miles—huge rafts with small huts lashed on them, fishing-boats, sampans and some odd-looking country boats with forked prongs and a sinister eye painted on the prow. The sun was pretty enough in the orange light, but now the river is nothing but a faint milky glow with the first mists wreathing across it. By morning, Jemma says, they will form into a solid bank of fog.

The motorboat is a disappointment. How we're all going to spend several days in it, I dread to think. It's smelly and noisy, difficult to steer, but it is of shallow draft, so we should be all right over shoals and sandbanks, of which we've heard so much from Jemma. The canvas awning, for the uprights, was missing, so we're all suffering from sunburn. Still, we're lucky. We passed sampans full of refugees, who will have to row if the wind drops. Rowing two hundred and forty miles in this heat isn't my idea of fun. The Bush Warfare group number ten, the same as us (now Tom has gone), and a very odd assortment they are. The C.O. is a captain of the Seaforth Highlanders who has been training irregulars in sabotage and intelligence in—as he said— "the establishment at Maymyo." But I never heard of a "Bush Warfare" establishment there. With him are four British other ranks, a White Russian from Harben who speaks Chinese, a Karen from the Burma Rifles, a Gurkha (from Maymyo, not Nepal) who in civil life is a strawberry-grower! The two Indians are V.C.O.'s, Viceroy's Commissioned Warrant Officers, and Hugh tells me I must address them as "Jemadar Sahib." They were sent to the Goteik Gorge to blow up the viaduct. They laid the charges and prepared for blowing but had to wait for the okay because the viaduct was part of the Burma Road System and under the control of the Chinese Government. God knows if the Chinese ever sent their permission. The Bush Warfare Group had to withdraw to avoid capture and, believe it or not, left the bridge intact for the Japs.

First hour everyone very chatty and friendly—as meetings between total strangers usually are. We heard about the soldiers' adventures "denying" treasuries, banks, power-stations, railway-yards and so on from Mandalay northwards. One was wounded when his own bullet ricocheted off the lock of the strong-room door of the Chartered Bank. Plastic charges finally blew the vault open and it was "an Aladdin's cave, stuffed full of jewellery, bars of gold, silver candlesticks."

So stiff after sitting squashed up on the bench for two hours, I asked if we could tie up and have a bathe and stretch our legs. The Captain looked at me as if I were mad. "We're not on a picnic, madam. We're approaching a village, and that's the last place I'd choose to stop." He made us crouch as we passed "the village"—a few primitive huts on stilts—revving up the engine so we shot past with maximum noise, enough to alert Japs for miles.

"What's the point of this?" Hugh asked. "We're bound to stop at villages for the night, and villagers are usually very friendly, especially in Kachin country."

The Captain glanced at the children but did not answer. It was Ken who did. "It's okay, sir, we're used to frights. Our train was ambushed. Are the Japs there, sir?"

"We're not sure, but we're taking no chances."

Hugh laughed. "You haven't much faith in Alexander, have you?"

The Captain answered, "If you mean, will Alex get out before we do? No, he won't. He's walking out, but if we make Myit-kyina, we'll get out by air."

Hugh shook his head. "We're not going to be thrown out of Burma, and General Alexander is not walking out. When you do get to Myitkyina you'll find Army Headquarters very busy and the Government functioning normally. I'm sure you won't want to fly out then."

It sounded as if Hugh suspected them of being deserters, and they seemed to take it that way because a hostile silence followed.

After a while they started chattering to the children but excluded Hugh and me. The person who won their attention was not, as it usually is, Ken or Mibs, but Jemma. She started off by saying she was glad in a way her father was dead because if he'd been alive and seen all his beautiful ships lying scuppered in Katha, it would have broken his heart. She spoiled the impression that her father owned the I.F.C. by going into her rather undistinguished antecedents. Her father was for some time the Buoying Superintendent, later the captain of a paddle-steamer. "We had our own piano in the saloon," she boasted. "I know every channel from Rangoon to Mandalay, and Mandalay to Myitkyina. I know the Chindwin too. I know them so well, I could pilot you in a fog because I can 'smell' them, like my daddy could. We never needed a pilot in the Defiles . . . Shall I tell you about the Defiles? They are . . ." But here I had to intervene and told her she was showing off and boring people who weren't on a conducted tour. The Captain butted in, "She's not boring me. Is she boring you?" He asked his men, and they obediently shook their heads. "She's a most knowledgeable young woman and she's going to be a great help when we travel at night." He made room for her beside him, and Jemma crossed over while Mibs sniggered and Ken pretended to be taken up with Butch. Hugh backed me by diverting attention from Jemma. "It's unheard of to travel by night. Even the I.F.C. steamers put in. I'm afraid I can't allow it."

One of the Tommies snorted, "Can't allow it! 'E'll 'ave to lump it, won't 'ee, sir, or do the other thing."

At this point, fortunately, Butch started barking and making frantic efforts to leap out. She had caught sight of otters on a sandbank. It took Ken as well as the three B.O.R.'s to keep her in the boat. The disturbance helped to restore friendly feelings. By the time the tips of Shwegu's pagodas appeared over the sandbanks—there are thousands of them, they line the banks for miles and cover one island—we were all so sticky and hungry there was no question of going further. But the soldiers' conviction that Japanese might be in the vicinity made us all jittery. No one wanted to go up the steps leading from the river into the town. We stood about indecisively until I said, "Mr Chapman is one of the Governor's advisers. He's the one to tackle local officials."

In other words, I established Hugh as the party's V.I.P., and from then he took charge. Interesting to observe the effect on him, but so it is with everyone, I think! Once a person is expected to dominate, dominate he does. I must say I liked it when Hugh expected me to obey him. It's a relief to hand over responsibility to someone else. I get so tired of having to control other people because they are either too stupid or too weak to exert their own wills. Hugh asked me to go with him to the Headman. Village surprisingly clean, and under a cat's cradle of palms, beautiful. Many refugees and Chinese soldiers about but none of the atmosphere of hysteria of Katha and Mandalay. The moment the Headman's wife saw us, she announced her husband was away, but when Hugh spoke Burmese and told her who he was, her manner changed and she invited us into her house, where, of course, we found the Headman. After drinking Shan tea in shallow bowls, the Headman led us to the forest bungalow. Elsewhere refugees were sleeping twenty to a room, he said. Mohammed Khan bought fish and vegetables for us and the soldiers, who were without money, said they'd been foraging and produced a lobster. Mohammed Khan included it in our fish stew, which we all shared, servants too, eating off leaf-plates. It was delicious. Afterwards, though dropping with fatigue, Hugh took me for a walk by the river while the soldiers and children had a sing-song. Hugh decided where everyone was to sleep—including the Tommies, who had to shake down on the verandah. They accepted his officiousness pretty calmly, I thought. There were only two rooms and no beds, only mats. Hugh, Ken, the Captain and the White Russian slept in one room, and the two girls, Fatima and I, in the other: at least that was the first arrangement. Then Hugh discovered a minute room at the back, which he said I could use. I was too exhausted to care where I slept but was glad to be saved from Fatima's pungent biri-betel-nut smell. As I was dropping off, my door opened stealthily and someone crept in beside me. Ken? A man's strong hand turned me over. It was Hugh.

NOTES FOR TWO DAYS.

Bhamo, May 5, and Talawgyi, May 6.

We weren't able to leave Shwegu till 9 A.M. because a bank of mist sat stubbornly on the river. I didn't care. Breakfast sitting next to Hugh, with electric currents passing between us wherever our bodies touched or hands and feet brushed against one another. We never exchanged glances but our awareness of each other was so intense it seemed strange everyone didn't notice it. Perhaps they did. I have an idea the children did—in particular, Mibs.

At the hottest time of the day we had engine-trouble, the breakdown taking place in one of the wide expanses of water between gorges, for we were passing through the famous Second Defile. (Jemma, "one of the seven wonders." Yesterday I could have contradicted her, but today I feel too benign, too happy.) I didn't ask anyone's permission to leave the boat this time but stood up, quietly dived straight in off the side! Everyone dumbfounded. Ken was in next, then one by one all of them, even Fatima, slid in. The old woman went in with anklets, armlets, everything. She held on to the boat with one hand while her nose-ring floated level with her cheeks.

All day a curious mood possessed me, without thought, aware only of light, colour, landscape. The glare off the water distorted reflections so that drifting meadows of water-hyacinth seemed to float in the dome of the sky and clouds to chase about among the pebbles. A black cormorant perched on floating timber held out its wings to dry, white sea-swallows screamed and flashed over the sandspits. It was inexplicably disconcerting to sail into the gorges, feel shadows engulf one, see the water, a moment before blue and dappled with clouds, change into grey oily whirlpools. The passage between the cliffs is so narrow it could be measured in yards. The cliffs themselves rise sheer for hundreds of feet, their lower rocks slimy, but halfway up, where the sun strikes them, covered in tawny grass, sprouting trees and an occasional pagoda.

How did anyone scale up there with bricks? This was my pre-occupation almost all day, and not the problem of the Bush War-fare men. They have left us—in Bhamo—where we spent the night in the P.W.D. [Public Works Department] bungalow. They picked up gossip—"and it's nothing but gossip," Hugh said—that Japanese patrols are infiltrating. They abandoned their plan to get flown out from Myitkyina and, with a map cut out from the *Daily Express*, spent all yesterday and most of today working out the best point to leave the boat. Jemma, who really does seem to know this river, told them to get out by the Mogaung River mouth and go up it by native craft to Mogaung and then to Kamaing, Maingkwan, and so into the Hukong. Hugh told them to do no such thing. He said even a properly equipped expedition—the kind taken annually by the political officers of the Frontier District—wouldn't get through so near the break of the monsoon. If caught in the Hukong in the rain, when the malaria mosquito breeds—"well, it's suicide," Hugh said. Their Captain listened politely, but when we reached the mouth of the Mogaung all ten got out.

They've gone, that's that. It doesn't seem to matter. Nothing seems to matter to me except Hugh and to try and fathom what's happened to us. One day I'll look back and know this time, idling along in this noisy, smelly motorboat, the children playing card-games with the servants, Hugh and I trailing our hands in the water—this time was the happiest in my life. I know it now. Few people are lucky enough to realize at the time that certain days, hours, minutes must be lived to the full, because they are the best one ever had. Most honeymoons are dismal, but ours is per-fect: we shall come back here, if H.E. can spare Hugh for a few days, after we are married. We've decided to try to find someone to marry us on our first day in Myitkyina. Everyone has sensed what is happening—even the Serang eyes me. The Serang smokes a pipe filled with toasted shreddings of banana leaves and opium. There's no secrecy or disgrace attached to this addiction, and I'm in such a strange mood I feel tempted to try the stuff.

Hugh says the Serang gets his daily ration from police outposts, or the District Commissioner's office.

"I had large black cakes of opium in my vaults in Kaikun. I wonder what Hamish did with the stuff?"

Hamish . . . not even Hamish can ruffle me. As for the children, they are suddenly no trouble. Our closeness has driven them towards Mohammed Khan, Nidhi Singh and Fatima. Since the soldiers left they have played cards with them at the other end of the boat, and I see Mibs resting her head against Fatima, while she watches us with sad, hostile eyes. Ken trimmed her hair with his dah—and then cut his own toenails with it.

I must try to be more understanding with them and try to help Mibs accept me. Something Hugh said at Shwegu sticks in my mind. After we had left the Headman he said, "You know, even though the Burmese are intolerant of foreigners—xenophobia is part of their history—they are always beautifully polite. This is because they are taught never to show disrespect of others."

Was Hugh sniping at me? If he was, I deserve it. All the cracks in my personality are beginning to show, even to me, and I'm determined to mend them. Falling in love is giving me insight. It really never occurred to me, I haven't respect for others.

22

When the first glimpse of Myitkyina revealed the silhouette of a town without a rug of smoke in the sky, without flames licking up from rooftops, Hugh's relief was greater than anyone else's. He had been playing with the Bush Warfare men, as with others, the old game of the official, reassuring in the interest of public morale when he himself felt far from secure.

The Irrawaddy doubled back on itself after giving them this initial view of their destination. For what seemed hours afterwards they were tantalized by miles of grey-green jungle baking in an endless plain. The river finally made a loop, resumed its northerly course, and on the left bank disclosed a town, primitive and straggling but made attractive by a background of distant hills. They approached down a channel nearer the right, or east, bank from where they could see sheds and huts marking a river ferry's embarkation area. What Hugh saw here filled him with alarm. Myitkyina's ferry connected the town with the earth-road from Bhamo, a road of great strategic importance if, as everyone believed, it would be the enemy's main invasion route. Hugh had expected to see the Military controlling this point, with police to keep refugees in order. But there was no evidence of authority of any kind. Landing-stage, road-approaches, river-banks were jammed with refugees, amongst whom groups of uniformed men could be distinguished. It looked too as if many hundreds had been waiting to cross to

Myitkyina for days, as there was a large encampment in the riverside jungle. As for the transport that blocked the road, it was of
every kind, military as well as civilian—from jeeps and armoured
cars to bicycles, bullock carts, trains of mules and a few elephants.

As the motorboat changed course for the west bank, the ferry-
boat could be seen leaving from the town jetty. Its departure
created excitement on the east bank. There were shouts, the
sound of engines revving up, and from every direction a surge
towards the landing-stage. The hubbub ended suddenly with the
crack of rifle-shots.

Jemma showed no concern. "Soldiers shooting refugees, I expect."

Ken was indignant. "Soldiers don't shoot refugees. Soldiers
never shoot their own side."

"They do. What about deserters? They have special firing
squads for deserters."

"You get everything wrong, purposely. They're firing above
their heads to make them behave, like Mr Waight makes his
police do in a riot."

Hugh said, "Will you kids shut up. Try and help. Try and
see what's going on in Myitkyina."

"Nothing's going on there, Daddy. It's a dirty old place with
houses on stilts and pigs running about underneath. I can't see
a single nice bungalow like Maymyo. Myitkyina is awful. Myitkyina is the end."

Miss Wadley said, "I think it's delightful. Look at that curious
hill, Ken. Doesn't it look like an extinct volcano?"

"Yes, Waddy, but with all those refugees—you can see them,
look, moving like sludge down the road—will there be room
for us? I mean Mibs is right. There are no nice bungalows. Will
we have to sleep on mats on the floor from now on?"

Hugh asked, "Which road?"

When Ken pointed it out Hugh answered, "That's a road leading out of the town, so all the more room for us. Don't worry.
We'll get a bungalow to ourselves. H.E.'s in the D.C.'s house, on

the river, and we'll probably be nearby in a nice riverside bungalow."

"See if you can spot the Governor's house," Miss Wadley said.
"There'll be a flagstaff, won't there, Hugh?"

"Expect so." Hugh was standing on the narrow quarterdeck
beside the serang, to whom he was doling out silver rupees from
a bag held by Mohammed Khan. "When we land, keep together.
I'll lead. Mohammed Khan can bring up the rear. Ken and
Jemma, will you two please make Fatima keep up?"

Whatever the pace, the cook's old mother managed to keep
up remarkably well, but always at a distance of twenty yards behind everyone else.

"But if the D.C.'s house is on the river, why don't we land
there? What's the point of landing in the town and battling our
way through crowds?" Miss Wadley asked.

"Daddy knows best," Mibs retorted.

"Don't be rude," Hugh snapped at his daughter. "Will you
kids behave! As if we hadn't enough on our plate." To Miss
Wadley he added, "You're right, but there's a chance we
wouldn't be allowed on shore there—there'd be sentries and
so on. Better present ourselves in the conventional way."

It took them an hour to reach the shady road which led to the
line of official residences built, as in Kaikun, overlooking the
river. Their scramble through the town unnerved them all, not
only because of distressing sights seen among refugees, but from
the alarming rumours they were spreading.

Hugh hesitated near the Circuit House, wondering whether to
book rooms in case no bungalow was immediately available. One
glance revealed a compound overrun by Indians of the poorest
kind, cooking, washing clothes, stringing them to dry between
trees: the place had become a refugee camp. An Indian youth
in a Gandhi cap came up to him. "You are wanting accommodation, no doubt?" Hugh explained they were on their way to
Government House.

"No Government House in Myitkyina, sar."

Hugh agreed, explaining he was going to the D.C.'s house,
now the Governor's residence.

"I can see you are also Government servant, sar, of executive rank, sar, kindly to help me. I am also Government servant of Department of Information and Broadcasting. I am receiving notice to depart from Maymyo to here and I am coming here with five A.I.O.s [Assistant Information Officers] for three weeks and much hardship, sar. Now . . ." He was becoming agitated, plucking at Hugh's sleeve. "What to do, sar? Much pay is due, six weeks' pay, and I am not finding Principal Information Officer to tell, sar. I have no money. I have not eaten for four days, sar." He looked at Hugh helplessly. "If we make deputation, sar, Governor Sahib is receiving us, you think, sar? Perhaps you are saying a word in the ear, sar. Six weeks' pay due . . . starving . . . so much hardship."

The Assistant Information Officer's words followed them as they hurried on towards a house where the tip of a flagstaff could be seen above trees.

"That's funny, no flag," Mibs said. "They always had a flag in Maymyo." Hugh had also noticed that none of the scarlet-and-gold-uniformed messengers whom one met on roads near a Governor's residence appeared to be about. Nor was there a sentry on duty. As they turned in at the drive they found the sentry-box lying on its side. It was quiet—too quiet. A crow cawed from a palm tree, and as they walked down the drive the crunching noise of gravel seemed abnormally loud. When the house and garden came into view, everyone halted. At first no one knew how to read the signs. On the steps of the house, on the drive, all over the garden packing-cases lay about, some nailed up, others half-packed, straw sticking out at the top. Here and there piles of china, books, silver, lay as if waiting to be packed. An old man, a Shan butler in black trousers and white jacket, was making feeble efforts to tidy up, picking up one article at a time. Under the trees a groom sat holding the reins of a fine-looking horse, and not far away lay the most incongruous sight of all, a large oval tray of silver on which stood silver teapot, milk-jug and sugar-basin.

What was happening? Was H.E. in residence, or wasn't he?

Had the place been looted? Was the Shan butler packing or un-packing?

Miss Wadley looked frightened. "We'll have to go in and see what's happening. We'd better take Mohammed Khan and Nidhi Singh—just in case."

"And leave us alone. Oh, Daddy! . . ." Mibs wailed.

Her father gave her a little shake. "Do stop that, darling, nothing's happening. The servants will stay here and look after you. Now, please don't start being troublesome."

As Hugh and Miss Wadley walked up the steps a small, silky-haired spaniel came out, took no notice of anyone but slumped down on the verandah, head on its paws. Butch bounded over to her and she obligingly rolled over on her back, but her interest soon evaporated and she rolled over again to stare morosely down the empty drive.

Hugh led Miss Wadley through two rooms, where carpets lay rolled up and the floor was cluttered with stacks of files and reams of official notepaper.

"Where's his bodyguard? Where's anyone?" Miss Wadley whispered. "If anything's happened, if he's been assassinated—what do we do?"

Hugh opened a door into a room, overlooking the river, where four white men sat at a table with glasses of beer, paper and pencils. Three were colleagues—Steve Halpern, Colonel Shean, and Bob Thorpe—with whom he had been working in Maymyo on the Governor's advisory staff: the fourth, Tom La Touche, was the District Commissioner of Myitkyina and an old friend.

"Where's H.E.?"

They stared at Hugh. Someone asked, "Where have you sprung from?"

"For God's sake—what's happened?"

"Late, aren't you?" That was Steve Halpern, a businessman, a wartime importation on the Governor's staff.

"Our coach was attacked. I got through to the station-master here on the twenty-eighth. He said H.E. arrived safely."

"Arrived safely and departed safely, old boy."

"When is he expected back?"

Halpern did not answer but drew up a chair for Miss Wadley. "Come and sit down. Find some beer, Bob."

Hugh interrupted him. "I asked—when's H.E. expected back?"

"Back? You *are* out of touch," La Touche said.

"I've been walking up the railway-line and from Katha got in an old motorboat."

"The Governor flew to India on the fourth," Halpern answered.

"The fourth? What's today?"

"Thursday the seventh. He governed Burma from Myitkyina for six days exactly."

Thorpe opened a bottle of beer for Hugh and another for Miss Wadley while Hugh sat in silence staring across the river.

"What went wrong?"

Colonel Shean sat back in his chair. "You remember the flap when Wavell came to Maymyo?"

Hugh nodded. "April first or second." It was obvious by that date that the Army would have to pull out of the oil-fields, so the C-in-C had flown out from India to work out new plans with General Alexander. The ramifications of the General's decision, where it applied to the civil administrators, had been a nightmare. For a start, joint Army and Civil H.Q. at Maymyo was changed, the Army leaving Maymyo for Shwebo but the Civil Government remaining there. If the invasion pushed the Army further north the General decided to set up H.Q. at Myitkyina, where the Civil authorities would also move all Government departments.

"Once the Army went off to Shwebo I knew they wouldn't keep in touch—we all said so—and they didn't," Halpern said.

The invasion had indeed pushed the Army further north. When Japanese tanks broke through at Loikaw it triggered the move—as arranged in early April—of the Civil Government to Myitkyina. It should also have triggered the move of Army H.Q. to Myitkyina—as agreed in early April between Alexander and Wavell.

Halpern went on, "Loikaw forced the generals to change the first plan. They thought up a new one—to get out. But they neglected to tell the poor bloody Civil Government. That's why H.E. came up here."

"Didn't inform H.E.!" It was inconceivable. "But there are liaison officers—Tom McNeil is one. Didn't he know?"

"Oh, some liaison officer did eventually find out, quite by mistake, I believe. But by then H.E. had gone into the blue. When they caught up with him he was sitting innocently somewhere in the Triangle, having a day's fishing."

"You mean he only heard the Army had pulled out *after* they'd pulled out? He'd no idea . . ."

"Neither H.E. nor a hundred thousand refugees. When H.E. found out he cabled Churchill, who told him to fly to India, and that's what he did on Monday."

"I see," Hugh said.

"*Do* you? That's good." La Touche smiled, but no one else did.

"Why didn't you four fly out with him?" Hugh asked. Bob Thorpe looked into the dregs of his glass. "One camp with five thousand refugees, another with four thousand, fifteen hundred coming in every day. Someone had to cope." Bob was an old Burma hand of Steel Brothers, who had spent season after season sweating it out in the Dry Zone. His skin was wrinkled and yellow; at sixty he looked like a man of eighty.

"How long have we got?" It was the first time Miss Wadley had spoken.

"Before the monsoon or the Japs? Before the monsoon, ten days; before the Japs, twelve days—that is, with luck."

"Where are we supposed to go?" she asked.

Bob Thorpe leaned across the table to push a pile of papers towards her. A diagrammatic route-map had been sketched and roneoed showing a zigzag line which started at a circle marked in hand-blocked capitals, "SHINBWIYANG," and ended after the bisection of numerous rivers in the top left-hand corner with another circle marked, "MARGHERITA," and a filled-in square marked, "LEDO."

"From Shinbwiyang to this point, Tagap-ga—"ga" means "village"—is plain sailing, over flat country. But beyond the Namyang River, no one really knows what's ahead. Fred Pooley of the Riffs volunteered to do a recce to Ledo with a couple of sub-edars, but it'll be two months before they're back."

"Two months!" Miss Wadley exclaimed, "How far *is* it to Ledo?"

"We've been trying to work it out. The map is not to scale, and we don't know what contours the trails follow . . ."

"Except in Naga country, and then it's straight up the sides of mountains, and straight down the other side."

"Yes—well, how far?" Miss Wadley sounded on edge. "Can't be all that far if you can see the Hukong Mountains from here."

"Who told you that? It isn't true. The Hukong is one place associated with Myitkyina, so people assume they're over there." Bob Thorpe pointed out of the window. "It's about three hundred miles before you get to the Hukong."

"Three hundred miles!"

"There's about a hundred miles of motor-road—but after the hundred-and-second milestone nothing but jungle-paths." He pointed to the names of the sketch-map. "Maingkwan's a hundred and twenty miles on, and from Maingkwan to Shinbwiyang it's forty miles. There's a good camp there, with a political officer in charge. We're asking for drops of food and medicine for Shinbwiyang. Once one gets there, there'll be a chance to rest and get fit before tackling the eighty miles of the Hukong. The Hukong starts at Tagap, and then there's the river, the Namyang, which is one of the worst."

"You speak as if you were expecting everyone, including yourselves, to walk out."

La Touche looked at Miss Wadley in a mischievous way. "What other way *is* there?"

"But—but—what about the airlift?"

"If everything with wings got airborne from India, a Dunkirk of the air, there still wouldn't be enough craft to get out a hundred thousand people." An impudent smile lit La Touche's young-old face. "If Myitkyina goes down in history, it will be as the Dunkirk that wasn't. We're lucky to get two planes a day, and that's no thanks to the R.A.F. or Civil pilots, Indian or British, but the Yanks and Chinese National Airways."

Miss Wadley picked up one of the maps. "May I have this?"

"Have two. As a matter of fact, you could help distribute them for us."

"I'll help, of course. You must tell me how to go about it." But she was hesitating, looking to Hugh to give her a lead.

"We'll both help," Hugh said. "Give us two rooms here for our party, and after we've had a wash and some food, we'll do whatever you want. But first . . ." He looked across at the District Commissioner. "May I have a word with you, Tom?"

La Touche nodded. The two men left the room followed by Miss Wadley.

Hugh looked from one to the other, hesitated. "First I'd better introduce you properly. This is Tom La Touche. We've known each other for years. And this is Miss Wadley, my fiancée."

La Touche shook hands. "Fiancée! So? I'd no idea."

"Look here, Tom, can you marry us?"

"Marry you?"

"You're the D.C. You're allowed to. As D.C. I find myself frequently marrying people."

"Well, yes, I can, but there are formalities. A period notice."

"Skip them, can't you? You'd be doing us a favour."

La Touche glanced at Miss Wadley, who was looking non-plussed as if this was the first she'd heard of Hugh's proposal. In fact, Hugh himself had planned nothing, but on the spur of the moment decided to make use of his friend's official powers.

"What about identity papers?"

"We've got passports. Have you yours here, Monica, dear?"

Not "darling." Nor was Hugh's slight hesitation lost on La Touche. Miss Wadley pulled her passport out of her Shan bag, handing it to him with a brisk, businesslike movement. The D.C. took it, but wavered, giving them both a questioning look. Here were two people, clearly strangers to one another, anxious to marry in a rush, at a time of crisis. Was it wise? Should he help them? He gave a scarcely perceptible shrug, which seemed to say, none of my business, and walked over to a cupboard. As he rummaged among stacks of official stationery and forms, Hugh winked at Miss Wadley.

"There's an official procedure and forms will have to be filled in. Then you'll have to sign the Marriage Register and pay the fee."

La Touche found the papers he wanted, placed them on the table and pulled out a chair for Hugh.

"It's very good of you to waive the period of notice," Hugh said.

"I don't suppose the Myitkyina Register will survive to be looked at. After you've signed I'll make out a certificate to vouch for your respectability."

When Hugh finished, Miss Wadley filled in the forms and then joined Hugh, standing behind the D.C.'s chair while their marriage-certificate was filled in.

They could hear the murmur of voices in the next room and the squeak of La Touche's brass nib as he copied details of their passports. Once they exchanged glances—Miss Wadley's serene, almost indifferent, Hugh's boyish and eager. He gave her another wink. He was the one who was behaving as people are expected to behave on their wedding-day. It puzzled Miss Wadley that she felt so little. No tremor of anticipation, no ache of love for Hugh, no pang for Tom. Her only positive thought was one of concern lest Hugh noticed the entry under "age." She had always told him she was thirty; now he would perceive she was thirty-five.

As the D.C. blotted the marriage-certificate a feeling of satisfaction seeped through her. Mrs Chapman! A married woman at last! So, she'd made it, and thirty-five wasn't too late for a couple of kids, if she felt like it. She couldn't help crowing over Guy Burnett and Tom, and one or two others who hadn't thought her good enough to marry. Someone had begged her to marry him, someone who was very nice too, whom she'd married because she loved, and not, as she might have done—for the sake of getting married.

La Touche stood up. "Congratulations! It'll cheer us all up. I'll find something more exciting than beer to celebrate."

He was assuming they would return to the meeting, Hugh too seemed keen to do so, but Miss Wadley had other ideas.

"May we join you later? We're so grubby. If you could let us have a couple of rooms for ourselves and our party, we'd freshen up, get something to eat." She smiled up at La Touche, who seemed now anxious to please her. "And later, I'd like to help. I'm afraid Hugh and I don't really feel like celebrating, not yet anyway." She added this looking across at Hugh, "Not until we've flown out to India."

When they found themselves alone for a few moments Hugh did not take her in his arms as he might have done but spoke sharply, "What was that about flying to India?"

"We must insist on it. With only two planes a day and thousands trying to fly out . . ."

"There's no question of insisting. No question of hinting or asking for any kind of priority whatever."

"You must be mad. We'll be stranded. If the Japs arrive—what'll happen to us?"

"Don't you see my position? It's unthinkable to ask for favours."

"*Your* position. *You!* Don't you consider me, and the children?"

"I do, but . . ." He turned away, distracted. "I've got to carry on like La Touche is, and the others. Can't possibly use my position to get my family out."

"Why not? Children and old people will get priority."

"If that's what they've arranged, okay, but it can't come from me."

Miss Wadley's expression hardened.

"Very well."

"You do understand?"

She had her head turned away. "Yes. Yes."

When he kissed her she appeared to respond, so he assumed she had come round to his point of view. "Don't worry, we'll manage somehow. In a week or so, when we're better organized, I daresay I can get you and the kids out."

When they had all bathed and changed into whatever each

possessed of clean clothes, Hanif appeared to tell them tea was ready on the lawn.

Hugh was touched when he saw to what trouble Mohammed Khan and Hanif had gone to please them. Damask white linen, expensive-looking cutlery, and the silver tea-service seen earlier were laid out on a table under the trees. There was an egg for each of the children and biscuits for them.

"All H.E.'s stuff. He took nothing but one small suitcase. I wonder who'll eventually inherit it all." Hugh turned over a jewelled cigarette-box that looked as if it had belonged to the Governor's wife.

After tea Hugh lay on the grass fondling Butch's ears while Mibs and Jemma pillowed their heads against his legs. His good humour had returned and he was making a great fuss of the children—preparatory to announcing the most important news of the day. Miss Wadley waited for him to tell the children of her new status, but he seemed to be putting off the moment. She noticed how he avoided referring to her either as "Miss Wadley" or "my wife."

"I'll have to get up now. Only wish I could lie here all afternoon. Mr La Touche has asked us"—he looked across at Miss Wadley—"to go to the airfield and help the Evacuation Officers."

"Are you going to leave us alone?" Mibs demanded.

"Mr La Touche is here—and the servants. I don't want any of you leaving the compound."

Miss Wadley poured Hugh a second cup of tea. "I thought of taking everyone with us."

Hugh started. "Why? There will be a seething mass all round the airfield. Much better for them to stay here."

She helped him to sugar. "I mean to take them, Hugh. There's just a chance of an empty seat at the last moment, and I could get one or two of them off."

"On a plane?" Ken asked. "To India? I wouldn't mind, provided Butch could come too."

Hugh said, "We've been over all this." He did not want to argue with Miss Wadley before the children and paused, uncertain what to do. He finished the cup of tea she had poured out for him, then walked slowly into the house. Miss Wadley called after him, "Please tell the servants to come here, darling." The word was said distinctly.

"I'm tired. I'm hot. I'm going to do what Daddy wants. I'm not going to the airfield."

Jemma threw herself on the grass beside Mibs, "Me too. All those people breathing and pushing! I trod on a cripple. He hadn't any legs and was going along like a frog. I didn't see him and I stepped on his back. It was awful. Let's stay here, please."

Miss Wadley left the tea-table, sauntered over to the girls, and stood looking down on them. Without raising her voice she said, "Get up, both of you. I want you to stand in the drive."

Neither stirred. Ken whistled to his dog and walked obediently to the gravelled path.

"Didn't you hear what I said, Jemma? Mibs? Get up. Get up at once! The planes will be here by four and we've a long walk to the airfield."

"Daddy told us to stay in the compound. Why are you always interfering?"

In sudden, savage loss of control, Miss Wadley struck at the girls, first pulled Mibs to her feet by hauling her upright with a fistful of clothing, and then attacked Jemma. Her strong hands twisted the clothing into knots held tightly against the bodies of the children so that when she shook them, shook and shook them, shook and shook them, they looked like rag-dolls, heads lolling to and fro.

"Stop, Waddy! Stop, please stop!"

Ken came pelting across the lawn, Butch at his heels.

The shrieks of the girls and Ken's cry were too much for the dog. What is a bull-terrier for? There is no meaning in life to a dog of the bull-terrier species unless it is in the glory of the fracas. Chunky, slothful, the rather boring Butch of peaceful life was transformed in an instant. Flabby muscles tightened, rolls of fat turned into bands of sinew, enormous jaws opened, fangs were displayed and from the deep chest came much noise. Butch's fighting technique was not, as with most dogs, to draw blood at once—that could wait—but to disconcert the enemy. Rolling into a missile as hard as a cricket-ball—but much larger—she launched herself at Miss Wadley, collided with her at shoulder level and tipped her off balance. Miss Wadley let go of the girls, who reeled away backwards while she herself fell sideways. Butch straddled her, fangs bared over her neck—small, merry, joyful eyes challenging her to move one inch. No blood was spilt, no clothing torn, but humiliation was complete.

"Oh Waddy, I'm sorry! I'm sorry! Butch, heel, you devil. Please forgive her, Waddy."

Ken yanked at his dog's collar and helped Miss Wadley to her feet. Both dog and victim were trembling.

From the steps of the D.C.'s bungalow the servants watched in horror: a white lady thumping white children! An old dog hurtling through the air to knock over the person who ruled them. Hugh reappeared, and having taken in the scene, seemed anxious to escape.

"Daddy, Miss Wadley started it! It wasn't Butch's fault. That beastly woman hit us."

"That's enough!" Hugh shouted and Mibs shouted back,

"But she did. You've got to believe us and tell her to stop it."

"Are you all right, my dear?" Hugh walked over to his wife and took her arm, but she was too angry to tolerate any conciliatory gestures. "Isn't it time you told these children about us?"

"Yes, all right, I'm sorry I haven't." He crossed to Mibs, Jemma and Ken, who stood together, Butch behind them, tongue lolling out and still trembling.

"I don't know what's been happening but you've upset—upset your mother. Go and apologize."

Mibs did not at first understand what her father meant. When she did, she flung herself upon him, fist beating his chest. "You've married her! You shouldn't have. Why did you? Oh Dad—dee!" She threw herself on the grass and sobbed with face pressed into the earth.

Miss Wadley was in no mood for further argument about who was going or not going to the airfield with herself and Hugh. No one, certainly not Hugh, was prepared to obstruct her now. Within minutes, servants and children were lined up on the lawn, each carrying a bundle or Shan bag with food and clothes. La Touche offered to save them the half-mile trudge by producing an army lorry. When it arrived they climbed in silently, Ken last of all.

"May I bring her, please, Waddy? She's sorry. She'll never be bad again."

Miss Wadley shrugged but did not object, so Ken heaved up his dog and climbed in after her. Jemma whispered, "Are you trying to suck up to her? Disgusting! Won't do you any good. You'll see—she'll get her own back."

Though the worst of the day's heat was over, the air flowed upwards in liquid waves, clear as water until it reached a whitish-orange blur, suspended about fifteen feet above the earth. This was a dust-cloud raised by thousands of feet, by the wheels of bullock-carts, by military and civilian cars, and vehicles of every kind, including a convoy of ambulances transporting patients from three Myitkyina hospitals. A multitude was converging on the airfield, for the promised mass air-evacuation, not only from the town, but from the south, where they arrived by foot up the railway-track, from the east, the direction of the river, and from the west, by the refugee tree-trails across-country from Shduzup.

When the airfield became visible from the road, Miss Wadley caught a glimpse through trees and sheds of two spots of yellow, as fragile as butterflies, alighting in the centre of a clearing.

"Those them?"

Hugh nodded. "Doesn't look hopeful. We want a miracle on the loaves-and-fishes scale to clear this horde."

"Or an air-raid."

"Yes, or an air-raid. Takes the Japs three days to obliterate completely. Toungoo, Meiktila, Mandalay, all flattened, Hern said, and they're busy now with Katha and Bhamo. So it won't be long now before Myitkyina gets hers unless the monsoon beats them." Hugh and his wife sat in front with the Gurkha driver.

Hugh spoke in undertones as much to ease tension between himself and his wife as to relieve his own distress by the latest war news. "The Japs aren't afraid of death. They die with great courage. But when it comes to disease—it's another story. They're scared stiff of malaria and dysentery and everything else that arrives with the monsoon. If we can hang on here till the monsoon comes, Bob Thorpe says, they'll stop the advance. He's right. With the first shower they'll call it a day, take cover, and start digesting what they've taken."

Hugh gave his wife another anxious glance. She appeared to have regained control of herself: the red flush from her neck had subsided and her manner seemed quiet. He touched her hand, "Look, I'm sorry about—what happened. No one's completely sane just now, so don't be too hard on them. There is something else—I must say it—and you mustn't mind. I do really mean what I said earlier. Please don't use my position to get them away. We must not try to jump the queue."

"Did you know La Touche has given me a chit to the E.O. [Evacuation Officer], telling him to get us all away if possible."

"I'd rather you didn't use it."

"You must be mad. Don't you want to help save our lives? If we don't get away today or tomorrow, we won't at all. We'll die in Burma—here or trying to walk out. Look at this mob, most of them are going to die here. And if you don't get us out, we'll die here too. You, me, Mibs and the others."

"It's something I can't argue about. We've got to take our chance with the rest."

"You make me sick."

They said no more until the lorry drew up at the wire fence enclosing the airfield. "Let's leave them in the lorry until we know what's happening," Hugh said. Miss Wadley agreed and gave the orders. "Get this under shade, driver. No one's to get out until I say."

The barrier of wire netting and the insufficient number of police were unable to control the refugees milling round the airfield. As the car was parked, a score or so of Anglo-Indian youths climbed over the netting, while soldiers with red hackles in their

Balmorals had backed army lorries up against the wire and were helping to slide over stretchers with wounded to comrades on the far side. Within the perimeter of the landing-ground, as well as outside it, there was chaos. Queues stretching for a quarter of a mile or so were broken by the stalls of Burmese traders, some selling produce, others dresses and other possessions bartered by refugees for food and drink. One of the traders was using the wire netting to display dresses. There was a trickle of people walking across the strip towards the aircraft, most of them women and children; some Anglo-Indian women and teenage girls were in evening dress; others with thin arms and legs had unnaturally thick bodies, thickened by several layers of clothing.

Miss Wadley and Hugh, wearing official badges, were allowed through the barrier, where, without a word and in sulky hostility, they parted, Hugh to walk to the furthest shed, Miss Wadley to enter the one where the long queue had formed.

It was surprising how little difficulty she encountered. She did not present herself before the three Evacuation Officers as a helper sent by the D.C. to relieve one of them, as, at that moment Hugh was doing. She walked briskly to the nearest man, an Anglo-Burmese. "I am Mrs Hugh Chapman," she said, "and the rest of the Governor's party is waiting in a lorry."

The Evacuation Officers looked up from interviewing the refugees seated opposite them. One exclaimed, "Governor's party? But the Governor left . . ."

"We're the people who travelled in H.E.'s special coach from Maymyo. We're the ones who were ambushed in mistake for him—luckily!" She smiled. The E.O.s smiled too. "Ambushed?" "You heard about the plot to capture H.E. and sell him to the Japs?" They had not heard but they nodded. "I've got a note from the D.C. asking you to get us off."

"Tomorrow. Too late today. Both aircraft are full to capacity, one with seventy, the other with seventy-five."

Miss Wadley answered calmly, "I'm quite willing to wait. I'd prefer it, but this has nothing to do with me. We're part of H.E.'s party, and so I suppose it's what H.E. has ordered."

"I see." They conferred together. "Can we divide your party, five in one plane, five in the other?"

"I'm afraid not," Miss Wadley said. "Please don't think I'm being difficult. All I'm doing is passing on instructions."

Again they conferred. One of them stood up. "Will you come with me?" As she followed him outside he explained, "I'll have to make ten people get out. They won't like it, can't be helped."

The children and servants followed Miss Wadley and the E.O. from the lorry across the airfield. Only Mibs cried, "Where's Daddy? I won't go without Daddy."

Miss Wadley told the E.O., "Mr Chapman is in the further shed. When we've got them in, would you kindly tell him to join us?"

The pilot stood by the plane. "I'm about to take off. I told you I couldn't take any more." When the E.O. explained, the pilot complained, "This is going to delay me." As he spoke the other aircraft started to taxi away.

Amongst the ten people ordered out by the E.O. was a pretty Anglo-Indian girl in a pink-sequin evening dress. She refused to leave unless her mother accompanied her, but her mother was not one of the ten asked to go and refused to budge. The girl started screaming "Mummy! Mummy! Don't go without me. Mummy stay behind with me!"

"Come along, there's a good girl. You'll join your mother to-morrow. I promise. You'll have the first seat tomorrow."

She hung on to the fuselage, screaming until the pilot shouted to the E.O., "Let her scream—fetch that other man and let's get off."

The other Hudson had taxied to the take-off point and was revving up engines as the E.O. ran to fetch Hugh. In a few moments Hugh could be seen racing across the field. The cabin-door remained open with the hysterical girl clutching it, Miss Wadley barring her entrance. When Hugh arrived his wife said, "Get in. I'll deal with her." Hugh entered the cabin, did not sit down but hurried down the cabin to the cockpit. He told the infuriated pilot that there had been a mistake and he could not take off until the nine people who had just embarked left the plane and restored their seats to those who had been deprived of them.

"I don't care who's in there—I don't care what the hell you do —but let me get this bloody ship off the ground."

The bewildered children and servants left the plane when Hugh told them to get out. Miss Wadley, however, did not move from her position by the door. She was still keeping out the girl in the pink dress. Hugh at last spoke to her: "Darling—you too. Go with them, with me. I want you to. I need you. Please." She let go of the door, and slowly, her face grim, walked down the small companionway. Hugh was about to follow her when the pilot shouted at one of the passengers who pushed Hugh back inside the cabin, pulled in the girl, and slammed the hatch.

"For God's sake—are you deaf? Air-raid siren!" As the plane taxied over the bumpy field, twenty Mitsu bombers flew low over the field. The Hudson transport about to take off was not hit, though bombs exploded all over the field. It lifted itself over the trees, changed course and went off on its westerly course for India while the Mitsus circled over the Irrawaddy and returned to strafe the refugees.

The second plane, the one in which Hugh was trapped, went creeping across the field like a small slow creature looking for a place to hide. The Mitsus hit it on their return run. From under the trees where the children had taken cover, Mibs saw black smoke and white flames spurt from it. Standing in the open Miss Wadley also stood watching. Both ran towards its pyre.

23

Hamish Waight had inferred at the Margherita Court that Miss Wadley had been too ill following cerebral malaria to keep accurate dates in her diary. In fact, this wasn't so. She was methodical by nature and had always jotted down location and date before making an entry: "Forest Bungalow, Kaikun, Christmas Day, 1941," . . . "Windermere Lodge, Maymyo, Good Friday, April 3, 1942," . . . and so on. She did not make daily notes but, according to her mood, recapitulated the events of many days in one account, sometimes covering several pages of her diary.

There were really only four entries which interested the Court. These were:

"School House, Sumprambum, May 7–8, 1942"
"Maingkwan, May 20, 1942"
"Patty's basha, Tagap, June 18, 1942" and
"Ngalang, same night."

School House, Sumprambum.
May 7–8, 1942.

They blame me. Fleeing from Myitkyina in lorry—every wooden house of bazaar blazing, trees round airfield in flames— they huddled together at one end, Mibs weeping against Fatima, the others staring at me. They didn't speak, but their eyes accused me—even the sweeper had the nerve to glare. Not one word of sympathy for me—only for Mibs. Yet I'm the one who suffers most. Hugh lost—all's lost for me. Hatred kept me from collapse. I glared back and didn't weep, but must have, without knowing it. Ken crept to my side—the only one—and his sticky hand wiped my face and I tasted salt of tears. Won't give in, won't indulge in self-pity: if I do, we're all done for. But for me we'd still be in Myitkyina. I made M.K. [Mohammed Khan] beat refugees out of lorry—twenty of them with a British Tommy at the wheel ready to drive off in our car. They refused to oust the cripple and the beggar woman, so we had them all the way. Three Englishmen, middle-aged, asked for lift, and I agreed. They brought bearers and luggage, but it turned out for best because their presence steadied us all and kept the Tommy in order. He drove off road (blocked by refugees) over paddy-fields and dried water-courses, and thanks to his mad handling of lorry, we had two breakdowns. But we got here, end of road, by 10 P.M. Englishmen must be officials because arranged for us to spend night under cover—everyone else camping in fields—also, they shared food with us. Am too worried and too miserable to sleep, so am writing this by candlelight. What's to happen to us? We have the bag of silver coins Hugh entrusted to M.K. Servants have a little rice. We have nothing but clothes we wear and one change and a few tins of food, enough to last flight to Calcutta. No tents, not even a groundsheet, not even a box of matches. The three Englishmen—who are very cagey about dis-closing names—have given me useful advice. When lorry-driver pulled up at 102nd milestone, where mass of refugees turned down jungle-track to Maingkwan, they told me fatal to join main exodus because cholera, dysentery, etc. bound to break out soon. They had decided to go more difficult but cleaner "Whiteman's" route via Fort Hertz and over Chaukan Pass. Had never heard of it, but immediately agreed. Over meal they also gave me more tips. I must draw up a schedule of miles per day, say ten, and how many minutes of rest per hour, and see they stick to it. The stricter the discipline I exert, they said, the less chance of collapse of morale. All this cheered me, and gave me

hope that they'd let us tag on to them. I'm alone now and depressed—and however hard I try, I can't help brooding over
Hugh.

May 8.

Woke at 5 A.M., so must have got an hour's sleep. Sky weird,
dark purple, and distant hills light yellow with flashes of lightning playing over them. Ready to start by 6 A.M., but a jeep tore
up and La Touche jumped out. He told us no one was allowed
to take Chaukan route—too dangerous—and he was going up to
Fort Hertz to turn back everyone who'd gone ahead. The three
Englishmen knew him and argued, but La Touche refused to let
us through. When La Touche saw me he came over and said
how sorry he was about Hugh. I nearly broke down. He nodded
towards the three men. "They'll look after you. Stick with them,"
and told me they are three High Court judges from Rangoon.
La Touche and I were standing in road where he was drawing a
map in the dust marking distances between main villages between our first main camp, Maingkwan, and a place he called
"Shin-way-bang" (Shinbwiyang). All round us people were
looking at the strange glow over the hills where lightning was
streaking up valleys and sprouting out of mountain tops like tiny
oaks. Quite suddenly there was a noise like machine-gun fire—
hail falling on corrugated iron roof of schoolhouse. Before we
realized what was happening, rain fell. I've never seen raindrops
like them, each making a round mark in the dust. In a few seconds
individual spots merged and water was flowing down the street.

La Touche climbed into his jeep and, standing up on the seat,
called us together. "This"—he didn't have to say the word "monsoon,"—"This means you can't get out to India." I'll never forget
those words. He went on to say Government had forbidden anyone to enter the Hukong Valley once the rains came. Someone
shouted, "What Government?" But he shouted back, "Don't be
a B.F. [bloody fool] and don't take it out on me. The Hukong's
still head-hunting area—and if that doesn't put you off, it's the
worst place anywhere in the world for the most pernicious

type of malignant malaria. You can fall unconscious for six weeks. If you get malaria, how can you hope to cross the Pangsau. The Pangsau Pass is about five thousand feet up and there may be snow."

"What about the tea-planters' camps?" one of the judges asked.

"They'll close. Can't possibly function in monsoon conditions."

The Judge shook his head and whispered to me, "Don't believe him."

There was more heckling when La Touche told us Government was ordering all refugees to the village of Shinbwiyang, where arrangements had been made for food, shelter, with a political officer and Dr Babu in charge. Some Indian telegraph clerks shouted, "Not desirous of dying in Burma, sar. We will proceed India, sar."

La Touche explained there really were adequate provisions for everyone in Shinbwiyang, because the Government had been expecting to feed a labour force of 250,000, due to start building a road on the Burma side of the Pangsau Mountain. He said, "I know for a fact there are 5000 tons of rice there in properly built rice godowns. The Government has also informed me the R.A.F. is making daily drops of food and medicine. Be reasonable. If you stay in Shinbwiyang the Government will see you are looked after. Getting that far will be quite hard enough. It's over 120 miles and through fairly bad jungle. You'll have had enough—believe me."

When La Touche left, the judges and I got together. They told me La Touche had convinced them camping at Shinbwiyang till the monsoon finished was the only sensible course. This was to be their plan and they advised me to do likewise. To help me, they said, they proposed to leave at once, and by forced marches arrive at Shinbwiyang ahead of the mass of refugees. This would enable them to commandeer a basha for themselves and one for us. When I realized what they were really saying was they wanted to get away on their own—and leave me to cope with my party—I could have wept. I would have willingly exchanged all their kindness for a chance to tag along behind them. I think perhaps they knew it, and to fob me off, overloaded me with provisions and good advice. They also took me to the hut of a Kachin woman trader, as there was no bazaar that day. Here they bartered some of their provisions for shoes for me and the children. They chose Bata canvas plimsoles because, they said, leather would retain water, and if one walked with feet in moisture foot rot would set in. They also gave me quinine and Dettol from their own stock, one groundsheet and a mosquito net.

Why wouldn't they let me join them? What's wrong with me? What puts people off? Am I too bossy? Or is it some weakness in me that compels me to latch on to people? Isn't that what I've been doing all my life? Guy, Tom, Hugh—latching on to men to make use of them? And these old men are too fly to let me.

We will leave by lorry tomorrow morning. The judges are so anxious to be rid of me they are leaving at once—and since I did not offer to send them in our lorry as far as the jungle turning, they must walk back down the road. Serve 'em right! Do they expect me to turn the other cheek? Damned if I will! Three Englishmen with plenty of food, money, servants and porters —yes, porters too! They've acquired a string of Kachins to carry their things—the only people who have. They are deliberately snubbing me, abandoning a lone woman with children. But why? That's what really worries me. What don't they like about me?

Maingkwan. May 20, 1942.

I'm entering my diary after ten days of jungle marching, writing in a shelter put up by Ken and Hanif. The rain is bucketing down, tall trees shut out the sky, the air is humid and there are mosquitoes shrilling close to my ear. Dim-dam flies, so small one can barely see them, are stinging my back through the rips in my bush-shirt.

I am writing this between attacks of ague. Ken has insisted on removing my shoes and is picking off leeches between my toes by dabbing them with his salt bag. Fatima is trying to relieve my aching body by shampooing my muscles. I must have lost two stone—we've all lost weight. Jemma is a skeleton, so is Ken. Mibs has fever; hers is worse than mine. I am strong enough to walk, but Mibs has had to be carried. Our Kaikun number of eight has increased to sixteen with Queenie and her girls. Queenie is one of the best-known characters of Rangoon's red-light district, and the seven girls, three pregnant, are from her house. It seems impossible that the person who lived at 7 Elsham Road and caught the 49a bus down the High Street, Kensington, should be the same woman who is slogging through jungle mud in such company, and yet it is the same person, but scoured of all the rubbish and stupidity of life. Sumprambum is only twelve days away, but it could be a hundred thousand light years distant. What we've seen and experienced has changed us all now and forever. Everyone has a different idea about the human race. But if it has nothing else, it has courage. I've seen people dragging themselves along with half a body, half a leg, small children trying to carry between them a dying mother or father, an old man with another old man on his back, and wounded soldiers staggering along with laden stretchers over slush two or three feet deep. We got across the Tanai Hka (upper reaches of the Chindwin) because five Gurkhas swam across with a liana rope—three got it across but two drowned.

I realize my fever is stimulating my mind, sending my thoughts whirling about all over the place, but what I've seen of other people's courage will change me for life. We came across the first dead two days from the main Myitkyina—Sumprambum Road. Since then, the number has increased each day. They drag themselves off the road to die—lie quietly under the dripping leaves and die there alone. Though the stench is terrible, there is nothing gruesome about these deaths—these poor leaderless, helpless, harmless people die so quietly. The kids have accepted these terrible circumstances in a way that seems to be heartless. Jemma: "What's Butch chewing?" Ken: "An old boot." "Is it an old boot, or the old man who was in the old boot?" This was not said facetiously but in a matter-of-fact way. The villages we've passed through are deserted—save for pigs, and the pigs are all fat. I've never known Ken attack animals, but he attacks them.

Thank God for our small store of tinned foods and rice. The Kachin villagers have all run away because of looting by Chinese troops. Even so, the Chinese we meet are the most ready to share what they have. A Chinese general exchanged a leg of salted pork for three boxes of matches. Our matches, given us by the judges, who bought them in Katha, are not faulty, like all matches bought in Myitkyina. Also, thanks to Patty, one of Queenie's "girls," we know how to keep them dry—by packing them in French letters.

My head is throbbing and I feel heavy, as if doped. It's not fever that makes me say I've not once been afraid in this place of death, only ashamed at what I am and have been. I'm sorry. Sorry that I am as I am, that I tried to grab Tom from Hla Gale and Ken. Sorry I "used" Hugh. But I won't—I can't—be like that again. I've behaved like a bullying, greedy child because I've felt undervalued—or that's what I tell myself. Perhaps I was, quite simply, a bully, and greedy. People have changed towards me because I have changed towards them.

At first they thought I was ordering them about because I enjoyed it, but when they realized the drill was imposed because I meant to keep them fit and walking, their dependence on me grew. The rules are those the judges suggested: not more than ten minutes' rest in every hour, no relaxing after the day's trek until every bit of mud and grit is washed off. When we halt to make camp we are all filthy, and unless we wash, our bites from mosquitoes, leeches, dim-dam flies and God knows what other insects are bound to become infected and might develop into the Naga sore. This is a horrible suppurating sore. Patty treated an Indian student whose flesh along the arch of his foot had been eaten to the bone. There's no cure, she says, save to cease being a refugee, to return to normal living conditions of good food and rest.

Queenie's girls have a genuine liking for me. It makes me feel strange—disarmed! I'm not at ease when people are being open and affectionate. I feel more at home if people feel hostile towards me, as I usually do towards them. Will Mibs and Jemma ever accept me, ever call me "Waddy" as my dear scrawny Ken does? If they can't, I won't blame them: I will blame myself. It was Hugh who opened my eyes. I doubt if he meant to: he wasn't subtle in that way. He was describing the Burmese character to me once, trying to explain why he admired it so much. He said, "I think it's because they respect people. The Burmese are conscious of each person's natural sense of dignity, and respect it." I remember thinking at the time, "Ah! That's one for me! That's what I haven't got—respect for people!" It's true I've never had it—till now!

Patty has arrived and is trying to bustle me into the deserted Naga Long House where she and Queenie and the girls are camping. She says I have a high temperature and will need nursing tonight. I dislike the idea of sharing their hut, but as I don't want to show it, I'll do as I'm told. In fact, I'm relieved to. I really am beginning to feel very ill.

Patty's hut, Tagap, June 10th—and afterwards.

I can't see the children, only hear them. Their voices rise from under the hut or just outside, near the ladder leading to the platform. When I first regained consciousness—about a week ago —I used to listen to them with amusement, and if one of them crept up the ladder to take a look at me, I used to pretend to be unconscious so that I could catch some more home-truths!

The first time I listened they were discussing the Golden Stairs, whether one climbed or descended them, whether they really ended on a station-platform as Fatima said, and if so, which station—Lekhapani, Ledo, Margherita? The Golden Stairs, journey's end for everyone in the Hukong, is a staple of refugee conversation. While nursing me I've heard Queenie and Patty murmuring, "When we reach the Golden Stairs we'll . . ."

Tagap must be about a hundred miles from Maingkwan, where I last noted in my diary, and that was a month ago. This hut is on the top of the hill; all the other Naga huts, including the Long House where the Naga bachelors lived, are scattered below. The villagers have run away except the Headman, who is old (and a businessman—he's in the looting racket with the Sikhs), and his daughter Ma Lu.

I can see nothing from this chung, the bamboo shelf on which I am lying, except treetops between the bumps of my feet under the sacking. Those grey trees and the drenched grey skies are terribly depressing—it's no wonder I perk up whenever these young devils gather under the hut. It's about the only time I snap out my lethargy.

In the past I've been hard on Mibs and Jemma because I've taken them too seriously—everyone too seriously. Those girls are really not the scheming minxes I've supposed them to be but likeable, plucky brats, and unconsciously very funny. They don't miss anything—nor does Ken, for all his sleepy ways. During the past week I've learned a great deal about the goings-on in Tagap from them.

The R.A.F. make two or three drops a week, canisters and sacks full of rice, dried milk, tinned fruit, biscuits, potatoes, medicines, magazines—and once a consignment of teddy-bears! The children's hero is Sergeant-Pilot Lord, one of the two who fly over from Digboi. He's very daring, comes in low and scoops up a rope strung between posts, on which messages are tied. There are several hundred refugees in the two Tagap villages, Upper and Lower Tagap, and thousands camping five miles down the hill on the banks of the Namyang River. Thanks to another of their heroes, a Sikh Subedar, no refugee gets any of this food free. This gentleman posts armed Sikh comrades round the dropping-zone to keep everyone off, collects everything and stores it in the Naga Long House (the kids refer to it as "Selfridge's"), where the Subedar sells it: rice is five rupees a pound, but tinned peaches can be as much as ten rupees. The kids like him because he gives them free American "K" rations. From what the children say, this dropping-zone concession and looted-food store, "Selfridge's," is coveted by Queenie. If—and when—the Sikhs move on, Queenie means to do a deal with them in partnership with the Tagap Headman! Another person who intrigues the children—particularly the girls—is Ma Lu, the Headman's daughter. I can only guess what she looks like—decked out in refugee cast-offs such as an evening dress of gold lace whose long skirt she wears bunched up round her waist to keep out of the mud—but I gather she is an Amazon. She has a small brown pony which fearlessly swims across the Namyang, while she "floats behind, clutching its tail." With Sergeant-Pilot Lord she appears to be Tagap's main contact with the world beyond the Hukong. It was she who brought the news (predicted and later confirmed by La Touche) that the refugee camps put up and run by tea-planters since April are all to close down. She could not discover why.

La Touche must have arrived here just about the time I was coming out of my coma. He looked in my hut, I hear, though I don't remember it, and left Patty a supply of quinine and marmite for me. He made himself unpopular when he called a meeting of refugees and told them no one was to attempt to cross the Namyang River on Government orders, also, on Government orders everyone was to return to the pest-hole of Shinbwiyang. This was the place Queenie refused to remain in for more than one night when she discovered refugees were dying of dysentery and malaria at the rate of five hundred per week. La Touche also confirmed Ma Lu's story about the end of food —medicines, stretcher-bearers, and tea-planter helpers—for refugees in the Hukong. According to Ma Lu, only one Road Commander, the Dukaba Major, has remained behind.

Lying here, not really involved with the world yet, I listen to the children in complete detachment. At times I wish this feeling of being cut off, aloof, could remain with me always. It's only when I get too close to events and people that I seem to lose my sense of humour. Nothing has shocked me about the chicaneries of the Sikhs, Queenie, Ma Lu. By normal standards the kids' comments on death and corpses should horrify me and make me loathe them, but I feel nothing except an amused affectionate indulgence.

I am listening to them now.

"It's funny she didn't die at Shinbwiyang. Nearly everyone else did." Mibs's voice. Jemma answered, "Everyone did *not* die. Only fifty people died the night we were there. At least she wasn't faking to get herself carried like some people."

Ken tried to keep the peace between them—as ever: "Mibs wasn't faking. Her malaria was jolly bad."

"And so were my sores. So was Ja-Bo's boil, but *we* didn't get carried. Mibs had only ordinary malaria and she was carried. Goodness knows what she'd have done with the proper malaria."

A pause. Mibs said, "Patty says she can't get over Miss Wadley. She says everyone she knows who had cerebral malaria died. So Miss Wadley still might die. If she does, bags I shove her off the cliff."

Ken said, "You wouldn't be allowed to. They only shove Indian corpses off the cliff."

"Then bags I help burn her."

"You can't burn her if she dies of malaria. Burning's for cholera. If she had died of cholera you could have burnt the hut with her."

Jemma laughed and Ken said crossly, "Nothing to giggle at. I don't want Waddy to die of anything."

"I wasn't thinking of your beastly Waddy. I was thinking of something else. Remember the old man we nearly burnt—the one who was alive."

Jemma's giggles shook the hut—literally. In rolling about she was barging into the bamboo piers.

June 12.

The children have gone. I cannot make myself believe it, but it must be true because Patty has just come up to tell me. Ken, Mibs, Jemma and the servants—all have gone, abandoned me, deserted me, left me with Queenie and Patty and the other whores. When I saw the sun shining this morning and heard the hubbub, different from the noise refugees make on rainy days, I got off the chung and struggled to the end of the hut. Refugees were streaming downhill, chattering, excited. If only I had understood the significance of something the kids said—Ma Lu had predicted a break of three days in the downpour. "That's when the Subedar will go down to the river. That's when Queenie will get 'Selfridge's.'" The break in the downpour brings down the flood-level. So with sunny days the refugees have a chance to cross the Namyang.

Patty says the children have gone off with the Sikhs—left me for a bunch of looters! When Patty came to tell me "the good news" (her words), I cried. Patty said, "There! There! You're still weak and you don't understand things yet. They're very lucky to go with the Subedar. We asked him to take them and didn't think he'd agree. He'll look after them. He'll get them to India. You can stay with us and go when we go, when you're stronger and when the rain stops.'

June 13.

Incredulity is turning to anger—how could they do this to me? I who brought them safely from Kaikun to Maymyo and from Maymyo here. So this is how they show gratitude! Not even Ken offered to stay with me. I don't believe it was Queenie's idea. It was Mibs and Jemma who conspired against me—perhaps Ken too. The servants probably egged them on to get rid of me because I imposed discipline. I made them clean themselves each night, and I rationed their food. They didn't like that, so they've bolted.

Later

Perhaps I'm to have the last laugh. Patty has just been here to tell me an elephant rider is in Tagap looking for "a boy with a white dog." It is Ko-Ni, sent by Hla Gale and Tom to take Ken back. Tom is in hiding in a remote Shan village where Hla Gale has joined him, Ko-Ni says.

Here's my chance to get even with them! I am still weak, can barely walk, but it won't matter if I can ride on Maung Khin.

I've announced my decision to go after Ken with Ko-Ni.

Queenie tried her utmost to stop me. Her reasons—my weakness, etc. When these did not deter me, she said it was forbidden to take elephants into the Hukong. "Who forbids it?" I asked, and I'm afraid I laughed. Everyone knows there is no law, no order in the Hukong. "The elephants have pulped the trails," said Queenie. "I'm thinking of the refugees." This from someone who is stealing Government food and selling it to starving people! However, I kept that to myself. Queenie and her girls saved my life, and I shall be forever grateful. When they saw I was determined, they packed up a parcel of food and Patty gave me a revolver which she loaded, packed in waterproof paper and stuffed into the pocket of my bush-shirt.

Ko-Ni and I set off next morning. Sun still shining, so Namyang will have gone down considerably. I was struck by the brilliant patches of colour dotted about Tagap village. At first I thought they were beds of flowers, but as the elephant approached they took wing—butterflies, myriads of them. When I saw what lay beneath, I felt sick. Patty told me butterflies feed on the juices of the dead.

It was a relief to get away from Tagap's smells. The emptiness of rolling wooded hills and smoking valleys, scent of resin and Artemisia, made me feel happy, and my anger against Ken and the others evaporated. After all, why shouldn't the kids leave without me? They knew how ill I've been, and I'm sure Queenie told them it was impossible for me to walk just yet.

I laughed when Maung Khin came to a clay slide, tested it with his feet and then tobogganed down it on his behind while I held on for dear life. At the foot of the slide Maung Khin stuffed bamboo leaves into his mouth, and flapped his ears as if to say it was all part of the day's work. I thought I heard thunder and pointed to the sky, but Ko-Ni shook his head. "Namyang!" Through a gap in the trees I caught sight of a stretch of khaki-coloured foam moving at the speed of an express train. Loaded with refuse, it bellowed over rocks, rolling great boulders as it tore along. I have never before seen the entire bed of a river on the move. As we went down the last few hundred feet the air became damp, gusts of wind brought the smell of rotting humus, and the forest lost its splendour. Trees festooned with long, trailing grey mosses like hair made it look like a forest of trembling old men.

In shadowy dips I saw strange lights, some softly glowing with the green of dying embers, others with greenish phosphorescent light.

Ko-Ni left it to Maung Khin to decide where he would cross the Namyang. As he made his investigations, taking a tentative step in, retreating, trying elsewhere, churning up pebbles, "aungying" a rock, Ko-Ni waited patiently and gave no orders. During these few minutes I saw three refugees, hanging onto the rope over the river, lose their grip and get carried away.

Maung Khin waded in, water rose over my legs, and there were excited shouts from the bank. I thought they were cheering us till I saw an uprooted tree with a fan of jagged roots lifted like a sail bearing down upon us. Even if it did not collide with the elephant, it would tangle with the guide rope and jeopardize the lives of those trying to cross, many carrying children.

Ko-Ni was aware of the peril but showed no alarm. He gradually changed Maung Khin's course, heading him downstream, parallel to the oncoming tree. The elephant was swimming steadily until he appeared to lunge and go under. Water swept over his back and carried away my parcel of food. When I could see through wet hair and bleary eyes, I realized Ko-Ni was guiding his beast into the tree. A branch loomed over my head. Ko-Ni shouted "Aung! Aung!" Maung Khin butted the fan of roots, twisted his trunk round one of them. Tree and elephant moved together, a grotesque mass of wrinkled grey hide and foliage. When at last Maung Khin started to wade, he pushed the tree along with him into the shallows, where its branches caught and held fast in a rock. How I wished Ken had been with me to watch his beloved, sagacious brother Khin! For some moments I was foolish enough to consider calling off my plan. Tender memories came back to me and I only wanted to see Ken's funny little face again. Fortunately, I recognized this as sentimentality and the tender feelings evaporated. Ken and his gang needed to be taught a lesson. For months I have devoted myself to them and given Ken all the love of my nature. He has repaid me by deserting me—as his father did.

We crossed the river and followed the trail to Namlip. No sooner had we entered a belt of forestland than the rain started to fall again and the clay, which had formed a thin crust after two dry days, cracked and dissolved into the consistency of porridge. Watching Maung Khin's wake, I could understand why elephants have been forbidden to use refugee paths. His weight formed footprints several feet deep and must have liquefied the clay to an even deeper level. We passed a child of about four struggling along by himself. He climbed the bank to avoid us but slipped and fell face downwards into one of Maung Khin's holes. I called out to people behind to help him struggling there like a fly in treacle. I hope they lifted him out before he suffocated.

Namlip's jumble of huts stood in black mud, pools of turgid water and slow-flowing slime. Nothing could have induced me to stay there the night. I saw the road climb steeply on the far side and was sure Ken and the Sikhs had gone to the mountaintop. It was time to get rid of Ko-Ni. I told him to make Maung Khin "hmit," as I wanted to make enquiries about the route Ken had taken. There were two ways out, I explained—one forking off from Namlip towards the west and Assam, the other going north, straight up to the Ngalang Ridge. "Let's hope Ken's taken the lower road," I said. "I've heard the climb to the Ridge is the worst in the Hukong, and elephants have been forbidden to use it."

I wasn't lying. There was indeed a road forking off from Namlip. What I kept to myself was the information Ma Lu had given me. This road, she said, at this season of the year became ten miles further up impassable to man and beast. It remained so, according to her, till the rains stopped. It was a dry-season route.

Even if I had not been determined to track Ken down, I would have been forced to climb the Ngalang Ridge. Like almost every refugee, I had lost all my food crossing the river—in fact, lost everything I possessed save the revolver, which I kept because

it could be bartered for food from Nagas later on. My chance
of survival lay in climbing the Ridge, because somewhere along
its summit there was another dropping-zone. And a dropping-
zone would certainly be the place where looting Sikhs would
camp.

When I rejoined Ko-Ni I said, "You know I've been ill—very
ill. Tell Thakin McNeil it was his son and servants who carried
me on a blanket between bamboo poles from Maingkwan to
Tagap—a hundred miles. Thanks to them, I'm still alive. But
you must understand I am still weak. I'm going to rest in Namlip, but I want you to go on and find Ken. When you've found
him, go back with him the most direct way."

Off he went—suspecting nothing. Once out of sight, I started
up the hill. My knees trembled so much I was forced to rest
continually. Eventually I begged a Gurkha soldier to cut me a
staff. He not only cut me one but helped me up the hill. Without
him I doubt if I could have gone more than a few yards. When
the trees started thinning out and we came out on grassy slopes,
I assumed we'd reached the summit and got rid of the Gurkha.
I rested for a few minutes. By this time I was ravenously hungry
and badly needed a drink. I started to cross the clearing when
a domed mountain-peak rose against the western sky. Above it
a speck of silver glinted in the paling light. It was then I realized
I'd come out on a false crest. The dropping-zone on the crown
of Ngalang was still miles away.

As other refugees were camping on this grassy place, I decided to cadge space in someone's shelter. A small lean-to looked
likely. I walked to it, round it, and came face to face with—
Fatima. She was trying to light a fire. Sprawling on the grass
round her lay the others—Mibs and Jemma with filthy matted
hair, in dresses made from sacks.

Ken yelped and made a dash for me. Waddy this! Waddy that!
You'd think I was his dearest friend. I disentangled myself from
his embraces.

"That's enough. I'm famished and thirsty—give me something
to eat and drink, please."

Mibs sauntered over. "I'm glad you're okay, Miss Wadley. Sorry we left you."

"Doesn't matter about that. Have you some water?"

"Waddy, Waddy! Please look at me. Say something nice. Look, here's Butch. She's still here. You're not cross we came away? They made us. They said . . ."

"I don't want to go into that, Ken. All I want at the moment is water—and a biscuit—anything."

Jemma stood staring at me. "We haven't a biscuit, and the only way to drink is to lick leaves."

"It's true, Waddy. We haven't had anything to eat or drink since we left Tagap. That's all yesterday and all today. But we will soon. Look." He pointed to the sky.

"You mean you people—my people—my Kaikun group—are relying on a bunch of looting Sikhs to bring you food!"

"The Sikhs are our friends and the food's from the R.A.F. and for everyone," Mibs said. "Look here, Miss Wadley, we've been getting on fine without you. We're glad you're well and all that, but we don't want you bossing us anymore."

I'm glad to say Ken hit Mibs. Then he came over to me. "I think I've got something for you, Waddy, only a tiny something . . ."

He dashed into the shelter and came out holding a small square of bully beef on the lid of a can, which he offered me. "Where's the rest?" I asked.

Butch had followed him out of the hut and was looking up expectantly. I guessed Ken was holding the tin, and the rest of the meat, behind his back.

"It's . . . it's . . ."

Jemma came between us.

"He's given you some—more than he's given any of us. And that's got to be enough because the rest belongs to Butch."

"Butch!" I shouted. "You desert me—and when I ask for food you say it's for Butch!"

"Well it is. It's her share—from the day before yesterday. We're all rationed, but we've eaten ours. Ken's kept her ration till today."

"Give me that tin, Ken," I said.

At that, Ken took to his heels, yelling, "Butch! Butch!"

That awful-looking old dog—with the head of a pig, the ears of a bat, and the body of an all-in wrestler—hasn't a brain in her head. She looked stupidly at me as if I had her tin of food.

Jemma grabbed her collar and hauled her after Ken. "Quick, Butchie, before that woman takes it." Ken emptied the contents of the tin on the ground, and pushed Butch's nose into it. Butch ate ravenously, gulping down chunks without chewing while Ken, Mibs and Jemma stood guard over her.

The servants, I noticed, watched me. When I drew the revolver from my pocket Fatima started to scream.

I told the children quietly, "If it's a choice between feeding a human being and feeding a dog—the dog must go."

Ken threw his body over the bull-terrier. "Waddy, don't! My Butch! My Butch!"

I fired over his head, and the cowardly dog wriggled away and ran towards the jungle. I followed and in the jungle fired a second shot.

Same night.

Left them. Lost my way. They are following me. To escape climbed down, down, but can't go further—sheer drop.

They have lanterns. See green strange lights all round me. Coming nearer. I am frightened.

Can't see their faces but they are there—behind the lanterns—giggling.

Look for my body. Mibs—Jemma—Ken.

Risley Hill's eyes were boring into Hamish. "I gather there was a blue notebook, a diary belonging to this Miss Wadley. The sweeper says he found it and gave it to the cook."

"What do you want it for?"

"For the case."

"To furnish evidence against these children?" Hamish made no effort to conceal his contempt.

"If you found it, you're bound to turn it in."

"If I did find it, I would not. Get that straight. I went to the Hukong to help, not to judge. It's not the kind of place anyone can sit in judgment on anyone else."

Hamish stalked off towards the children, who had remained where he had left them. Their immobility struck him unpleasantly, reminding him of people found standing in groups after volcanic disasters petrified in larva.

Because he was upset he barked at them with unnecessary harshness, "Snap out of it! Straighten up! Smile!" Ken and Mibs did not respond, but Jemma, oddly enough, perked up as if Hamish's rough voice had broken through her insensibility. She pushed back a strand of hair, grinned, tasted clay on her mouth and wiped it with the back of her hand. Seeing her smile, Hamish scooped her off her feet, held her up for an instant, her face level with his own. He wanted to tell her something but could not find the words, so gave her an affectionate shake before heaving her over his shoulder.

When Risley Hill saw the children again, some ten days later, he did not immediately recognize them. In bazaar-made clothes, with clean skins, minor sores healing, worse ones covered with lint, the change in them was not wholly brought about by these external details but by a different way of holding themselves, of moving and looking about them. Also, they were squabbling —and over Hamish. For Hamish was there too, striding down the street in his idea of jungle uniform, the absurd cane-bowler, Bata hockey-boots, bush-shirt, storm-lantern and staff. Mibs, the fair-haired little girl whom Risley Hill liked best, held one of Hamish's hands, the boy the other, which left the third child, the narrow-faced black-haired chit of a girl, Jemma, with no hand to grasp. She jigged backwards in front of Hamish, getting in his way as she attacked first the fair girl, then the boy in an attempt to dislodge one or other from Hamish's side.

"What are you gawping at?"

Risley Hill started. "Hello! How are you? You've cleaned them up, I see."

"Didn't you think I would?"

"I didn't mean—oh, come off it, Hamish! I'm glad you did. They look fine."

"No thanks to you." Hamish glowered at the liaison officer, who smiled back, refusing the challenge to fight.

Risley Hill replied sweetly, "I was only doing my job. Anyway, here you all are, and I'm glad the kids are looking so well."

But Hamish wasn't prepared to be friendly quite so quickly. "As a matter of fact it *is* thanks to you. After your threats I buttoned it up. No one can have a go at them without first having a go at me. I'm their legal guardian now."

Risley Hill persisted in his efforts to make amends. "I heard you'd applied for custody, and glad you fixed it. I've been wanting to see you—no, don't get angry. That's all past. I only wanted to pass on gossip that might interest your—your children. Some porters brought a story down from the Pangsau . . ." His eyes shifted to take in the children. "No, not the Pangsau. A ridge. You kids would probably know . . . Is there a steep ridge called the Ngalang?"

The children stiffened, their attitudes assuming that petrified stillness which had once so distressed Hamish.

Risley Hill went on easily, "Don't worry. It's only about a strange object seen on the ridge. Oblong, white, with ears of a bat. The porters say the Nagas found it sheltering under a nat shrine. You know the ones—little houses on stilts. Because it was under a nat shrine the Nagas took the object to be a nat too, and have started worshipping it, bringing it offerings of rice and flowers.

Ken, still rigid, fists clenched asked, "A bat, sir?"

"A bat, a white pig, the Nagas couldn't make out what it really was."

Jemma and Mibs drew in their breath. It was Ken who spoke again. "Could it have been a dog, sir? A white dog?"

Risley Hill nodded and turned to Hamish. "I shouldn't bank on it, but it's worth looking into. When I heard the story it occurred to me that's just what it could be—a white dog."

J16